Loveless

Books by Alice Oseman

SOLITAIRE

RADIO SILENCE

I WAS BORN FOR THIS

LOVELESS

WINNER OF THE YA BOOK PRIZE 2021

Novellas by Alice Oseman

NICK AND CHARLIE

THIS WINTER

Graphic novels by Alice Oseman

HEARTSTOPPER VOLUME 1

HEARTSTOPPER VOLUME 2

HEARTSTOPPER VOLUME 3

HEARTSTOPPER VOLUME 4

Loveless

Alice Oseman

HarperCollins *Children's Books*

First published in Great Britain by
HarperCollins *Children's Books* in 2020
HarperCollins *Children's Books* is a division of HarperCollins*Publishers* Ltd
1 London Bridge Street
London SE1 9GF

www.harpercollins.co.uk

4 6 8 10 9 7 5

HarperCollins*Publishers*
1st Floor, Watermarque Building, Ringsend Road
Dublin 4, Ireland

ISBN 978-0-00-824412-5

CHILDREN'S FICTION

Alice Oseman asserts the moral right to be identified as the author of the work.

Typeset in 11/15pt Bembo by Palimpsest Book Production Ltd,
Falkirk, Stirlingshire
Printed and bound in India by Thomson Press India Ltd

If it proves so, then loving goes by haps:
Some Cupid kills with arrows, some with traps.

Much Ado About Nothing, William Shakespeare

PART ONE

PART ONE

LAST CHANCE

There were literally three separate couples sitting around the fire making out, like some sort of organised kissing orgy, and half of me was like, *ew*, and the other half was like, *Wow, I sure do wish that was me.*

To be fair, it's probably what I should have expected from our prom afterparty. I don't go to parties very often. I hadn't been aware this actually was the culture.

I retreated from the firepit and headed back towards Hattie Jorgensen's giant country house, holding up my prom dress in one hand so I didn't trip, and dropped Pip a message.

Georgia Warr
i could not approach the fire and retrieve the marshmallows because there were people kissing around it

Felipa Quintana
How could you betray and disappoint me like this Georgia

When I entered the kitchen and located Pip, she was leaning against a corner cupboard with a plastic cup full of wine in one hand and her phone in the other. Her tie was half tucked into her shirt pocket, her burgundy velvet blazer was now unbuttoned and her short curls were fluffy and loose, no doubt due to all the dancing at prom.

'You OK?' I asked.

'Might be a tad drunk,' she said, her tortoiseshell glasses slipping down her nose. 'And also I *do* fucking love you.'

'More than marshmallows?'

'How could you ask me to make such a choice?'

I slung my arm round her shoulders and we leant back together against the kitchen cupboards. It was almost midnight, music was thumping from Hattie's living room, and the sound of our classmates chatting and laughing and shouting and screaming resonated from every corner of the building.

'There were three separate couples making out around the fire,' I said. 'Like, in unison.'

'Kinky,' said Pip.

'I sort of wished I was one of them.'

She gave me a look. '*Ew.*'

'I just want to kiss someone,' I said, which was odd, because I wasn't even drunk. I was driving Pip and Jason home later.

'We can make out if you want.'

'That wasn't what I had in mind.'

'Well, Jason's been single for a few months now. I'm sure he'd be up for it.'

'Shut up. I'm serious.'

I *was* serious. I really, really wanted to kiss someone. I wanted to feel a little bit of prom-night magic.

'Tommy, then,' said Pip, raising an eyebrow and smiling evilly. 'Maybe it's time to *confess*.'

I'd only ever had a crush on one person. His name was Tommy. He was the 'hot boy' of our school year – the one who could actually have been a model if he'd wanted. He was tall and skinny and conventionally attractive in a Timothée Chalamet sort of way, though I didn't really understand why everyone was in love with Timothée Chalamet. I had a theory that a lot of people's 'celebrity crushes' were faked just to fit in.

Tommy had been my crush ever since I was in Year 7 and a girl had asked me, 'Who d'you think is the hottest boy at Truham?' She'd shown me a photo on her phone of a group of the most popular Year 7 boys at the boys' grammar over the road, and there was Tommy right in the middle. I could tell he was the most attractive one – I mean, he had hair like a boy-band star and was dressed pretty fashionably – so I'd pointed and said *him*. And I guess that was that.

Almost seven years later, I'd never actually talked to Tommy. I'd never even really *wanted* to, probably because I was shy. He was more of an abstract concept – he was hot, and he was my crush, and nothing was going to happen between us, and I was perfectly fine with that.

I snorted at Pip. 'Obviously not Tommy.'

'Why not? You like him.'

The thought of actually following through on the crush made me feel extremely nervous.

I just shrugged at Pip, and she dropped the discussion.

Pip and I started to walk out of the kitchen, arms still slung round each other, and into the hallway of Hattie Jorgensen's fancy country home. People were slumped on the floor in the corridor in their prom dresses and tuxes, cups and food scattered around. Two people were kissing on the stairs, and I looked at them for a moment, unsure whether it was disgusting or whether it was the most romantic thing I'd ever seen in my life. Probably the former.

'You know what I want?' Pip said, as we stumbled into Hattie's conservatory and collapsed on to a sofa.

'What?' I said.

'I want someone to spontaneously perform a song to declare their love for me.'

'What song?'

She gave this some thought.

'"Your Song" from *Moulin Rouge*.' She sighed. 'God, I am sad, gay and alone.'

'Solid song choice, but not as attainable as a kiss.'

Pip rolled her eyes. 'If you want to kiss someone that much, just go talk to Tommy. You've liked him for seven years. This is your last chance before we go to uni.'

She might have had a point.

If it was going to be anyone, it was going to be Tommy. But the idea filled me with dread.

I folded my arms. 'Maybe I could kiss a stranger instead.'

'Fuck off.'

'I'm *serious*.'

'No you're not. You're not like that.'

'You don't know what I'm like.'

'Yes I do,' said Pip. 'I know you more than anyone.'

She was right. About knowing me and about me not being like that and about tonight being my last chance to confess the crush I'd had for seven years, and the last chance to kiss someone while I was still a schoolkid, while I had a chance to feel the teenage-dream excitement and youthful magic that everyone else seemed to have had a little taste of.

It was my last chance to feel that.

So maybe I would have to bite the bullet and kiss Tommy after all.

ROMANCE

I loved romance. Always had. I loved Disney (especially the under-appreciated masterpiece that is *The Princess and the Frog*). I loved fanfiction (even fanfics for characters I knew nothing about, but Draco/Harry or Korra/Asami were my comfort reads). I loved thinking about what my own wedding would be like (a barn wedding, with autumn leaves and berries, fairy lights and candles, my dress – lacy and vintage-looking, my soon-to-be-spouse crying, my family crying, me crying because I'm so, so happy, just, so happy that I have found *the one*).

I just. Loved. *Love*.

I knew it was soppy. But I wasn't a cynic. I was a dreamer, maybe, who liked to yearn and believed in the magic of love. Like the main guy from *Moulin Rouge*, who runs away to Paris to write stories about truth, freedom, beauty and love, even though he should probably be thinking about getting a job so he can actually afford to buy food. Yeah. Definitely me.

I probably got this from my family. The Warrs believed in *forever love* – my parents were just as in love now as they were back in 1991 when my mum was a ballet teacher and my dad was in a band. I'm not even joking. They were literally the plot of Avril Lavigne's 'Sk8er Boi' but with a happy ending.

Both sets of my grandparents were still together. My brother married his girlfriend when he was twenty-two. None of my close relatives had been divorced. Even most of my older cousins had at least partners, if not whole families of their own.

I hadn't ever been in a relationship.

I hadn't even kissed anyone.

Jason kissed Karishma from my history class on his Duke of Edinburgh expedition and dated a horrible girl called Aimee for a few months until he realised she was a knob. Pip kissed Millie from the Academy at a house party and also Nicola from our youth theatre group at the dress rehearsal for *Dracula*. Most people had a story like that – a silly kiss with someone they sort of had a crush on, or didn't really, and it didn't necessarily go anywhere, but that was a part of being a teenager.

Most people aged eighteen have kissed someone. Most people aged eighteen have had at least one crush, even if it's on a celebrity. At least half of everyone I knew had actually had sex, although some of those people were probably lying, or they were just referring to a really terrible hand job or touching a boob.

But it didn't bother me, because I knew my time would come. It did for everyone. *You'll find someone eventually* – that was what everyone said, and they were right. Teen romances only worked out in movies anyway.

All I had to do was wait, and my big love story would come. I would find *the one*. We would fall in love. And I'd get my happily ever after.

PIP, JASON AND ME

'Georgia has to kiss Tommy,' Pip said to Jason as we slumped down next to him on a sofa in Hattie's living room.

Jason, who was in the middle of a game of Scrabble on his phone, frowned at me. 'Can I ask why?'

'Because it's been seven years and I think it's time,' said Pip. 'Thoughts?'

Jason Farley-Shaw was our best friend. We were kind of a trio. Pip and I went to the same all-girls grammar school and met Jason through the annual school plays, where they'd always get a few of the boys from the boys' grammar school to join in, then after a couple of years he joined our school, which was mixed in the sixth form, and joined our youth theatre group too.

No matter what production we put on, whether it was a musical or a play, Jason usually played essentially the same role: a stern older man. This was mostly because he was tall and broad, but also because, at first glance, he did give off a bit of a strict dad vibe. He'd been Javert in *Les Mis*, Prospero in *The Tempest* and the angry father, George Banks, in *Mary Poppins*.

Despite this, Pip and I had quickly learnt that underneath his stern exterior, Jason was a very gentle, chilled-out dude who seemed to enjoy our company more than anyone else's. With Pip being a harbinger of chaos and my tendency to feel worried and awkward about pretty much everything, Jason's calmness balanced us out perfectly.

'Uh,' Jason said, glancing at me. 'Well . . . it doesn't really matter what *I* think about it.'

'I don't know if I want to kiss Tommy,' I said.

Jason looked satisfied and turned back to Pip. 'There you go. Case closed. You have to be sure about these things.'

'No! Come on!' Pip squawked and turned to face me. 'Georgia. I know you're shy. But it's *totally normal* to be nervous about crushes. This is literally the *final* chance you have to confess your feelings, and even if he rejects you, it doesn't matter, because he's going to uni on the other side of the country.'

I could have pointed out that this meant a relationship would be pretty difficult should he respond positively, but I didn't.

'Remember how nervous I was telling Alicia I liked her?' Pip continued. 'And then she was like *sorry, I'm straight*, and I cried for like two months, but look at me now! I'm thriving!' She kicked one leg into the air to make her point. 'This is a no-consequence scenario.'

Jason was looking at me through all of this, like he was trying to suss out how I felt.

'I dunno,' I said. 'I just . . . don't know. I guess I do like him.'

A flash of sadness crossed Jason's features, but then it was gone.

'Well,' he said, looking down at his lap, 'I guess you should just do what you want.'

'I guess I do want to kiss him,' I said.

I looked around the room and, sure enough, Tommy was there, standing in a small group of people near the doorway. He was just far enough away that I couldn't quite focus on the details of his face – he was just the concept of a person, a blob, a generic attractive guy. My seven-year crush. Seeing him so far away and blurry took me right back to being in Year 7, pointing at a photo of a boy I thought was probably attractive.

And that made up my mind. I could do this.

I could kiss Tommy.

I'd had times when I'd wondered whether I'd end up with Jason. I'd had times when I'd wondered whether I'd end up with Pip too. If our lives were in a movie, at least two of us would have got together.

But I'd never felt any romantic feelings for either of them, as far as I could tell.

Pip and I had been friends for almost seven years. From day one of Year 7, when we'd been sat together in our form-room seating plan and forced to tell each other three interesting facts about ourselves. We learnt we both wanted to be actors and that was it. Friends.

Pip was always more sociable, funnier, and generally more interesting than me. I was the listener, the supportive one when she'd had her am-I-gay crisis at the age of fourteen, and then her I-don't-know-whether-to-do-acting-or-science crisis last year, and then her I-really-want-to-cut-my-hair-short-but-I'm-scared crisis several months ago.

Jason and I had met each other later, but we bonded faster than I'd ever thought possible, given my poor track record for forming friendships. He was the first person I met who I could sit quietly with and it wouldn't feel awkward. I didn't feel like I had to try to be funny and entertaining with him; I could just be me, and he wouldn't dislike me because of it.

We'd all had what felt like a thousand sleepovers with each other. I knew exactly where the broken springs were in Pip's bed. I knew that Jason's favourite glass in my cupboard was a faded Donald Duck one I got at Disneyland when I was twelve. *Moulin Rouge* was the movie we always watched when we hung out – we all knew it word for word.

There were never any romantic feelings between Pip, Jason and me. But what we did have – a friendship of many years – was just as strong as that, I think. Stronger, maybe, than a lot of couples I knew.

TRUTH OR DARE

In order to get me physically closer to Tommy, Pip forced us to join a group game of truth or dare, which both Jason and I protested against, but Pip obviously won.

'Truth,' I said when it was my turn to suffer. Hattie, who was leading the game, grinned evilly and selected a card from the 'truth' pack. There must have been about twelve of us, all sitting on the living-room carpet. Pip and Jason were sitting on either side of me. Tommy was opposite. I didn't really want to look at him.

Pip handed me a crisp from the bowl for support. I gratefully accepted it and stuffed it in my mouth.

'What's the worst romantic or sexual experience you've had with a guy?'

A couple of people chorused '*Oooh*', one guy whistled, and one girl just laughed, one short burst of 'ha' that I found more embarrassing than anything else.

Thankfully, I wouldn't see most of the people at this party ever again in my life. Maybe on Instagram, but I muted most people's Instagram stories and I already had a mental list of all the people

I was going to unfollow after A-level results day. There were a few people at school that me, Pip and Jason got along with. People we'd sit with at lunch. A little gang of theatre kids we'd hang out with in school play season. But I knew already that we would all go to uni and forget about each other.

Pip, Jason and I would not forget about each other, though, because we were all going to Durham University in October, as long as we got the grades for it. This actually hadn't been planned – we were a trio of high-achieving nerds, but Jason had failed to get into Oxford, Pip had failed to get into King's College London, and I was the only one for whom Durham was actually my first choice.

I thanked the universe every day that it'd worked out like that. I *needed* Pip and Jason. They were my lifeline.

'That's too far,' Jason immediately interjected. 'Come on. That's way too personal.'

There were cries of outrage from the rest of our peers. People didn't give a shit about it being personal.

'You must have *something*,' drawled Hattie in her super-posh accent. 'Like *everyone's* had a terrible kiss or something by now.'

I was very uncomfortable about being the centre of attention, so I thought it'd be better to just get this over with.

'I've never kissed anyone,' I announced.

When I said it, I didn't think I was saying anything particularly odd. Like, this wasn't a teen movie. Virgin-shaming wasn't *really* a thing. Everyone knew that people did these things when they were ready, right?

But then the reactions began.

There were audible gasps. A pitying '*aww*'. Some of the guys started laughing and one of them coughed the word '*virgin*'.

Hattie brought her hand to her mouth and said, horrified, 'Oh my God, *seriously*?'

My face started to burn. I wasn't weird. There were lots of eighteen-year-olds who hadn't kissed anyone yet.

I glanced at Tommy, and even he was looking at me with sympathy, like I was a little kid – like I was a child who didn't understand anything.

'It's not *that* unusual,' I said.

Hattie pressed her hand to her heart and stuck out her bottom lip. 'You're so pure.'

A guy leant over and said, 'You're, like, eighteen, right?'

I nodded at him, and he said, 'Oh my *God*,' like I was disgusting or something.

Was I disgusting? Was I ugly and shy and disgusting and *that* was why I hadn't kissed anyone yet?

My eyes were starting to water.

'All right,' Pip snapped. 'You can all stop being dickheads right the fuck now.'

'It *is* weird, though,' said a guy I knew from my English class. He was addressing Pip. 'You've got to admit it's *weird* to have got to eighteen without having kissed anyone.'

'That's rich coming from a guy who admitted to having a wank over the princesses in *Shrek 3*.'

There were cackles of glee from the group, momentarily distracted from laughing at me. While Pip continued to berate our classmates, Jason very subtly took hold of my hand and pulled me up and out of the room.

Once we were in the corridor, I was about to cry so I said I needed to pee and went upstairs to find the loo. When I reached the bathroom, I examined my reflection, rubbing under my eyes so my mascara didn't smudge. I swallowed the tears down. I wasn't going to cry. I did not cry in front of anybody.

I hadn't realised.

I hadn't realised how *behind* I was. I'd spent so much time thinking that my one true love would just *show up* one day. I had been wrong. I had been so, so wrong. Everyone else was growing up, kissing, having sex, falling in love, and I was just . . .

I was just a child.

And if I carried on like this . . . would I be alone forever?

'Georgia!'

Pip's voice. I made sure my tears were gone by the time I exited the bathroom. And she didn't suspect a thing.

'They're so fucking dumb,' she said.

'Yeah,' I agreed.

She tried to smile warmly at me. 'You know you'll find someone eventually, right?'

'Yeah.'

'You *know* you'll find someone eventually. Everyone does. You'll see.'

Jason was looking at me with a sad expression on his face. Pitying, maybe. Was he pitying me too?

'Am I wasting being a teenager?' I asked them. And they told me *no*, like best friends would, but it was too late. This was the wake-up call I'd needed.

I needed to kiss someone before it was too late.

And that someone had to be Tommy.

TOMMY

I let Pip and Jason go back downstairs to get drinks, using the excuse that I wanted to get my jacket from one of the guest bedrooms because I was cold, and then I just stood in the dark corridor, trying to breathe and collect my thoughts.

Everything was OK. It wasn't too late.

I wasn't weird or disgusting.

I had time to make my move.

I located my jacket, and also found a bowl of cocktail sausages balanced on a radiator, so picked those up too. As I walked back down the corridor, I saw that another bedroom door was ajar, so I peered inside, only to get an absolute eyeful of someone very clearly getting fingered.

It sent a sort of shockwave through my spine. Like, wow, OK. I forgot people actually did that in real life. It was fun to read about in fanfics and see in movies, but the reality was kind of just like, *Oh. Yikes. I'm uncomfortable, get me out of here.*

That aside – surely you'd think to shut the door properly if someone was going to put a body part inside of you.

It was hard to picture myself in a situation like that. Honestly,

I loved the idea in theory – having a sexy little adventure in a dark room in someone else's house with someone you've been on-and-off flirting with for a couple of months – but the reality? Having to actually touch genitals with someone? Ew.

I guess it took time for people to be ready for stuff like that. And you'd have to find someone you felt comfortable with. I'd never even interacted with anyone I wanted to kiss, let alone someone I wanted to . . .

I looked down at my bowl of cocktail sausages. Suddenly I was not very hungry any more.

And then a voice broke the silence around me.

'Hey,' said the voice, and I looked up, and there was Tommy.

This was the first time I had talked to Tommy in my life.

I'd seen him a lot, obviously. At the few house parties I'd been to. Sometimes at the school gate. When he joined our school for sixth form, we didn't take any of the same subjects, but we occasionally passed in the corridor.

I'd always felt sort of nervous when he was nearby. I figured this was because of the crush.

I didn't really know how I was supposed to act around him.

Tommy pointed at the bedroom. 'Is anyone in there? I think my coat's on the bed.'

'I think someone's getting fingered in there,' I said, hopefully not loud enough for the people in question to hear.

Tommy dropped his hand. 'Oh. Right. OK, then. Um. I guess I'll get it later.'

There was a pause. We stood awkwardly outside the door. We couldn't hear the two people inside the bedroom, but just knowing it was happening, and we were both aware of it, made me want to die.

'How are you?' he asked.

'Oh, you know,' I said, holding up the bowl of sausages. 'I have sausages.'

Tommy nodded. 'Good. Good for you.'

'Thanks.'

'You look really nice, by the way.'

My prom dress was sparkly and lilac, and I felt fairly uncomfortable in it compared to my usual patterned knits and high-waisted jeans, but I thought I looked nice, so it was good to have confirmation. 'Thanks.'

'Sorry about the truth or dare game.' He chuckled. 'People can be such twats. For the record, I didn't have my first kiss until I was seventeen.'

'Really?'

'Yeah. I know it's kind of late, but . . . you know, it's better to wait until it feels right, isn't it?'

'Yeah,' I agreed, but I was just thinking that if seventeen was 'late', then I must be basically geriatric.

This all felt weird. Tommy had been my crush for seven years. He was talking to me. Why wasn't I jumping for joy right now?

Thankfully at that moment my phone buzzed. I retrieved it from my bra.

Felipa Quintana
Sexcuse me buts where are you
Haha sex
I said sex accidentally
And BUTS
Haha butts

Jason Farley-Shaw
Please return before pip has another glass of wine

Felipa Quintana
Stop subtweeting me in our own group chat when I'm standing right next to you

Jason Farley-Shaw
For real though Georgia where are you

I quickly switched my phone screen off before Tommy thought I was ignoring him.

'Uh . . .' I began, not quite knowing what I was going to say before I said it. I held up my oversized denim jacket. 'If you're cold, you can borrow my jacket.'

Tommy looked at it. He seemed unfazed that it was technically a 'girl's' jacket, which was good, because if he'd protested, that probably would have been it for my crush.

'You sure?' he asked.

'Yeah!'

He took the jacket and put it on. It made me feel a bit uncomfortable, just knowing that some guy I really didn't know very well was wearing my favourite jacket. Shouldn't I have been pleased about this development?

'I was just gonna go sit by the fire for a bit,' said Tommy, and he slouched against the wall, leaning ever so slightly towards me with a smile. 'D'you . . . wanna come with?'

That was when I realised he was trying to flirt with me.

Like, this was working.

I was actually going to get to kiss Tommy.

'OK,' I said. 'Let me just message my friends.'

Georgia Warr
hanging out with tommy lol

School romance was on my list of favourite fanfiction tropes. I also loved soulmate AU, coffee shop AU, hurt/comfort and temporary amnesia.

I figured school romance was the most likely one that would happen to me, but now that the possibility of it happening was more than zero, I was freaking out.

Like, heart racing, sweating, hands shaking freaking out.

This was what crushes felt like, so this was normal, right?

Everything was totally normal.

KISSING

When we got to the fire, we were the only people there. No kissing orgy in sight.

I picked a seat near the blanket pile and Tommy sat next to me, balancing a beer bottle on his chair arm. What would happen now? Would we just start making out? God, I hoped not.

Wait, wasn't that what I wanted?

A kiss had to happen, anyway. That much was clear to me. This was my last chance.

'So,' Tommy said.

'So,' I said.

I thought about how I was going to initiate the kiss. In fanfics, they just say *Can I kiss you*, which is very romantic to read but sounded so embarrassing in my head when I imagined saying it out loud. In movies, it just seems to sort of happen without any discussion beforehand, but both parties go into it knowing exactly what's happening.

He nodded at me, and I glanced at him, waiting for him to speak.

'You look really nice,' he said.

'You said that already,' I said, smiling awkwardly, 'but thanks.'

'S'weird we didn't really speak much at school,' he continued. As he spoke, he put his hand on the top of my chair, so his hand was weirdly close to my face. I don't know why that made me feel so uncomfortable. His skin was just *there*, I guess.

'Well, we weren't really friends with the same people,' I said.

'Yeah, and you're pretty quiet, aren't you?'

I couldn't even deny that. 'Yeah.'

Now that he was so close, I was struggling to even see what exactly I'd been attracted to for seven years. I could *tell* that he was conventionally attractive, like you can tell pop stars or actors are attractive, but nothing about him really made me feel *butterflies*. Did I know what butterflies felt like? What exactly was I supposed to be feeling right now?

He nodded as if he already knew everything about me. 'That's all right. Quiet girls are nice.'

What was that even supposed to mean?

Was he being creepy? I couldn't tell. I was probably just nervous. Everyone gets nervous around their crushes.

I glanced towards the house, feeling like I didn't really want to look at him any more. And I spotted two figures hovering in the conservatory, watching us – Pip and Jason. Pip immediately waved at me, but Jason looked kind of embarrassed and pulled Pip away.

They both wanted to see what would happen with Georgia and her seven-year crush.

Tommy leant a little closer to me. 'We should talk more, or something.'

I could tell he didn't mean that. He was just stalling. I knew what was supposed to happen next.

I was supposed to lean in, nervous, but excited, and he'd brush my hair out of my face and I'd look up at him beneath my eyelashes, and then we'd kiss, gently, and we'd be one, Georgia and Tommy, and then we'd go home, giddy and happy, and maybe it'd never happen again. Or maybe he'd message me, and we'd decide to go on a date, just to see what would happen, and at the date we would decide to try going out, and on our third date we would decide to be boyfriend and girlfriend, and a couple of weeks after that we would have sex, and while I was at university he would text me good morning and come to visit every other weekend, and after university we would move in together in a little flat by the river and get a dog, and he'd grow a beard, and then we would get married, and that would be the end.

That was what was supposed to happen.

I could see every single moment of it in my head. The simple route. The easy way out.

I could do that, couldn't I?

If I didn't, what would Pip and Jason say?

'It's OK,' he said. 'I know you haven't kissed anyone before.'

The way he said it was like he was talking to a newborn puppy.

'OK,' I said.

It irritated me. He was irritating me.

This was what I wanted, wasn't it? A cute little moment in the dark?

'Hey, look,' he said, a pitying smile on his face. 'Everyone has a first kiss eventually. It doesn't mean anything. It's OK to be new at, like, romance and all that.'

New at romance? I wanted to laugh. I'd been studying romance like an academic. Like an obsessive researcher. Romance would be my *Mastermind* topic.

'Yeah,' I said.

'Georgia . . .' Tommy leant in close, and then it hit me.

The disgust.

A wave of absolute, unbridled disgust.

He was so close I felt like I wanted to scream, I wanted to smash a glass and throw up at the same time. My fists tightened on the arms of my chair and I tried to keep looking at him, keep moving towards him, *kiss him*, but he was *so close to me* and it felt *horrific*, I felt *disgusted*. I wanted this to end.

'It's OK to be nervous,' he said. 'It's kind of cute, actually.'

'I'm not nervous,' I said. I was disgusted by the thought of him near me. Wanting things from me. That wasn't normal, was it?

He put his hand on my thigh.

And that's when I flinched, shoving his hand away and sending his drink toppling off the side of the chair, and he swung forwards to grab it and fell out of his seat.

Right into the firepit.

ON FIRE

There'd been signs. I'd missed all of them because I was desperate to fall in love.

Luke from Year 5 was the first. He did it via a note in my coat pocket during playtime. *To Georgia. You're so beautiful, will you be my girlfriend? Yes [ ] No [ ] From Luke.*

I ticked *No* and he cried all through numeracy.

In Year 6, when all of the girls in my class decided they wanted boyfriends, I felt left out, so asked Luke if he was still up for it, but he was already going out with Ayesha, so he said no. All the new couples played together on the climbing frame during the leavers' barbecue, and I felt sad and lonely.

Noah from the school bus was the second, in Year 9, although I'm not sure he counts. He asked me out on Valentine's Day because that was what people did on Valentine's Day – everybody wanted to be in a couple on Valentine's Day. Noah scared me because he was loud and enjoyed throwing sandwiches at people, so I just shook my head at him and went back to staring out of the window.

The third was Jian from the boys' school. Year 11. A lot of

people thought he was extremely attractive. We had a long conversation at a house party about whether *Love Island* was a good show or not, and then he tried to kiss me when everyone was drunk, including both of us. It would have been so easy to go for it.

It would have been so easy to lean in and do it.

But I didn't want to. I didn't fancy him.

But the fourth turned out to be Tommy, who I knew from school and who looked like Timothée Chalamet, and I didn't really know him that well, but this was the time that broke me a little, because I'd thought I really liked him. But I couldn't do it, because I didn't fancy him.

My seven-year crush on him was entirely fabricated.

A random choice from when I was eleven, and a girl held up a photo and told me to choose a boy.

I didn't fancy Tommy.

Apparently, I hadn't ever fancied anyone.

I screamed. Tommy screamed. His entire arm was on fire.

He rolled over and suddenly Pip flew out of nowhere, grabbing a blanket, and falling straight on top of Tommy, stifling the flames while Tommy was saying, '*Holy shit, holy shit,*' over and over and I was just standing over him, watching him burn.

The first thing I felt was shock. I felt frozen. Like this wasn't really happening.

The second thing I felt was anger about my jacket.

That was my favourite fucking jacket.

I should never have given it to some boy I barely knew. Some boy I didn't even *like*.

Jason was there too, asking Tommy if he was hurt, but he was sitting up and shaking his head, pulling off the ruins of my favourite jacket, looking at his unscathed arm and saying, 'What the fuck?' And then he stared up at me and said it again. 'What the fuck?'

I looked down at this person I had picked at random from a photo and said, 'I don't like you like that. I'm really sorry. You're nice, but I just – I don't like you like that.'

Jason and Pip both turned to me in unison. A little crowd was starting to form, our classmates wandering outside to see what the commotion was about.

'What the *fuck*?' said Tommy a third time, before he was swarmed by his friends, coming to see if he was OK.

I was just staring at him thinking, *that was my fucking jacket* and *seven years* and *I never liked you at all.*

'Georgia,' said Pip. She was next to me, pulling on my arm. 'I think it's time to go home.'

LOVELESS

'I never liked him,' I said in the car as we pulled up outside Pip's house and I cut the engine. Pip was next to me. Jason was in the back. 'Seven years and I just lied to myself the whole time.'

They were both being weirdly silent. Like they didn't know what to say. In a horrible way, I almost blamed them. Pip, anyway. She'd been the one pushing me to do this. She'd been teasing me about Tommy for seven years.

No, that was unfair. This wasn't her fault.

'This is my fault,' I said.

'I don't *understand*,' said Pip, gesturing wildly. She was still fairly tipsy. 'You . . . you've had a crush on him for years.' Her voice got quieter. 'This was your . . . your *big chance*.'

I started laughing.

It's wild how long you can trick yourself. And everyone around you.

The door to Pip's house opened, revealing her parents in matching dressing gowns. Manuel and Carolina Quintana were just another of the perfectly-in-love, incredibly-romantic-backstory couples I knew. Carolina, who'd grown up in Popayán, Colombia, and Manuel, who'd grown up in London, met when Manuel went to visit his dying grandma in Popayán when he was seventeen. Carolina was literally the girl next door, and the rest was history. These things just happened.

'I've never had a crush on anyone in my entire life,' I said. It was all sinking in. I'd never had a crush on anyone. No boys, no girls, not a single person I had ever met. What did that *mean*? Did it mean anything? Or was I just doing life wrong? Was there something wrong with me? 'Can you believe that?'

There was a pause again, before Pip said, 'Well, s'fine. S'fine, man. You know you'll find someone —'

'Don't say it,' I said. 'Please do not say it.'

So she didn't.

'You know, the idea — the *idea* of it is nice. The *idea* of liking Tommy and kissing Tommy and having some cute little moment by the fire after prom. That's *so* nice. That's what I wanted.' I felt myself clench the steering wheel. 'But the reality *disgusts me*.'

They didn't say anything. Even Pip, who'd always been a chatty drunk. Even my best friends couldn't think of a single comforting word.

'Well . . . This has been a good night, right?' Pip slurred as she stumbled out of my car. She held the front passenger door open and pointed dramatically at me, the streetlamps reflecting in her glasses. 'You. Very good. Outstanding. And you —' she prodded Jason in the chest as he moved into the front seat — 'excellent. Really excellent work.'

'Drink water,' said Jason, patting her on the head.

We watched her walk up to her front door and get gently chastised by her mum for being drunk. Her dad waved at us, and we waved back, and then I started the engine and we drove away.

It could have been a good night. It could have been the best night of my life, if I'd actually had a crush on Tommy.

The next stop was Jason's. He lived in a house built by his dads, who were both architects. Rob and Mitch had met at university – they were doing the same course – and ended up competing for the same architecture apprenticeship. Rob won, which he claims he earned, but Mitch always claims he let Rob win because he liked him.

When we arrived, I said, 'Most people our age have kissed someone.'

And he said, 'That doesn't matter.'

But I knew it did. It mattered. It was not random that I was the one who was falling behind. Everything that had happened that night was a sign that I needed to try harder, or I would be alone for the rest of my life.

'I don't feel like a real teenager,' I said. 'I think I failed at it.' And Jason clearly didn't know what to say to that, because he said nothing.

Sitting in my car on the drive of my family home, the ghost of a boy's hand on my thigh, I made a plan.

I was going to university soon. A chance to reinvent myself and become someone who could fall in love, someone who would fit in with my family, with people my age, with the world. I'd make a load of new friends. I'd join societies. I'd get a boyfriend. Or a girlfriend, even. A partner. I'd have my first kiss, and I'd have sex. I was just a late bloomer. I wasn't going to die alone.

I was going to try harder.

I wanted forever love.

I didn't want to be loveless.

PART TWO

CHANGE

The drive to Durham University was six hours long, and I spent most of it replying to Pip's barrage of Facebook messages. Jason had already travelled up there a couple of days earlier, and Pip and I had hoped to go together, but it turned out that my bags and boxes had taken up the whole of my dad's car boot and most of the back seats. We settled for messaging and trying to spot each other on the motorway.

Felipa Quintana
New game!!!!!
If we spot each other on the motorway we get 10 points

Georgia Warr
what do we get if we have the most points

Felipa Quintana
Eternal glory

Georgia Warr
love me a sweet cup of eternal glory

Felipa Quintana
DUDE I JUST SAW YOU!!!!!!!!!!!!
I waved but you didn't see me
Rejection
A modern tragedy by Felipa Quintana

Georgia Warr
you'll get over it

Felipa Quintana
I'll need intense therapy
You're paying

Georgia Warr
i'm not paying for your therapy

Felipa Quintana
Rude
I thought you were my friend

Georgia Warr
use your 10 points to pay for therapy

Felipa Quintana
MAYBE I WILL

The drive was hideously long, actually, even with Pip's messages for company. Dad was asleep for most of it. Mum insisted she got to choose the radio station since she was driving, and it was all motorway, flashes of grey and green, with only one stop at a service station. Mum bought me a packet of crisps, but I was too nervous about the day ahead to eat them, so they just sat in my lap, unopened.

'You never know,' Mum had said, in an attempt to cheer me up, 'you might find a lovely young man on your course!'

'Maybe,' I said. *Or a lovely young woman. God, anybody. Please. I'm desperate.*

'Lots of people meet their life partner at university. Like me and Dad.'

Mum regularly pointed out boys she thought I would find attractive, as if I could just go up to someone and ask them out. I never thought any of her choices were attractive anyway. But she was hopeful. Mostly out of curiosity, I think. She wanted to know what sort of person I would choose, like when you're watching a movie and waiting for the love interest to appear.

'Yeah, maybe,' I said, not wanting to tell her that her attempt at cheering me up was just making me feel worse. 'That'd be nice.'

I was starting to feel a bit like I was going to be sick.

But everyone probably felt this way about starting university.

Durham is a little old city with lots of hills and cobbled streets, and I loved it because I felt like I was in *The Secret History* or some other deep and mysterious university drama where there's lots of sex and murder.

Not that I was particularly on track to experience either of those.

We had to drive into a huge field, queue up in the car, and

wait to be summoned, because Durham University's colleges are all tiny and they don't have car parks of their own. Lots of students and their parents were getting out of their cars to talk to each other while we all waited. I knew I should get out and start socialising too.

My running theory was that my shyness and introversion were linked to my whole 'never fancying anyone' situation — maybe I just didn't talk to enough people, or maybe people just stressed me out in general, and that was why I'd never wanted to kiss anyone. If I just improved my confidence, tried to be a bit more open and sociable, I'd be able to do and feel those things, like most people.

Starting university was a good time to try something like that.

Felipa Quintana
Hey are you in the queue
I've befriended my car next door neighbour
She brought a whole-ass fern with her
It's like five feet tall
Update: the fern's name is Roderick

I was about to reply, or maybe even get out of the car and meet Pip's acquaintance and Roderick, but it was then that Mum turned the engine on.

'They're calling us,' she said, pointing up ahead at where someone in a high-vis vest was waving.

Dad turned round to smile at me. 'You ready?'

It'd be hard, sure, and it'd be scary and probably embarrassing, but I *would* become someone who could experience the magic of romance.

I knew I had *my whole life ahead of me*, and *it'd happen one day*, but I felt like if I couldn't change and make it happen at university, it'd never happen at all.

'Yeah,' I replied.

Also, I didn't want to wait. I wanted it now.

ROONEY

'Oh no,' I said, standing outside the door of what would be my bedroom for the next nine months, and slightly dying inside.

'What?' asked Dad, dropping one of my bags on to the floor and pulling his glasses down from the top of his head.

'Oh, well,' said Mum, 'you knew there was a chance of this happening, darling.'

On the front of my bedroom door was my photo and underneath it was written 'Georgia Warr' in Times New Roman. Next to that was another photo – of a girl with long brown hair, a smile that looked positively candid in its naturalness, and perfectly threaded eyebrows. Underneath that was the name 'Rooney Bach'.

Durham was an old English university that had a 'college system'. Instead of halls of residence, the university was made up of 'colleges' spread around the city. Your college was where you slept, showered and ate, but it was also a place you showed your allegiance to through college events, your college sports teams, and running for the college's executive student roles.

St John's College – the one that I had been accepted into –

was an old building. And because of that, a few of the students living there had to share rooms.

I just hadn't thought it would be me.

A wave of panic flooded through me. I couldn't have a roommate – hardly anyone in the UK had roommates at uni. I needed *my own space*. How was I supposed to sleep or read fanfic or get dressed or do *anything* with someone else in the room? How was I supposed to relax when I had to socialise with another person every moment I was awake?

Mum didn't even seem to notice I was panicking. She just said, 'Well, let's get cracking, then,' and opened the door for me.

And Rooney Bach was already there, wearing leggings and a polo shirt, watering a five-foot fern.

The first thing Rooney Bach said to me was, 'Oh my God, are you Georgia Warr?' like I was a celebrity, but she didn't even wait for affirmation before casting her watering can aside, grabbing a large strip of aqua-blue fabric – which I determined to be a rug – from her bed, and holding it up to me.

'Rug,' she said. 'Thoughts?'

'Um,' I said. 'It's great.'

'OK, *amazing*.' She whooshed the rug into the air and then laid it down in the centre of our room. 'There. It just needed that splash of colour.'

I think I was in shock a little bit, because only then did I take a proper look around our room. It was large, but pretty gross, as I'd expected it would be – bedrooms are never nice at old English universities. The carpet was a mouldy grey-blue, the furniture was beige and plastic-looking, and our beds were singles. Rooney's already had bright, flowery bedsheets on it. Mine looked like it belonged in a hospital.

The only nice part of the room was a large sash window. The paint on the wooden frame was peeling and I knew it'd be draughty, but it was sort of lovely, and you could see all the way down to the river.

'You've done up the place nicely already!' Dad was saying to Rooney.

'Oh, d'you think so?' said Rooney. She immediately started narrating a tour of her side of the room to Mum and Dad, showing off all the key features – her illustrated print of some meadows (she liked going on country walks) and one of *Much Ado About Nothing* (her favourite Shakespeare play), her fleece duvet topper (also aqua, to match the rug), her house plant (whose name was – I hadn't misheard – *Roderick*), an aqua desk lamp (from John Lewis) and, most importantly, a giant poster that simply read 'Don't Quit Your Daydream' in a swirly font.

The whole time, she was smiling. Her hair, up in a ponytail, swished around, as my parents tried to keep up with how fast she was talking.

I sat down on my bed in the grey half of the room. I hadn't brought any posters with me. All I'd brought were a few printed-out photos of me, Pip and Jason.

Mum looked at me from the other side of the room and gave me a sad smile, like she knew that I wanted to go home.

'You can message us any time, darling,' said Mum, as we were saying goodbye outside the college. I felt empty and lost, standing there in the cobbled street in the October cold, my parents about to leave me.

I don't want you to go, was what I wanted to say to them.

'And Pip and Jason are just down the road, aren't they?' continued Dad. 'You can go and hang out with them any time.'

Pip and Jason had been placed in a different college – University College, or 'Castle' as it was commonly referred to by the students here, since it literally was part of Durham Castle. They'd stopped replying to my messages a couple of hours ago. Probably busy unpacking.

Please don't leave me here alone, I wanted to say.

'Yeah,' is what I said.

I glanced around. This was my home, now. Durham. It was like a town out of a Dickens adaptation. All of the buildings were tall and old. Everything seemed to be made of lumps of stone. I could see myself walking down the cobbles and into the cathedral in my graduation gown already. This was where I was supposed to be.

They both hugged me. I didn't cry, even though I really, really wanted to.

'This is the start of a big adventure,' said Dad.

'Maybe,' I mumbled into his jacket.

I couldn't bear to stay and watch them walk away down the road towards the car – when they turned to go, so did I.

Back in my room, Rooney was Blu Tack-ing a photo to the wall, right in the centre of her posters. In the photo was Rooney, maybe aged thirteen or fourteen, with a girl who had dyed red hair. Like, Ariel from *The Little Mermaid* hair.

'Is that your friend from home?' I asked. This was a good conversation starter, at least.

Rooney whipped her head round to look at me, and for a moment I thought I saw an odd expression cross her face. But then it was gone, replaced by her wide smile.

'Yeah!' she said. 'Beth. She's – she's not here, obviously, but . . . yeah. She's my friend. Do you know anyone else in Durham? Or are you here all alone?'

'Oh, erm, well, my two best friends are here, but they're in Castle.'

'Oh, that's so nice! Sad you didn't get into the same college, though.'

I shrugged. Durham took your choice of college into consideration, but not everyone could get their first choice. I'd tried to get into Castle too, but I'd ended up here. 'We tried, but, yeah.'

'You'll be OK.' Rooney beamed. 'We'll be friends.'

Rooney offered to help me unpack, but I declined, determined to at least do this one thing by myself. While I was unpacking, she sat on her bed and chatted to me, and we learnt that we were both studying English. She then declared that she'd done none of the summer reading. I'd done all of it but didn't mention that.

Rooney, I was quickly learning, was extremely chatty, but I could tell that she was putting on some sort of happy, bubbly persona. Which was fair enough – I mean, it was our first day of university. Everyone was going to be trying really hard to make friends. But I couldn't get a sense of what sort of person she really was, which was mildly concerning because we were going to be living with each other for almost a full year.

Were we going to be best friends? Or were we going to awkwardly put up with each other before leaving for the summer and never speaking again?

'So . . .' I scanned the room in search of something to talk about, before landing on her *Much Ado* poster. 'You like Shakespeare?'

Rooney's head snapped up from her phone. 'Yeah! Do you?'

I nodded. 'Um, yeah, well, I was in a youth theatre group back home. And I did a lot of the school plays. Shakespeare was always my favourite.'

This actually caused Rooney to sit up, eyes wide and sparkling. '*Wait.* You *act?*'

'Um . . .'

I did act, but, well, it was a bit more complicated than that now.

When I was in my early teens, I'd wanted to be an actor – which was why I'd joined the youth theatre group that Pip already went to and started auditioning for the school plays with her. And I was good at it. I got top marks in drama class at school. I usually got a pretty solid speaking part in the plays and musicals that I did.

But as I got older, acting just started to make me nervous. I got *more* stage fright the more plays I did, and eventually, when I auditioned for *Les Misérables* in Year 13, I was shaking so much that I got relegated to a role with only one line, and even then, come showtime, I threw up before every single performance.

So maybe a career in acting wasn't for me.

Despite this, I was planning to continue with acting at uni. I still enjoyed figuring out roles and interpreting scripts – it was the audiences I had problems with. I just needed to work on my confidence. I'd join the student theatre society and maybe audition for a play. I needed to join *one* society, at least, if I was going to *branch out* and *open up* and *meet new people*.

And find someone to fall in love with.

'Yeah, a bit,' I said.

'Oh. My. God.' Rooney clapped one hand to her heart. 'This is amazing. We can go join the DST together.'

'The DST . . .?'

'Durham Student Theatre. They basically run all of the drama societies in Durham.' Rooney flipped her ponytail back. 'The Shakespeare Soc is literally the main society I wanna join. I know most freshers do the Freshers Play but I had a look at what plays they've done the past few years and they're all kind of boring? So I'm at least gonna try and join Shakespeare. God I'm *praying* they'll do a tragedy. *Macbeth* is literally my *dream* . . .'

Rooney rambled on without seeming to care whether I was actually listening or not.

We had something in common. Acting. This was good.

Maybe Rooney would be my first new friend.

A NEW FRIENDSHIP

'Oh, *wow*!' said Jason later that day as he and Pip stepped into my – well, my and Rooney's room. 'It's the size of my garden.'

Pip stretched out her arms and did a twirl on the spot, emphasising the unnecessary amount of empty space in the room. 'I didn't realise you'd joined the college of the bourgeoisie.'

'I don't understand why they couldn't just . . . build a wall in the middle,' I said, pointing at the gap between mine and Rooney's sides of the room, which was currently only occupied by Rooney's aqua rug.

'How very Trump of you,' said Jason.

'Oh my God, shut *up*.'

Rooney had left a while ago with a group of people she'd befriended on our corridor. They'd invited me, but honestly, I needed some down time – I'd been trying my best to say hi to new people for most of the day, and I really, really wanted to see some familiar faces. So I'd invited Jason and Pip to come hang in my room for a bit before this evening's freshers' events at our separate colleges, and thankfully, they'd both finished unpacking and didn't have anything else to do.

I'd already told them a little bit about Rooney – that she liked theatre and was generally quite nice – but her side of the room was a much better summary of her personality.

Jason surveyed it, then looked over my side. 'Why does her side look like an Instagram influencer's bedroom and yours looks like a prison cell? You brought so many bags with you!'

'It's not *that bad*. And a lot of the bags had books in them.'

'Georgia, my dude,' said Pip, who had slumped on to my bed. 'Her side looks like Disneyland. Yours looks like a stock photo.'

'I didn't bring any posters,' I said. 'Or fairy lights.'

'You – *Georgia*, how the *hell* did you forget fairy lights? They're an essential element of university room décor.'

'I don't know!'

'You'll be sad without fairy lights. Everyone's sad without fairy lights.'

'I think Rooney's got more than enough for both of us. She's already letting me share a rug.'

Pip looked down at the aqua and nodded approvingly.

'Yes. It's a good rug.'

'It's just a rug.'

'It's a shaggy one. That's sexy.'

'*Pip*.'

Pip suddenly leapt out of the bed, staring at Rooney's fern in the corner of the room. 'Hang on – wait one fucking second. That plant . . .'

Jason and I turned to look at Roderick.

'Oh,' I said. 'Yeah. That's Roderick.'

And it was at that moment that Rooney Bach returned to our room.

She swung the door wide open, kicked her Norton Anthology

in front of it to act as a doorstop, and turned to face us with a Starbucks in her hand.

'Guests!' she said, beaming at the three of us.

'Um, yeah,' I said. 'These are my friends from home, Pip and Jason.' I pointed at each of them. 'And this is my roommate, Rooney.' I pointed at Rooney.

Rooney's eyes widened. 'Oh my God. This is *them*.'

'It's us,' said Pip, one eyebrow raised.

'And we've met already!' Rooney gave Pip a once-over, her eyes flicking briefly up and down from her tortoiseshell glasses down to the stripy socks visible beneath her rolled-up jeans, before striding towards her and holding out her hand with such force that Pip looked, for the briefest second, afraid.

She shook the hand. She gave Rooney a once-over in return – from her Adidas Originals all the way up to the hairband just visible at the top of her ponytail. 'Yes. I see Roderick has settled in.'

Rooney's eyebrow quivered, like she was surprised and pleased that Pip's immediate reaction was *banter*. 'He has. He's been enjoying the northern air.'

She turned to Jason and held out her hand again, which he took. 'We haven't met, but I like your jacket.'

Jason glanced down at himself. He was wearing the fluffy brown teddy jacket he'd owned for years. I truly believed it was the most comfortable item of clothing to exist on this planet. 'Oh, right. Yeah, thanks.'

Rooney smiled and clapped her hands together. 'It's *so* nice to meet you both. We're going to *have* to become friends, now that me and Georgia are friends.'

Pip gave me a look as if to say, *friends? Already?*

'As long as you don't steal her away from us,' Jason joked,

though Pip whipped her head round to him, seemingly taking the statement very seriously indeed.

Rooney noticed this happen, and a small curl of a smile appeared at the side of her mouth.

'Of course not,' she said.

'I've heard you're interested in theatre,' Pip said. There was a nervous tone to her voice.

'Yes! Are you?'

'Yeah! We all went to the same youth theatre group. And we did school plays together.'

Rooney seemed genuinely excited by this prospect. Her love for theatre was definitely *not* fake, even if some of her smiles were. 'So you'll be auditioning for a DST play?'

'Obviously.'

'A lead role?'

'Obviously.'

Rooney grinned, and after taking a sip from her Starbucks cup she said, 'Good. We'll be competing, then.'

'I . . . I guess we will,' said Pip, flustered, surprised and confused all at the same time.

Rooney suddenly made a concerned face and checked her phone. 'Oh, sorry, I have to head out again. Got to meet this girl I've been chatting to on the English Soc Facebook group down at Vennels. I'll meet you back here at six for the Freshers' Barbecue?'

And then she was gone, while I was wondering what Vennels was, and why I didn't know what Vennels was, and how Rooney already knew what Vennels was when she'd only been here for less than one day, just like me.

When I turned back to my friends, Pip was standing very still with a startled expression on her face that made her look a bit like a cartoon scientist, post-explosion.

'What?' I asked.

Pip swallowed and shook her head a little. 'Nothing.'

'*What?*'

'Nothing. She seems nice.'

I knew that look. It was a Pip look I knew well. I'd seen it when she had to be gymnastics partners with Alicia Reece – one of her most intense crushes – in Year 11 PE. I'd seen it when we went to a Little Mix meet and greet and Pip got to hug Leigh-Anne Pinnock.

Pip didn't fancy a lot of girls – she was quite picky, actually. But when Pip *did* fancy someone, it was very, very obvious. To me, anyway. I could always tell when people had crushes on each other.

Before I could make a comment, Jason interrupted. He was peering at the photo of Rooney and Mermaid-hair Beth. 'It's so odd that you ended up with a roommate. What did you write on your personality quiz?'

We'd had to fill in personality quizzes after we got accepted into Durham, so that if we ended up having to share rooms, they'd try to match us with someone we'd get along with.

I strained to remember what I'd written on mine – and then it clicked.

'Shakespeare,' I said. 'The quiz – one of the questions was about your interests. I wrote Shakespeare.'

'So?' said Jason.

I pointed at Rooney's *Much Ado About Nothing* poster.

'Oh my *God*,' said Pip, her eyes widening. 'Is she also a Shakespeare stan? Like us?'

'So she says.'

Jason nodded, seemingly pleased. 'That's good! You can bond over that.'

'Yes,' said Pip, much too quickly. 'Befriend her.'

'I mean, we're roommates. So hopefully we will be friends.'

'That's good,' Jason repeated. 'Especially since we won't get to hang out all the time any more.'

This made me pause. 'Won't we?'

'Well – no? I mean, at least this week. We're at different colleges.'

I genuinely hadn't thought about that. I'd had this idea that we'd meet up every day, hang out, explore Durham, *begin our university journeys together*. But all our freshers' events were at our own colleges. We were all on different courses – I was doing English, Jason was doing history, and Pip was studying natural sciences. So he was right. I probably wouldn't see much of Pip and Jason at all this week.

'I guess,' I said.

Maybe this could be OK. Maybe this would be the kick I needed to *branch out* and find *new people* and *have experiences*.

Maybe this could all be part of *the plan*. The romance plan.

'Right,' said Pip, slapping her thighs and bouncing to her feet. 'We should head. I still haven't finished unpacking all my shirts.'

I let Pip bundle me into a hug before she trotted out of the room, leaving just me and Jason. I didn't want Jason and Pip to go. I hadn't wanted my parents to go. I didn't want to be left here alone.

'I wish I was at Castle too,' I said. I sounded like a five-year-old.

'You'll be OK,' said Jason, in his usual calming tone. Nothing fazed Jason. He had whatever the opposite of anxiety was. Absolute, unerring peace of mind.

I swallowed. I really, really did want to cry. Maybe I could have a quick cry before Rooney got back.

'Can I have a hug?' I asked.

Jason paused. Something unreadable crossed his face.

'Yeah,' he said. 'Yeah. C'mere.'

I crossed the room and let him envelop me in a warm hug.

'You'll be OK,' he said again, rubbing his hands gently over my back, and I don't know if I believed him, but it felt nice to hear anyway. And Jason always gave the warmest, cosiest hugs.

'OK,' I mumbled into his jacket.

When he stepped back, his eyes darted away.

He might even have blushed a little bit.

'I'll see you soon?' he said, not looking at me.

'Yeah,' I said. 'Message me.'

My friendships with Pip and Jason wouldn't change. We'd made it through seven years of secondary school, for God's sake. Whether we hung out all the time or not – we would always be friends. Nothing could ruin what we had.

And getting to focus on a new friendship with Rooney Bach – a fellow Shakespeare enthusiast who was significantly more sociable than me – could only be a good thing.

ROMANTIC THINKING

At the St John's College Freshers' Barbecue, Rooney moved around the courtyard like an ambitious businesswoman at an important networking event. She befriended people in a quick, easy way that left me in awe and, to be honest, very jealous.

I had no option but to trail her like a shadow. I didn't know how to mingle solo.

University was where most people made friendships that actually *lasted*. My parents still met up with their uni friends every year. My brother's best man had been one of his uni friends. I knew I had Pip and Jason, so it wasn't like I was going in friendless in the first place, but I still figured that I might meet some more people I got along with.

And at the barbecue, people were on the *hunt* for friendships. Everyone was being extra loud, extra friendly and asking way more questions than is normally socially acceptable. I tried my best, but I wasn't great at it. I'd forget people's names as soon as they said them. I didn't ask enough questions. All the posh private-school boys in zip-neck jumpers blended in with each other.

I thought about trying to make progress with my *finding love* situation, but no particular romantic feelings arose for anyone I met, and I was too anxious to try and force myself to feel them.

Rooney, on the other hand, *flirted*.

At first, I thought I was just seeing things. But the more I watched, the more I could see her doing it. The way she'd touch guys on the arm and smile up at them – or smile down, because she was *tall*. The way she'd listen when they spoke and laugh at their jokes. The way she'd give the guy direct, piercing eye contact, the sort of eye contact that made you feel like she *knew* you.

It was absolutely masterful.

What I found interesting was that she did this to several guys. I wondered what her goal was. What was she looking for? A potential boyfriend? Hook-up options? Or was she just doing it for fun?

Either way, I thought about it a lot while I was trying to fall asleep later that night in a new room and a new bed, with a person already asleep a few metres away from me.

Rooney seemed to know exactly what to do. I'd watched her master the set-up. The romance pre-game. She did it the same way she befriended people – with the precise expertise of someone who'd had a lot of practice and a lot of success. Could I do that? Could I copy her?

Would she teach me how to do it?

It seemed to take Rooney a monumental amount of effort to wake up on Monday morning. I thought *I* was bad at waking up in the mornings, but Rooney had to hit snooze at least five times before she managed to drag herself out of bed. All of the alarms were 'Spice Up Your Life' by the Spice Girls. I woke up at the first one.

'I didn't know you wore glasses,' was the first thing she said to me after she'd finally arisen.

'I wear contacts most of the time,' I explained, and it reminded me of how surprised Pip had been, aged eleven, to find out that I was short-sighted after six whole months of being friends. I'd started wearing contact lenses the summer before secondary school.

When I awkwardly asked her if she wanted to head down to the cafeteria for breakfast, she looked almost like I'd suggested throwing ourselves out of the window, before replacing the expression with a broad smile and saying, 'Yeah, that sounds good!' And then she changed into sportswear and became the bubbly, extroverted Rooney I'd met the day before.

I stuck close to Rooney throughout our first official day of Freshers' Week, through our introductory English lecture to our afternoon off. In the lecture, she effortlessly befriended the person sitting next to her, and in the afternoon, we went out for coffee with a few people who also did English. She made friends with all of them, too, and broke away to talk to this one guy who was obviously attractive in a conventional sort of way. She flirted. Touching his sleeve. Laughing. Looking into his eyes.

It looked so easy. But even imagining myself doing it made me feel a bit nauseated.

I hope this doesn't sound like I thought badly of Rooney for flirting and making connections and setting herself up for, without a doubt, some sort of grand university romance that she'd be able to tell her grandchildren about when she was an elderly over-sharer.

I was just very, very jealous that I wasn't her.

The main event of the Tuesday of Freshers' Week was 'College Matriculation', a bizarre pseudo-religious ceremony that took place in Durham Cathedral, at which we were welcomed into the university. We all had to wear posh outfits and our college gowns, which made me feel very sophisticated.

I stuck with Rooney until, on the way out of the cathedral, I spotted Pip and Jason, walking together across the grass, no doubt heading to their own matriculation ceremony. They saw me, and we ran to each other through the graveyard in what felt like slow-mo with the *Chariots of Fire* music playing in the background.

Pip leapt on me, almost drowning me in her college gown. She was dressed as fancy as she'd been dressed at prom – full suit and tie, a halo of carefully styled curls, and she was wearing a cologne that smelt like a forest after the rain. She felt like *home*.

'I'm going to write St John's a letter of complaint,' she said into my shoulder, 'to tell them to let you transfer to Castle.'

'I don't think that will work.'

'It will. D'you remember when I complained to Tesco and they sent me five packets of Maltesers? I know how to pen a strongly worded letter.'

'Just ignore her,' said Jason. Jason was also suited up – he looked fancy too. 'She's still hungover from last night.'

Pip stepped back, adjusting her collar and tie. She did look a little less chipper than usual.

'Are you OK?' she asked. 'Is your roommate being normal? Are you dying of stress?'

I thought about these questions and replied, 'No to all.'

Speaking of Rooney, I glanced over Pip's shoulder to see how far ahead Rooney had walked, only to find that Rooney had actually stopped at the edge of the graveyard and was looking back. Right at us.

Pip and Jason turned to look.

'O-oh, she's there,' Pip mumbled, and immediately started adjusting her hair. But Rooney was still looking at us, and she smiled and waved, seemingly directly at Pip. Pip awkwardly raised a hand and waved back with a nervous smile.

I wondered suddenly whether Pip had a chance with Rooney. Rooney *seemed* pretty straight, judging by how many guys I had seen her flirt with and that she hadn't tried flirting with any girls, but people could surprise you.

'You getting along with her OK?' asked Jason.

'She's really nice, yeah. She's better than me at, like, everything, which is annoying, but she's fine.'

Pip frowned. 'Better than you at what?'

'Oh, you know. Like, making friends, and, I dunno. Talking to people.' *Flirting. Romance. Falling in love, probably.*

Neither Jason nor Pip seemed impressed by this answer.

'OK,' said Pip. 'We're coming round tonight.'

'You really don't have to.'

'No, I know a cry for help when I hear it.'

'I'm not crying for help.'

'We need a pizza night, urgently.'

I saw through her immediately. 'You just want to have an opportunity to talk to Rooney again, don't you?'

Pip gave me a long look.

'Maybe so,' she said. 'But I also care about you. And I care about pizza.'

'So she's just, like, insanely good at getting people to like her?' said Pip through a mouthful of pizza later that evening.

'That's pretty much it, yeah,' I said.

Jason shook his head. 'And you want to be like her? Why?'

The three of us were sprawled on Rooney's aqua rug, pizza

in the middle. We'd had a minor debate about whether to watch our group favourite, *Moulin Rouge*, or Jason's favourite, the live action *Scooby-Doo* movie, but we eventually settled on *Scooby-Doo* and were playing it on my laptop. Rooney was out for the night at some sort of themed bar night, and had I not already made plans with my friends, I probably would have gone with her. But this was better. Everything was better when Jason and Pip were here.

I couldn't admit to them how desperately I wanted to be in a romantic relationship. Because I *knew* it was pathetic. Trust me. I completely understood that women should want to be *strong and independent* and you don't need to find love to have a successful life. And the fact that I so desperately wanted a boyfriend – or a girlfriend, a partner, whoever, *someone* – was a sign that I was not strong, or independent, or self-sufficient, or *happy alone*. I was really quite lonely, and I wanted to be loved.

Was that such a bad thing? To want an intimate connection with another human?

I didn't know.

'She just finds it so easy to talk to people,' I said.

'That's just what life is like when you're abnormally attractive, though,' said Pip.

Jason and I looked at her.

'Abnormally attractive?' I said.

Pip stopped chewing. 'What? She is! I'm just stating facts! She's got that sort of "I could step on you and you would enjoy it" energy.'

'Interesting,' Jason said, raising an eyebrow.

Pip started to go a bit red. 'I'm literally just making an observation!'

'. . . OK.'

'*Don't look at me like that.*'

'I'm not.'

'*You are.*'

Since the events of prom, I'd given some solid thought as to whether I might actually be a lesbian, like Pip. It would make sense. Maybe my lack of interest in boys was because I was, in fact, interested in girls.

That'd be a fairly sensible solution to my situation.

According to Pip, the hallmarks of realising you're a lesbian were: firstly, getting a little intensely obsessed with a girl, mistaking it for admiration, and sometimes thinking about holding their hand, and secondly, having a subconscious fixation on certain female cartoon villains.

Jokes aside, I'd never had a crush on a girl, so I didn't really have any evidence to support that particular theory.

Maybe I was bi or pan, since I didn't even seem to have a preference at this point.

The next couple of hours were spent talking, snacking, and occasionally glancing at my laptop screen to watch the movie. Pip rambled at length about how interesting her introductory chemistry lab class had been, while Jason and I both mourned how dull our first lectures had been. We all shared our thoughts about the people we'd met in college – how many posh private-school kids there were, how bad the drinking culture already seemed to be, and how there really should be more cereal options at breakfast. At one point, Pip decided to water Roderick the house plant, because, in her words, 'He's looking a bit thirsty.'

But soon it was eleven o'clock, and Pip decided it was time to make some hot chocolate, which she insisted on doing on the stove rather than using the kettle in my bedroom. We all headed out of the room towards the tiny kitchen on my corridor, which was shared between eight people but had been empty the few times I'd been in there thus far.

Tonight, it was not empty.

I knew this from the moment Pip glanced through the door window and made a face like she'd been given a mild electric shock.

'Oh *shit*,' she hissed, and as Jason and I joined her, we finally saw what was going on.

Rooney was in the kitchen.

She was with a guy.

She was sitting on the kitchen counter. He was standing between her legs, his tongue in her mouth, and his hand up her shirt.

To put it lightly: they were both very much enjoying themselves.

'Oh,' I said.

Jason immediately stepped away from the situation, like any normal person would, but Pip and I just stood there for a moment, watching this go down.

It became clear to me in that moment that the only way I was going to make any progress in my *finding love* mission was if I asked Rooney for help.

I was not going to be able to do it on my own, ever.

I'd *tried*. I promise I'd tried. I'd tried to kiss Tommy when he went in for one, but the *Kill Bill* sirens started going off in my mind and I just couldn't. I just *couldn't*.

I'd tried to talk to people at the Freshers' Barbecue, and when we were huddling outside the lecture halls, and at lunch and dinner when I sat with Rooney and all the people she had befriended. I'd tried, and I wasn't terrible at it, I was polite, and nice, and people didn't seem to hate me.

But I would never be like Rooney. Not naturally, anyway. I would never be able to kiss some guy just because it was fun, because it made me feel good, because I could do what I wanted. I would never be able to manufacture that spark that she seemed to have with almost everyone she met.

Unless she told me how.

Pip finally tore her eyes away from the window. 'That's got to be unhygienic,' she said, making a disgusted face. 'That's where people make their *tea*, for God's sake.'

I murmured my agreement before moving away from the door, our hot chocolate plans abandoned.

Pip had this look on her face like she'd seen this coming.

'I'm so dumb,' she muttered.

I knew almost everything about romance. I knew the theory. I knew when people were flirting, I knew when they wanted to kiss. I knew when people's boyfriends were being shitty to them, even when they couldn't tell it themselves. I'd read infinite stories of people meeting and flirting and awkwardly pining, hating before liking, lusting before loving, kissing and sex and love and marriage and partners for life, till death us do part.

I was a master of the theory. But Rooney was a master of the practice.

Maybe fate had brought her to me. Or maybe that was just romantic thinking.

SEX

In the middle of the night, between Tuesday and Wednesday, I woke up to hear someone having sex in the room above ours.

It was a sort of rhythmic thumping. Like a headboard hitting a wall. And a creaking, like the bend of an old bedframe.

I sat up, wondering if I was just imagining it. But I wasn't. It was real. People were having sex in the room above us. What else would that sound be? There were only bedrooms up there, so unless someone had decided to do some 3 a.m. DIY, there was only one thing that sound could be.

Rooney was fast asleep, curled up on her side, her dark hair splayed around her on the pillow. Utterly oblivious.

I knew this sort of thing would happen at university. In fact, I knew this sort of thing happened at school – well, not *physically* at school, hopefully, but among my schoolfriends and classmates.

But hearing it happen, in the flesh, not just knowing and imagining, chilled me to the core. Even more than when I saw that person getting fingered at Hattie's party.

It was a jarring sort of *oh, God, this thing is actually real, it's not just in fanfics and movies. And I'm supposed to be doing that too.*

COLLEGE MARRIAGE

'College families' were a new concept to me. At Durham, students in their second and third years paired up to act as a mentor team, or 'college parents' for a small group of incoming freshers, who were their 'college children'.

I kind of loved it. It made a romance out of something absolutely mundane, which was something that I was incredibly experienced at.

Rooney and I, plus four other students who I only knew from their Facebook profiles, had arranged to gather with our college parents at Starbucks. This had all been organised in a group chat on Facebook last week in which I'd been too scared to say anything other than 'Sounds great! I'll be there ☺'.

But when we got there, only one of our parents was there – Sunil Jha.

'So,' said Sunil, crossing one leg over the other in his chair. 'I'm your college parent.'

Sunil Jha had a warm smile and kind eyes, and although he was only two years older than us he seemed infinitely more mature. He was also dressed incredibly well – slim trousers with

Converse, a T-shirt tucked in and a bomber jacket with a subtle grey tartan pattern.

'Please don't refer to me as your college mother or father,' he continued, 'not just because I'm non-binary, but also because that feels like a scary amount of commitment.'

This earned some chuckles. On his jacket were several enamel pins – a rainbow flag, a tiny old radio, a pin featuring a boyband logo, one that read 'He/They', and another pride pin, this one with black, grey, white and purple stripes. I was sure I'd seen that one before, online somewhere, but I couldn't remember what it meant.

'In a strange turn of events, your college mother decided that university wasn't for her and dropped out at the end of last term. So we're going to be a single-parent family this year.'

There were some more chuckles, but then silence. I wondered when Rooney was going to bust out the questions, but it seemed even she was a little intimidated by Sunil's third-year confidence.

'Basically,' said Sunil, 'I'm here if you have literally *any* questions or worries about anything while you're here. Alternatively, you can just do what you want and forget I ever existed.'

More laughs.

'So. Does anyone have anything you want to chat about while we're here?'

After a short moment, Rooney was the first to jump in. 'I was wondering, like . . . how the college marriage thing worked? I heard something about *college proposals* but I don't really know what that is.'

Oh, yeah. I was glad she'd asked that.

Sunil laughed. 'Oh my God, yes. OK. So. College marriage.' He linked his fingers together. 'If you want to form a mentor team with another student, you get college married. One of you proposes to the other and usually it's a big, dramatic proposal. There'll be lots happening this term.'

Rooney was nodding, fascinated. 'What d'you mean by "big and dramatic"?'

'Well . . . let me put it this way. My proposal involved me filling her bedroom with glitter-filled balloons, getting forty-odd people to wait in there and surprise her, and then get down on one knee in front of everyone with a plastic ring in the shape of a cat.'

Oh. God.

'Does everyone . . . um . . . does everyone get college married?' I asked.

Sunil looked at me. He really did have kind eyes. 'Most people. Usually friends do it, since it's just for fun. Sometimes couples do it, though.'

Friends. Couples.

Oh no.

Now I *really* needed to actually meet people.

The discussion broadened out into other aspects of university – our studies, the best clubs, good times to use the library, the Bailey Ball at the end of term. But I didn't say anything else. I just sat there, stressing out about college marriage.

It didn't matter if I didn't do that. Right? That wasn't what I was here for.

'Now, I'm going to be escorting you to a club this evening, apparently,' said Sunil, as we were all packing up to leave. 'So meet in reception at nine p.m., OK? And don't worry about dressing up too much.' As he continued he met my eyes and smiled, warm and gentle, 'And you don't have to come if you don't want to, all right? It's not mandatory.'

As Rooney and I walked back to college, I messaged Pip and

Jason about 'college marriage'. Their responses were pretty much what I expected from them:

Felipa Quintana
OMG WE HAVE THAT TOO
Literally cannot wait till someone proposes to me
Or I propose to someone
It's gonna be dramatic af
I hope someone showers me with confetti then recites a poem
to me on a boat in front of a hundred onlookers before releasing
a pair of doves into the sky

Jason Farley-Shaw
I think the concept seems kind of archaic, idk

Rooney, however, didn't have anything to say about college marriage, because she was much too focused on going out to a club.

'I'm so excited for tonight,' she said.

'Really?'

She smiled. 'I'm ready for my *uni experience*, you know?'

'Yeah,' I said, and I meant it. I was ready for my uni experience too. Sure, the idea of going to clubs was horrifying, and I still couldn't quite imagine the scenario in which I would fall for someone, but I was *going* to make it happen, and I was *going* to enjoy it. 'Me too.'

'So,' she said, and looked at me with her big dark eyes. She was objectively very pretty. Maybe she'd be my endgame. Roommate romance like in a fanfiction. This was university, for God's sake. Anything could happen. 'D'you like going out?'

By 'going out', she meant clubbing, and honestly, I didn't know.

I'd never been to a club. There weren't many nice ones in rural Kent, and neither Pip nor Jason were into that sort of thing.

Clubbing. College marriage. Sex. Romance.

I knew all this stuff was optional.

But I wanted to have a completely normal university experience, just like everyone else.

BABY'S FIRST CLUB

'Oh my God!' said Rooney, once I'd finished straightening my hair. 'You look so nice!'

'Ah, thanks!' I said awkwardly. I'm terrible at taking compliments.

Mum and I had gone clothes shopping a couple of weeks ago so I would have things to wear for club nights, and I'd picked out a couple of dresses and a pair of chunky shoes. I put one of the dresses on with black tights and honestly didn't think I looked too bad, but next to Rooney, I just felt like a child. She was wearing a velvet red jumpsuit – a deep V at the front and flared legs – with heeled boots and huge hooped earrings. She'd piled half her hair up in a messy bun on top of her head, the rest flowing down her back. She looked really fucking cool. I . . . didn't.

Then I felt bad because Mum and I had chosen this dress together. I felt a million miles away from Mum and our local shopping centre.

'Did you go out much back in Kent?' Rooney asked from where she was sitting on her bed, applying some final touches to her make-up in front of her pedestal mirror.

I wanted to lie and say I was super experienced at clubbing, but there was really no use. Rooney was already becoming acutely aware that I was a shy person and much, much worse at socialising than she was.

'Not really,' I said. 'I . . . I dunno. I didn't really think it was my sort of thing.'

'You don't have to go out if you don't want to!' She patted highlighter over her cheekbones before shooting me a smile. 'It's not everyone's scene.'

'No, no,' I said. 'I mean . . . I want to at least try it.'

She smiled some more. 'Good! Don't worry. I'll look after you.'

'Have you been out clubbing lots, then?'

'Oh, God, yeah.' She laughed, going back to her make-up.

OK. She sounded confident. Was she a party girl, like so many people I knew back at home? Was she the sort of person who would go out to clubs all the time and hook up with random people?

'Have you got Find My Friends on your phone?' she asked.

'Oh, um, I think so.'

I got my phone out and, sure enough, I did have the app downloaded. The only people I had on there were Pip and Jason.

Rooney held out her hand. 'Let me add myself. Then if we lose each other, you can find me again.'

She did so, and soon there was a little dot with Rooney's face on the map of Durham.

She suggested we took a selfie together in our bedroom mirror. She knew exactly how to pose, chin hidden behind a raised shoulder, eyes looking up enticingly beneath her lashes. I put one hand on my hip and hoped for the best.

If I was fully honest with myself, I just wanted to be Rooney Bach.

Sunil met us in the reception area, and it looked like most, if not all of the John's freshers had shown up to get their first taste of university nightlife. Despite the fact that he'd told us we didn't have to get dressed up, Sunil was wearing a tight-fit shirt in a bright paisley pattern with skinny trousers. I did notice, however, that he was wearing shoes that looked like they'd been trampled on and dragged through a muddy field, which probably should have prepared me for what I was about to face at the club.

We were shepherded to the club through the cold streets of Durham by Sunil and some other third years. Rooney had already attracted a small crowd of 'friends', if you could call them that yet, and I hovered towards the back of her group, apprehensive.

Everyone seemed so excited.

Nobody else seemed nervous.

Most people my age had been to clubs by now. Most people I'd known in Year 13 had frequented the club in our nearest town, which from what I'd heard was a sticky, terrifying hellhole of regrets. But *I* was the one regretting not having gone with them, now. This was just another example of something I had utterly failed to experience during my teenage life.

The entrance was down an alleyway, and it was free to get in before 11 p.m. They didn't need IDs as we were all wearing freshers' wristbands. Inside, it was as if someone had designed me my own personal hell – a tight-packed crowd, sticky floors and music so loud it took Rooney repeating herself three times before I realised she was asking me if I wanted to go to the bar.

I listened to what she ordered so I'd know what to ask for – vodka and lemonade. Then there was chatting, and more chatting, and more chatting. Well, shouting, actually. Mostly people wanted to talk about *what are you studying*, and *where are you from*, and *how are you finding it all*. I started repeating sentences word for word to multiple people. Like a robot. God. I just wanted to make a friend.

And then there was dancing. I started to notice just how many of the songs were about romance or sex. How had I never noticed that before? Like, almost all songs ever written are about romance or sex. And it felt like they were taunting me.

Rooney tried to get me to dance with her, just in a casual, fun way, and I tried, I swear I tried, but she gave up quickly and found someone else. I bobbed along the side of various people I'd had conversations with. I was having fun.

I was having fun.

I was not having fun.

It was nearing eleven o'clock when I messaged Pip, mostly because I wanted someone to talk to without having to shout.

Georgia Warr
HEY how are you this evening

Felipa Quintana
Everything is absolutely fine why do you ask
I may have smashed a wine glass

Georgia Warr
pip . . . .

Felipa Quintana
Let me live

Georgia Warr
how come you're drinking

Felipa Quintana
Because I am the master of my own fate and I live for chaos
Jk our corridor is having a pizza and alcohol night
Btw I think I left my jacket in your room last night?

Georgia Warr
oh no!!! i'll bring it when i visit you, don't worry

'Who you texting?' Rooney shouted in my ear.

'Pip!' I shouted back.

'What's she saying?'

I showed Rooney the message about Pip's smashed glass. Rooney grinned at it, and then laughed.

'I like her!' she shouted. 'She's so funny!' And then she went back to dancing.

Georgia Warr
anyway guess where I am

Felipa Quintana
Omg where

Georgia Warr
A CLUB

Felipa Quintana

ARE YOU JOKING

I never thought I would see this day

Baby's first club!!!

Wait was this Rooney's idea? Is she peer pressuring you???

Georgia Warr

no i wanted to go haha!!

Felipa Quintana

Okay well be safe!!!!! Don't do drugs!!!!! Watch out for nasty men!!!!!!!

I hung in there, bobbing, until Rooney wanted to get some fresh air. Well, as much fresh air as you could get in the smoking area out the back of the club.

We leant against the brick wall of the building. I shivered, but Rooney seemed fine.

'So?' she asked. 'What's your official clubbing verdict?'

I made a face. I couldn't help it.

She threw her head back against the wall and laughed.

'At least you're honest about it,' she said. 'A lot of people hate it and still go anyway.'

'I guess.' I sipped my drink. 'I just wanted to try it. I wanted to be a part of the uni experience. You know.'

She nodded. 'Gross clubs are an important staple of university life, yes.'

I couldn't tell whether she was being sarcastic.

I was a little drunk, to be fair.

'I just want . . . I want to *meet people*, and . . . do normal things,' I said, throwing back the last of my drink. I didn't even like it that much, but everyone was drinking, and I'd look weird if I wasn't, wouldn't I? 'I don't have a great track record of doing that very well.'

'Don't you?'

'Nope. I have hardly any friends. I've always had hardly any friends.'

Rooney's smile dropped. 'Oh.'

'I've never even had a boyfriend. Or even kissed anyone.'

The words just came on out before I could stop them.

I immediately cringed at myself. Shit. That was the thing I wasn't supposed to tell anyone any more. That was the thing people had made fun of me for.

Rooney's eyebrows raised. 'Wow, *really*?'

She wasn't being sarcastic. That was pure, genuine shock. I don't know why I was surprised – people's reactions during truth or dare on prom night must have been how everyone felt. But it really got to me in that moment. The weird looks. The people who'd suddenly see me as a child, as *immature*. The movies where the main characters freaked out about being virgins at the age of sixteen.

'Really,' I said.

'Do you feel bad about it?'

I shrugged. 'Yeah.'

'And you want to change it? Now that you're at uni?'

'Ideally, yes.'

'OK. Good.' She turned so she was facing me, leaning against the wall with one shoulder. 'I think I can help.'

'O . . . K . . .'

'I want you to go in there and find one person you think is hot. Or a few. More chance of this working.'

I already absolutely hated this idea. 'Oh.'

'Try and get their name, or at least memorise what they look like. And then I'll help you get with them.'

I did not like this scheme. I did not like this at all. Survival Mode was kicking in throughout my body. I wanted to run.

'Oh,' I repeated.

'Trust me,' she grinned. 'I know a *lot* about relationships.'

What did *that* mean?

'OK,' I said. 'So I just pick a person and . . . you'll set us up?'

'Yes. Sound good?'

'. . . Yeah.'

If the university experience was all about bad decisions, at least I was doing something right.

I felt a bit like David Attenborough.

I circled the club on my own, leaving Rooney at the bar, focusing on the guys first. There were a lot of hoodies. Sweat-patches on T-shirts. A lot of them had the same hairstyle – short sides, longer on top.

I kept looking. Surely I'd find someone I fancied *eventually*. The club was packed – there had to be a good couple of hundred people crammed into this room alone.

And yet, I found no one.

There were guys who were objectively 'attractive', of course, by modern-day media standards. There were guys who clearly worked out a lot. There were guys who had fun hair or good fashion or a nice smile.

But I wasn't *attracted* to any of them.

I didn't feel any sort of *desire*.

When I tried to picture standing close to them, kissing them, *touching them* . . .

I grimaced. Disgusting, disgusting, *disgusting*.

I decided to change tactics and look at the girls instead. Girls are all pretty, to be honest. And they have much more variety in appearance.

But on a basic, physical level, did I feel attraction?

No.

Lots of people had started hooking up already – kissing each other underneath the flashing lights and the love songs playing louder than the voices in our heads. It was a little gross, but it had an element of danger that made it beautiful. Kissing a stranger you'd never see again, kissing someone whose name you didn't even know, just to feel a little high in that moment. Just to feel the warmth of someone's skin on yours. Just, for a while, to feel purely alive.

God. I wished I could do that.

But the idea of trying to get with any of these people – no matter their gender – was, honestly, unnerving. It made me feel itchy. Shivery, maybe. It filled my stomach with a weird, horrible dread, and a warning siren went off in my brain. It felt like my antibodies were fighting it off.

What was I going to say to Rooney?

Out of hundreds of students, I couldn't find anybody I thought was hot. Sorry.

Maybe she could just choose someone for me. God, that would be so much easier.

It would be so much easier if I had someone to just tell me what to do and who to be with and how to act and what love actually was.

I abandoned my search. Tonight I would remain kiss-less. Romance-less. And that was fine. Right? That was fine.

I didn't know whether I'd wanted it or whether I hadn't.

Honestly, it might have been a little bit of both. Just like with Tommy.

Wanting and not wanting at the same time.

It wasn't until an hour later that I spotted Rooney again through the blurry, flashing mass of bodies. She was in the middle of the dance floor, making out with a tall guy wearing ripped skinny jeans.

His arms were round her waist. One of her hands was on his face.

It was a picture of passion. Movie romance. Desire.

How.

How could a person reach that point in the space of an hour?

How could she do in one single hour what I was unable to force myself to do in my whole teenage life?

I hated her. I wanted to be her. I hated myself.

It all hit me then, suddenly. The music was so loud I felt like my vision was blurring. I shoved through people to get to the edge of the room, only to find myself pressed up against the wall, which was wet with condensation. I looked wildly around for the door, then started barging my way towards it, and out, into the chilly, empty October air.

I breathed.

I wasn't going to cry.

Three of the John's third years were having a conversation in the smoking area, leaning against the wall, including, to my surprise, Sunil.

He was my college parent – I knew he'd help me. I could ask him to walk me back. But as I stepped forward, I felt embarrassed. I was an absolute failure. A child. Sunil turned, glanced at me curiously and I willed him to ask me if I wanted to go back to college and whether I wanted him to walk back with me. But he didn't say anything. So I just left.

After a couple of hours in the noisy club, the high street's silence felt like it was echoing around me. I could barely remember the way back to college because I'd been so stressed on the way here that I hadn't been paying attention to where we'd been walking, but thankfully, I found myself on the cobbled path and walking back up the hill, past the castle, then the cathedral, and then I could see the stone steps of St John's College.

'There's something wrong with you,' I said under my breath. Then I shook my head, trying to get the thought out. That was a bad thought. There was nothing wrong with me. This was just who I was. *Stop thinking about it. Stop thinking about any of it.*

I could message Pip and – what would I even tell her? That I was terrible at clubbing? That I could have tried to kiss someone but decided not to? That I was utterly failing at my new start? Pathetic. There was nothing to even tell her.

I could talk about it with Jason, but he'd probably just tell me I was being silly. Because I was. I knew this whole thing was ridiculous.

So I just walked. I kept my head down. I didn't even know what was wrong. Everything. Myself. I didn't know. How come everyone else could function and I couldn't? How could everyone live properly yet I had some sort of error in my programming?

I thought about all the people I'd met in the past few days. Hundreds of people my age, all genders, appearances, personalities.

I couldn't think of a single one I was attracted to.

I opened the door to college so loudly that the man in the little office gave me a stern look. I suppose he thought I was a drunk fresher. God, I wished I was. I looked down at my dress, the one Mum had seen in River Island and said, *Oh, isn't that perfect?* And I'd agreed, and she'd bought it for me, so I could look nice and feel nice during Freshers' Week. I started to well up. God, not yet, please not yet.

My room was empty – of course it was. Rooney was out there living her life and having experiences. I grabbed my washbag and pyjamas, went straight to the bathroom, got in the shower and had a cry.

HIGH STANDARDS

'So you have *very high standards*,' Rooney said to me the next morning while I was eating a bagel in bed and she was doing her make-up in front of her mirror.

We would have talked about it last night, but I fell asleep in the middle of reading a Steve/Bucky Regency Era AU fic, only to wake up a few hours later to find Rooney returned, fast asleep, her make-up still on and her boots discarded in the middle of the aqua rug.

'That's . . . accurate,' I confirmed. I did have high standards. I wasn't sure what exactly my standards were, but they were undoubtedly very high.

'Don't worry,' she said, seemingly unfazed. 'We've got *loads* more chances to find you someone. It won't be that hard.'

'Won't it?'

'Nope.' Her mouth dropped open as she did her mascara. 'Loads of people are looking to hook up this week. There are *so* many opportunities for you to meet people. It won't take us that long to find you someone you like.'

'OK.'

'You'll see.'

'OK.'

'What's your type?' Rooney asked at lunch.

Lunch at college was just like lunch at school – cafeteria food and sitting round tables and benches – but ten times worse due to the added pressure of socialising with a bunch of people I didn't know very well. As irritating as I found Rooney's effortless ability to thrive at university, I was actually very glad to have her in situations like this.

Thankfully, however, this was the first meal that Rooney and I had showed up to in which we didn't spot anyone Rooney knew, so we were able to sit just us.

'Type?' I asked, my mind immediately going to Pokémon types, and then wondering whether it was a food question of some sort and looked down at my pasta.

'Type of *guy*,' said Rooney, mouth full.

'Oh.' I shrugged and speared a piece of pasta. 'I don't really know.'

'Come on. You must have *some* idea. Like, what sort of guys do you find yourself liking?'

None of them, is what I probably should have said. *I never like anyone.*

'No type in particular,' is what I actually said.

'Tall? Nerdy? Sporty? Musicians? Tattoos? Long hair? Boys who look like pirates?'

'I don't know.'

'Hm.' Rooney chewed slowly, looking at me. 'Girls?'

'What?'

'D'you prefer girls?'

'Um.' I blinked. 'Well . . . I don't think so? Not really.'

'Hm.'

'What?'

'It's just interesting.'

'What is?'

Rooney swallowed, smirking. 'You, I guess.'

I was about eighty per cent sure she was using 'interesting' as a synonym for 'weird', but, oh well.

'I had an idea,' Rooney said to me in a very earnest tone that evening. I would have taken her seriously were she not dressed as a sexy fried egg in preparation for the John's college bar fancy-dress party. This comprised a body piece in the shape of a fried egg, but with thigh-high socks and giant heels. I was actually quite impressed – it was an incredible way to say 'I want to look good, but also let you know that I have a sense of humour'.

I was not going to the fancy-dress party. I'd told Rooney I needed a night to just be on my own and watch *About Time* swiftly followed by *La La Land*, and, to my surprise, she'd said that was fair enough.

'An idea?' I said from my bed. 'About . . .?'

Rooney walked over and flopped down next to me on my bed. I shuffled up so the fried-egg body piece wasn't literally crushing my torso.

'Your no-romo situation.'

'I'm really not that bothered,' I said, which was obviously a lie. I was extremely and consistently bothered, but after yesterday's fiasco I was ready to give up rather than put myself through that again.

Rooney held up her phone. 'Have you tried any dating apps?'

I looked at the phone. I'd never met anyone our age who used a *dating app*. I hesitated. 'Do people our age use dating apps?'

'I've used Tinder since I turned eighteen.'

I knew what Tinder was, at least. 'I don't really think Tinder is for me.'

'But how will you know if you don't try?'

'I don't think I need to try everything to know I don't like it.'

Rooney sighed. 'Look, OK. This is just an idea, but Tinder is a really good way to just have a look at what guys are actually out there, like, *in the vicinity*. You don't actually have to talk to them, but, like, it might at least help you get an idea of what sort of guy you want to go for.'

She opened Tinder on her phone and immediately showed me a picture of the first guy who popped up. 'Kieran, 21, Student'.

I looked at Kieran. He looked a bit like a tall rat. Which, you know. That sort of look does it for some people.

'I don't think this is my thing,' I said.

Rooney rolled off my bed with a sigh, her egg costume nearly knocking over the glass of water on my bedside table. 'It's just an idea. Do it if you get bored tonight.' She walked over to her own bed and grabbed her bag. 'Swipe left is no, swipe right is yes.'

'I don't think I'll –'

'It's just an idea! You don't have to, like, *love* them, but just look out for anyone you see who you wouldn't mind finding more about.'

And then she was out the door.

I was half an hour into *About Time* when I picked up my phone and downloaded Tinder.

I definitely wasn't going to talk to anyone. I was just curious.

I just wanted to know if I would ever see a guy and think, *Yeah, he's hot.*

So I made a Tinder profile. I picked five of my best selfies from Instagram and spent another half an hour trying to think what to write in my 'About' section, before settling on 'Cheesy-romcom connoisseur'.

The first guy who popped up was 'Myles, 20, Student'. He had brown hair and a leer. In one picture he was playing snooker. I got a bad vibe and swiped left.

The second guy was 'Adrian, 19, Student'. His bio said he was an adrenaline junkie who was looking for his 'manic pixie dream girl', which got an instant swipe left.

I swiped left on four more guys, then realised that I wasn't even looking at them properly – I was just reading the bios and making an assessment as to whether I thought we'd get on. That wasn't the point. I was supposed to be finding someone I was *physically attracted to*.

So after that I tried to properly focus on their appearances. Their faces, their eyes, their mouths, their hair, their style. These were the things you were supposed to like. What did *I* like? What was *my* standard? What were *my* preferences?

After ten minutes of this, I stumbled upon a guy who looked like a model, so I was unsurprised when I looked at his info and read 'Jack, 18, Model'. He had a sharp-cut jawline and a symmetrical face. His main photo was clearly from a magazine advert he'd done.

I tried to picture myself dating Jack, 18, Model. Kissing him. Having sex.

Like, if it was gonna be anyone, based on appearance alone, surely it would be Jack, 18, Model, with his cool denim jacket and dimples.

Imagine kissing that face.

Imagine him leaning in.

Imagine his skin near you.

My thumb hovered over the screen for a moment. Trying to ignore the nauseated feeling in my stomach at the pictures I was conjuring in my head.

Then I swiped left.

Georgia Warr
hello fried egg i have an update
i swiped left on all of them lol

Rooney Bach
Haha what do you mean all of them

Georgia Warr
just all the ones i looked at

Rooney Bach
And how many was that?

Georgia Warr
idk like . . . forty?
tinder isn't for me i think lol
sorry to disappoint

Rooney Bach
I'm not disappointed haha I just hoped it would help
FORTY
Wow!!
Okay!

Georgia Warr
so that's a lot to swipe left on??

Rooney Bach
You really do have high standards
That's not necessarily a bad thing but at least we've got that
sussed

Georgia Warr
so what do i do now

Rooney Bach
Might have to go back to good old-fashioned Meeting People In
Real Life

Georgia Warr
ew
hate that for me

I deleted Tinder from my phone, then hit play on *About Time* again, wondering why picturing myself in any sort of romantic or sexual situation made me feel like I was going to vom and/ or run a mile, while romance in movies felt like the sole purpose of being alive.

PRIDE

Rooney was right about one thing: meeting people in real life was probably the only way this was going to work for me. Fortunately, it was Freshers' Week, and I still had many opportunities to meet people, which continued on the Friday when Rooney and I went to the Freshers' Fair.

'I'm going to join *so many* societies,' Rooney said, and I didn't take her that seriously, but when we went round all the stalls in the Student Union building, she collected so many flyers that she made me start carrying some of them for her.

I'd arranged to meet Pip and Jason there too but wasn't sure where to find them because the Student Union building was *huge*. They'd have to wait. The most important task at hand was *joining university societies*. Alongside clubbing, which I had epically failed at, societies were a staple of university life and supposedly one of the easiest ways to make friends with like-minded people.

But as we walked round the stalls, I started to feel nervous. Maybe a little overwhelmed. I tentatively signed up to English Soc with Rooney, but apart from that, I could barely even remember what I was interested in. Creative Writing Soc? I didn't really enjoy writing that much – the few occasions I'd tried writing my own fanfic were *disastrous*. Film Soc? I could just watch movies in bed. There were even super-niche things like Anime Soc, Quidditch Soc and Snowboarding Soc, but they all seemed like they catered for a specific group of friends who just wanted an excuse to hang out and do their favourite hobby together. I didn't know what my hobbies were any more, except yearning for romance and reading fanfiction.

In fact, the only other society I wanted to join was the Durham Student Theatre. I could see its giant stall at the end of the hall.

I'd definitely meet new people if I was in a play this year.

Rooney ended up walking on ahead, excited to chat to all the people on the stalls. I ambled along, feeling increasingly like I just didn't really fit anywhere, until I realised I had reached the stall of Durham's Pride Society.

It stood out boldly with a giant rainbow flag behind it and had quite a sizeable gathering of freshers standing near it, chatting excitedly to the older students behind the table.

I picked up one of their leaflets to have a look. Most of the front page was decorated with some of the identities it supported in arty fonts. The ones I knew well were at the top – lesbian, gay, bisexual, transgender – and then, to my surprise, it moved into ones I'd only really heard on the internet – pansexual, asexual, aromantic, non-binary. And more. I didn't even know what some of them meant.

'College child?' said a voice, and I looked up and was faced with Sunil Jha, my college parent.

On his woolly jumper he was wearing all his pins again, and he was smiling warmly at me. He was definitely the nicest person I'd met at Durham so far, not counting Rooney. Could he be my friend? Did college parents count as friends?

'Interested in signing up?' he asked.

'Um,' I said. To be honest, I didn't really want to join. What right did I have to join a society like this? I mean, to be fair, I didn't really know what I was. And yes, sure, I had considered the possibility that I was not into guys. *Strongly* considered. Then again, I didn't really seem to like girls either. I didn't seem to like anyone. I hadn't met anyone I liked yet, felt the nice stomach butterflies, and been able to proudly declare 'Aha! Of course! *This* is the gender that I like!' I didn't even have a particular gender preference when it came to smutty fanfiction.

Sunil held out a clipboard and pen. 'Write down your email! It just puts you on our mailing list.'

There wasn't really any way to say no, so I mumbled an OK and wrote down my email address. I immediately felt like a fraud.

'It's Georgia, isn't it?' asked Sunil while I was writing.

'Y-yeah,' I stammered, honestly taken aback that he'd remembered my name.

Sunil nodded approvingly. 'Sweet. I'm the Pride Rep at John's.'

Another girl behind the stall leaned over to us and added, '*And* Sunil's the president of Pride Soc. Always forgets to mention that because of *modesty* or something.'

Sunil laughed gently. He definitely gave off an air of modesty, but self-confidence too. Like he was very good at his job but didn't want to boast about it.

'This is Jess, one of the vice-presidents,' he said. 'And this is Georgia, one of my college children.'

I looked at the third-year girl. She had hip-length braids, a big smile, and was wearing a colourful dress that had lollipops on it. She had a little badge that said 'she/her' on it.

'Aw!' she said. 'This is your college child?'

Sunil nodded. 'They sure are.'

Jess clapped her hands together. 'And you're joining Pride Soc. This was actually meant to be.'

I forced a smile.

'*Anyway*,' said Sunil, shaking his head at her with a sort of fondness, 'we're here for any freshers who wanna get involved in queer stuff at Durham, basically. Club nights, meet-ups, formals, film nights. Stuff like that.'

'Cool!' I said, trying to sound enthusiastic. Maybe I *should* try and get involved. Maybe I'd go to the Pride Society, see a girl, have a big lesbian awakening, and finally feel some romantic feelings for another human being. I was sure I'd read a fanfic with that exact plot.

I handed the clipboard back.

'Our welcome gathering is happening in a couple of weeks,' said Sunil with a smile. 'Maybe we'll see you there?'

I nodded, feeling a little bit embarrassed, like I'd been exposed somehow, which was dumb, because there was really nothing interesting about me to expose, and I already knew that I wasn't going to go to any of Sunil's Pride Soc events.

PUTTING YOURSELF OUT THERE

Our final stop of the Freshers' Fair was Durham Student Theatre, which had the largest stall in the entire Student Union, and Pip and Jason were standing right in front of it.

Rooney had already stormed ahead to the stall, which was decorated with a big red curtain and papier-mâchéd comedy–tragedy masks. The DST seemed to be a sort of umbrella organisation that supported and funded lots of smaller theatre groups – the Musical Theatre Soc, the Opera Soc, the Freshers' Drama Soc, Student Comedy, and more.

The students behind the stall, even from afar, all seemed loud and confident – it had none of the calming vibe of the Pride Soc stall. But that didn't put me off. Theatre was something familiar. It had been a part of my life for over seven years and, despite my stage fright, I didn't want to give it up.

Plus, Pip and Jason would be doing it with me. So I'd be OK.

'Pip? Jason?'

Their heads turned to reveal a confused-looking Pip Quintana, holding a flyer and pushing her tortoiseshell glasses up her nose, and a definitely hungover Jason Farley-Shaw, who had bags under his eyes and looked like he was trying to burrow and make a nest inside his teddy-bear jacket.

'GEORGIA!' Pip shrieked, running up to me and bundling me into a hug.

I hugged her back until she stepped away. She was smiling wide. So little had changed; she was still Pip, dark hair fluffed up in all different directions and drowning in an oversized sweatshirt. But, of course, we'd only been in Durham for five days. It already felt like a lifetime. Like I was already a different person.

'Hey,' said Jason. His voice sounded gravelly.

'You OK?' I asked him.

He made a grunting noise and pulled his jacket round him. 'Hungover. And we couldn't find you. Check your phone.'

I quickly glanced at the screen. There were several unread messages in the group chat asking where I was.

Pip folded her arms and gave me a discerning look. 'I assume you haven't been checking your phone because you've been really busy putting yourself out there and joining loads of societies?

'Um . . .' I tried not to look too guilty. 'I joined English Soc?'

I didn't confess to Pip that I'd signed up to Pride Soc's mailing list. Probably because I didn't feel like I actually belonged there.

Pip made a face. 'Georgia. That's *one society*.'

I shrugged. 'I could join some later.'

'*Georgia.*'

'What have you joined?'

She counted them on her fingers. 'I've joined Durham Student Theatre, obviously, and also Science Soc, Latin American Soc, Pride Soc, Chess, Ultimate Frisbee and I think I signed up for, like, Quidditch?'

Of course Pip had joined Pride Soc too. I wondered what she'd say if I randomly showed up to a Pride Soc event.

'Quidditch?' I asked.

'Yeah, and if the brooms don't actually fly, we're going to be really fucking disappointed.'

'We?' I looked at Jason. 'You also joined Quidditch? You don't even like *Harry Potter*.'

Jason nodded. 'The Quidditch president was incredibly persuasive.'

'What else did you join?'

'DST, History Soc, Film Soc and Rowing.'

I frowned. 'Rowing?'

Jason shrugged. 'Loads of people are doing it, so. Thought I'd give it a go –' He stopped speaking abruptly, peering past my shoulder. 'What is Rooney doing?'

I turned. Rooney seemed to be having a heated conversation with the girl behind the stall.

'I don't understand,' Rooney was saying. 'What d'you mean it *closed*?'

The girl behind the stall looked a little desperate. 'I-I think they didn't have any members in second or first year, so when the third years left, it just – it just disappeared.'

'And I can't start it up again?'

'Um . . . I don't know . . . I don't really know how it works . . .'

'Are you the president? Can I talk to the president?'

'Um, no, she's not here . . .'

'Oh, never mind. I'll sort this out another time.'

Rooney stormed towards us, eyes filled with fire. Out of sheer instinct, I cowered backwards.

'Can you *believe*,' she said, 'the Shakespeare Society is just . . . fucking . . . *gone*? Like, that was the *one* society I really wanted to join, and now it's just . . .' She stopped, realising that Pip and

Jason were standing next to me, staring at Rooney with what could only be described as fascination. 'Oh. Hello.'

'All right,' said Pip.

'Hi,' said Jason.

'How's Roderick?' said Pip.

Rooney's mouth twitched with amusement. 'I like that your mind immediately went to my house plant rather than asking how *I* am.'

'I care about plant welfare,' Pip replied.

I noticed the cooler tone to her voice immediately. Gone was the flustered way she'd babbled around Rooney back in our bedroom. She wasn't blushing and adjusting her hair any more.

After what she'd seen in our kitchen, Pip was on the defensive now.

It made me feel sad. But this was what Pip did when she got a crush on someone who couldn't like her back: she shut down the feelings with sheer willpower.

It protected her.

'Are you going to call plant social services on me?' asked Rooney, smiling cheekily. She seemed to be immensely enjoying having someone to banter with, like it was a welcome break from having to be peppy and polite.

Pip tilted her head. 'Maybe I am plant social services and I'm just in disguise.'

'It's not a very good disguise. You look exactly like the sort of person who's got at least six cactuses on your bookcase.'

This seemed to be the last straw for Pip, because she snapped back, 'I only have three, actually, and it's *cacti* not *cactuses* –'

'Uh . . .' The two girls were interrupted by Jason, who, if he'd not had a headache before, definitely had one now. 'So, are you actually gonna sign up to DST, or . . .?'

'Yes,' I said immediately, if only to end whatever weirdly aggressive verbal sparring was occurring between Pip and Rooney.

'I don't even know what the point is any more,' said Rooney with a dramatic sigh. 'Shakespeare Soc doesn't even exist. Something about it running out of members.'

'Can't you just join something else?' said Pip, but Rooney looked at her like she'd suggested something infinitely idiotic.

Jason hadn't even bothered to stay involved in this conversation and had walked over to the DST mailing list. I followed him and he handed me the pen.

'I didn't think you'd want to join DST,' he said, 'after all the throwing-up during *Les Mis*.'

'I still love theatre,' I said. 'And I need to join more than just the English Soc.'

'But you could pick something that *didn't* make you throw up.'

'I'd rather throw up surrounded by friends than join a society alone and be sad.'

Jason paused, then said, 'I think that sounded more profound in your head than it did in real life.'

I finished writing my email address and put the pen down, glancing up at Jason. He did genuinely seem a bit concerned about me.

'I want to do this,' I said. 'I . . . I really want to try and . . . you know. Meet new people and . . . have a good university experience.'

Jason paused again. Then he nodded, face full of understanding. 'Yeah. That makes sense.'

We stepped aside to let Pip and Rooney write down their emails on the list, all the while they were having some sort of inane argument about which DST society they should join, and each of them seemed determined to establish that their choice was the correct choice and the other person's choice was utterly wrong. After several minutes of this, Jason eventually decided to end it by suggesting we all go to get pizza from the Domino's stand, which was giving out free slices.

'I'm gonna carry on looking around for a bit,' said Rooney. She moved her gaze from Pip to me. 'Meet you at the entrance in like twenty minutes?'

I nodded.

'Fab.' Rooney looked back at Pip again and said as if Jason didn't even exist, 'How about we all meet up at John's bar tonight? It's *so* fun down there, it's this tiny little basement bar . . .'

Most people would not have been able to tell what was up with Pip, but I'd known her for over seven years, and she had this *look*. A slight narrowing of the eyes. Her shoulders hunched.

The fact of the matter was: Pip had decided to hate Rooney.

'Yeah, we'll be there,' said Pip, folding her arms.

'*Yay,*' said Rooney, smiling wide. 'Can't *wait.*'

Rooney wandered off into the mass of stalls again. Pip, Jason and I headed towards the Domino's stand, Pip's eyes never leaving the back of Rooney's head, and Jason asking Pip, 'What the *fuck* was that?'

SHAKESPEARE AND HOUSE PLANTS

A bonding opportunity for my only three friends was definitely a good idea, but this was somewhat counteracted by the fact that Rooney seemed to delight in irritating Pip, while Pip seemed to be infuriated by her mere existence in all of our lives, and I had already discovered that I was not a fan of clubs and bars.

Felipa Quintana
THE VIBES, GEORGIA. THE VIBES.

Georgia Warr
what of them

Felipa Quintana
THEY ARE BAD
I should have seen it when we met
She's full of bad vibes

Georgia Warr

rooney's actually quite nice

are you just saying this because you saw her hooking up with someone?? no slut-shaming is allowed in this group chat

Felipa Quintana

OBVIOUSLY NOT. She can hook up with whoever she likes however much she wants, I have no problems with people who enjoy casual hooking up

I'm just getting a bad vibe

 . . . . . . She made fun of my cacti

Jason Farley-Shaw

In other news

Where are we meeting and what time??

I don't know where John's Bar is!!

Georgia Warr

i'll come pick you both up from pip's room

i'm concerned about pip arriving by herself and making a scene as soon as she sees rooney

Jason Farley-Shaw

Oh that's good thinking. Smart. 👍

Felipa Quintana

FUCK you both

'I'm perfectly capable of going to a bar and not making a scene just because I don't like *one* person,' said Pip as she opened her door to me later that evening.

I'd been given specific directions but still ended up having to call her and be verbally directed around the winding corridors of Castle. And if that wasn't enough chaos to deal with on a Friday evening, Pip's bedroom was in definite competition for *messiest bedroom in Durham*. There were more clothes on the floor than there appeared to be in her open wardrobe, her desk was piled high with incredibly boring-looking science books and pieces of paper, and her bedsheets were smushed into a corner, several feet away from her bed.

'Sure you are,' I said, patting Pip on the head.

'*Don't* patronise me, Georgia Warr. Did you bring my denim jacket?'

'Your denim jacket?' I smacked my head. I could picture exactly where Pip's jacket was in my room – on the back of my desk chair. 'Oh, no, sorry, I totally forgot.'

'Don't worry,' said Pip, but she glanced down at her outfit nervously. 'I was gonna wear it tonight, but . . . do you think I look OK without it? Or maybe I could wear a bomber jacket.'

She looked really good, actually – she was wearing a stripy short-sleeved shirt, tucked in at the hips into a pair of ripped black skinny jeans, and her hair was carefully styled. And she looked very much like *herself*, which I thought was more important.

Pip had always been kind of insecure about how she looked. But now that she was actually dressing how she'd always wanted to dress, and had cut her hair and all that, she exuded a sort of confidence that I could never hope to achieve – a confidence that said *I know exactly who I am*.

'You look really nice,' I said.

She smiled. 'Thanks.'

I'd decided to wear something slightly more casual than my last attempt at 'going out' – some high-waisted jeans and a tight-fit crop top – but I still felt a little like I was wearing a costume. My usual comfy knitwear style wasn't really suitable for bars and clubs.

Jason arrived minutes later, wearing his teddy-bear jacket on top of his standard T-shirt–jeans combo. He took one look at the floor and immediately started picking up items of clothing and folding them. 'Jesus fucking Christ, Pip. Learn to tidy.'

'It's absolutely fine how it is. I know where everything is.'

'Maybe so, but it won't be absolutely fine when you start getting spiders birthing underneath your sweatshirts.'

'*Ew*, Jason. Don't say "birthing".'

We did a quick tidy of Pip's room before leaving. It was only a few minutes' walk from Castle to St John's – we had to cross Palace Green, past the cathedral, and down a little side street – and in that time, I decided to confront Pip about the exact reason for her declaration of 'bad vibes'.

'I *don't* have a crush on her,' said Pip instantly, which confirmed the fact that she definitely had a crush on Rooney. 'I *don't* get crushes on straight girls. Any more.'

'So you've decided that she's your mortal enemy because . . .?'

'You know what it is?' Pip folded her arms, pulling her bomber jacket round her. 'She's the sort of person who just thinks she's better than *everyone*, purely because she goes to clubs and bars and she has a giant house plant and she likes *Shakespeare*.'

'You like Shakespeare and you have house plants,' said Jason. 'Why's she not allowed to like Shakespeare and house plants?'

Pip just gave him an irritated look.

Jason glanced at me, eyebrows raised. We could both tell that Pip was making up silly reasons to dislike Rooney in an attempt to deflect her feelings. But we also knew we should probably just let it happen because, in all honesty, it was probably the best course of action.

We'd seen Pip through several straight–girl crushes. They were not fun for her. The sooner she could get over those feelings, the better.

'You could have just said no to hanging out tonight,' I pointed out.

'No I couldn't,' said Pip, 'because then she'd *win*.'

Jason and I stayed silent for a moment.

Then I said, 'She's been giving me some advice about stuff.'

Pip frowned. 'Advice? About what?'

'Well . . . you know I was feeling kind of bad about, like . . .' God. This stuff was always so awkward to talk about. 'You remember at the prom afterparty I was feeling really down about not having kissed anyone, and . . . you know. Rooney's been helping me try and put myself out there a bit.'

Pip and Jason stared at me.

'*What?*' Pip shook her head in disbelief. 'You don't – Why is she making you do that? You don't have to do that shit . . . just – *God*. You need to just go at your own pace, man. Why is she making you? . . . What? Is she trying to persuade you to start getting with people at bars? That's fine if *she* wants to do that, but that's not who you are.'

'She's not making me do anything! She's just helping me open up to people a bit, and, like . . . take chances.'

'But you shouldn't have to force this stuff! That's not who you *are,*' she repeated, frowning.

'Well, what if that's who I *want* to be?' I snapped back. I felt immediately bad about it. Pip and I never argued.

Pip shut her mouth. She didn't seem to have an answer for that.

Eventually she said, 'I don't like Rooney because she's disrupting the dynamics of our friendship group. And she's very annoying to me specifically.'

I didn't even bother to answer her.

Jason was flattening his hair awkwardly. 'Uh . . . It's good that you've made a friend, though, Georgia.'

'Yeah,' I said.

I felt my phone buzz in my bag and withdrew it to take a look.

Rooney Bach
I'm at the bar!
Hey maybe we could hook you up with someone tonight . . .

I sent her a thumbs-up emoji.

CHAOTIC ENERGY

Rooney had managed to bagsy an entire table for us in John's bar, which deserved a medal, because it was *heaving*. The bar was a tiny basement area in college, super old and very hot. I could practically feel people's sweat in the air as we squeezed through the crowd to get to the table.

Rooney had dressed up for the night: jumpsuit, heels, hair curled into loose waves. She probably had other plans after hanging out with us at the very childish hour of 9 p.m. And while she had been waiting for us, she seemed to have befriended a large group of people sitting at the next table.

'Darlings,' said Rooney in a fake posh drawl as we all sat down, turning away from her new friends. 'You all look *so* nice.' She looked directly at Pip. 'So stripes are your thing, Felipa?'

Pip narrowed her eyes at the use of her unshortened name. 'Have you been Facebook-stalking me?'

'Instagram, actually. I enjoyed the photo of you dressed up as a crayon for Halloween.'

This earned a smug smile from Pip. 'You scrolled *very* far back then.'

We had to suffer several minutes of irritating banter between Pip and Rooney before Jason and I could even contribute to the conversation. In that time, I did some people-watching, looking around the room at our fellow students. There were people on a regular night out, some dressed up and others just in their college sweatshirts and jeans. There were people in fancy dress – a lot, actually, but it was still Freshers' Week, so that made sense.

'So how did you all become friends?' asked Rooney.

'School,' I said. 'And we all went to the same youth theatre group.'

'Oh my *God*, that's right! You're all theatre kids! I forgot!' Rooney's face lit up. 'This is amazing. We can all go to the welcome meeting together next week!'

'It's sad about your society getting shut down,' Jason said.

'Yeah! Shakespeare Soc. I was *so* set on joining it, but . . . it just doesn't exist any more. Surely that's some sort of crime against Britain.'

'So you like Shakespeare?' asked Pip. She sounded *sceptical*, almost.

Rooney nodded. 'Yeah! *Love* it. Do you?'

Pip nodded back. 'Yeah. I've been in a few at school.'

'Same. I was in *Romeo and Juliet, Much Ado, Comedy of Errors*, and *Hamlet* at school.'

'We did *Romeo and Juliet, Midsummer Night's Dream* and *The Tempest*.'

'So I have more experience?' Rooney said, and the curl of her lips was unmissable. It was like she was starting a fight.

Pip's jaw twitched.

'I guess,' she said.

I caught eyes with Jason over the table, and the way his eyes widened told me that I wasn't imagining this. Jason could tell what was going on too.

Here they were, Rooney and Pip, two very different sorts of chaotic energy colliding before my very eyes. I felt overwhelmed.

'So, are you and Georgia, like, best friends now?' asked Pip with a weak chuckle.

I was about to protest being dragged into whatever this was, when Rooney replied instead.

'I'd say we're pretty good friends already,' said Rooney, smiling and looking at me. 'Right?'

'Right,' I said, because there was really nothing else I could have said.

'We do live together,' Rooney continued, 'so, yes. Why? Jealous?'

Pip went a little red. 'I was just wondering whether we'd have to fight for the title of Georgia's ultimate best friend.'

'Am I not even a contender?' Jason pointed out, but both the girls ignored him.

Rooney took a long sip of her beer, then leant closer to Pip. 'You don't strike me as much of a fighter.'

'Is that a dig at my height?'

'Just saying. I think you might be naturally at a disadvantage compared to most people.'

'Ah, but I have the Short Person Anger advantage.'

Rooney smirked. 'Can't relate.'

'Hey,' I said loudly, and Pip and Rooney both looked at me. 'We're supposed to be having fun and getting to know each other.'

They blinked at me.

'Isn't that what we're doing?' said Rooney.

'I need a *drink*,' Jason said loudly, standing up. I stood up with him, giving him a supportive squeeze on the arm, and we left Rooney and Pip to their bizarre banter competition.

I knew that relying on alcohol to relieve anxiety was not great. On a physical level, I didn't even enjoy the taste that much. Unfortunately, I had grown up in a place where almost everyone my age drank, and I'd accepted drinking as 'normal', like a lot of other things, even though often it wasn't really what I wanted to do at all.

Jason ordered a cider and I ordered a double vodka and lemonade, and also two beers for Pip and Rooney.

'I know she's done the whole deflecting-feelings-by-being-angry thing before,' said Jason grimly as we waited at the bar for our drinks. 'But I haven't seen her like this since Kelly Thornton in Year Ten.'

'This is definitely worse,' I said, thinking back to the time with Kelly – a lengthy feud over a stolen pencil – which had ended in Pip throwing a half-eaten apple at her head and getting two weeks of detention. 'I just want everyone to be friends.'

Jason chuckled and nudged me with his shoulder. 'Well, you've got me. We're relatively drama-free.'

I looked up at Jason. His big brown eyes and soft smile were so familiar to me. We'd never had any drama. So far, anyway.

'Yes,' I said. 'Relatively.'

FOREVER ALONE

I proceeded to get drunk in record time. Maybe because I'd skipped dinner in favour of reading fanfic and eating a bagel in bed, or maybe because I drank the equivalent of six shots in forty-five minutes, but whatever it was, by ten o'clock, I felt genuinely relaxed and happy, which was definitely a sign that I was not in my right mind.

To reiterate: I'm not advocating this sort of thing. But, at the time, I didn't know how else to deal with what a long, stressful week it had been, and the prospect of many more long, stressful weeks I had to come over the next three years.

I suppose it's fair to say I was not enjoying my *university experience* thus far.

We headed into town at around ten o'clock. Rooney was insistent. I would have protested, but I did want to see if clubbing was any better if you went with your friends. Maybe I would enjoy it if Pip and Jason were there.

Pip and Rooney were both at least a bit tipsy and had been dominating around eighty per cent of the conversation. Jason had been kind of quiet, which wasn't unusual, and he didn't seem to mind when I slotted my arm through his as we walked into the centre of Durham, to try and minimise the amount of swaying I was doing as I walked.

Rooney kept swapping between bantering with Pip, then turning round to me, her long hair flying about in the gusty October air, and shouting, 'We need to get you a MAN, Georgia! We need to find you a MAN!'

The word 'man' grossed me out because it made me picture a guy far older than me – no one our age was a *man* yet, were they?

'I'll find one eventually!' I shouted back, even though I knew that was bullshit and nothing in life is certain and I didn't 'have time to figure things out' because I might just have a brain aneurism at any moment and then I'd be dead, without having fallen in love, without having even figured out who I was and what I wanted.

'You don't have to find a man, Georgia,' Pip slurred at me once we were inside the club, queueing for the bar.

It wasn't the dank, sticky club from the other day, but a new one. It was fancy, modern, and out of place in historic Durham. It was playing cool indie-pop – Pale Waves, Janelle Monáe, Chvrches – and we were surrounded by people dancing under neon lights. I had a bit of a headache, but I wanted to try and enjoy it. I wanted to push myself.

'I know,' I said, thankfully out of earshot of Rooney, who was talking intensely to Jason about something. Jason looked moderately overwhelmed.

'I've already accepted that I'll never find anyone,' said Pip, and it took a moment for the full implications of that to sink into my brain.

'What? What happened to *you'll find someone eventually because everyone does?*'

'That's a straight-people rule,' Pip said, and that shut me up for a moment. Every time she'd told me 'you'll find someone eventually' . . . had she even believed it about herself? 'It doesn't apply to me.'

'Wh— don't say that. There just weren't many out girls when we were at school. You didn't have many options.'

Pip had kissed two girls during the time we'd known each other – one of whom repeatedly denied it ever happened, and the other told Pip she didn't actually like her that way, she'd just thought it was a joke between friends.

Pip looked down on to the sticky bar surface. 'Yeah, but, like . . . I don't even know how to, like . . . date. Like how does that even *happen?*'

I didn't know what to say to her. It wasn't like I had the answers, and even if I did, we were both too tipsy to make much sense of them.

'Is there something bad about me?' she said suddenly, looking me right in the eyes. 'Am I . . . really annoying . . . am I just really annoying to everyone?'

'Pip . . .' I wrapped one arm round her shoulders. 'No, God – no, of course you're not. God. Why d'you think that?'

'I dunno,' she grumbled. 'Just thought there might be a specific reason as to why I'm forever alone.'

'You're not forever alone when I'm here. I'm your best friend.' She sighed. '*Fine.*'

I squeezed her, and then our drinks arrived.

'D'you think, since I'm your best friend, you could try *not* despising Rooney with every fibre of your being? At least for tonight?'

Pip sipped her cider. 'I will *attempt it*. I can make no promises.'
That would have to be good enough.

As soon as we'd finished our drinks, Rooney started dancing. She also seemed to be on speaking terms with various people in the club, so kept vanishing to socialise elsewhere. I felt bad for thinking it, but I actually didn't mind, because I got to have some time to myself with my best friends.

And it turned out that clubbing *was* slightly better when you were with people you know and love. Pip managed to get us to do our usual stupid dance moves, and after that I was smiling, and laughing and almost felt *happy*. Rooney even joined us, and Pip managed to keep her dagger-eyes to a minimum. If it weren't for the scary older students crowded around us and the ever-present threat of Rooney trying to set me up with a guy, I would have been having a genuinely good time.

Unfortunately, this only lasted half an hour before Rooney intervened.

Me, Jason and Pip had gone to sit down on some leather sofas when Rooney appeared with a guy I didn't know. He was wearing a Ralph Lauren shirt, peach chinos and boat shoes.

'Hey!' Rooney shouted at me over the music. 'Georgia!'

'Yeah?'

'This is Miles!' She pointed at the guy. I looked at him. He smiled in a way that immediately annoyed me.

'Hi?' I said.

'Come dance with us!' Rooney held out a hand to me.

'I'm tired,' I said, because I was.

'I think you and Miles would really get along!' said Rooney. It was painfully obvious what she was trying to do.

And I did not want to go along with it.

'Maybe later!' I said.

Miles didn't seem too bothered, but Rooney's smile dropped a little. She stepped close to me so that Miles couldn't hear us.

'Just give him a try!' she said. 'You could just kiss him and *see*.'

'She's fine,' said Jason's voice from one side. I hadn't realised he was listening in.

'I'm just trying to help –'

'I know,' said Jason. 'But Georgia doesn't want to. You can see it on her face.'

Rooney struck him with a long stare.

'I see,' she said. 'Interesting.'

Miles had already wandered off towards some friends, so Rooney turned to Pip, who was also listening to the conversation with a stern expression, and said, 'Quintana? Shall we dance?'

She said it like she was challenging Pip to a duel, so Pip of course accepted and went to dance with Rooney like she had a point to prove. Rooney wasn't sober enough to understand the point that Pip was trying to make: Rooney hadn't got to her. Except she obviously had. I sank back into the sofa with Jason and we watched Rooney and Pip dance.

It almost looked like Pip was having fun, were it not for the Mr Darcy-like grimace on her face every time Rooney got too close to her. Lights flashed around them, and every few seconds they would be hidden from view by other dancing bodies and smiling faces – but then they'd return, and they'd be a little closer to each other, moving to the music. Rooney towered over Pip, mostly because of her giant heeled boots, but she was a few inches taller normally anyway, and when Rooney put her arms round her, I felt suddenly worried that they'd both just fall over, and then Pip started to protest, but must have found herself ignored, realising she'd got herself into this situation and now had to deal with it.

For a moment I thought Rooney was going to lean in and kiss her, but she didn't.

Pip shot a glance at me, and I just smiled at her, then stopped watching them. They weren't going to murder each other. Hopefully.

Jason and I ate a packet of crisps Jason had procured from the bar and we talked, and it reminded me of what we'd do on the school play dress-rehearsal days when we weren't needed in a scene. Pip was always a lead role so she was busy the whole day, but Jason and I would get to sneak off and sit behind a curtain somewhere, eating snacks and watching TikTok compilations on my phone, trying not to laugh too loud.

'D'you miss home?' Jason asked.

I thought about it. 'I don't know. Do you?'

'I don't know,' he said, closing his eyes and leaning his head back. 'I mean, I'm a bit homesick, I guess.' He chuckled. 'I miss my dads, even though they've called me every day. And I've already watched the *Scooby-Doo* movie four times. For comfort. But school was hell. I don't miss school.'

'Mm.' Uni wasn't any better so far. For me, anyway.

'What?'

'I like being *here*,' I said.

'At uni?'

'No, here. With you.'

Jason opened his eyes again and turned to me. He smiled. 'Me too.'

'GEORGIA!' screeched Rooney, stumbling over to us from the dance floor. 'You've found a MAN.'

'No,' I said. 'This is my friend Jason. Remember?'

'I know who he is,' she said, crouching down in front of us. 'I know exactly what's going on here.' She pointed a finger at me.

'*You.*' She pointed at Jason. 'And *him.*' She clapped her hands together. 'Big. Messy. Feelings.'

I just shook my head, and I felt Jason shift a tiny bit away from me while he laughed awkwardly. What was Rooney talking about?

Rooney patted Jason on the shoulder. 'S'nice. You should just tell Georgia, though.'

Jason didn't say anything. I checked to see if he knew what Rooney was talking about, but his face didn't give anything away.

'I don't get it,' I said.

'You're very interesting,' said Rooney to Jason, 'and very boring at the same time because you never *do* anything.'

'I'm going to the loo,' said Jason, standing up with an expression on his face I only saw on him when he was drunk – deep irritation. But he wasn't drunk. He was genuinely pissed off. He walked away from us.

'That was really rude,' I said to Rooney. I think I was genuinely pissed off too.

'Are you aware that Jason is into you?'

The words hit me like lightning.

Are you aware that Jason is into you?

Jason. One of my best friends in the entire world. We'd known each other for over four years, we'd hung out more times than I could count, I knew his face as well as my own. We could tell each other anything.

But he hadn't told me *that.*

'What?' I croaked, my breath gone.

Rooney laughed. 'Are you joking? His crush on you is so obvious it's actually painful to watch.'

How was this *possible*? I was excellent at recognising romantic feelings. I could always tell when people were flirting with me, or each other. I *always* knew when Pip and Jason had crushes on people.

How had I missed this?

'He's a really lovely guy,' said Rooney, her voice softer, as she sat on the sofa beside me. 'Have you really not considered him?'

'I . . .' I started to tell Rooney that I didn't like him like that, but . . . did I even know what romantic feelings felt like? I thought I'd had a crush on Tommy for seven years and that turned out to be nothing.

Jason *was* a really lovely guy. I mean, I loved him.

And suddenly the idea was swirling around my brain and I couldn't stop myself *wondering*. Maybe this was like all those American romcoms I'd spent my whole teenage life watching; maybe Jason and I were *meant to be* like the two leads from *13 Going On 30* or *Easy A*, maybe 'he'd been there all along', maybe I just hadn't tapped into my romantic feelings because I felt so comfortable and safe around Jason and I'd just written him off as 'best friend' when in fact he could have been 'boyfriend' instead.

Maybe, if I reached out, if I *pushed myself* – maybe Jason was the love of my life.

'Wh . . . what do I do?' I whispered.

Rooney put her hands back in her pockets. 'I'm not sure yet. But –' she stood up, her hair falling around her shoulders like a superhero cape – 'I think we're going to be able to solve your little *never kissed anyone* situation.'

IMMATURE

I was woken from a dream that night when Rooney returned to our room. She'd told us to go back to college without her. I couldn't see her very well without my glasses on, but she seemed to be tiptoeing around like a cartoon character. She flicked the kettle on to make her post-night-out cup of tea, and when she opened her wardrobe, various hangers fell down, making a very loud clatter. She froze and said, 'Oh no.'

I put my glasses on just in time to see her turn to me with a guilty expression.

'*Sorry*,' she whispered loudly.

'S'fine,' I mumbled, croaky from sleep. I checked my phone. *5:21a.m.* How. *How* did any human stay awake, let alone stay out *clubbing* for that long? I had my late-night 200k fanfic mistakes but that was just sitting in bed reading. 'Didn't know anywhere stayed open this late.'

Rooney chuckled. 'Oh, no, it doesn't. I was at this guy's place.'

I frowned, a little confused. But then I understood. She was at a guy's place, having sex.

'Oh,' I said. 'Cool.'

I did actually think this was quite cool. I was always a bit envious of people who were super sex-positive and felt comfortable enough to just bang whoever they fancied. I couldn't even imagine feeling comfortable enough to let someone kiss me, let alone going to an absolute stranger's home and getting naked.

She shrugged. 'Wasn't that great, to be honest. Bit of a letdown. But, you know. Why not! Everyone's up for it this week.'

I was curious as to what way the guy had been a letdown but felt it might be a bit intrusive to ask.

Rooney then let out a dramatic gasp, swung her body round and whispered, '*I forgot to water Roderick,*' before quickly filling a mug with water, running over to her house plant, and pouring it into his pot.

'D'you think . . .' I began, but then stopped. Sleepiness was making me want to be honest.

I didn't like being honest.

'What?' she said, having finished tending to Roderick. She walked over to her bed and wrenched her heels off.

'D'you think I'm immature?' I asked, bleary-eyed, my brain not fully awake.

'Why would I think that?' She started unzipping her jumpsuit.

'Because I haven't had sex or kissed anyone or . . . any of that. And I'm not . . . getting with guys and . . . you know.' Being you. Doing what you do.

She looked at me. 'Do *you* think you're immature?'

'No. I just think a lot of other people think I am.'

'Have they told you that?'

I thought back to the prom afterparty.

'Yeah,' I said.

Rooney tugged off her jumpsuit and sat down on her bed in just her underwear. 'That's horrible.'

'So . . . am I?'

Rooney paused. 'I think it's pretty amazing that you haven't felt peer-pressured into doing anything by now. You haven't made yourself do anything you didn't want to do. You haven't kissed anyone just because you're scared of missing out. I think that's one of the most mature things I've ever heard, actually.'

I closed my eyes and thought about telling her what had happened with Tommy. I'd almost gone through with that.

But when I opened my eyes again, I found her just sitting there on the bed, looking at the photo of her and Mermaid-hair Beth. Beth must have been a really good friend. It was the only photo Rooney had put on the wall.

Then her head whipped round to face me and she said, 'So are you going to try dating Jason?'

It all came flooding back, and that was all it took.

A suggestion.

Rooney saying, 'You'll never know until you try.'

Rooney saying, 'He's really cute. Are you sure you don't like him maybe, like, a little bit? You get along *really* well.'

Rooney saying, 'You honestly act like you're made for each other.'

That was all it took for me to think . . .

Yeah.

Maybe.

Maybe I could fall in love with Jason.

WE SURE DO LOVE DRAMA

Durham Student Theatre's introductory meeting took place four days later – the Tuesday of my second week at university – inside the Assembly Rooms Theatre. Rooney almost had to physically drag me there after I spent the whole weekend in our room, worn out from five days of intense socialising, but I kept reminding myself that I had to do this, I *wanted* to do this, to put myself out there and have experiences. And Jason and Pip would be there, so it couldn't be all bad.

The seats were almost completely full already, since a *lot* of people were interested in being a part of the DST, but me and Rooney spotted Pip sitting alone near the back of the stalls, so we went to join her. I probably should have sat politically in between Rooney and Pip, but Rooney ended up walking into the row of seats ahead of me, leading to a very awkward greeting between them.

Moments later, Jason arrived. He was panting and looked a little bit sweaty.

I wondered whether I should find that attractive in a sort of post-workout way.

'Is . . . this seat . . . taken?'

I shook my head. 'Nope.' I paused while he shook his T-shirt away from his chest, and then shrugged off his teddy-bear jacket. 'Are you OK?'

He nodded. 'I just ran . . . all the way from the library . . . and now I'm dying.'

'Well, you made it in time.'

'I know.' He turned and looked at me properly then, flashing a warm smile. 'Hello.'

I smiled back. 'Hi.'

'So you're sure about doing this then?'

'Yep. And even if I wasn't, I think I'd have been press-ganged into it by these two.' I pointed towards Rooney and Pip, who were steadfastly ignoring each other.

'True.' He crossed one leg over another, then didn't give me the chance to say anything more before he started rummaging in his rucksack. After a moment, he drew out a family-size open packet of salted popcorn and held it out to me. 'Popcorn?'

I dug in and scooped up a handful. 'Salted. You're a hero.'

'We must all play our part in this bitch of a world.'

I was about to agree, but then the lights dimmed, as if we were about to watch a real play, and Durham Student Theatre's first meeting of the year began.

The president's name was Sadie and she had the brightest, most engaging voice I'd ever heard. She explained the system of DST, which was incredibly complicated, but the fundamental idea was that each society within DST got a certain amount of funding to put on a production of their own, created entirely by the students within that society. Rooney took a lot of notes while Sadie was explaining.

The meeting went on for an hour, and Jason and I sat and

shared popcorn the whole time. Was this supposed to mean something? Was this what flirting was? No. No, this was just what friends, did, right? This was just me and Jason being normal.

I thought I *got* this sort of thing. I *understood* flirting. But now, when it came to Jason, I had no idea what to think.

When the meeting finally ended, Rooney and Pip went down to join the queue of freshers who had something to ask President Sadie. They walked together but didn't look at each other.

Jason and I stayed in our seats and we reminisced about some of our funniest youth theatre anecdotes. *Hairspray* when the music director downloaded a knock-off version of the score and all the songs sounded wrong. *Dracula* when Pip slipped on some fake blood and tore down the stage curtains. *Romeo and Juliet* when me and Jason had been painting the set and got stuck on the balcony for two hours because everyone went for dinner and forgot we were there.

Maybe it was the fact that I'd been surrounded by loud theatre people for the past hour.

Maybe it was because I genuinely liked Jason in that way.

Whatever it was, it gave me the confidence to say, 'Hey, I was thinking . . . we should . . . do something.'

He raised his eyebrows, intrigued. 'Something?'

Oh God. Why was I doing this? *How* was I doing this? Had I been possessed by the spirit of someone with an actual shred of self-confidence?

'Yeah,' I said. 'I dunno. Go see a movie, or . . .' Wait. What fun things did people do on dates? I racked my brain, but all the fanfic I'd read had suddenly deleted itself from my mind. 'Eat . . . food.'

Jason stared at me. 'Georgia, what are you doing?'

'I just − we could − hang out.'

'We hang out all the time.'

'I mean just us.'

'Why just us?'

There was a pause.

And then he seemed to get it.

His eyes widened. He shifted back from me a little, then forward again.

'Are you . . .' He let out a tiny, disbelieving chuckle. 'You sound like you're asking me out, Georgia.'

I made a face. 'Um. Well, yeah.'

Jason said nothing for a moment.

And then he said, 'Why?'

It was not exactly how I'd expected him to react.

'I just . . .' I paused. 'I think . . . I don't know. I want to. Go out with you. If you also want to.'

He just kept on staring.

'If you don't want to, that's fine. We can just forget about it.' I could feel my cheeks heating up. Not because Jason was making me particularly flustered, just because I was a disaster and everything I did was a tragic mistake.

'OK,' he said. 'Yeah. Let's – let's do it.'

'Yeah?'

'Yeah.'

We looked at each other. Jason was an attractive guy, and he was a good person too. He was clearly the sort of person who I should like romantically. Who I *could* like romantically. He looked like a boyfriend.

I loved his personality. I'd loved his personality for years.

So I could fall *in love* with him. With a little bit of effort. Definitely.

★

Jason had to go, to run to a lecture, leaving me a little shell-shocked that I had been able to do what I had just done, but I was soon distracted by the raised voices at the front of the auditorium. Voices that belonged to Rooney and the DST president, Sadie.

There was hardly anyone in the theatre now, so I wandered down to where Rooney and Pip were just in front of the stage with Sadie. Pip was sitting in the front row, watching the conversation – or argument, I wasn't yet sure – go down.

'We only have enough funding for one new society this year,' said Sadie firmly. 'That's already been taken by the Mime Society.'

'*Mime Society?*' Rooney spluttered. 'Are you joking? Since when is *mime* more important than *Shakespeare?*'

Sadie gave her a look like she was very, very tired of dealing with people like Rooney. 'We also don't appreciate snobbery in the DST.'

'I'm not being *snobby*, I just . . .' Rooney took a breath, clearly trying not to shout. 'I just don't understand why you got rid of the Shakespeare Soc in the first place!'

'Because it didn't have enough members to continue,' said Sadie coolly.

I sat down next to Pip in the front row. She leant over to me and whispered, 'I just wanted to ask what the Freshers' Play would be this year.'

'What is it?'

'No idea yet. This is still happening.'

'What if I funded the society myself?' Rooney asked.

Sadie raised an eyebrow. 'I'm listening.'

'I-I don't need any of DST's money. I just want to put on a Shakespeare.' She looked genuinely *desperate*. I hadn't realised she cared that much about this, honestly.

'Do you know how much it costs to put on a play?'

'Um . . . no, but –'

'Hiring the theatre? Costumes? Set? Rehearsal space? All using the DST's time and resources?'

'Well, no, but I –'

Sadie sighed again.

'You need five members to count as a society,' she said. 'And we'll hire the theatre for you for *one* performance.'

Rooney closed her mouth. Blinked once. Then said, 'Wait, really?'

'Not gonna lie, I am just doing this so you'll stop bothering me.' Sadie whipped a notepad out from the stack of flyers she had with her on the stage. 'Who are your members?'

'Rooney Bach,' said Rooney, then looked around at me and Pip. We didn't even have time to protest.

'Felipa Quintana,' said Rooney.

'Hang on, no,' said Pip.

'Georgia Warr.'

'Wait, what?' I said.

'And Jason Farley-Shaw.'

'Is this legal?' said Pip.

'Who's the fifth?' Sadie asked.

'Um . . .' Rooney faltered. I figured she would just conjure up the name of one of her many friends, but she didn't seem to be able to think of anyone. 'Er, I guess we haven't got the fifth member yet.'

'Well, you'd better get one quick, OK? We're giving you funding for this. I need to know you're serious.'

'I will.'

'Put on a good enough production by the end of the year and I'll consider giving you full funding next year. Does that sound reasonable?'

'Um. Yes. Yeah.' Rooney unfolded her arms. 'Th-thank you.'

'You're welcome.' Sadie reached around her for a plastic bottle and took a deep swig from it — one that made me think that whatever was inside wasn't water. 'I don't think you realise how much work it is putting on a production. It needs to be *good*, OK? Some of our plays go to the Edinburgh Fringe.'

'It will be good,' said Rooney, nodding. 'I promise.'

'OK.' Sadie looked directly at me when she said, deadpan, 'Welcome to Durham Student Theatre. We sure do love drama.'

'I don't understand why you can't just let me have this one and be in my play,' Rooney snapped at Pip as we walked back to college. 'What were you gonna do? Join the Mime Society?'

'I was going to do the Freshers' Play like a *normal* fresher,' Pip snapped back. 'They're doing *The Importance of Being Earnest*, for God's sake. A classic.'

'Shakespeare means a *lot* to me, OK? It was basically one of the only things that I enjoyed at school —'

'What, and I'm supposed to drop my interests and hobbies just because you've got a sob story? This isn't the fucking *X Factor*.'

I walked a few paces behind them as Pip and Rooney bickered, their voices getting gradually louder and louder. People around us on the street started turning to observe the scene as they passed.

Pip wrapped her bomber jacket tightly round her body and ran a hand through her hair. 'I get that you were, like, a star performer at your school, but, like, so was I, and you don't get to come here and pretend like you're better than me just because you like Shakespeare.'

Rooney folded her arms. 'Well, *I* think putting on a Shakespeare is a bit more noteworthy than some little comedy play.'

'*Some little comedy play?* Apologise to Oscar Wilde right the fuck now!'

Rooney halted, bringing us all to a stop. I was contemplating diving into the nearest café. She stepped slightly towards Pip, then seemed to change her mind, and stepped back again, keeping a safe distance between them.

'You're just here to *have fun*. Well, I'm here to actually do something that means something.'

Pip shook her head. 'What the *fuck* are you *talking about,* dude? This is a theatre society. Not a political party.'

'Ugh, you're so *annoying*.'

'So are you!'

There was silence for a moment.

'Please be in my society,' said Rooney. 'I need five members.'

Pip looked at her, expression unchanging. 'Which play are you doing?'

'I don't know yet.'

'Can it be a comedy? I'm not doing this if we're doing any of the boring-ass history plays.'

'It'll be a comedy or a tragedy. No history plays.'

Pip narrowed her eyes.

'I'll think about it,' she said.

'Yeah?'

'Yeah. But I still don't like you.'

Rooney smiled broadly. 'I know.'

Pip headed off towards Castle, leaving Rooney and me alone on the cobbled street by the cathedral.

'What just happened?' I asked her.

Rooney let out a long breath. Then she smiled.

'We're putting on a play.'

DATING SKILLS

I had somehow asked out one of my best friends, and there was absolutely no way for me to take that back, which meant that I probably needed to follow through and actually go on a date with Jason Farley-Shaw.

He ended up messaging me about it the day after the DST meeting.

Jason Farley-Shaw
Hey ☺ so how's about that movie/food?

I got the message while Rooney and I were in an intro to poetry lecture, and instead of listening to the lecturer drone on about Keats, I spent the hour analysing this message. I didn't open it, but I could read all of it from my home screen. I didn't want to open it, because I didn't want him to know that I'd read it, because if he knew I'd read it, I'd have to reply so he didn't think I was ignoring him, and for some reason, the idea of continuing this incredibly new and incredibly weird flirtation with Jason was making me want to abandon my degree and become my brother's plumbing apprentice.

The very ordinary smiley-face emoji and the single, sensible question mark were extremely *not* like Jason, which suggested that he, too, had been overthinking this conversation. How should I reply? Should I be grammatically rule-abiding and polite? Or should I just start sending him memes straight away, like normal? How was this supposed to work?

To be absolutely and completely honest, I didn't want to go on a date with him at all.

But I did want to *want* to go on a date with him.

And that was the crux of my problem.

'Why are you staring at your phone like you're trying to make it explode with your mind?' asked Rooney once we'd walked back to our room after the lecture.

I decided to be honest. Rooney would probably know how to approach this.

'Jason messaged me,' I said.

'Oh!' She dumped her bag on the floor and rolled on to her bed, kicking off her Converse and pulling her hair out of its ponytail. 'Nice. What's he saying?'

Sitting on my own bed, I held up my phone to her. 'I kind of asked him out yesterday.'

Rooney leapt off her bed.

'You did *WHAT*?'

I paused. 'Um. I asked him out. Was that . . . wrong?'

She stared at me for a long time.

'I don't understand you at all,' she said finally.

'. . . OK.'

She sat back down, pressing her fingers to her lips.

'OK, well . . . good. This is good.' She took a breath. 'How did this *happen*?'

'I dunno, I was just thinking about it after what you said, and – I mean, I guess I just thought – like, I *realised* . . .' I folded my arms. 'I do.'

'You do what?'

'Like him.'

'Romantically?'

'Mm.'

'Sexually?'

I made a spluttering noise because I was suddenly picturing having sex with Jason. 'Who thinks about sex that quickly?'

Rooney snorted. 'Me.'

'Anyway, I do like him.' *I do.* I did. I probably did.

'Oh, I *know* you do. I saw this coming from the moment I met him.' She sighed happily. 'It's like a movie.'

'I don't know what to text him back,' I said. 'Help me.'

I felt a little bit embarrassed. This was simple stuff, for Christ's sake. This was twelve-year-old-level Dating Skills.

Rooney blinked. Then she got up from her bed, walked over to me, and gestured for me to budge up. I obeyed, and she flopped down on to the duvet beside me, taking my phone from my hands. She opened the message before I could stop her.

I watched her read it.

'OK,' she said, and then she typed out a message for me and sent it.

Georgia Warr
Yes for sure! You free at all this week?

'Oh,' I said.

She slapped my phone back into my hands.

I expected her to ask why I couldn't accomplish such a simple task. I expected her to maybe laugh, in a nice way, about how much I had been panicking about this.

She gave me a long look and I waited for her to ask: *Was that so hard? Why couldn't you do that yourself? Do you even want to talk to Jason? Was your panic because you have a crush on him or are you panicking because you're not even sure what you're doing, or why you're doing it, or whether you even want to be doing it? Are you panicking because if you can't even want to do this, you might never be able to want to do this?*

But instead she just smiled and said, 'No prob.'

STRAIGHT OUT OF
A ROMANCE NOVEL

Jason and I arranged our date for that Saturday, which meant I had five whole days to panic about it.

Thankfully, my second week at university was a welcome distraction.

Both Rooney and I were now faced with *actual university work* – real lectures and tutorials and reading ten whole books in four weeks. And we were settling into our new life living together too. We'd always go to lectures together and go to lunch together, but she liked to go down to the bar in the evenings or go out to a club with other friends, while I preferred to sit in bed with biscuits and a fanfic. Sometimes Rooney would talk to me about ideas for her Shakespeare play, chatting excitedly about how she would do the set and the costumes and the staging, and other times we would just talk about whatever – TV shows. College gossip. Our home lives.

I didn't really understand why Rooney had chosen me. Clearly, she could have anyone she wanted as whatever she wanted – friend, partner, hook-up, even someone to playfully banter with.

But despite being able to befriend anyone, and having fifty acquaintances already, it was me she ate with, and walked through Durham with, and hung out with when she wasn't partying.

I was probably just convenient. That was the nature of roommates.

But all in all, it was OK. I was *OK*. Maybe I wasn't the socialite I'd come to university hoping I could be, but living with Rooney was *OK*, and I'd even managed to secure a date with someone. An actual romantic date.

Things were looking up.

As it turned out, there was nothing interesting to do in Durham apart from eat out, drink, and go to the cinema. Unless you particularly like looking at old buildings. But even that got tiring after you'd walked past them every day on your way to Tesco.

I wanted to think of something actually fun to do with Jason, like ice skating or bowling or one of those cool bars that doubles up as a mini-golf place. But Jason immediately suggested going to the little ice-cream café on Saddler Street, and I didn't have anything better to suggest, so I agreed. Plus, ice cream is nice.

'You're going on your date?' Rooney asked, just as I was about to leave our room on Saturday afternoon, about ten minutes before we'd agreed to meet. She looked my outfit up and down.

'Yes?' I said, looking at myself.

I was just wearing my normal clothes – mom jeans, a cropped woolly jumper, and my coat. I thought I looked quite good, actually, in my usual sort of cosy bookseller way. We were only going for ice cream, for God's sake.

'You look cute,' said Rooney, and I felt like she really did mean it.

'Thanks.'

'Are you looking forward to it?'

I actually hadn't really been looking forward to it. I guessed this was due to nerves. Everyone gets nervous about a first date. And I was *very* nervous. I knew that I needed to chill out and be myself, and if I didn't feel that spark after a while then we just weren't meant to be.

But I also knew that this was a chance for me to actually experience romance and be someone who has fun, quirky experiences and doesn't die alone.

No pressure, I guess.

'Pistachio,' said Jason, looking at my choice of ice cream as we sat down at a table. He was wearing his teddy-bear jacket again, which I loved for its sense of familiarity and cosiness. 'I forgot that you're literally a disgusting gremlin when it comes to ice cream.'

The café was cute, tiny and decorated with pastel colours and flowers. I admired Jason for suggesting it. It was straight out of a romance novel.

I glanced at his selection of ice cream. 'Vanilla, though? When they had cookies-and-cream?'

'Don't bash vanilla. Vanilla is a classic.' He popped a spoonful into his mouth and grinned.

I raised my eyebrows. 'I forgot how basic you are.'

'I'm not basic!'

'It's a basic choice. That's all I'm saying.'

We sat at our little round table in the ice-cream café and talked for an hour.

We talked about university for most of that. Jason explained that his history lectures were already a bit dull, and I lamented about the length of my reading lists. Jason admitted that he didn't think the drinking-clubbing lifestyle was really for him, and I said I felt the same. We spent a long time talking about how we both felt Freshers' Week was a monumental let-down – marketed to be the best week of your whole university life, only to turn out to be a week of endless drinking, visiting gross clubs and failing to make real friends.

Eventually conversation dwindled a little, because we'd known each other for years, and we'd already had dozens, if not hundreds, of deep chats. We were already at the point where silence didn't feel awkward. We *knew* each other.

But we didn't know how to do this.

Be romantic.

Date.

'So this is weird, isn't it?' said Jason. We'd long since finished our ice cream.

I was leaning on my hand, elbow on the table. 'What's weird?'

Jason looked down. A little embarrassed. 'Well . . . the fact that we're . . . you know . . . doing this.'

Oh. Yeah.

'It's . . .' I didn't really know what to say. 'I guess it is. A bit.'

Jason kept his eyes firmly down, not looking at me. 'I've been thinking about it all week and I just . . . I mean, I didn't even know you might like me like that.'

Neither had I. But then I had no idea what 'liking someone like that' was even supposed to feel like. If it was going to be with anyone, it was probably going to be with him.

His voice grew a little quieter and he smiled awkwardly, like he didn't want me to see how nervous he was. 'Are you just doing this because of what Rooney said when we all went out that night?'

I sat up a little. 'No, no – well, I mean, maybe a little bit? I think her saying it made me properly, um . . . *realise* that I wanted to. So . . . I guess I *started* thinking about it after that, and . . . yeah. It just felt like . . . I guess it just felt right.'

Jason nodded, and I hoped I'd made sense.

I just needed to be honest. Jason was my best friend. I needed to make this work and do it at my own pace.

I loved Jason. I knew I could be honest with him.

'You know I've never done this before,' I said.

He nodded again. Understanding. 'I know.'

'I . . . want to go slow.'

He went a little red. 'Yeah. Of course.'

'I like you,' I said. At least I thought I did. I might have if I tried, if I *encouraged* it, if I pretended it was real until it *was*. 'I mean, I-I think I could – I want to give this a chance, and I don't want to regret anything when I'm on my deathbed.'

'OK.'

'I just don't really know what I'm doing. Like. Theoretically, yes, but in practice . . . no.'

'OK. That's OK.'

'OK.' I think I was going a bit red too. My cheeks felt hot. Was it because I felt flustered around Jason or because this whole thing was a bit awkward to talk about?

'I don't mind going slow,' said Jason. 'Like, all my romantic experiences until now have been a bit shit.'

I knew all about Jason's past romantic experiences. I knew about his first kiss with a girl he thought he really liked, but the kiss was so terrible it actually put him off doing it again. And I knew about the girlfriend he'd had for five months when we were in Year 13 – Aimee, who went to our youth theatre group. Aimee was kind of annoying in a *Jason is my property and I don't like anyone else hanging out with him* sort of way, and Pip and I never liked her, but Jason was happy for a little while, so we supported the relationship.

Or, at least, we did until we figured out that Aimee had been making all sorts of comments to Jason about how he wasn't allowed to hang out with certain people, and he needed to stop talking to other girls – including me and Pip. Jason put up with that for *months* until he realised that she was, in fact, a shithead.

Jason had sex for the first time with her, and it pissed me off that he'd had that experience with someone like that.

'This won't be shit,' I said, then rephrased. 'This . . . won't be shit, will it?'

'No,' he said. 'Definitely not.'

'We'll go slow.'

'Yeah. This is new territory.'

'Yeah.'

'And if it doesn't work out . . .' Jason began, then seemed to change his mind about what he was going to say.

I'll be honest: I still wasn't even sure that I was into Jason. He was super nice, funny, interesting and attractive, but I didn't know whether I was *feeling* anything other than platonic friendship.

But I would never know unless I persisted. Unless I tried.

And if it didn't work out, Jason would understand.

'. . . we'll still be friends,' I concluded. 'No matter what.'

'Yes.' Jason leant back in his chair and folded his arms, and God, I was glad that I was doing this with Jason and not some random person who didn't know me, who didn't understand, who would expect things from me and would think I was weird when I didn't want to . . .

'There's one other thing we should probably talk about,' said Jason.

'What?'

'What are we going to tell Pip?'

There was a silence. I honestly hadn't even thought about how Pip would feel about this.

Something told me she wouldn't be happy about her two best friends getting together and majorly distorting the dynamics of our friendship group.

'We should tell her,' I said. 'When we find a good time.'

'Yeah. Agreed.' Jason looked relieved that I'd said it. That he didn't have to be the one to suggest it.

'Best to just be honest about it.'

'Yeah.'

When we left the ice-cream café, we hugged goodbye, and it felt like a normal hug for us. A normal Jason and Georgia hug, the sort of hug we'd been having for years.

There wasn't any sort of weird moment when we felt like we should kiss. We hadn't reached that point yet, I guessed.

That would come later.

And I was fine with that.

That was what I *wanted*.

I thought.

Yeah.

THE SPARK

When Rooney returned to our room that night, she wanted to hear every detail of my date with Jason. I would have been fine with this, were it not 4.38 a.m.

'So it went well, then?' she asked after I'd finished giving her the rundown from where I was wrapped up like a burrito in my duvet.

'Yeah?' I said.

'Are you sure?' she asked. She was sitting on her bed, cup of tea in one hand and make-up wipe in the other.

I frowned. 'Why?'

'You just . . .' She shrugged. 'You don't sound very enthusiastic.'

'Oh,' I said. 'I mean . . . I guess I just . . .'

'What?'

'I'm not sure if I really like him like that yet. I dunno.'

Rooney paused. 'Well, if the spark's not there, the spark's not there.'

'No, I mean, we get along really well. Like, I love him as a person.'

'Yeah, but is the spark there?'

How was I supposed to know that? What the fuck was *the spark*? What did *the spark* even feel like?

I thought I'd understood what all these romantic things would feel like – *butterflies* and *the spark* and just *knowing* when you liked someone. I'd read about these feelings hundreds of times in books and fanfic. I'd watched way more romcoms than was probably normal for an eighteen-year-old.

But now I was starting to wonder whether these things were just made up.

'. . . Maybe?' I said.

'Well, you might as well just wait and see how it goes, then. When you know, you know.'

That sort of made me want to scream. I didn't know *how* to know.

Honestly, if I'd had any sort of feelings for girls, I *would* have wondered whether I wasn't straight. Maybe *boys* in general were the problem.

'What does it feel like when *you* get the spark?' I asked. 'Like . . . tonight. You – I assume you were with a guy?'

Her expression dropped instantly. 'That's different.'

'Wait – how? Why?'

She stood up from her bed and turned round, grabbing her pyjamas. 'That's just different. That's nothing like this situation.'

'I'm just asking –'

'Me having sex with some random guy is not similar to you dating your best friend. Completely different scenarios.'

I blinked. She was probably right about that.

'So why do you have sex with random guys?' I asked. As soon as I said it, I realised what a blunt and invasive question it was. But I *did* want to know. It wasn't like I was judging her – honestly, I wished I had her confidence. But I didn't understand how she did it, really. *Why* she wanted to do it. Why would someone go to a stranger's house and take their clothes off when you could just stay home and have a safe, comfortable wank? Surely the end result was exactly the same.

Rooney turned back round. She gave me a long, unreadable look.

'Honestly?' she asked.

'Yeah,' I said.

'I just *enjoy* having sex,' she said. 'I'm single and I like sex, so I have sex. It's fun because it feels good. I don't feel a "spark" because it's not about romance. It's a casual physical thing.'

I got the sense that she was telling the truth. That really was all there was to it.

'Anyway,' she continued, 'we've got *much* more important things to think about right now.'

'Like what?'

'Like the Shakespeare Society.' Rooney finished changing into her pyjamas, grabbed her washbag, and headed towards our bedroom door. 'Go to sleep.'

'OK.' And I did. But not before I spent a while thinking about the spark. It sounded magical. Like something out of a fairy tale. But I couldn't imagine what it felt like. Was it a physical feeling? Was it just intuition?

Why had I never felt it? *Ever?*

On the Sunday of that second week, Rooney and I were chilling in our bedroom when someone knocked on the door. When Rooney opened it, at least thirty of her acquaintances entered, carrying balloons and party poppers and streamers, and then a guy got down on one knee in front of everyone and asked Rooney to be his college wife.

Rooney screamed and jumped on him, smothering him in a tight hug, agreeing to be his college wife. And that was that. I watched the whole thing go down from my bed, actually entertained. It was kind of lovely.

Once everyone had cleared out, I helped Rooney clean up the remains of the party poppers and streamers. It took a whole hour.

She'd gone out a few evenings that week, and she always came back with a *story* – a hook-up, or a drunken escapade, or some college drama. And I'd always listen, fascinated and, confusingly, jealous. Some part of me wanted that excitement in my life, but at the same time the idea of a night like that filled me with horror. I knew I didn't *really* want to drunkenly hook up with a stranger, as fun as that seemed from the outside. I didn't need to, anyway, now that I had my thing with Jason.

I'd wanted to *be* Rooney when I first met her. I thought I needed to copy her.

Now, I wasn't so sure I could hack it.

A SHORT BUT COMPELLING
PRESENTATION BY
ROONEY BACH

Rooney gave me a long look as we sat down opposite each other in the Student Union café on the Wednesday of our third week of university. She then withdrew her MacBook from her bag.

'What's this about?' I asked.

'Oh, you'll see. You will *see*.'

She'd dragged me here after this morning's Heroic Age lecture but had refused to tell me why, explaining that she wanted to build up the tension. This only succeeded in irritating me.

'I assume this is a Shakespeare Soc thing,' I said.

'You are correct.'

While joining the Shakespeare Society had not exactly been my idea, I had genuinely been quite excited to be involved. It felt like I was actually putting myself out there, trying something new, and it would hopefully result in a year of fun rehearsals, meeting new people, and enjoying my *university experience*.

But now it seemed that it would be a society of only four

people, all of whom I already knew, and without enough members we probably wouldn't even get to function as a real society anyway.

'Have you decided what play we're doing?'

'Even better.' She grinned.

Before I had the chance to ask what that meant, Pip arrived, Kanken slung over one shoulder, giant chemistry book in one arm and her button-up shirt baggy round her torso.

She pushed up her glasses and sat down next to me. 'I assumed you would have found an excuse to get out of this. Like dropping out of university or running away to become a goat herder.'

'Hey!' I made a disappointed face. 'I want to be here! I want to have fun university experiences and make memories!'

'Memories like throwing up four times in one evening?'

'I'm sure that was just a one-time thing.'

Rooney, ignoring both of us, checked her watch. 'Now we're just waiting for Jason.'

Pip and I looked at her.

'You actually got Jason to agree to do this?' Pip said. 'He didn't tell me he'd agreed to this.'

'I have my ways,' said Rooney. 'I'm very persuasive.'

'More like very irritating.'

'Same difference.'

It was then that Jason, the fourth member of our Shakespeare troupe, wandered into the union café and sat down next to Rooney, shrugging off his teddy-bear jacket. Beneath, he was wearing full sports attire, including a sweatshirt that had a 'University College Rowing Club' logo on it.

'Hello,' he said.

Pip frowned at him. 'Mate, since when did you join the *rowing club*?'

'Since the Freshers' Fair. You were literally there when I wrote my name down.'

'I didn't think you'd actually *go*. Don't they have practices at like six a.m. every day?'

'Not every day. Only on Tuesdays and Thursdays.'

'Why would you put yourself through that?'

Jason huffed out a laugh, though I could tell he was a little annoyed. 'Because I wanted to try something new? Is that so bad?'

'No, no. Sorry.' Pip nudged him with an elbow. 'It's cool.'

Rooney clapped her hands together loudly, halting their conversation. 'Attention, please.' She flipped up her MacBook. 'The presentation will now commence.'

'The what?' said Pip.

'Jesus,' I said.

On the screen was the first slide of a PowerPoint presentation.

A Shakespeare Medley: A short but compelling presentation by Rooney Bach

'Short . . . but compelling . . .' I repeated.

'I relate,' said Pip.

'What's happening?' asked Jason.

Rooney clicked to the next slide.

Part 1: The Premise
- a) A medley of several Shakespeare scenes (only good ones) (NO history plays)
- b) We each play different roles in various scenes from various plays
- c) All the scenes explore the theme of LOVE and it feels very deep and meaningful

This did actually pique my interest. And it seemed to interest Jason and Pip too, as they both leant forward to watch as several images appeared on screen: Leonardo DiCaprio and Claire Danes looking traumatised in their *Romeo and Juliet* movie, followed by David Tennant and Catherine Tate lounging around in their West End production of *Much Ado About Nothing*, then a picture of someone with a donkey mask on, which was presumably from *A Midsummer Night's Dream*.

'I have decided,' said Rooney, 'that instead of just doing one play, we're doing the best bits of a load of them. Only the good ones, obviously.' She glanced at Pip. 'None of the history plays. Comedies and tragedies only.'

'I hate to say it,' said Pip, 'but that's actually a fun idea.'

Rooney flicked her ponytail back with a triumphant expression. 'Thank you for admitting that I'm right.'

'Hang on, that's not what I —'

Jason interrupted her. 'So we'll get to play lots of different parts?'

Rooney nodded. 'Yes.'

'Oh. Cool. Yeah, that actually does sound fun.'

I raised my eyebrows at him. I'd thought he'd rather join the Musical Theatre Soc, honestly. He'd always preferred musicals to plays.

Jason shrugged at me. 'I want to be in a show this year, and you know if we try and audition for the Freshers' Play or Musical Theatre Soc, we either won't get in because so many people want to be in it, or we might get relegated to a tiny role. You remember in Year Ten when I had to be a tree in *A Midsummer Night's Dream*.'

I nodded. 'A thrilling experience for you.'

'I don't particularly feel like wasting a year of my life turning up to rehearsals just to stand still and wave my arms around occasionally.' Jason glanced at Rooney. 'At least with this we know we'd get lead roles and a decent amount of lines. And we'd be doing it with friends. It'd be *fun*.' He slapped his thigh and leant back in his seat. 'I'm in.'

Rooney was beaming wide. 'I should have hired you to do the presentation.'

'Oh my God,' said Pip, folding her arms. 'I can't believe you've converted Jason to your side already.'

'It's my charm and intelligence.'

'Fuck off.'

Rooney moved on to the next slide.

Part 2: The Plan
   a) I will decide on the plays and scenes we're doing
   b) I will direct
   c) Weekly rehearsals until our performance in March
      (YOU MUST ATTEND ALL OF THEM)

'Hang on,' Pip spluttered, running a hand through her curls. 'Who made you *supreme overlord* of the Shakespeare Soc?'

Rooney smirked at her. 'I think that'd be me, actually, considering it was all my idea.'

'Yes, well . . .' Pip went a little red. 'I . . . I think we should have some say in who directs.'

'Oh really?'

'Yes.'

Rooney leant forward over the table so she was staring directly at Pip's face. 'And what's your say?'

'I –' Pip cleared her throat, not quite able to maintain eye contact. 'I want to co-direct with you.'

Rooney's smirk dropped. She said nothing for a moment. And then –

'Why?'

Pip stood her ground. 'Because I want to.'

That wasn't the reason. I knew exactly why Pip was doing this. She wanted to one-up Rooney. Or at least be her equal.

'That's my condition,' she said. 'If you want me to be a part of this, I want to co-direct.'

Rooney pursed her lips. 'Fine.'

Pip smiled wide. She'd won this round.

'Moving on,' said Rooney, and clicked to the next slide.

Part 3: The Fifth Member
   a) Find them
   b) Lure them in
   c) Shakespeare Soc gets approved as a full society
   d) SUCCESS

'*Lure them in?*' I said.

'Yikes,' said Pip.

Jason chuckled. 'Sounds like we're trying to persuade people to join a cult.'

'Yes, well . . .' Rooney huffed. 'I didn't know how else to phrase it. We just need to find a fifth person,' she went on. 'Can you all ask around and see if anyone's interested? None of this matters if we can't recruit a fifth person. I'll ask around too.'

The three of us agreed we'd ask people we knew, though I wasn't sure exactly who I'd be able to ask, since all of my friends were sitting with me at the table.

'You've really thought about all this,' said Pip.

Rooney smiled. 'Impressed?'

Pip folded her arms. 'No, just – not really, no. You've done the bare minimum of what's required as a director –'

'Admit it. You're impressed by me.'

Jason cleared his throat. 'So . . . rehearsal this week?'

Rooney's smile turned into a wide grin. She smacked her hands down on the table, drawing the attention of most of the people in the room. '*Yes!*'

We all agreed the date and time, then Pip and Jason had to leave – Pip to a lab, and Jason to a tutorial. As soon as they'd left the café, Rooney stood up and flung herself over the table to hug me. I just sat there, letting it happen.

That was our first ever hug.

I was just about to move my arms to hug her back when she pulled away, sitting down and smoothing her ponytail. Her face returned to her usual Rooney face: an effortless smile.

'It's going to be amazing,' she said.

Our troupe consisted of two star performers who both wanted to be in charge, one girl who threw up every time she acted, and one boy who might possibly be the love of my life.

It was going to be an absolute disaster, but that wasn't stopping any of us.

PALM TO PALM

'This is perfect,' said Rooney, at the exact moment Jason tried to walk into the room and smacked his head on the top of the doorframe so hard that he let out a noise like a startled cat.

To her credit, Rooney had *tried* to book a decent room for our first ever Shakespeare Soc rehearsal. She'd attempted to book one of the giant rooms in the university buildings near the cathedral where lots of the music and drama societies practised. She'd also tried to book a classroom in the Elvet Riverside building where we had our lectures and tutorials and would take our exams at the end of the year.

But Sadie was failing to reply to Rooney's emails, and without the DST's clearance, Rooney was not allowed to book rooms for the Shakespeare Society.

I'd pointed out that we could probably just rehearse in our bedroom, but Rooney insisted we find a proper rehearsal space. 'To get us in the zone,' she'd said.

And that's how we ended up in a rickety room in the centuries-old college chapel with such a low ceiling that Jason, who is six foot three, had to actually crouch a little to walk around in. The carpet was faded and worn and there were decaying Sunday School posters on the walls, but it was quiet and free to use, which was all we really needed.

Pip was on FaceTime to her parents as she entered the room, talking in Spanish too fast for my GCSE-level skills to keep up with, looking somewhat exasperated as her mum kept interrupting her.

'She's been talking to them for an hour,' Jason explained as he sat down, rubbing his head. I sat down on the chair next to him. Pip's parents had always been somewhat overprotective in a very endearing way. I hadn't spoken to my parents since last week.

'Who are you talking to?' said Rooney, skipping over to Pip and sneaking a glance over her shoulder.

'*Who's this, nena?*' I heard Pip's dad say. '*Have you finally got yourself a girlfriend?*'

'NO!' Pip immediately squawked. 'She's – she's definitely not!'

Rooney waved at Pip's parents with a wide grin. 'Hi! I'm Rooney!'

'Look, I have to go,' Pip snapped at her phone.

'*What do you study, Rooney?*'

She leant in closer to the phone, and closer to Pip as a result. 'I do English literature! And me and Pip are in the Shakespeare Society together.'

Pip started adjusting her hair, seemingly as a way to put her whole arm in between her body and Rooney's. 'I'm going now! I love you! *¡Chau!*'

'Aw,' said Rooney as Pip hung up the call. 'Your parents are so cute. And they liked me!'

Pip sighed. 'They're going to ask about you every single time they call me, now.'

Rooney shrugged and walked away. 'Clearly they can see I would make a good girlfriend. Just saying.'

'And why's that?'

'My charm and intelligence, obviously. We've been through this.'

I expected Pip to snap back, but she didn't. She went a little red and then laughed, like she'd found Rooney properly amusing. Rooney turned round, her ponytail flying through the air as she did so, to watch, with an unreadable expression on her face.

It took us twenty minutes to actually get the rehearsal underway, largely because Pip and Rooney would not stop bickering. First about who would play Romeo and Juliet, then about which part of *Romeo and Juliet* we would perform, and then about how we would perform it.

Even after they agreed to cast Jason and me as Romeo and Juliet, Pip and Rooney spent another fifteen minutes stomping around the room, plotting out the scene and vehemently disagreeing with each other about literally everything, until Jason decided that we should probably intervene.

'This isn't working,' he said. 'You are not co-directing.'

'Er, *yes*, we are,' said Pip.

'We have some minor artistic differences,' said Rooney. 'But aside from that, this is working absolutely fine.'

I snorted. Pip glared at me.

Rooney put one hand on her hip. 'If Felipa could just *compromise* a little, then things would be a bit more straightforward.'

Pip squared up to Rooney. Or, at least, she tried to, but couldn't quite because Rooney was several inches taller, even with Pip's hair height.

'You do *not* have permission to call me Felipa,' she said.

'This is bad,' I muttered to Jason. He nodded in agreement.

'How about we just wing it?' said Jason. 'Just let me and Georgia have a go at the scene, and we can go from there.'

The two co-directors reluctantly agreed, and all was right for a small moment.

Until I realised that I was about to act a *Romeo and Juliet* scene with Jason Farley-Shaw.

I loved acting. I loved getting to step into a character and pretend to be someone else. I loved getting to say stuff and behave in ways that I never would in real life. And I knew I was good at it too.

It was *the audience* that made me nervous, which in this case was Pip and Rooney. And with the added pressure of *performing a romantic scene with Jason, my best friend who I was almost dating*, it's hopefully understandable that I was *very* nervous going into this scene.

Jason and I had copies of *Romeo and Juliet* in our hands – well, mine was sort of in my arm because I was using my giant *Oxford Anthology of Shakespeare* – and he had the first line. Pip and Rooney were sitting on chairs with one seat between them, watching.

'*If I profane with my unworthiest hand,*' began Jason, '*this holy shrine, the gentle sin is this: my lips, two blushing pilgrims, ready stand to smooth that rough touch with a gentle kiss.*'

OK. In the zone. I am a romantic lead.

'*Good pilgrim,*' I said, focusing on reading the words in the book and trying not to overthink it, '*you do wrong your hand too much –*'

'OK, Georgia?' Pip cut in. 'Can we have you a bit further away from Jason? Just to emphasise the *yearning.*'

'And then you could step a little closer to him as you speak,' said Rooney. 'Like, this is your first proper meeting and you're already *obsessed* with each other.'

Pip looked at her. 'Yeah. Good idea.'

Rooney returned her gaze with a slight twitch of her eyebrow. 'Thank you.'

I did as they instructed and carried on.

'*Which mannerly devotion shows in this; for saints have hands that pilgrims' hands do touch, and palm to palm is holy palmers' kiss.*'

'Definitely a hand touch there,' said Rooney.

Jason held out his hand to me, and I touched it with mine.

I felt a wave of nerves flow through me.

'*Have not saints lips,*' said Jason, staring right at me, '*and holy palmers too?*'

I could feel myself going red. Not because I was flustered or because of the romance of the scene. But because I felt *uncomfortable*.

'*Ay, pilgrim,*' I replied, '*lips that they must use in prayer.*'

'Georgia,' said Pip, 'can I be honest?'

'Yeah?'

'That was supposed to be a super flirty line, but you just look like you need a shit.'

I spluttered out a laugh. 'Wow.'

'I know it's just a read-through but, like . . . be romantic?'

'I'm trying.'

'Are you?'

'Oh my *God.*' I snapped the book shut, kind of annoyed, honestly. I wasn't a bad actor. Acting had been one of the few things I'd actually *excelled* at. 'You're being so harsh.'

'Can we start again from the beginning?'

'Fine.'

Jason and I reset and I opened up my book again.

OK. I was *Juliet*. I was in love. I had just met this super-hot forbidden boy and was obsessed with him. I could *do this*.

We read through until we got up to the 'lips' bit again, Jason's hand holding mine.

'*O, then, dear saint,*' said Jason, '*let lips do what hands do; they pray, grant thou, lest faith turn to despair.*'

Jason was giving his *everything*. God, I felt uncomfortable.

'*Saints do not move, though grant for prayer's sake.*'

'*Then move not, while my prayer's effects I take.*'

Jason suddenly glanced at me kind of awkwardly, then turned to Rooney and Pip and said, 'Presumably we kiss there.'

Rooney clapped her hands in delight. '*Yes.*'

'Definitely,' said Pip.

'Just a little one.'

'I dunno. I think it could be a proper kiss there.'

Rooney waggled her eyebrows. 'Ooh. Felipa's *into* this.'

'I would prefer it,' said Pip, 'if you did not call me that.'

Pip really, really didn't like being called Felipa. She'd gone by Pip ever since I'd known her. She always said she preferred a more masculine-sounding name, and – with the exception of it being used by her family members – Felipa just didn't feel like her.

Sensing the change of tone in Pip's choice, Rooney's smirk dropped.

'OK,' said Rooney, more genuinely than I'd heard her talk to Pip so far. 'Sure. Sorry.'

Pip ruffled her hair and cleared her throat. 'Thank you.'

They stared at each other.

And then Rooney said, 'How about I call you *Pipsqueak* instead?'

Pip instantly looked like she was about to erupt, but Jason spoke before they could start having a full-blown argument. 'So, the kiss.'

'You don't have to do it now,' said Pip quickly.

'No,' Rooney agreed. 'In future rehearsals, but not now.'

'OK,' I said, and stepped back a little, relieved.

Obviously I didn't want to kiss Jason in front of people. And I didn't want my first kiss to be in a play.

That was probably why I felt awkward. That was probably why I wasn't doing my best acting right now.

That was probably why being Juliet, one of the most romantic roles in literary history, made me feel sort of nauseated.

'That wasn't . . . like . . . awkward or anything, was it?' Jason whispered to me as we were packing up twenty minutes later.

'What? No. No, it was – it was fine. Great. It was great. You were great. We'll be great.' Too much, Georgia.

He sighed in relief. 'OK. Good.'

I took a moment to think about it, then before I could talk myself out of it, I said, 'I don't want our first kiss to be in a play.'

Jason froze in the middle of stacking chairs. Just for a second. His cheeks flushed. 'Um, no. No, definitely not.'

'Yeah.'

'Yeah.'

When we turned round, I saw Pip looking at us from across the room, her eyes narrowed suspiciously. But before she could say anything, Rooney spoke.

'Did anyone ask around to try and find our fifth member?'

'I don't have any other friends,' I said immediately, as if everyone wasn't already fully aware of this.

Jason stepped out of the room so he could finally stand up to his full height. 'I can try and ask some of my Castle friends, but . . . I'm not sure they're really the acting sort.'

'I've already asked my Castle friends,' said Pip. 'They said no.' She turned to Rooney. 'Don't you have, like, fifty best friends? Can't you find someone?'

Rooney's expression suddenly dropped and for a brief moment

she seemed genuinely angry. But then it was gone. She rolled her eyes and said, 'I don't have fifty friends.' But didn't say more than that.

I had to agree with Pip. It was a little weird that Rooney, who was out partying at least twice a week and was down in the college bar most other days, didn't have a single other person she could get to join.

'What about your college husband?' I suggested. They must have been friends, at least.

Rooney shook her head. 'I don't think he's really into theatre.'

Maybe she wasn't really as close to those people as I'd thought.

As we all stood in the autumn cold on the cobbled street outside and said our goodbyes, I wondered why Rooney cared so much about this in the first place. So much that she would go to all this effort – starting a new society, being the director, putting on her own play.

We'd known each other for a few weeks now. I knew that she was a sex-positive party girl and a Shakespeare enthusiast who could put on a smile to make you like her.

But as for *why* she did any of the things she did?

I had no idea.

ELEPHANT IN THE ROOM

GEORGIA WARR, FELIPA QUINTANA

Felipa Quintana
ROONEY

Georgia Warr
my name is georgia, actually

Felipa Quintana
I just want to know how a person so hot can be so fucking annoying

Georgia Warr
oh good
are we finally going to talk about the elephant in the room

Felipa Quintana
What elephant???

Georgia Warr
your ginormous crush on rooney bach

Felipa Quintana
Uh wait wait wait
I mean she's OBJECTIVELY hot
I'm not into her

Georgia Warr
aldkjhgsldkfjghlkf

Felipa Quintana
I DON'T CRUSH ON STRAIGHT GIRLS

Georgia Warr
lol

Felipa Quintana
We would murder each other if we dated
Which we wouldn't because she's straight
And I don't like her like that
And she's super annoying and she has to have her way all the time
And I'm doomed to be a lonely gay 4 life

Georgia Warr
you're digging yourself so far into this hole

Felipa Quintana
I'M CHANGING THE SUBJECT
I have a question

Georgia Warr
fire away my dude

Felipa Quintana
I may be like . . . totally making this up, but . . . is there something
going on between you and Jason???
He told me you met up just you two the other day and like
Idk it sounded almost like a date or something hahaha

Georgia Warr
would you find that weird? if we dated?

Felipa Quintana
Idk
It'd be a change

Georgia Warr
well i guess i don't really know what's going on with that yet

Felipa Quintana
So you do like him??

Georgia Warr
i don't really know?
maybe?
we've decided to see what happens

Felipa Quintana
Hm
Okay

GEORGIA WARR, JASON FARLEY-SHAW

Georgia Warr
i just told pip that we're potentially seeing each other

Jason Farley-Shaw
Oh SHIT okay!
Wow
What did she say?

Georgia Warr
she just said 'Hm okay'

Jason Farley-Shaw
Oh god she's mad then

Georgia Warr
i don't think she's angry
she's probably just confused

Jason Farley-Shaw
Fair enough I guess!!
It is kind of a sudden development

Georgia Warr
she'll get over it though right?
i mean she'll be all right with it?

Jason Farley-Shaw
Yeah
Definitely

GEORIGA WARR, ROONEY BACH

Georgia Warr
hey fried egg where are you??

Rooney Bach
Out!!!! ☺

Georgia Warr
you coming back tonight?
i have things to discuss

Rooney Bach
Oooooo THINGS
What things I love things

Georgia Warr
well
idk what to do next with jason
so i am summoning you to assist
unless you wanna stay out, no pressure haha

Rooney Bach
Nah people are just being boring and drunk and I'm not in the
mood to get with anyone
Fried egg is on her way

Georgia Warr
be hasty, egg

THE LETTER 'X'

'There,' said Rooney as I tapped send on my message.

Georgia Warr
Sooooo d'you wanna meet up again this weekend?

We were sitting next to each other against the headboard of my bed, Rooney still in full going-out clothes and me in some Christmas pyjamas, despite the fact that it was early November.

'What do I do on the date?' I asked, looking at the message, waiting for Jason to see it.

She sipped her post-night-out cup of tea. 'Whatever you want.'

'But do we have to kiss on the second date?'

'You don't *have* to do anything.'

I turned to Rooney, but we were sitting too close, so I just got an eyeful of dark hair curled into loose waves. 'Would *you* kiss on the second date?'

Rooney snorted. 'I don't go on dates.'

'But you've been on a date before.'

She stayed silent for a moment.

'I guess so,' she said finally. 'But generally, I prefer just sex.'

'Oh.'

'Don't get me wrong, being in a relationship would be *nice*, probably. And sometimes I meet people and I think, maybe . . .' She halted mid-sentence, then rolled off my bed and walked over to her own. 'It's . . . well, I always fall for the wrong people. So what's the point?'

'Oh.'

She didn't say anything more than that, and it felt rude to push it and ask for details. Instead, she started changing into her pyjamas, and I definitely saw her shoot a glance at her photo of her and Mermaid-hair Beth.

Maybe Beth was an ex-girlfriend. Or an old crush. I didn't have any evidence that Rooney liked girls, but it wasn't impossible.

'There's nothing wrong with just having sex,' she said, once she'd got into bed.

'I know,' I said.

'Relationships just aren't for me, I think. They never end well.'

'OK.'

She suddenly leapt up from the bed, muttering '*Roderick*,' and running over to water him. Roderick was looking a little the worse for wear, to be honest – Rooney seemed to be forgetting to water him quite frequently. After she'd finished, she was asleep five minutes later, while I stayed up, alternating between staring at the blue-tinged ceiling and scrolling through my phone, stressing about whether I was supposed to kiss Jason on our second date.

What if I really *didn't* like guys and *that* was why this whole thing felt so difficult to navigate?

As soon as the thought popped into my head, I had to investigate further. I opened Safari on my phone and typed in, 'am I gay'.

A bunch of links popped up, mostly useless internet quizzes

that I already knew would be unhelpful and inaccurate. But one thing caught my eye – *the Kinsey Scale test.*

I started reading about the Kinsey Scale. Wikipedia explained that it was a scale of sexuality which went from zero, 'exclusively heterosexual', to six, 'exclusively homosexual'.

Curious, and frustrated with myself, I took the test, trying to just answer the questions instinctively and not overthink anything. When I finished, I clicked 'submit answers', and waited.

And instead of a number, the letter 'X' popped up.

You did not indicate any sexual preference. Try adjusting your answers.

I read and reread those lines.

I'd . . . done the test wrong.

I must have done the test wrong.

I went back to my questions and started to look for where I could change my answers, but couldn't find any I'd answered inaccurately, so just decided to exit the browser.

It was probably just a faulty test.

MR SELF-CONFIDENCE

'You look nice!' was one of the first things he said to me when we met outside the Gala cinema on Saturday afternoon.

'Oh, er, thank you?' I said, looking down at myself. I had selected some khaki overalls with a Fair Isle jumper underneath, though most of the outfit was hidden by my giant coat because Durham was already dipping below ten degrees and I did not deal well with the cold.

Jason, on the other hand, was wearing his teddy-bear jacket and black jeans, which was his look pretty much all year round.

'I was thinking,' he said as we walked inside the building, 'the cinema was probably a terrible idea for a – for, like, a meet-up.'

He'd been about to say 'for a date'. He knew it was a date too, then.

It was *on*.

I chuckled. 'Yeah. Let's meet up and ignore each other for two hours.'

'Basically. I mean, it sounds pretty relaxing, to be honest.'

'That's true.'

'I think the perfect marriage would be made up of two people who can sit in comfortable silence with each other for extended periods of time.'

'Steady on,' I said. 'We're not married yet.'

This made him let out a spluttery, somewhat scandalised laugh. Nice. I could flirt. I was *acing* this.

We were half an hour into the movie when the fire alarm went off.

Until that point, things were going rather well. Jason had not attempted to hold my hand, put his arm round me, or, thank *God*, kiss me. We were simply two friends watching a movie at the cinema.

Obviously I didn't want him to do any of those things because they would have been terribly cliché and almost kind of sleazy.

'So, now what?' he asked as we stood in the cold outside the cinema. Nobody else seemed to know whether the fire was real, but it didn't seem like we'd be getting back inside any time soon. A staff member had just come outside and was giving out cinema vouchers.

I pulled my coat a little tighter round me. This was not how I'd hoped this afternoon would go. I had hoped we would sit next to each other in silence for two hours, watch a nice movie and then go home.

But we couldn't end the date now. That would be awkward. That would not be date-like behaviour.

'Erm . . . I guess we could just go back to college and have tea, or something?' I said. That seemed to be the thing people did to socialise at uni. Tea in our bedrooms.

Oh wait. Bedroom. Was going to a bedroom a good idea? Or would that mean –

'Yeah!' Jason smiled, slotting his hands into his pockets. 'Yeah, that sounds good. D'you wanna come to mine? We could watch a movie in my room, or something?'

I nodded too. 'Yeah, that sounds good.'

OK.

It was OK.

I could do this.

I could be normal.

I could go back to a boy's room on a date and do whatever was usually involved in that. Talking. Flirting. Kissing. Sex, maybe.

I was brave. I didn't have to listen to my own thoughts. I could do all of it.

I actually don't like tea, which obviously Jason knew, and he automatically made me a hot chocolate instead.

He had his own room, like Pip and most students at Durham, which meant it was small. It was probably a third of the size of mine and Rooney's, with one single bed. The décor was much the same though – a crusty old carpet, yellow breeze-block walls, and IKEA furniture. His sheets were plain blue. He had a laptop and some books on his bedside table, and a few pairs of shoes were tidily lined up underneath the radiator.

But it wasn't any of this that I noticed first. It was the wall that I noticed first.

The wall was entirely blank apart from a framed photograph of Sarah Michelle Gellar and Freddie Prinze Jr in *Scooby-Doo 2: Monsters Unleashed*.

I looked at it.

Jason looked at me looking at it.

'I have questions,' I said.

'Understandable,' he said, nodding and sitting down on his bed. 'Er, d'you remember Edward? From my old school? He gave it to me.'

He finished his sentence, as if this was the end of the story.

'Go on,' I said.

'So . . . OK, you're gonna have to come sit down if I'm gonna explain this.' He patted the space next to him on the bed.

This made me a little nervous. But it wasn't like there was anywhere else to sit in the room, and he didn't do it in a particularly flirty way, so I guessed it was fine.

I sat down next to him on the edge of the bed, holding my hot chocolate.

'So, we all know I'm a Scooby-Doo stan.'

'Obviously.'

'And also a Sarah Michelle Gellar and Freddie Prinze Junior stan.'

'I mean . . . OK, sure.'

'OK. So, at my old school, like, before I moved to ours for sixth form, I was kind of known as the guy who'd never kissed anyone.'

'What?' I said. 'You never told me that.'

'Well, you know I left that school, because, like . . .' He made a face. 'A lot of the guys there . . . I mean, it was an all-boys school and people would just rip the shit out of each other for every tiny thing.'

'Yeah.'

Jason had told us a little bit about that before. How people at his old school were kind of nasty, generally, and he didn't want to be in that sort of environment any more.

'So they all picked on me for having never been kissed. And I guess I got teased about it a lot. Nothing serious, but, yeah, it was a thing. Everyone thought it was pretty weird.'

'But you've kissed people now,' I said. 'Like . . . you've had a girlfriend before.'

'That was all after. Before then, that was *the thing* people would pick on me about. And you know . . . people would say it was because I was ugly and I had acne and I liked musical theatre and just stupid shit like that. That sort of thing doesn't bother me now, but I guess it did when I was younger.'

'Oh,' I said, but my voice felt hoarse all of a sudden. 'That's horrible.'

'When we left in Year Eleven, Ed gave me this framed photo.' He pointed at the photo. 'Sarah and Freddie. And Ed was like, *this is a good luck charm to help you get a girlfriend*. We both really loved the *Scooby-Doo* movies, and it became an ongoing joke that Sarah Michelle Gellar and Freddie Prinze Junior were, like, the pinnacle of romance, because they're real-life married *and* on-screen love interests. Every time someone we knew got into a relationship, we'd be like, *but are you at Sarah and Freddie's level, mate.* I . . . yeah. OK. It sounds weird when I try to explain it.'

'No, it's funny,' I said. 'I just hope they don't get divorced any time soon.'

He nodded. 'Yeah. That would kind of mess the whole thing up.'

'Yeah.'

'Anyway, after he gave it to me, I had my first kiss like a week later.' Jason chuckled. 'I mean, it was a shit kiss, but . . . I guess I got it out of the way. So now it *is* a good luck charm.'

Jason told this story like it was a funny anecdote that I was supposed to be laughing at. But it wasn't funny.

It was really fucking sad.

I remembered the story of his first kiss with a girl he didn't really like that much. He'd told me and Pip that it wasn't great, but he was glad he'd got it out of the way but hearing all this from Jason now made me realise what had actually happened.

He'd felt pressured into having his first kiss. Because people were bullying him for not having kissed anyone, he forced himself to do it, and it was bad.

A lot of teenagers did that. But hearing it from Jason made me really, really angry.

I knew what it was like to feel bad about not having kissed anyone.

And to feel pressured into doing it because everyone else was.

Because you were weird if you hadn't.

Because this was what being a human was all about.

That was what everyone said.

He looked up at the picture. 'Or maybe it isn't a good luck charm. I guess my romantic experiences until now haven't been . . . great.' He looked away. 'A shit first kiss and then . . . Aimee.'

'Yeah, Aimee was a disgusting human being.'

'I think I only stayed with Aimee for so long because I was scared of being single and, like . . . being that person again. People had been shitting on me for years because I was . . . I dunno, *unlovable* or something. If I broke up with Aimee, I thought I was gonna be, like, unlovable forever.' His voice quietened. 'I really believed she was the best I deserved.'

'You deserve more,' I said immediately. I knew this to be true because I loved him. Maybe I wasn't *in love* with him, not yet, but I did love him.

'Thanks,' he said. 'I mean, I know. I know that now.'

'OK, Mr Self-Confidence.'

He laughed. 'Just wish I could tell that to sixteen-year-old me.'

I was a hypocrite.

I was doing exactly what Jason had forced himself to do all those years ago. Have experiences, kisses, relationships – all because he was scared to be different. He was scared to be the guy who hadn't kissed anyone.

That was exactly what I was doing. And I was going to end up hurting him.

Maybe I should just tell him now. Tell him we should stop this, end it, just stay as friends.

But maybe, if I just held on for a little bit longer, we would fall in love, and I would not hate myself any more.

Before I had the chance to speak again, Jason had already moved to the headboard and opened up his laptop. 'Anyway. A movie?' He patted the bed next to him and pulled a blanket from underneath him. 'You can choose, since I chose the cinema movie.'

I moved next to him to survey the movie options. He pulled the blanket over our legs. What if this was all a precursor to us having sex? Or even just kissing? This was the normal time when we would start kissing, right? People who were on a date didn't just sit through a movie. They got ten minutes in and then started making out. Was I going to have to do that? Just thinking about it made me want to cry.

I chose something and we watched in silence. I kept fidgeting. I didn't know what to do. I didn't know what I *wanted* to do.

'Georgia?' Jason asked after about twenty minutes. 'You . . . OK?'

'Erm . . .' I was freaking out. I was majorly freaking out. I liked Jason and I wanted to chill out and watch a movie with him. But I didn't want to do any of the other stuff. What if my sexuality was just the letter 'X', like the Kinsey Scale had told me? 'Actually, I'm feeling a bit unwell.'

Jason sat up from the headboard. 'Oh no! What's wrong?'

I shook my head. 'Nothing bad, I just . . . I'm just a bit headachy, to be honest.'

'Do you wanna call it a day? You should go take a nap, or something.'

God. Jason was so nice.

'Would that be OK?' I asked.

He nodded earnestly. 'Of course.'

When I left, there was a short moment of overwhelming relief.
But after that, I just hated myself.

SUNIL

I didn't even end up going back to St John's.

I went straight downstairs and out of Castle college, thinking I was going to go to Tesco to get some comfort food for the evening. But then I just sat down on the steps and couldn't move.

I was utterly, utterly messing this up.

I was going to end up hurting Jason.

And I was going to end up alone. Forever.

If I couldn't like a guy who was lovely, kind, funny, attractive, *my best friend* . . . how could I ever like anybody?

It didn't play out like this in movies. In movies, two childhood best friends would eventually realise that, despite everything, they had been made for each other this whole time, that their connection went beyond just attraction, and then they'd get together and live happily ever after.

Why wasn't this playing out like that?

'Georgia?' said a voice from behind me. I twisted my body, startled that someone whose voice I didn't immediately recognise knew who I was. I was startled again to see that it was Sunil, my college parent, who had the self-confidence of a member of Queer Eye.

'Sunil,' I said.

He chuckled. He was wearing a thick colour-block coat over a classic black tux.

'Correct,' he said.

'How come you're at Castle?'

'Music practice,' he said, smiling warmly. 'I'm in the student orchestra and needed to run through a couple of things with the other cellists.' He sat down next to me on the steps.

'You play the cello?'

'I do. It's quite enjoyable, but orchestra is stressful. The conductor doesn't like me because me and Jess always get caught chatting.'

'Jess . . . from the Pride Soc stall? She's in it too?'

'Yup. Viola, so she wasn't there today. But we pretty much do everything together.'

I thought that was a cute thing to say, but I was struggling to feel any positive emotions about literally anything, so I just tried to force a smile, which obviously failed.

'You OK?' he asked, raising his eyebrows.

I opened my mouth to say yes, I was absolutely fine, but I started hysterically laughing instead.

I think that was the closest thing I had to crying in front of someone else.

'Oh no,' said Sunil, eyes widening in alarm. 'You're definitely not OK.'

He waited for me to say something.

'I'm fine,' I said. If I was a doll, that would be one of my pre-recorded phrases.

'Oh *no*.' Sunil shook his head. 'That was the worst lie I've ever heard in my life.'

That actually did make me laugh for real.

Sunil waited again to see if I was going to elaborate, but I didn't.

'You didn't come to the Pride Soc Freshers' Week club night,' he continued, turning to me a little.

'Oh, er, yeah.' I shrugged weakly. 'Er . . . club nights aren't really my thing.'

I'd got the email about it, of course. It'd been two weeks ago. *Pride Soc Welcomes You! Come Party with Your New Family of QUILTBAGs!* I had to Google what QUILTBAG meant, but even while doing that, I knew I wouldn't go. Even if I liked drinking and clubbing, I wouldn't go. I didn't belong. I didn't know whether I was a QUILTBAG or not.

He nodded. 'You know what? Same.'

'Really?'

'Yep. Can't stand alcohol. It gives me the shakes and I'm *such* a lightweight. I'd much rather have a queer film night or a queer tea party, you know?'

As he spoke, I glanced down at his jacket and found that he was wearing those badges again. I homed in on the one with the purple, black, grey and white stripes. God, I'd meant to look up what that meant. I really did want to know.

'Speaking of Pride Soc,' he said, gesturing at his tux, 'I'm heading off to its autumn formal. The rest of the exec team are setting it up right now and I'm *hoping* there haven't been any disasters.'

I didn't know what possessed me to ask, but the next thing I said was, 'Can I come?'

He raised an eyebrow. 'You want to come along? You didn't RSVP to the email.'

I'd received that email too. I hadn't deleted it. I'd imagined quite vividly what it would be like to attend something like that, confidently a part of something.

'I could . . . help set up?' I suggested.

I liked Sunil. I really did. I wanted to hang out with him a little more.

I wanted to see what the Pride Soc was like.

And I wanted to forget about what had just happened with Jason.

He looked at me for a long moment, and then he smiled. 'You know what? Why not. We could do with an extra person to help blow up balloons.'

'Are you sure?'

'Yeah!'

Suddenly I felt myself getting cold feet. I looked down at my overalls and woolly jumper. 'I'm not dressed for a formal.'

'No one gives a shit what you're wearing, Georgia. This is the Pride Society.'

'But you look sexy and I look like I just rolled up to a nine a.m. lecture.'

'Sexy?' He laughed like he had a private joke with the word, and then he stood up and held out a hand.

I didn't know what else to do or say, so I took it.

COULD HAVE GONE HARDER
WITH THE PRIDE FLAGS

Sunil held my hand all the way through Durham. In a slightly odd, but nonetheless comforting way, I felt like I was hanging out with one of my parents. I supposed, in a way, I was.

He didn't seem to feel the need to talk. We just walked. Sometimes he would swing my hand. About halfway there, I wondered what I was doing. I wanted to be curled up in bed, reading the Jimmy/Rowan Spider-Man AU fanfic I'd started last night. I shouldn't be at this formal. I didn't deserve to be at this formal.

I needed to message Jason and explain.

I needed to explain what was wrong with me.

I needed to say sorry.

'Here we are,' said Sunil, smiling. We had reached a red door leading into one of Durham's many old Dickensian buildings. I looked at the shop it was connected to.

'Gregg's?'

Sunil snorted. 'Yes, Georgia. We're having our society formal dinner at *Gregg's*.'

'I'm not complaining. I love sausage rolls.'

He opened the door, revealing a narrow corridor leading to a stairway and a sign: *Big's Digs: Restaurant and Bar*.

'We've rented out Big's for the evening,' said Sunil cheerfully, leading me up the stairs and into the restaurant. 'The club nights are fine, obviously, but I insisted we have formals as well this year. Not everyone is into clubbing.'

It wasn't a huge space, but it was a beautiful one. It was one of Durham's old buildings, so the ceiling was low, adorned with wooden beams and soft, warm lighting. All the tables had been arranged in neat squares, laden with white tablecloths, candles, shiny cutlery and colourful centrepieces that featured all sorts of different pride flags – some I recognised, some I didn't. A few multicoloured balloons hung from the corners of the room and streamers bordered the windows. Right at the back, overlooking the whole room, was a big rainbow flag.

'Could have gone harder with the pride flags,' Sunil said, narrowing his eyes. I couldn't tell whether he was joking.

We weren't alone in the room – there was a small gathering of people putting a few final touches on the decorations. I quickly spotted the other third year I met on the stall, Jess, although her braids were styled into an updo. She was wearing a dress with tiny dogs on it. She waved, skipped over to Sunil, and swung her arm round him.

'Oh my God, *finally*,' she said.

'How's it going?'

'Good, actually. We're just arguing about whether to do place cards or not.'

'Hm. People will want to sit with their friends, though.'

'That's what I think. But Alex thinks that'll cause chaos.'

They discussed place cards while I stood slightly behind Sunil, like a toddler behind their parent's leg at a family gathering. The students setting up all appeared to be third years. Some were dressed in bright, quirky outfits – sequins, patterned suits and big heels – while others wore more ordinary dresses and tuxes. I felt entirely out of place in my overalls, no matter what Sunil had said.

'Oh, and I've brought Georgia along to help set up,' said Sunil, interrupting my thoughts. He gave me a squeeze round my shoulders.

Jess smiled at me. I felt a little panicked – was she going to ask why I was here? What was my sexuality? Why hadn't I come to any of their other events?

'Can you blow up balloons?' she asked.

'Um, yeah.'

'Thank *God*, because I literally can't, and Laura is moaning about doing it because she's apparently got a cough.' And then she handed me a packet of balloons.

Sunil had to go off to assist with the evening's preparations, and I quickly started to feel like I'd made a terrible mistake by coming and that I was going to be forced into talking to a load of people I really didn't know. But Jess seemed happy for me to tag along, working my way through the balloons, as she caught up with her friends and acquaintances, and I even got to know her a little, asking her about the orchestra and playing the viola and her friendship with Sunil.

'I honestly did not have a real friend here until I met him,' she said, after we'd finished tying up the last cluster of balloons. 'We got sat next to each other at orchestra and we just immediately started gushing about what each other was wearing. And we've been glued at the hip ever since.' She smiled, watching Sunil chatting to some timid-looking freshers. 'Everyone loves Sunil.'

'Well, he's really nice, so that makes sense,' I said.

'Not just that, but he's actually a really good president. He won the Pride Soc election by a landslide. Everyone was really fed up with the president last year – he didn't want to use anyone else's ideas except his own. Oh, speaking of.' Jess hopped over to Sunil and quietly said, 'Lloyd's here. Just a heads-up.' She pointed towards the entrance.

Sunil glanced towards the door where a skinny blond guy wearing a velvet tux was standing. An expression I hadn't seen on Sunil before flashed across his features – annoyance.

Lloyd looked over to him, unsmiling, then walked away towards a table on the other side of the room.

'Lloyd *hates* Sunil,' said Jess, as Sunil rejoined his conversation with the group of freshers. 'So, that's a bit of a thing there.'

'Drama?' I asked.

Jess nodded. 'Drama.'

For some reason – pity, or genuine kindness, I wasn't sure – I ended up sitting next to Sunil at his table throughout the dinner. By eight o'clock, the room was packed and lively, and waiters were serving drinks and starters.

Between courses Sunil made an effort to move around the room and talk to people on every table, especially the freshers. The newbies seemed genuinely excited to meet him. It was sort of wonderful to watch.

I managed to chat a little to the other people on my table, but I was relieved when Sunil returned for dessert, and I could get to talk to him properly. He told me that he was studying music, which he thought was probably a mistake, but he was enjoying it. He was from Birmingham, which explained the very slight tinge in his accent, which I hadn't been able to place. He had no idea what he was doing after Durham yet, despite this being the final year of his degree.

I told him about our Shakespeare Society and how it was probably going to be a disaster.

'I did a little bit of acting when I was at school,' said Sunil when I told him about us needing a fifth member. He launched into a story of the time he played a minor role in a school production of *Wicked*, and concluded it by saying, 'Maybe I could be in your play. I do miss the theatre.'

I told him that would be amazing.

'I'm so busy, though,' he said. 'I just . . . have a lot on all of the time.' And judging by the tired expression on his face, he wasn't exaggerating, so I told him it'd be OK if he couldn't.

But he said he'd think about it.

I hadn't met a lot of openly queer people before. There'd been a crowd of people at school who Pip hung out with from time to time, but there could only have been about seven or eight of them, max. I don't know what I expected. There was no particular type of person, no particular style or *look*. But they were all so friendly. There were a few obvious friendship groups, but mostly, people were happy to chat to whoever.

They were all just *themselves*.

I don't know how to explain it.

There was no pretending. No hiding. No faking.

In this little restaurant hidden away in the old streets of Durham, a bunch of queer people could all show up and just *be*.

I don't think I'd understood what that was like until that moment.

After dessert, tables were moved to the side and the real mingling began. The lights were dimmed and the music was turned up, and almost everyone was standing, chatting, laughing and drinking. I quickly realised my socialising reserves had been utterly depleted by what had honestly felt like the longest day of my life, and I'd also drunk enough alcohol to be in that weird space where everything feels like a dream, so I found an empty seat in a corner and huddled there with my phone and a glass of wine for half an hour, scrolling through Twitter and Instagram.

'Hiding in the corner, college child?'

I raised my head, startled, but it was only Sunil, a glass of lemonade in hand. He looked like a celebrity in his tux, his hair pushed neatly back. I supposed he was a celebrity here.

He sat down in the chair next to me. 'How are you doing?'

I nodded at him. 'Fine! Yeah. This has been really nice.'

He smiled and gazed out at the room. Happy people having fun. 'Yes. It's been a success.'

'Have you organised anything like this before?'

'Never. I was part of the society's leadership team last year, but events like this weren't my call. Last year it was literally all bar crawls and club nights.'

I grimaced. Sunil saw, and laughed. 'Yeah. Exactly.'

'Is it stressful? Being the president?'

'Sometimes. But it's worth it. Makes me feel that I'm doing something important. And that I'm *part of* something important.' He let out a breath. 'I . . . I did things on my own for a long time. I know how it feels to be totally alone. So now I'm trying to make sure . . . no queer person has to feel like that in this city.'

I nodded again. I could understand that.

'I'm not a superhero, or anything. I don't want to be. A lot of the freshers see me as this, like, queer angel sent down to fix all their problems, and I'm not, I'm really, really not. I'm just a person. But I like to think I'm making a positive impact, even if it's a small one.'

I suddenly got the sense that Sunil had been through a lot before he'd become this person – confident, eloquent, wise. He hadn't always been the self-assured president of a society. But whatever he'd been through, he'd done it. He'd survived. And he was making the world a better place.

'But I'm very tired all the time,' he said with a small chuckle. 'I think sometimes I forget about . . . looking after myself. Just . . . bingeing a show or, I don't know. Baking a cake. I hardly ever do stuff like that. Sometimes I wish I could spend a little more time just doing something utterly pointless.' He met my eyes. 'And now I'm oversharing!'

'I don't mind!' I blurted. I really didn't. I liked deep chats and I felt like I was getting to know Sunil properly. I knew that he, as my college parent, was supposed to be my mentor here at Durham, but I already wanted to know him better than that. I wanted us to be friends.

But that was when I heard the voice.

'Georgia?'

I looked up, though I didn't need to, because I knew the voice almost as well as my own.

Pip, wearing a black tux not dissimilar from Sunil's, was staring down at me with a baffled expression.

'What are you doing here?'

PIP

I looked at Pip. Pip looked at me. Sunil looked at Pip. Then he looked at me. I looked down at my hands, struggling to know what to do or how to explain why I had attended a Pride Soc formal when I was supposed to be dating Jason and Pip had no reason to believe I wasn't straight.

'I–I ran into Sunil,' I said, but didn't know where to go from there.

'I'm her college parent,' said Sunil.

'Yeah.'

'So . . .' Pip smiled awkwardly. 'You just . . . decided to come along?'

There was a silence.

'Actually,' said Sunil, sitting up in his chair, 'I asked Georgia to come along to help out. We were a bit short on numbers for setting all this up.' He turned to me with a smile that looked a tiny bit sinister. Probably because he was lying out of his ass. 'And, in return, I'm going to be in Georgia's play.'

'Oh!' Pip immediately brightened, her eyes widening. 'Shit! Yes! We really needed a fifth member!'

'You're in it too?'

'Yeah! Well, I was sort of forced into it, but yes.'

As soon as I had processed the fact that Sunil had just volunteered himself to be in our play, he had been called over by another group of people, had given me a pat on the shoulder, and bidden farewell to both of us.

Pip met my eyes again. She still seemed a bit confused. 'Shall we . . . go to the bar?'

I nodded. I'd had too much wine and I needed some water, badly. 'Yeah.'

It actually took us around twenty minutes to get to the bar, because people kept stopping to talk to Pip.

Pip had made a huge number of new friends here at Pride Soc, which shouldn't have surprised me. She'd always been good at making friends, but she was selective, and back in our home town, there hadn't actually been many people she'd wanted to hang out with. There'd been the other girls in our form when we were in the lower school, and she'd had a handful of queer mates in the sixth form, but there was no Pride Soc at our school. Rural Kent didn't have any sort of queer areas or shops or clubs like in the big cities.

She came out to me when we were fifteen. It wasn't the most dramatic, or funny, or emotional of coming-outs, if films or TV were anything to go by. 'I think I might like girls instead,' was what she'd said while we were scouring the high street shops for new schoolbags. There'd been some build-up. We'd been talking about boys who went to the all-boys school. I'd been saying how I didn't really understand the hype. Pip agreed.

It goes without saying that Pip had a shit time, generally. And while Pip had many, many other acquaintances who she could definitely have deepened friendships with, she always came to me to talk about difficult things. I don't know if that's because she trusted me or just because I was a good listener. Maybe both. Either way, I became a safe place. I'd been happy to be one then, and I still was now.

I was happy to give that to her.

'Sorry about that,' she said, once we'd finally sat down on the bar stools and had ordered two glasses of apple juice, neither of us particularly in the mood to continue drinking alcohol. She was smiling.

'No you're not.' I grinned back. 'You're extremely popular.'

'OK, you got me.' She crossed her legs, revealing stripy socks peeping out from underneath her trousers. 'I'm extremely popular now and I am loving it. Don't worry; you and Jason are still my joint number ones.'

I looked back at the little crowds of Pride Soc members, some just standing and chatting, others dancing, others sitting in corners with drinks, whispering intimately.

'I've been going to LatAm Soc as well,' Pip said. 'They had a welcome social a few days ago.'

'Oh! How was it?'

Pip nodded excitedly. 'Actually awesome. My mum basically forced me to go, because, like, I wasn't super enthused about it. I didn't really know what you'd actually *do* in it. But it was really nice to make some friends there. And they genuinely do *so* much stuff. Like, I met this other Colombian girl, and she was telling me about this little gathering they did last December for *Día de las Velitas*.' She smiled. 'It made me feel like . . . I dunno. It reminded me of when I lived in London.'

Back in our home town, sometimes Pip had felt alone in a way that Jason and I just couldn't make better. She often said she wished her family hadn't moved out of London, because at least there she'd had her grandparents and a big community around her. When she moved to our tiny Kentish town aged ten, that community was gone. Pip was the only Latina in our school year.

With that, and figuring out that she was gay, Pip had definitely drawn the short straw in terms of *people in her vicinity who she could relate to and bond with on a deep level due to shared life experiences*.

'I'd forgotten how good it felt to be surrounded by so many Latinx people, you know?' she continued. 'Our school was so *white*. And even being here in Durham – Durham as a whole is so white. Even Pride Soc is pretty white overall!'

She gestured around her, and when I looked, I realised how correct she was – with the exception of Sunil, Jess, and a handful of others, most faces in the room were white.

'I'm starting to feel how much it affected me to just . . . be around white people all the time. Like, being gay *and* Latina meant that I just . . . didn't know *anyone* like me. As good as it felt to finally have a few queer friends in sixth form, they were all white, so I just couldn't fully relate to them.' She chuckled suddenly. 'But I met this gay dude at LatAm Soc and we had a massive chat about being gay and Latinx, and I swear to God I'd never felt so understood in my *life*.'

I found myself smiling. Because my best friend was *thriving* here.

'What?' she said, seeing the smile on my face.

'I'm just happy for you,' I said.

'God, you actual sap.'

'I can't help it. You're one of the very few people I actually care about in the world.'

Pip beamed like she was very pleased about this fact. 'Well, I am a very popular and successful lesbian. It's an honour to know me.'

'*Successful?*' I raised an eyebrow. 'That's a new development.'

'Number one, how dare you?' Pip leant back on her stool with a smug expression. 'Number two, yes, I may have got with a girl at the Pride Soc club night.'

'Pip!' I sat up straight, grinning. 'Why didn't you tell me that?'

She shrugged, but she was clearly very pleased with herself. 'It wasn't anything serious, like, it wasn't like I wanted to date her or anything. But I wanted to kiss her – we both wanted to kiss, so, like . . . we just did.'

'What was she like?'

We sat at the bar and Pip relayed the whole encounter to me about the girl in second year at Hatfield College who studied French and was wearing a cute skirt, and how it didn't mean anything in particular but it had been fun and good and silly and everything she'd wanted from being at university.

'This is so dumb, but it just . . . it just gave me hope. Just a little bit.' Pip let out a breath. 'Like . . . I might not be alone forever. Like I might have the chance to . . . be properly myself here. To feel like being myself is a *good* thing.' She laughed, then brushed her curls out of her eyes. 'I don't know if I ever felt like being me was . . . good.'

'That's a mood,' I replied in a jokey way, but I guessed I sort of meant it.

'Well, if you ever consider becoming gay, let me know. I could very quickly hook you up with someone. I have contacts now.'

I snorted. 'If only sexuality worked like that.'

'What, choosing it?'

'Yeah. I think I'd choose to be gay if I could.'

Pip didn't say anything for a moment, and I wondered if I'd said something weird or offensive. It was the truth, though. I would have chosen to be gay if I could.

I knew liking girls could be hard when you're also a girl. It usually was, at least for a while. But it was beautiful too. So fucking beautiful.

Liking girls when you're a girl was *power*. It was *light*. Hope. Joy. Passion.

Sometimes it took girls who liked girls a little while to find that. But when they found it, they flew.

'You know,' said Pip. 'Straight people don't think shit like that.'

'Oh. Really?'

'Yeah. Thinking shit like that is, like, step one to realising you're a lesbian.'

'Oh. Right.' I laughed awkwardly. I was still pretty sure I wasn't a lesbian. Or maybe I was and I was just really repressed. Or maybe I was just 'X' on the Kinsey Scale. Nothing.

God. I was regretting not ordering more alcohol.

We sat in silence for a moment, neither of us wanting to really push the issue. Normally Pip was nosy as hell whenever we started talking about *deep stuff*, but she probably knew there were some things that it wasn't cool to be nosy about.

I wished she had been nosy.

I wished I could find the words to talk about all of this with my best friend.

'So, you and Jason,' said Pip, and I thought, *oh no*.

'Uh, yeah?' I said.

Pip snorted. 'Have you kissed yet?'

I felt myself go a bit red. 'Uh, no.'

'Good. I can't imagine you kissing.' She narrowed her eyes and looked off into the distance. 'It'd be like . . . I dunno. Like seeing my siblings kiss.'

'Well, we're probably going to end up doing it at some point,' I said. *Definitely*. We definitely were.

Pip looked at me again. I couldn't read her. Was she annoyed? Did she just find it weird?

'You've never really been interested in anyone before,' she said. 'I mean, the Tommy thing . . . that was all . . . you just *made up* that crush. By accident.'

'Yeah,' I agreed.

'But you . . . you just like Jason now?'

I blinked at her. 'What? Don't you believe me?'

She leant forward a little, then back again. 'I'm not sure I do.'

'Why not?'

She didn't want to say it. She knew it'd be disrespectful to say it, to *assume* anything about my sexuality, but we were both thinking it.

We were both thinking that I probably just didn't like men.

I didn't know what to say, because I didn't disagree.

I wanted to tell Pip that I didn't feel sure about anything, and I felt so weird all the time, to the point that I hated myself, being a kid who knew all about sexuality from the internet but couldn't even vaguely work out what I was, couldn't even come up with a ballpark estimate, when everyone else seemed to find it so, so easy. Or if they didn't find it easy, they got through the hard bit at school, and by the time they were my age, they were already kissing and having sex and falling in love as much as they wanted.

All I could manage to say was: 'I don't really know how I feel.'

Pip could tell I wasn't saying everything that was in my head. She could always tell.

She grabbed my hand and held it.

'That's OK, my guy,' she said. 'That's fine.'

'Sorry,' I mumbled. 'I'm . . . shit at explaining it. It sounds fake.'

'I'm here to talk whenever you want, man.'

'OK.'

She pulled me into a side hug, my face pressing against her collar. 'Date Jason for a bit if you want. Just . . . don't hurt him, OK? He acts all calm and collected, but he's really sensitive after all that shit with Aimee.'

'I know. I won't.' I lifted my head. 'You're really OK with it?'

Her smile was forced and pained, and it nearly broke my heart.

'Of course. I love you.'

'Love you too.'

MIRAGE

I decided to leave after that. Pip kept getting dragged into conversations with people I didn't know, and I didn't have any energy left to talk to new people. Jess was busy mingling, and Sunil was nowhere to be seen.

I checked my phone. It was only twenty past ten. I wondered whether Jason was OK.

He was probably still sitting in his room, all alone, wondering whether I'd really had a headache or I just didn't like him.

I didn't want to think about love any more.

As I walked out of the restaurant and down the narrow stairway, I heard a pair of hushed voices at the bottom. I stopped, realising that one of the voices belonged to Sunil.

'I'm the president now,' he was saying, 'and if that pisses you off *so* much, you don't have to come to the society events any more.'

'What, now you're trying to kick me out?' said the second voice. '*Classic.* I shouldn't be surprised by this point.'

'And now you're trying to pick a fight again.' Sunil let out a long sigh. 'Don't you ever get *tired*, Lloyd? Because I do.'

'It's my right to voice my concerns about the society. You've changed all the events we do and now you're letting in way too many people!'

'Letting in too many – what planet are you *on*?'

'I saw the fucking flyers you were handing out at the Freshers' Fair! *Asexual* and *bigender* and whatever. You're just gonna let in anyone who thinks they're some made-up internet identity?'

There was a short silence, and then Sunil spoke again, his voice hardened.

'You know what, Lloyd? Yes. Yes, I am. Because Pride Soc is inclusive, and open, and loving, and *not run by you any more*. And because there are still sad little cis gays like you who seem to take other queers' mere existence as a threat to your civil rights, even *freshers* who are showing up here for the first time – some of them likely *never* having been to a queer event in their whole lives – just trying to find somewhere they can relax and be themselves. And I don't know if you're aware of this, Lloyd, because I know you don't recognise any pride flag that isn't the fucking rainbow, but I actually happen to *be* one of those *made-up internet identities*. And guess what? I'm the president. So get the fuck out of my formal.'

I heard the sound of footsteps moving away and the swing of the door opening and closing.

I waited a moment, but there was no way to pretend I hadn't heard that conversation, so I descended the steps. Sunil looked up as I approached. He was leaning against the wall, fingers tightly clenching his upper arms.

'Oh, Georgia,' he said, forcing a smile, but I must have looked guilty because he immediately said, 'Ah. You heard some of that.'

'Sorry,' I said as I reached the bottom step. 'Are you OK? Do you . . .' I struggled to think of a way I could help. 'Do you want a drink or something?'

Sunil chuckled. 'You're sweet. I'm OK.'

'He . . . sounded like a . . . disgusting person.'

'Yes. He very much is. Just because you're gay doesn't mean you can't be a bigot.'

'I think you pretty much annihilated him, though.'

He laughed again. 'Thanks.' He unfolded his arms. 'You heading home?'

'Yeah. It's been really nice.'

'Good. Great. You're welcome to come along any time.'

'Thank you. And . . . thanks for what you said to Pip about . . . you know, why I was here.'

He shrugged. 'No biggie.'

'You don't have to be in our play.'

'Oh, no, I am definitely being in your play.'

My mouth dropped open. 'You . . . are?'

'Definitely. I've really needed to do something like this – something *fun*. So, I'm in.' He put his hands in his pockets. 'If you'll have me.'

'Yeah! Yeah, we sort of need five members or the society gets scrapped.'

'Well, there we have it, then. Message me the details?'

'Yeah, definitely.'

There was a pause.

I could have left. It would have made sense for me to head home. But instead I found myself talking.

'I was sort of on a date today,' I said. 'When you found me.'

Sunil raised his eyebrows. 'Oh really?'

'But it . . . didn't go very well.'

'Oh. Why? Were they awful?'

'No, it was . . . the guy is really lovely. It's me that's the problem. I'm weird.'

Sunil paused. 'And why are you weird?'

'I just . . .' I laughed nervously. 'I don't think I can ever feel anything.'

'Maybe he's the wrong person for you.'

'No,' I said. 'He's wonderful. But I never feel anything for anyone.'

There was another long pause.

I didn't even know how to begin to explain it properly. It felt like something I'd made up in my head. A dream I couldn't quite remember properly.

And a word.

A word that Lloyd had spoken with such malice, but Sunil had defended.

A word that had sparked something in my brain.

I'd finally made the connection.

'Uh . . .' I was grateful I was a little tipsy. I pointed at his pin – the one with black, grey, white, and purple stripes. 'Is that . . . the flag for, um . . . being asexual?'

Sunil's eyes widened. For the briefest moment, he seemed genuinely shocked that I was not certain what his pin meant.

'Yes,' he said. 'Asexuality. Do you know what that is?'

Now, I had definitely *heard* of asexuality. I'd seen a few people talking about it online, and many people with it in their Twitter or Tumblr bios. Sometimes I even came across a fanfic with an asexual character. But I'd hardly ever heard people use the word in real life, or even on TV or in movies. I figured it was something to do with not liking sex. But I didn't know for sure.

'Erm . . . not really,' I said. 'I've *heard* of it.' I immediately felt embarrassed by this admission. 'You really don't have to spend time explaining it to me, I can just – I could just go and look it up . . .'

He smiled again. 'It's OK. I'd like to explain it. The internet can be a bit confusing.'

I shut my mouth.

'Asexuality means I'm not sexually attracted to any gender.'

'So . . .' I thought about this. 'That means . . . you don't want to have sex with anyone?'

He chuckled. 'Not necessarily. Some asexual people feel that way. But some don't.'

Now I was just confused. Sunil could tell.

'It's OK,' he said, and it genuinely did make me feel like it was OK that I didn't understand. 'Asexuality means I'm not sexually *attracted* to any gender. So I don't look at men, or women, or anyone, and think, *wow, I want to do sexy stuff with them.*'

This made me snort. 'Does anyone actually think stuff like that?'

Sunil smiled, but it was a sad smile. 'Maybe not in those exact words, but yes, most people think stuff like that.'

This shook me. 'Oh.'

'So, I just don't feel those feelings. Even if they're someone I'm dating. Even if they're a model or a celebrity. Even if, on a basic, objective level, I can tell that they're conventionally attractive. I just don't feel those feelings of attraction.'

'Oh,' I said again.

There was a pause. Sunil looked at me, contemplating what to say next.

'Some asexuals still enjoy having sex, for a whole variety of reasons,' he continued. 'I think that's why a lot of people find it confusing. But some asexuals don't like sex at all, and some are just neutral about it. Some asexuals still feel romantic attraction to people – wanting to be in relationships, or even kiss people, for example. But others don't want romantic relationships at all.

It's a big, big spectrum with a whole range of different feelings and experiences. And there's really no way to tell how one specific person feels, even if they openly describe themselves as asexual.'

'So . . .' I knew it was a little invasive to ask, but I just *had* to. 'Do *you* still want relationships?'

He nodded. 'Yes. I identify as gay as well. Gay asexual.'

'As . . . as well?'

'The technical term is homoromantic. I still want to be in relationships with guys and masculine folks. But I feel very indifferent about sex, because I have never looked at men or any gender and felt sexual attraction to them. Men don't turn me on. Nobody does.'

'So romantic attraction is *different* from sexual attraction?'

'For some people they feel like different things, yes,' said Sunil. 'So some people find it useful to define those two aspects of their attraction differently.'

'Oh.' I didn't know how I felt about that. What I felt was so *whole* – it didn't feel like two different things.

'Jess – she's aromantic, meaning she doesn't feel *romantic* attraction for anyone. She's also bisexual. She won't mind me telling you that. She finds a lot of people physically attractive, but she just doesn't fall in love with them.'

Isn't that sad? was what I wanted to ask. *How is she OK with that?* How would *I* be OK with that?

'She's happy,' said Sunil, like he'd read my mind. 'It took her some time to feel happy with herself, but . . . I mean, you met her. She's *happy* with who she is. Maybe it's not the heteronormative dream that she grew up wishing for, but . . . knowing who you are and *loving* yourself is so much better than that, I think.'

'This is . . . a lot,' I said, my voice quiet and a little croaky.

Sunil nodded again. 'I know.'

'*A lot* a lot.'

'I know.'

'Why do things have to be so complicated?'

'Ah, the eternally wise words of Avril Lavigne.'

I didn't know what to say after that. I just stood there, processing.

'It's funny,' said Sunil after a few moments. He looked down, as if remembering an old joke. 'So few people know what asexuality or aromanticism are. Sometimes I think I'm so wrapped up with Pride Soc that I forget there are people who've just . . . never even heard these words. Or have any idea that this is a real thing.'

'I-I'm sorry,' I said instantly. Had I offended him?

'Oh my God, you have nothing to be sorry about. It's not in films. It's hardly ever in TV shows, and when it is, it's some tiny subplot that most people ignore. When it's talked about in the media, it gets trolled to hell and back. Even some queer people out there hate the very concept of being aro or ace because they think it's unnatural or just *fake* – I mean, you heard Lloyd.' Sunil smiled sadly at me. 'I'm glad you were curious. It's always good to be curious.'

I was curious now, that's for sure.

And I was also terrified.

I mean, that wasn't me. Asexual. Aromantic.

I still wanted to have sex with someone, eventually. Once I found someone I actually liked. Just because I'd never liked anyone didn't mean I never *would* . . . did it?

And I wanted to fall in love. I really, really did.

I definitely would someday.

So that couldn't be me.

I didn't want that to be me.

Fuck. I didn't know.

I shook my head a little, trying to dispel the hurricane of confusion that was threatening to form inside my brain.

'I should . . . go home,' I stammered, feeling suddenly like I was being a huge bother to Sunil. He probably just wanted to have a nice evening, but here I was, asking for a sexuality lesson. 'I mean – back to college. Sorry – um, thank you for explaining about . . . all of that.'

Sunil gazed at me for a long moment.

'Sure,' he said. 'I really am glad you came along, Georgia.'

'Yeah,' I mumbled. 'Thank you.'

'Pride Soc is here for you,' he said. 'OK? Nobody was ever there for me, until . . . until I met Jess. And if I hadn't met her . . .' He trailed off, something crossing his expression that I couldn't read. He replaced it with a familiar calm smile. 'I just need you to know that people are here for you.'

'OK,' I said hoarsely.

And then I was gone.

I guess it's fair to say a lot was spiralling in my brain on that walk home.

I was going to hurt Jason, or Jason and I were going to die together wearing wedding rings. Pip was thriving – maybe she didn't need me any more. Why couldn't I feel anything for anyone? Was I what Sunil and Jess were? Those super long words that most people hadn't even heard of?

Why couldn't I fall in love with anyone?

I passed the shops and cafés, the history department and Hatfield College, drunk students and locals stumbling around, and the cathedral, lit up gently in the dark, and that made me stop and think about how I had walked this path with Jason only a few hours earlier, and we had been laughing, and I had almost been able to imagine that I was someone entirely different.

When I got back to my room, the people upstairs were having sex again. Rhythmic thumping against the wall. I hated it, but then I felt bad, because maybe it was two people in love.

In the end, that was the problem with romance. It was so easy to romanticise romance because it was everywhere. It was in music and on TV and in filtered Instagram photos. It was in the air, crisp and alive with fresh possibility. It was in falling leaves, crumbling wooden doorways, scuffed cobblestones and fields of dandelions. It was in the touch of hands, scrawled letters, crumpled sheets and the golden hour. A soft yawn, early morning laughter, shoes lined up together by the door. Eyes across a dance floor.

I could see it all, all the time, all around, but when I got closer, I found that nothing was there.

A mirage.

PART THREE

I LOVE NONE

'GEORGIA,' a voice said – or screeched, rather – as I entered the Shakespeare Soc rehearsal several days later.

It was our first rehearsal in a real rehearsal room. We were inside one of the many large, old buildings by Durham Cathedral that contained nothing but classrooms, which were available to rent out as society activity spaces. I imagined this building was what most private schools felt like – wooden and unnecessarily large.

The screech in question was one I was coming to know well.

Rooney appeared out of a classroom doorway wearing a burgundy boiler suit, which looked immensely fashionable on her, but if I'd worn it, would have made me look like a car-wash employee.

She grabbed both my arms and started leading me into the room. Inside was mostly empty apart from one table set up at the far end, upon which Pip and Jason were sitting. Jason appeared to be doing some of his course reading, while Pip looked up and stared at Rooney with nothing less than disdain.

'I'm dying, Georgia,' said Rooney. 'Literally. I'm going to explode.'

'Please calm down.'

'No, I am. I was up until six a.m. this morning planning the rest of the show.'

'I know. We live together.'

Since I had informed Rooney that Sunil was on board, she'd gone a little bit overboard on the play preparation – staying up late to plan, scheduling weekly rehearsals for the rest of the year, and bombarding all of us in our new group chat that Pip had named 'A Midsummer Night's Dab'. Rooney argued with Pip about the group chat name in the group chat for several hours.

'We have to get the first couple of scenes ready before the Bailey Ball,' Rooney continued. 'That'll keep us on target.'

'That's only a few weeks away.'

'*Exactly.*'

The Bailey Ball – the upcoming ball at St John's in early December – was completely irrelevant to our society, but Rooney had decided to use it as a target anyway. Probably just to scare us into attending the rehearsals.

'What if Sunil doesn't want to come after all?' She lowered her voice to a whisper. 'What if he thinks it's a shit idea? He's a *third year*. He *knows things.*'

'He's really not the sort of person who's going to criticise a student play, to be honest.'

It was then that Sunil entered the room, wearing dark chinos with a red stripe up each side, a tight polo and a denim jacket. Somehow he appeared not to be freezing to death in November's brutal northern temperature.

He smiled as he approached, and I felt an uncomfortable wash of guilt that he might just be here because I asked.

Pip and Jason joined us to say hi.

'You're the only one I haven't met already,' said Sunil to Jason, holding out his hand.

Jason shook it. He looked intimidated. He was probably in awe of the sheer coolness that radiated from Sunil at all times. 'Hi. I'm Jason.'

'Hi! I'm Sunil. You're very tall, Jason.'

'Uh . . . I suppose I am?'

'Congrats.'

'Thanks?'

Rooney clapped her hands together loudly. 'OK! Let's start!'

Jason and Sunil got sent to the other side of the room to go through a scene from *A Midsummer Night's Dream* while Pip, Rooney and I sat down in a circle on the floor with copies of *Much Ado About Nothing* laid out in front of us.

Much Ado is probably one of the best Shakespeares because the plot is exactly like an enemies-to-lovers fanfic, with a lot of confusion and miscommunication along the way. The premise is: Beatrice and Benedick *hate* each other, and their friends find this hilarious, so they decide to trick them into falling in love, and it works much better than anyone expected.

Amazing.

I had again been chosen by Pip and Rooney to play one of the romantic leads – Benedick. Pip was playing Beatrice. We sat down in a circle to read the scene, and I hoped I'd do better this time. Maybe it had just been awkward with Jason. Now I was acting with Pip in a much funnier scene.

'*I wonder that you will still be talking, Signor Benedick,*' Pip drawled with an eye-roll. '*Nobody marks you.*'

I put on my best sarcasm and responded, '*What, my dear Lady Disdain! Are you yet living?*'

'Less angry, I think,' said Rooney. 'Like, Benedick's teasing her. He thinks it's hilarious.'

I *loved* enemies-to-lovers romances. But I was struggling to *get into* this. I'd much rather just watch someone else perform it.

I let Pip read her next line before I chipped in again, this time trying to sound less annoyed.

'*Then is courtesy a turncoat. But it is certain I am loved of all ladies, only you excepted,*' I said. '*And I would I could find in my heart that I had not a hard heart; for, truly, I love none.*'

'Hm,' said Rooney.

'Look,' I said. 'This is the first time we're reading it through.'

'It's OK. Maybe this role just isn't for you.'

This *and* Juliet? Was it just the romantic roles I couldn't do? Surely not – I'd played plenty of romantic roles in the past in school plays and youth theatre shows and I was fine.

Why was I psyching myself out about romantic roles now?

'Hey!' Pip barked at Rooney. 'Stop insulting Georgia!'

'I'm the director! I've got to be honest!'

'Uh, I'm *also* the director and I think you're being a bitch!'

'Drama,' said Jason from the other side of the room. I turned to see Sunil raise his eyebrows at him, and then they both started snickering.

'If you think Georgia is *sooo* shit –' said Pip.

'That's not what she said, but OK,' I said.

'Then let me see *you* do it better, Rooney Bach. If you've got no problems with getting gay for a scene.'

'Oh, I have no problems with *getting gay*, pipsqueak,' said Rooney, seeming to imply something else entirely, which Pip noticed, and recoiled a little in surprise.

'OK then,' said Pip.

'OK,' said Rooney.

'OK.'

Rooney slammed her copy of *Much Ado* on to the floor. '*OK.*'

I went to sit with Sunil and Jason so we could all watch Pip and Rooney act out Beatrice and Benedick's first argument from *Much Ado About Nothing*. I predicted that it was going to either be absolutely hilarious or an utter mess. Possibly both.

Rooney stood tall and sneered down at Pip. '*I would I could find in my heart that I had not a hard heart; for, truly, I love* none.' She wasn't even looking at her copy of *Much Ado*. She knew it off by heart.

Pip laughed and turned away, as if addressing an onlooker. '*A dear happiness to women! They would else have been troubled with a* pernicious *suitor.*' She turned back to Rooney, narrowing her eyes. '*I thank God and my cold blood I am of your humour for that: I had rather hear my dog bark at a crow than a* man *swear he* loves *me.*'

Rooney's mouth twitched. It was shockingly similar to the way it did when she *wasn't* acting.

She stepped slightly closer to Pip as if to emphasise her height advantage. '*God keep your Ladyship still in that mind!*' She pressed a hand on to Pip's shoulder and squeezed. '*So some gentleman or other shall 'scape a predestinate scratched face.*'

'*Scratching could not make it worse,*' Pip bit back immediately with a cock of her head and a cheeky grin, '*an 'twere such a face as yours were.*'

How did they both know this scene off by heart already?

Rooney leant right in, her face mere centimetres from Pip's.

'*Well,*' she breathed in a low tone, '*you are a rare parrot-teacher.*'

Pip took in a sharp gulp of air. '*A bird of my tongue is better than a beast of yours.*'

And Rooney, the absolute maniac, let her eyes drop down to Pip's mouth.

'*I would my horse had the speed of your tongue*,' she murmured, '*and so good a continuer.*'

The silence that followed was earth-shattering. Jason, Sunil and I just stared, entranced. The air in the room was beyond electric — it was on *fire*.

We waited for the moment to end, and it was Pip who finally broke. She wrenched herself out of the moment, red-faced.

'And that's how it's done, kids,' she said, with a bow. We clapped.

Rooney turned away and started fixing her ponytail, oddly quiet.

'So you two are gonna play Benedick and Beatrice, right?' said Jason.

Pip shot a glance at me. 'Well, if Georgia doesn't mind . . .'

'No, of course not,' I said. 'It was great.'

Perhaps a little *too* great, if the flush on Pip's cheeks was anything to go by.

'What?' said Pip, looking back to Rooney, who was still busying herself with pulling out and retying her ponytail. 'Was the scene too sexy for you?'

'Nothing's too sexy for me,' she shot back. But she didn't turn round. She was hiding.

Pip smirked. I could tell she felt like she'd won.

We spent our remaining rehearsal time helping Rooney and Pip plot out the scene, adding in a few props, before running through a couple more times. They seemed to get more flustered each time, along with increasing the amount of intense eye contact and touching in the scene.

At the end of the two hours, me, Sunil and Jason stacked the chairs, then went to wait near the door while Pip and Rooney stood in the centre of the room and bickered over a couple of lines towards the end of the scene. Jason shrugged his teddy coat on.

'So,' he said to Sunil. 'Regrets?'

Sunil laughed. 'No! It was fun. I'm very glad I got to witness . . .' he gestured vaguely towards Pip and Rooney, '. . . whatever *this* is.'

'We're very sorry about them,' I said.

He laughed again. 'No, honestly. This has been fun. It's actually a welcome change to the general chaos and drama of Pride Soc. And the stress of third year.' He put his hands in his pockets and shrugged. 'I don't know, I think – I think I've needed to do something like this. University has been stressful. Like, when I was a fresher, I was just . . . in a really bad place, and then I spent all of second year doing things for Pride Soc, and . . . well, obviously that continued into this year. Orchestra is a good time but stressful as hell. I don't think I ever really take the time to just . . . pursue something just because it's *fun*. You know?' He looked up, as if surprised we were still standing there, listening to him. 'Sorry, now I'm oversharing.'

'No, it's fine,' I said, but that didn't feel like enough. 'We're . . . really glad you're here.'

Jason patted him on the shoulder. 'Yeah, you need to come for pizza with us sometime. Cast bonding.'

Sunil smiled at him. 'I will. Thank you.'

We said goodbye to Sunil, who had a tutorial to get to, and Jason and I leant against opposite sides of the doorframe, waiting for Pip and Rooney.

Jason started flicking through the pages of his copy of the play. '*Much Ado* is such a good play. Although I don't get the appeal of relationships where they're mean to each other at the start.'

'It's all just build-up to the point where they inevitably have really wild sex,' I said, thinking fondly of some of my favourite enemies-to-lovers fics. 'It makes the eventual sex more exciting.'

'I suppose it makes a good story.' Jason flipped over a page. 'It's funny how much stuff revolves around sex. I don't even think I'd need it in a relationship.'

'Wait, really?'

'Like, it's fun, but . . . I don't think it's a deal-breaker. If the other person didn't want to do it that much. Or at all, I guess.' He looked up from behind the book. 'What? Is that weird?'

I shrugged. 'No, that's just a cool way to think about it.'

'If you really loved someone, I just think you wouldn't really . . . *care* so much about things like that. I dunno. I think everyone's been kind of conditioned to be obsessed with it, when in actual fact . . . you know, it's just a thing people do for fun. You don't even need it to make babies any more. It's not like you'd die without it.'

'Die without what?' asked Pip, who was suddenly only a couple of metres away from us, pulling her bomber jacket on.

Jason snapped the book shut. 'Pizza.'

'Oh my God, can we get pizza right now? I *will* die without pizza right now.'

They left the room together, chatting, while I waited for Rooney, who was tying her shoelaces.

Was there some kind of third choice when it came to mine and Jason's relationship? Could we be together and just . . . not have sex?

I stood there in the doorway trying to picture it. No sex, but still a romance. A *relationship*. Kissing Jason, holding hands with Jason. Being in *love*.

I'd spent a lot of time thinking about how I felt about love, but not much about *having sex* – I'd just assumed that sex would automatically be a part of it. But it didn't have to be. Sunil had told me that some people didn't want sex but were perfectly happy in relationships without it.

Maybe I *did* like Jason romantically – I just didn't want to have sex with him.

WANK FANTASY

Obviously, I spent the rest of the day thinking about sex. Not even in a fun way. Just in a *confused* way.

I hadn't given much thought to how I felt about sex until the prom afterparty. That had been when I'd started to wonder whether I was *weird* for not having done all the things other people claimed they'd done – including having sex.

We all know that the concept of 'virginity' is dumb as hell and invented by misogynists, but that didn't stop me feeling like I was, essentially, missing out on something really great. But *was* I missing out? Sunil said he felt *indifferent* about sex. I'd never heard anyone talk about sex like that before. Like it was a takeaway cuisine you thought was OK, but you wouldn't personally choose it.

All I'd felt about sex so far was shame for not having had it.

That night, in bed, I decided I needed to talk to someone who actually knew a bit about it. Rooney.

I rolled over to face her across the room. She was typing on her MacBook, most of her body concealed by her duvet.

'Rooney?' I said.

'Mm?'

'I've been thinking about . . . you know . . . my thing with Jason.'

This immediately got her attention. She sat up a little, shutting her MacBook, and said, 'Yeah? Have you kissed yet?'

'Um – well, no, but –'

'Really?' She raised her eyebrows, clearly thinking this was weird. 'How come?'

I didn't know what to tell her.

'Don't stress about it,' she said with a wave of her hand. 'It'll happen. When it's the right time, it'll just *happen*.'

This annoyed me. Was kissing really so *vague*?

'I guess,' I said, feeling like I should just be honest, 'I . . . don't even know whether . . . you know, I'm attracted to men in general, or . . . something like that.'

Rooney blinked. 'Really?'

'Yeah.'

'OK,' said Rooney. She nodded, but I could see on her face that this was a surprise to her. 'OK.'

'I'm not sure, though. I've been thinking a lot about, um . . . well, how I'd feel about . . . physical stuff.'

There was a pause, and then she said, 'Sex?'

I should have guessed she'd just be blunt about it. 'Well, yeah.'

'OK.' She nodded again. 'Yeah. That's good. Sexual attraction is just figuring out who you want to have sex with.' She paused to think, and then she turned fully to face me. 'Right. We're going to figure this out.'

'What d'you mean?'

'I mean, let's get to the bottom of your feelings and figure out whether you're attracted to Jason or not.'

I had absolutely no idea where this conversation was going, and I was scared.

'Question One. Do you wank?'

I'd been right to be scared.

'Oh God.'

She held up her hands. 'You don't have to answer, but I think this might be a pretty good way of figuring out if you really like Jason.'

'I'm so uncomfortable.'

'It's just me. I've heard you fart in bed.'

'No you *haven't.*'

'I have. It was loud.'

'Oh *God.*'

I knew I could just shut this conversation down if I really wanted to. It *was* a bit rude of Rooney to ask such personal things when, really, we'd only known each other for a month and a half. But I *did* want to talk about stuff like this with someone. And I *did* think that talking about it might help me figure some stuff out.

'So,' Rooney continued. 'Masturbation.'

I wasn't the sort of person who thought it was a 'guy thing'. I'd been on the internet long enough to know that masturbation was all-gender.

'Doesn't . . . doesn't everyone masturbate?' I mumbled.

'Hm, no, I don't think so.' Rooney tapped her chin. 'I had a friend back at home who said she just didn't like doing it.'

'Oh. That's fair enough.'

'So I assume you do it then.'

Yes, I did. I wasn't gonna just lie about it. I knew it wasn't something to be ashamed of, obviously, but it still felt excruciating to talk about.

'Yeah,' I said.

'OK. So, what d'you think about when you masturbate?'

'Rooney. Oh my fucking God.'

'Come on! We're doing a scientific study to determine where your attraction lies. Oh my God, we should get Pip to help! She does science!'

I didn't particularly want Pip to get involved in this already awkward conversation. 'No, we shouldn't.'

'Do you think about men? Women? Both? Any/or?'

The honest answer was:

Any.

Literally anything.

But I knew that would just confuse things. And here's why.

My usual masturbation situation was just whenever I was in the mood to read a smutty fanfic. It felt like a safe, fun way to get turned on and have a good time. So I would just think about the characters in the fic I was reading. Whatever combination of genders that involved – I wasn't fussy, as long as the writing was good.

It wasn't about bodies and genitals for me. It was about chemistry. But that wasn't anything unusual, I thought.

People didn't *really* just look at boobs or abs and get turned on. Did they?

'Georgia,' said Rooney. 'Come on. I'll tell you mine if you tell me yours.'

'Fine,' I said. 'I . . . the gender doesn't really matter.'

'Oh my God! Same!' Rooney gestured between us. 'Wank fantasy sisters!'

'Never say that again.'

'No, but it's cool to know I'm not alone in that.' She wrapped her covers a little tighter round her. 'Like, I know I only go out with guys, but . . . you know. It's fun to think about other stuff.'

Maybe I was bi or pan, then. Maybe we both were. If gender didn't matter to us, that would make sense, right?

'There are still some specific scenarios I have to picture,' she continued. 'Like, I can't just imagine myself doing anything with anyone. I still think I have . . . preferences. But not limited to gender.'

Something she'd said struck me.

'Wait,' I said. 'I-I mean, I don't imagine *myself* with any gender.'

She paused. 'Oh. What?'

It clicked in my brain what I was trying to say.

'I don't think about *myself* having sex,' I said.

Rooney frowned, then she snorted, and then, upon realising I wasn't joking, she frowned again. 'What do you think about then? Other people?'

'. . . Yeah.'

'Like . . . people you know?'

'Ew, no. Oh my God. More like . . . made-up people in my brain.'

'Hm.' Rooney let out a deep breath. 'So . . . you don't think about having sex with Jason?'

'No!' I exclaimed. The thought of having sex with Jason freaked me out. 'People don't – people don't actually do that, do they?'

'What, fantasise about someone they have a crush on?'

As soon as she said it, I realised how obvious it was. Of course people did that. I'd seen it dozens of times in movies and on TV and in fanfics.

'This is going to be harder than I thought,' said Rooney.

'Oh.'

'OK, so. Question Two. Who was the celebrity you last got off to?'

I blinked. 'People *definitely* don't do that.'

'Do what?'

'Get off to pictures of celebrities.'

'Uh, yes they do. I have a folder of shirtless pics of Henry Cavill on my laptop.'

I laughed.

Rooney did not.

'What?' she asked.

I genuinely thought she was joking. 'I thought that was just a movie thing. You really just . . . look at abs and that does it for you?'

'I mean . . . yeah.' Rooney looked a little put out. 'What, is that not normal?'

I had no idea what was normal. Maybe nothing was normal. 'I just don't get the appeal. Like . . . abs are just lumpy stomachs.'

This made Rooney laugh loudly. 'OK. Fine. Question Three –'

'How are there more questions –'

'Sex dreams. What happened in your last sex dream?'

I stared at her. 'Seriously?'

'Yes!'

I started to say that I'd never had a sex dream, but that wasn't strictly true. I'd had a dream a couple of years back where in order to pass my exams I had to have sex with a guy in my class. He was waiting on my bed, naked, and I kept walking in and out of my bedroom, fully clothed, not quite able to work up the courage to go through with it. It wasn't a nightmare, but it gave me that same feeling of a nightmare where you're trying to run away from a demon but your legs are moving like they're stuck in sludge, and the demon is catching up with you, but you can't move properly, and you're about to die.

On second thoughts, I wasn't sure that counted as a sex dream.

'I don't have sex dreams,' I said.

Rooney stared back at me. 'What . . . ever?'

'Does everyone have sex dreams?'

'Well . . . I don't know, now.' Rooney looked almost as confused as me. 'I assumed it was kind of an everyone thing, but . . . I mean, I guess it's not.'

I almost regretted bringing this up with her. For someone who'd had a lot of sex, Rooney didn't seem to understand it any better than I did. Making a snap decision, I grabbed my phone again. 'I am going to message Pip.'

'*Yes*. Please get her involved. I want to know what she thinks.'

I gave Rooney a look. 'You're very interested in what Pip thinks about sex, huh?'

Rooney spluttered. 'Uh – no, actually, no. I just – I just wanted a third opinion and she's the most likely person to overshare.'

Georgia Warr
apologies for the late-night message but i have a question, dear friend

Felipa Quintana
It better not be about the group chat name because I will defend 'a midsummer night's dab' until I die

Georgia Warr
i respect the dab, it's not about that
sooooooo
me and rooney are having a conversation about sex right now

Felipa Quintana
OOOOH
Okay I'm in

Georgia Warr
my question is . . . . . .
do you have sex dreams?

Felipa Quintana
Lol WOW

Georgia Warr
you don't have to answer if it's too personal haha
but also i have seen you pee multiple times
we know each other probably too well by this point
for the record, rooney is here and wants to know your answers

Felipa Quintana
Wow hi rooney
Yeah I've had sex dreams
Not like looooads
But occasionally
I mean that's pretty normal right??

'She says she's had sex dreams,' I said to Rooney.

'Ask her about masturbating,' Rooney hissed from across the room.

'Rooney.'

'It's for science!'

Georgia Warr
that's basically what we're trying to determine
a second question – when you have a wank do you think about
YOURSELF having sex?? And if so . . . with what gender??
rooney says the gender doesn't matter for her

Felipa Quintana

JESUS georgia what is this conversation omg
Wait Rooney thinks about being with girls??????

Georgia Warr

yeah

Felipa Quintana

Okay . . . . . . Okay interesting
Well firstly, yeah I do think about myself? Idk what else I would
think about?? I guess unless you're literally just having a wank
to porn . . . but even then it's like at least a little bit about you
and your fantasies too
And obviously I just think about girls haha . . . the thought of
being with a guy just disgusts me
I mean I am very much a lesbian. We've established this
This is interesting though

'She said she does think about herself having sex,' I said.

Rooney nodded, though she'd started adjusting her hair so I couldn't read her expression. 'Yeah. I mean, that's what most people do, I think.'

Georgia Warr

i won't tell rooney this one, this is just a question from me
do you fantasise about other people?? like real people? like if
you get a crush or meet someone really hot, do you fantasise
about having sex with them????

Felipa Quintana

Georgia how come you wanna know all this?

Are you okay??

Are you and Jason having SEX

Oh god I don't know if I want to know

Georgia Warr

calm down i'm not having sex

just trying to understand some stuff

Felipa Quintana

Okay

Yeah I guess I do sometimes

Not eeeevery single hot person I meet but if I really liked someone . . .

I mean sometimes I just can't help it I guess haha?

'What are you saying to her?' Rooney asked.

I was staring at my phone screen.

And then I chucked it across my bed.

'This has to be a fucking *joke*,' I blurted.

Rooney paused. 'What?'

I sat up, pushing the covers off my body. 'Everyone has to be fucking JOKING.'

'What d'you –'

'People are really out there just . . . thinking about having sex all the time and they can't even *help it*?' I spluttered. 'People have dreams about it because they want it *that much*? How the – I'm losing it. I thought all the movies were exaggerating, but you're all really out there just craving genitals and embarrassment. This has to be some kind of huge joke.'

There was a long silence.

Rooney cleared her throat. 'I guess we're not wank fantasy sisters.'

'For fuck's sake, Rooney.'

I don't think this conversation had gone to a place that either of us were expecting it to.

I'd never fantasised about myself having sex. And that was different from most people. *I* was different. How had I never realised this before?

Picturing fanfic characters having sex? Great. Fine. Sexy. But picturing *myself* having sex with anyone, guy, girl, whoever, didn't interest me.

No – it was more than that. It was an immediate fucking turn-off.

Was that what Sunil had told me about? Was that how he felt?

'I don't really know what to say or how to help,' Rooney said. Then, with more sincerity than I was used to from Rooney, she followed up with, 'Don't do anything you don't want to do, OK?'

'. . . OK.'

'I mean with Jason.' She looked so serious all of a sudden, and I realised how rare it was for me to see an expression like that on Rooney's face. 'Just don't do anything you're not comfortable with. Please.'

'Yeah. OK.'

Felipa Quintana

Hey, you sure you're okay? This was a weird conversation

Georgia Warr
i'm okay
sorry
this was weird

Felipa Quintana
I don't mind!!! I love weird
I hope I helped??

Georgia Warr
you did

COUNTDOWN TIMER MUSIC

'So . . . I guess this is properly a date, then,' I said to Jason over our pancakes.

Our third date was at a pancake café. It was situated up a hill about a ten-minute walk out of Durham's town centre and was so tiny that I felt claustrophobic. That was probably why I was so uncomfortable, I reasoned.

My statement seemed to fluster him for a moment, but eventually he cracked a smile. 'I guess it is.'

He'd made an effort today, just like I had. His hair was extra fluffy, and he was wearing a fashionable Adidas sweatshirt with his usual black jeans.

'Did the other two times count?' I asked.

'Hm . . . I don't know. Maybe the second one?'

'Yes. Us getting kicked out of the cinema then me getting a migraine does sound like a pretty good first date.'

'One to tell the grandkids, I suppose.' As soon as he said it, he looked very embarrassed, unsure whether this was an appropriate joke to make yet. I laughed to put him at ease.

We ate our pancakes and talked. We talked about the play, about our courses, about the upcoming Bailey Ball, which I'd managed to score Pip and Jason guest tickets to. We talked about politics and decorating our bedrooms and the new Pokémon game that was coming out soon. God, it was easy to talk to Jason.

That was all it took to ease my doubts. To stop thinking about that conversation with Rooney and Pip. To forget about what Sunil had told me.

Jason and I laughed about some little joke. And I thought – maybe. Maybe it could work if I just tried one more time.

'You know what Rooney said?' I said to Jason once we'd made it back to college. We were sitting in his corridor's kitchen, and Jason had already made me a hot chocolate.

Jason stirred sugar into his tea. 'What?'

I had made the decision on the walk back here to take my shot. Despite what Rooney had concluded at the end of our chat, I needed to treat this situation realistically – I was going to have to make an effort to force myself to like Jason. But I could do that, right? I could do it.

'She thought it was weird we hadn't kissed yet.'

OK, that wasn't *exactly* what she'd said just before our big sex conversation. But it was what she'd implied.

Jason stopped stirring his tea. For a moment, his face was unreadable.

Then he continued stirring.

'Did she?' he said, with a small twitch of his mouth.

'I think she's had a lot more relationships than us, though,' I said with an awkward chuckle.

'Has she?' Jason responded, again unreadable.

'Yeah.'

Shit. Was I making this weird? I was making this weird.

'Well . . .' Jason tapped the spoon on the side of his mug. 'That's . . . I mean, everyone does these things at different paces. We don't need to rush it.'

I nodded. 'Yeah. True.'

OK. That's fine. We didn't need to kiss today. I could try again another day.

Relief washed over me.

Wait, no.

I couldn't give up that easily, could I?

Fuck.

Why was this so fucking hard?

Rooney had said it just *happened*. But if I didn't do anything, nothing would happen. If I didn't try, I'd be like this forever.

Jason finished making his tea. We'd decided to go chill in his room for a bit with a movie – it was a late Sunday afternoon and that felt like the thing to do.

But just as I went to pull open the door, someone on the other side pushed it towards me so fast that I tripped backwards over my own feet and fell on to Jason and his boiling mug of tea.

We didn't go down, but the tea went *everywhere*.

The person who'd opened the door backed away immediately with an apologetic 'Sorry, I'll come back in a bit.' I was only lightly splashed, and I was still wearing my coat anyway. I turned to Jason, who had sat down on a nearby chair, to survey the damage.

His jumper was soaked. But that didn't seem to bother him – he was staring, alarmed, at his left hand, which had also been covered in tea. Fresh, boiling tea.

'Oh fuck,' I said.

'Yeah,' he said, just staring at his hand.

'Does that hurt?'

'Er . . . slightly.'

'Cold water,' I said immediately. I grabbed his wrist, pulled him over towards the sink, turned on the cold tap, and held his hand under the water.

Jason just stared, dumbfounded. We waited, letting the icy water do its work.

After a moment, he said, 'I was looking forward to that tea.'

I let out a sigh of relief. If he was making jokes, it probably wasn't too bad.

'Does tea wash out?' He looked down at the stained fabric, and then just chuckled. 'I'll look it up.'

'I'm really sorry,' I blurted out, realising that this was probably my fault.

Jason nudged me with his elbow.

We were standing very close in front of the sink.

'It wasn't your fault. That guy who came in, he's in my corridor. I swear he never looks where he's going. I've bumped into him like five times.'

'Are you – is it OK? We don't need to go to A&E or anything?'

'I think it's fine. I should probably just stand here for a few minutes, though.'

We fell into silence again, listening to the sound of running water.

Then Jason said, 'Er, you don't have to hold my hand if you don't want to.'

I was still holding his wrist, keeping his hand under the tap. I quickly let go, but then realised that maybe that had been a sort-of-flirty line, and he wanted me to keep holding his hand . . . or maybe he didn't and it didn't mean anything? I wasn't sure. It was too late.

I turned my head to find him staring down at me. He quickly

looked away, but almost immediately turned back again so that we were holding each other's gaze.

It was like a siren suddenly going off everywhere around me.

Like a burglar alarm that wakes you up so hard you can't stop shaking for half an hour.

Looking back, it was almost hilarious.

Whenever someone tried to kiss me, I went headfirst into a fight or flight response.

His eyes focused on my lips, then darted back up. He wasn't like Tommy. He was trying very hard to work out whether this was something I wanted. He was looking for the *signals*. Had I been giving off the signals? Maybe it would have been easier for him to just ask, but how do people phrase that in a non-cheesy way? And to be honest, I was glad he didn't ask, because what would I have said?

No. I would have said no, because it turned out I just couldn't lie to anyone except myself.

As he moved towards me, only a fraction of an inch, I imagined the *Countdown* timer music starting to play.

I wanted to try.

I *wanted* to want to kiss him.

But I didn't actually want to kiss him.

But maybe I should do it anyway.

But I didn't want to.

But maybe I wouldn't know until I tried.

But I knew that I already knew.

I already knew what I felt.

And Jason could tell.

He moved back again, clearly embarrassed. 'Uh ... sorry. Wrong moment.'

'No,' I found myself saying. 'Go on.'

I wanted him to just do it. I wanted him to rip the plaster off. Yank the bone back into shape. Fix me.

But I already knew there was nothing to fix.

I was always going to be like this.

He met my eyes, questioning. Then he leant in and pressed his lips to mine.

BRAINWASHED

My first kiss was with Jason Farley-Shaw in the November of my first year of university, standing in front of a college kitchen sink.

As much of a romantic as I was, I hadn't given much thought to what my first kiss would be like. Looking back, that probably should have been an indicator of me not really wanting to kiss anyone, but years of films, music, TV, peer pressure, and my own craving for a big love story had brainwashed me into believing this was going to be something amazing, as long as I gave it a shot.

It was not amazing.

In fact, I hated it. I think I would have felt less uncomfortable if someone had dared me to start singing on public transport.

It was not Jason's fault that it was not amazing. I didn't have anyone to compare him to, obviously, but objectively, he was perfectly fine at kissing. He didn't do it too deep or forcefully. There were no teeth incidents, or, God forbid, tongue.

I knew what sorts of feelings kissing was *supposed* to bring up. I'd read hundreds, possibly *thousands* of fanfics by this point. Kissing someone you like was supposed to make your head spin, your stomach twist, your heart speed up, and you were supposed to enjoy it.

I didn't feel any of that. I just felt a deep, empty dread in the pit of my stomach. I hated how close he was. I hated the way his lips felt against mine. I hated the fact that he wanted to do this.

It only lasted for a few seconds.

But those were some very uncomfortable seconds for me.

And, from the look on his face, they were for him too.

'You look like that was terrible,' I found myself saying. I didn't know what else to say but the truth by this point.

'So do you,' said Jason.

'Oh.'

Jason looked away with a pained expression. He opened his mouth, then closed it again.

'Well, I fucked that up,' I said.

He shook his head immediately. 'No, it's my fault. Sorry. Shit. It was the wrong moment.'

I wanted to laugh. I wished I could explain just how much it was my fault.

Maybe I *should* try to explain.

But Jason ended up speaking first.

'I don't think you're into me,' he said.

When he looked at me, it was like he was pleading. Begging me to tell him otherwise.

'I . . . I didn't know whether I was,' I said. 'I thought if . . . if I *tried* then I could make it happen – I just wanted to see if I could fall in love, and you were the person I thought I could fall for, like, if I tried?'

As I said it, I realised exactly the weight of what I'd done.

'You . . . just used me as an experiment, then,' said Jason, looking away. 'Knowing full well that I really liked you.'

'I didn't want to hurt you.'

'Well, you did.' He laughed. 'How did you think you were going to do that and *not*?'

'I'm sorry,' was all I could say.

'Fuck.' Then he laughed a horrible, sad laugh. 'Why did you do this to me?'

'Don't say that,' I said hoarsely.

Jason turned the tap off and studied his hand, comparing it with his other hand. It looked several shades redder than it should be. 'OK. I think it's OK.'

'Are you sure?'

'Yeah. I might go and wrap it in something, just to be safe.'

'Oh. God, yeah, of course.' I stood there awkwardly. 'Do you want me to come?'

'No.'

Fuck. This was all going to shit.

'I'm really sorry,' I said, not sure whether I was apologising for the burn or for the kiss. Both, probably.

Jason was shaking his head. It almost seemed like he was annoyed with himself, but nothing that had happened this afternoon had been his fault. 'I . . . I just need to go.'

Jason headed for the door.

'Jason,' I said, but he didn't stop.

'I'm just gonna need you to leave me alone for a while, OK, Georgia?'

And then he was gone.

Jason didn't deserve any of this.

Jason was . . .

Jason had real feelings for me.

He deserved someone who was actually able to reciprocate.

FANTASY FUTURE

It wasn't just that I'd hurt Jason. It wasn't even having to accept that I was some kind of sexual orientation that barely anyone had heard of, that I would have to find some way to explain to my family and everyone else. It was knowing, with absolute certainty, that I was never, ever going to fall in love with anybody.

I had spent my whole life believing that romantic love was waiting for me. That one day I'd find it and I would be totally, finally *happy*.

But now I had to accept that it would never happen. None of it. No romance. No marriage. No sex.

There were so many things that I would never do. Would never even *want* to do or feel *comfortable* doing. So many little things I'd taken for granted, like moving into my first place with my partner, or my first dance at my wedding, or having a baby with someone. Having someone to look after me when I'm sick, or watch TV with in the evenings, or going on a couples' holiday to Disneyland.

And the worst part of it was – even though I'd longed for these things, I knew that they'd never make me happy anyway. The idea was beautiful. But the reality made me sick.

How could I feel so sad about giving up these things that I did not actually want?

I felt pathetic for getting sad about it. I felt guilty, knowing that there were people out there like me who were *happy* being like this.

I felt like I was grieving. I was grieving this fake life, a fantasy future that I was never going to live.

I had no idea what my life would be like now. And that scared me. God, that scared me so, so much.

MIRROR WORLD

I didn't tell Pip.

I didn't want to disappoint her too.

The day after my date with Jason, I started to wonder whether he would tell Pip, and Pip would hate me. But then she messaged me that afternoon with a link to a really funny TikTok, which definitely meant that Jason hadn't told her.

The day after that, Pip messaged me asking if I wanted to meet up with her for a study session in the big university library because she hated doing uni work by herself in her room, and I agreed. Jason, she explained, had rowing practice so couldn't come. We didn't chat much while we were there – I had an Age of Chivalry assignment, and she was doing chemistry work that looked ten times more difficult than my essay on 'Destiny in Chrétien de Troyes' *Perceval*'. I was glad we didn't talk much. Because if she'd asked me about Jason, I wouldn't have been able to lie.

It was nearly nine o'clock at night by the time we'd both finished, so we decided to get some fish and chips, then head back to my room to catch up on *Killing Eve*.

It probably would have been a normal evening. It probably

would have cheered me up a bit, after everything that had happened.

If we hadn't entered my bedroom to find Rooney crying.

She was curled up under her sheets, clearly trying to hide the fact that she was upset but failing utterly because of how loudly she was sniffing. My first thought was that Rooney was *never* in our room at this time of the evening. My second thought was, *Why is she crying?*

Pip had frozen next to me. There was no escaping the situation. We could see Rooney was crying. She knew that we knew. There was no pretending this wasn't happening.

'Hey,' I said, properly entering the room. Pip hovered in the doorway, clearly trying to decide whether to stay or go, but just as I turned to her to tell her to leave, she came inside and closed the door behind her.

'I'm fine,' came the teary response.

Pip laughed, then seemed to instantly regret it.

At the sound of Pip's voice, Rooney peered over her covers. Upon seeing Pip, her eyes narrowed.

'Can you leave,' she said, immediately less tearful and more *Rooney*.

'Um . . .' Pip cleared her throat. 'I wasn't laughing at you. I was just laughing because you said you were fine when you're clearly not. I mean, like, you're literally crying. Not that that's *funny*. It was just a bit *stupid* –'

Rooney's face, very clearly tear-stained, hardened. 'Leave.'

'Um . . .' Pip rummaged into her bag of fish and chips and withdrew a large clump of paper napkins. She jogged over to Rooney's bed, placed them right at the bottom of the duvet, then jogged back to the door. 'There.'

Rooney looked at the napkins. Then up at Pip. And, for once, she didn't say a thing.

'I, er . . .' Pip ran a hand through her hair and looked off to one side. 'I hope you feel better soon. And if you need any more tissues, erm . . . I can go get some?'

There was a pause.

'I think I have enough now, thank you,' said Rooney.

'Cool. I'll just go then.'

'Cool.'

'Are you . . . are you OK?'

Rooney stared at her for a long moment.

Pip didn't wait for an answer. 'Yeah. No. Sorry. I'm going.' She swung round and practically ran from the room. As soon as the door clicked shut, Rooney slowly sat up, picked up one of the napkins, and dabbed her eyes.

I sat down on my own bed, dropping my bags on to the sheets.

'*Are* you OK?' I asked.

This made her raise her head. Her eye make-up was smeared down her cheeks, her ponytail falling out of place, and she was wearing normal going-out clothes – a bardot top and tight skirt.

There was a moment of silence.

And then she started crying again.

OK. I was going to have to deal with this situation. Somehow.

I stood up and walked over towards her kettle, which she kept plugged in on her desk. I filled it up from our bedroom sink, then put it on to boil. Rooney liked tea. The first thing she did after getting back to our room was always to make a cup of tea.

While waiting for it to boil, I cautiously sat on the edge of her bed.

I suddenly noticed there was something on the floor under my feet – the photo of Rooney and Mermaid-hair Beth. It must have fallen off the wall. I picked it up and put it on her bedside table.

What was this about? The play, maybe? That was about eighty per cent of what she talked about.

Maybe it was a relationship thing. Maybe she'd had an argument with a guy. Or maybe it was a family thing. I didn't know anything about Rooney's family, or her life back home at all, really.

I've always hated being asked if I'm 'OK'. The available answers are either to lie and say *I'm fine*, or to massively and embarrassingly overshare.

So instead of asking Rooney that again, I said, 'Do you want me to get your pyjamas?'

For a moment, I wondered if she hadn't heard me.

But then she nodded.

I leant back and grabbed her pyjamas from the end of the bed. She always wore matching button-up ones with cute patterns.

'Here,' I said, holding them out for her.

She sniffed. Then she took them.

While she was changing, I went over to the kettle and made her some tea. When I returned, she had transformed into Bedtime Rooney, and accepted the mug.

'Thanks,' she mumbled and sipped it immediately. People who drink tea must not have any sensation left on their tongues, I swear to God.

I linked my fingers together awkwardly in my lap.

'Do you . . . want to talk about it?' I asked.

She snorted, which was at least slightly better than the sobbing.

'Is that . . . a no?' I said.

She sipped again.

There was a long pause.

I was about to give up and go back to my own bed, when she said,

'Had sex with some guy.'

'Oh,' I said. 'What . . . recently?'

'Yeah. Like a couple of hours ago.' She sighed. 'I was bored.'

'Oh. Well . . . good for you.'

She shook her head slowly. 'No. Not really.'

'It . . . was bad?'

'I just did it to try and fill a hole.'

I considered this.

'I may be a virgin,' I said, 'but I *sort of* thought that filling a hole was usually the point.'

Rooney let out a cackle. 'Oh my *God*. You did *not* just make that joke.'

I glanced at her. She was grinning.

'Are you referring to a different hole?' I asked. 'A non-vaginal one?'

'*Yes*, Georgia. I'm not talking about my fucking *vagina*.'

'OK. Just checking.' I paused. 'I thought you were all sex-positive and stuff. There's nothing wrong with casual sex.'

'I know that,' she said, then shook her head. 'I still believe in all that. I'm not saying that having casual sex makes me a bad person, because it doesn't. And I really do enjoy it. But tonight . . . it was just . . .' She sipped her tea, her eyes filling with tears again. 'You know when you eat too much cake and it makes you feel sick? It was sort of like that. I thought it'd be fun, but it just made me feel . . . lonely.'

'Oh.' I didn't want to pry, so I just remained silent.

Rooney drank the rest of her tea in a few big gulps.

'D'you wanna watch some YouTube?' she asked.

This threw me. 'Er . . . sure.'

She put down her mug, stood up, threw open the duvet and slipped inside. She shuffled over to one side and patted the space next to her, indicating for me to get in.

'I mean . . . you don't have to,' Rooney said, sensing my hesitation. 'D'you have a lecture in the morning, or something?'

I didn't. I had a fully free day of no contact time tomorrow.

'Nah. I have to eat my fish and chips anyway.' I retrieved my dinner, then lay down next to her. It felt right and wrong at the same time – a mirror world. The same as my own bed but everything was opposite.

She smiled and pulled her floral duvet over us and huddled towards me to get comfy, then grabbed her laptop from her bedside table.

She opened up YouTube. I didn't really watch any YouTubers – I only used YouTube for trailers, fan videos, and TikTok compilations. But Rooney seemed to be subscribed to dozens upon dozens of channels. It surprised me. She hadn't seemed like the sort of person to be into YouTube.

'There's this really funny YouTuber I watch a lot,' she said.

'Sure,' I said. 'D'you want some chips?'

'God, yes.'

She found the channel and searched through the videos until she found one she wanted. And then we lay together in her bed and watched it, Rooney sharing my chips.

It was a pretty funny video, to be fair. It was just this YouTuber and his friends playing a weird singing game. I kept giggling aloud, which made Rooney laugh, and before I knew it, we'd been watching for twenty whole minutes. She immediately found another video she wanted to show me, and I was happy to let her. Halfway through, she rested her head on my shoulder, and . . . I don't know. That was probably the calmest I'd ever seen her.

We watched silly videos for another hour or so until Rooney shut her laptop and put it aside, then snuggled back down into the bed. I wondered whether she'd fallen asleep, and if so, should

I just go back to my own bed, because I definitely wasn't going to be able to sleep here in such close proximity to another person, but then Rooney spoke.

'I used to have a boyfriend,' she said. 'A long-term boyfriend. From when I was fourteen until I was seventeen.'

'Wow. Really?'

'Yeah. We broke up when I was in Year Twelve.'

I'd assumed that Rooney had always been like Rooney. That she'd always been this carefree, fun-loving, passionate person who wasn't bothered about commitment.

A *three-year-long* relationship?

That wasn't what I'd expected.

'Things with him . . . were very bad,' she said. 'I . . . it was a very bad relationship in . . . a lot of ways, and . . . it really . . . put me off wanting them.'

I didn't ask her to elaborate. I could imagine what she meant.

'I haven't liked anyone since then,' she mumbled again. 'I've been scared to. But I might . . . be starting to like someone new.'

'Yeah?'

'I really . . . don't want to be doing that.'

'Why?'

'It just won't end well.' She shook her head. 'And she hates me, anyway.'

I knew instantly that she meant Pip.

'I don't think she hates you,' I said gently.

Rooney said nothing.

'Anyway, you're only eighteen, you've got so much time –' I started to say, but didn't know how to continue. What did I mean when I said that? That she'd *definitely* find the perfect relationship someday? Because I knew that wasn't true. Not for me. Not for *anyone*.

It was something adults said all the time. *You'll change your mind when you're older. You never know what might happen. You'll feel differently one day.* As if we teenagers knew so little about ourselves that we could wake up one day a completely different person. As if the person we are *right now* doesn't matter at all.

The whole idea that people always grew up, fell in love and got married was a complete lie. How long would it take me to accept that?

'I'm nineteen,' she said.

I frowned. 'Wait, are you? Did you have a gap year?'

'No. It was my birthday last week.'

This confused me more. 'What? When?'

'Last Thursday.'

Last Thursday. I could barely remember anything about it – uni days were all blurring into one endless stream of lectures and meals and sleep.

'You . . . didn't say anything,' I said.

'No.' She laughed, partly muffled by her pillow. 'I started thinking what would happen if people knew it was my birthday. I'd just end up going on another night out with a bunch of people I really don't know that well, and they'd all pretend to be my friend and sing happy birthday and take fake-happy selfies for Instagram before we'd all separate and hook up with different people, and I'd just end up in some stranger's bed after having below-average sex, hating myself again.'

'If you'd told me, we could have done . . . none of that.'

She smiled. 'What would we have done?'

'I dunno. Sat in here and eaten pizza. I could have forced you to watch *Bridesmaids*.'

She snorted. 'That's a shit movie.'

'It's not the best, but the romance is literal perfection. They sit on a car and eat *carrot sticks* together.'

'The dream.'

We lay there in silence for a little while.

'You . . . don't like having casual sex any more,' I said, realising what she'd been trying to say earlier. It wasn't that casual sex had hurt her, or that it made her a bad person – it didn't. 'You want . . .' It wasn't even that she wanted a relationship. Not really. She wanted what a relationship would *give* her.

'You want someone to know you,' I said.

She stayed silent for a moment. I waited for her to tell me how wrong I was.

Instead, she said, 'I'm just lonely. I'm just so lonely all the time.'

I didn't know what to say to that, but I didn't need to, because she fell asleep a few minutes later. I looked over her head and saw that Roderick had significantly wilted – Rooney was definitely forgetting to water him. I stared up at the ceiling and listened to her breathing next to me, but I didn't want to leave the bed, because even though I couldn't sleep, and I was paranoid about drooling on her or rolling on top of her by accident, Rooney needed me for some reason. Maybe because, despite all of her friends and acquaintances, nobody really knew her like I did.

BUT IF SHE CANNOT LOVE YOU

Jason still showed up to our next Shakespeare Soc rehearsal the following week.

I didn't think he would. I had messaged him to apologise again, to try and explain, even though I was shit at articulating any of my thoughts and feelings.

He'd read it but didn't reply.

I spent most of my lectures that week zoned out, not taking enough notes, wondering how I was going to salvage our friendship out of the chaos I'd created. Jason liked me romantically. I'd taken advantage of that to figure out my sexual identity, despite knowing I didn't like him like that in return. Selfish. I was so selfish.

He looked exhausted when he rolled up to our rehearsal in full rowing club kit, a heavy rucksack hanging off his shoulder. His teddy jacket was absent. I was so used to him wearing it that he seemed sort of vulnerable without it.

He walked straight past me, without looking at me, mouth clamped shut, and sat down next to Pip, who was going over today's scene.

Sunil arrived moments later. He was wearing checked trousers with a black shearling jacket and a beanie.

He took one look at Jason and said, 'You look exhausted.'

Jason grunted. 'Rowing.'

'Oh, yes. How are the six a.m. practices?'

'Freezing and wet.'

'You could quit,' said Pip. She seemed a little hopeful at the prospect.

Jason shook his head. 'Nah, I do enjoy it. I've made a lot of friends there.' He shot a quick glance at me. 'It's just been a lot.'

I turned away. There was no way to make this better.

In true Jason tradition, he was assigned the role of a stern older man. This time it was Duke Orsino from *Twelfth Night*, another of Shakespeare's romcoms.

The premise of *Twelfth Night* is a big, messy love triangle. Viola is shipwrecked in the land of Illyria and, since she has no money, disguises herself as a boy called Cesario so that she can get a job as a servant to Duke Orsino. The duke is in love with a noble lady of Illyria, Olivia, so he sends Viola to express his love for her. Unfortunately, instead of accepting the duke's feelings, Olivia falls in love with Viola, who is disguised as Cesario, a guy. And, doubly unfortunate, Viola falls in love with the duke. It's not *technically* gay, but let's be real: this play is very, very gay.

Sunil had already volunteered to be Viola, saying, 'Just give me all of the roles that mess around with gender, please.'

Pip and I huddled next to each other against the wall with my coat over our legs. It was freezing cold in our giant rehearsal room today.

'You two run through the scene,' said Rooney. 'I need to go and get some tea or I will actually die.'

She'd had another of her nights out last night.

'Get me a coffee!' shouted Pip as Rooney went to leave.

'I would literally rather stomp on a nail!' Rooney shouted back, and I was interested to see that this made Pip *laugh* instead of her usual gritted-teeth annoyance.

Jason and Sunil were amazing. Jason was well-practised, having done a lot of Shakespeare before, and Sunil was equally good, despite the fact that the only acting he'd done was a minor role in a school production of *Wicked*. Jason was all, '*Once more, Cesario,*' and Sunil was all, '*But if she cannot love you, sir,*' and, overall, it was a very successful run-through.

I sat and watched, and it almost took me out of my head, making me forget about everything that had happened in the past couple of months. I could just live in the world of Viola and Orsino for a while.

'*I am all the daughters of my father's house,*' said Sunil. One of the final lines of the scene. '*And all the brothers too.*' He glanced up at me and Pip with a smile, momentarily breaking character. 'That's such a good line. New Twitter bio.'

Sunil really seemed to be enjoying being in the production. Maybe more than any of us, to be honest. He and Jason went off to work on the scene on their own, and with nothing to do, I stayed sitting against the wall, knees tucked up to my chin waiting for Rooney to come back from her tea run.

'Georgia?'

I looked up at the voice to find Pip scooting over to me, her open copy of *Twelfth Night* in one hand.

'I had an idea,' she said. 'About what you could do in the play.'

I was really, really not in the mood to actually do any acting today. I wasn't sure I could act as well as I'd thought, anyway.

'OK,' I said.

'There's another character in *Twelfth Night* who has quite a big thematic role — the clown.'

I snorted. 'You want me to be the clown?'

'Well, that's just what he's called in the text. He's more of a court jester.' Pip pointed at the scene in question. The clown had some lines leading up to the scene that Jason and Sunil were currently working on. 'I thought it might be really cool to have you do some of these bits before this Viola–Orsino scene.'

I read the lines, sceptical. 'I don't know.' I glanced at her. 'I . . . my acting's been pretty shit lately.'

Pip frowned. 'Dude. That's not true. Those roles just . . . weren't *right* for you. You're not *shit* at anything.'

I didn't reply.

'How about you just give it a go? I promise I will be nothing but supportive. And I'll throw something at Rooney if she says anything negative about you.' As if to demonstrate, Pip pulled her boot off and held it aloft.

This made me laugh. 'OK. Fine. I'll try.'

'I'm back!' Rooney galloped into the room, somehow not spilling hot drinks everywhere. She slumped down next to me and Pip, putting her tea on the floor, and handing a coffee to Pip.

Pip stared at it. 'Wait, you actually got me one?'

Rooney shrugged. 'Yeah?'

Pip looked up at Rooney, genuine surprise, and something almost akin to fondness on her face. 'Thanks.'

Rooney stared back, then seemed to have to wrench her head away. 'So how's the scene going? It's only two weeks until the Bailey Ball, we need to get this one locked down before then.'

'I had an idea,' said Pip. 'We could add in the clown.'

I half-expected Rooney to immediately protest this, but instead, she sat down next to Pip and leant towards her so she could read her copy of *Twelfth Night*. Pip made a face of moderate alarm, before relaxing, though not without very quickly adjusting her hair.

'I think that's a good idea,' said Rooney.

'Yeah?' asked Pip.

'Yeah. You do sometimes have good ideas.'

Pip grinned. 'Sometimes?'

'Sometimes.'

'That means a lot.' Pip nudged her. 'Coming from you.'

And I swear to God Rooney went redder than I had ever seen her.

It'd been a long time since I'd stood on a stage alone. Well, it wasn't *technically* a stage, but the way the other four were sitting in front of me, watching, while I was standing in front of them, had the same effect.

In *Twelfth Night*, the clown, whose name is actually Feste, shows up periodically to either provide some light comic relief, or to sing a song relevant to the themes of the story. Right before Jason and Sunil's scene, Feste sings a song, 'Come away, death', about a man who dies, possibly of heartbreak because a woman doesn't love him back, and he wants to be buried alone because he's so sad. It's basically just a fancy way of saying that unrequited love is pretty rough.

We all decided that I should recite it as a monologue rather than sing, which I was grateful about. But I was still nervous.

I could do this. I wanted to *prove* that I could do this.

'*Come away, come away, death*,' I began, and I felt my breath catch in my throat.

I can do this.

'*And in sad cypress let me be laid.*' I kept my voice soft. '*Fly away, fly away, breath; I am slain by a fair cruel maid.'* And I read the rest of the song. And I felt all of it. I just felt . . . all of it. The mourning. The wistfulness. The fantasy of something that could never happen.

I'd never experienced unrequited love. I never would. And Feste, the clown, wasn't even talking about himself – he was telling someone else's story. But I felt it anyway.

'Lay me, O, where sad true lover never find my grave, to weep there.'

There was a pause before I closed my book and looked up at my friends.

They were all staring at me, transfixed.

And then Pip just started clapping. 'Fucking YES. Absolutely fucking yes. I'm a genius. You're a genius. This play is going to be *genius.'*

Rooney joined in with the applause. So did Sunil. And I saw Jason very subtly wipe his eye.

'That was OK?' I asked, although that's not really what I wanted to ask. *Was I good? Will I be OK?*

Everything in my life was upside down, but did I still have this? Did I still have one thing that brought me happiness?

'More than OK,' said Pip, smiling wide, and I thought, *Yeah, OK.* I hated myself right now for a lot of reasons, but at least I had this.

TWO ROOMMATES

In the two weeks between that rehearsal and the Bailey Ball, we had three more rehearsals, during which we completely surpassed Rooney's aim of getting one scene done. We got all three done – *Much Ado About Nothing* with Pip and Rooney, *Twelfth Night* with Jason, Sunil and me, and *Romeo and Juliet* with Jason and Rooney, having decided that I wasn't the best choice for Juliet. We even had time for the pizza night we'd promised Sunil. He and Jason seemed to be fast friends, getting immersed in a discussion about musicals they'd seen, and Rooney and Pip managed to make it through a whole movie without making a single snide comment to each other. At one point, they were even sitting with their shoulders pressed together, amiably sharing a packet of tortilla chips.

Despite everything that was happening behind the scenes, it was coming together. We were actually making a production.

Thank God I had that to hang on to. Without it, I would have probably just stayed in bed for two weeks, because figuring out my sexuality had unearthed a new kind of self-hatred I hadn't been ready for. I'd thought figuring that out was supposed to make you feel proud, or something. Clearly not.

Something was up with Rooney too. Something had changed in her after that night we'd walked in to find her crying. She'd stopped going out in the evenings, instead spending them watching YouTube videos or TV shows, or just sleeping. I'd got used to the clacking of her frantic typing next to me in our English lectures, but it had stopped, and I often caught her just sitting very still, staring into the distance, not listening to the lecturers at all.

Sometimes she seemed fine. Sometimes she was 'normal' Rooney, directing the play with an iron fist, being the shiniest person in the room, chatting to twelve different people at dinnertime in the college cafeteria. She was at her best when Pip was around – exchanging banter and jokes with her, lighting up in a way she didn't with anyone else – but even with her, I sometimes noticed Rooney turn away, put physical distance between them, like she didn't want Pip to even see her. Like she was scared what would happen if they got too close.

I could have checked if she was OK, but I was too wrapped up in my own feelings, and she didn't check if I was OK either, because she was too wrapped up in hers. I didn't blame her, and I hoped she didn't blame me.

We were just two roommates dealing with things that were difficult to talk about.

THE BAILEY BALL

'If you send me the photos of you in your dress,' said Mum on Skype the afternoon of the Bailey Ball, 'I'll get them printed out and sent to all the grandparents!'

I sighed. 'It's not the same as prom. I don't think there will be official photography.'

'Well, just make sure you get at least *one* full-length pic of you in your dress. I bought it so I need to see it in action.'

Mum had bought me my Bailey Ball dress, though it had been my choice. I hadn't actually planned on getting it because it was too expensive, but when I was sending links of potential dresses to her while we chatted on Messenger, she offered to pay for it. It was really nice of her, and honestly, it made me feel a pang of homesickness more intense than I'd experienced so far at uni.

'Did any boys ask you to be their date to the ball?'

'Mum. British universities don't do that. That's American schools who do that.'

'Well, it would have been nice, wouldn't it?'

'Everyone just goes with their friends, Mum.'

Mum sighed. 'You're going to look *so beautiful*,' she cooed. 'Make sure you do your hair nicely.'

'I will,' I said. Rooney had already offered to do it for me.

'You never know – you might meet your future husband tonight!'

I laughed before I could stop myself. Two months ago, I *would* have been dreaming of a perfect, magical meet-cute at my first university ball.

But now? Now I dressed for myself.

'Yeah,' I said, clearing my throat. 'You never know.'

Rooney was silent while she did my hair with some thick curling tongs, her eyebrows furrowed in concentration. She knew how to do those big loose waves that you always see on American TV shows, but I found absolutely impossible to replicate by myself.

Rooney had already done her own hair. It was swept back from her forehead and perfectly straightened. Her dress was blood red and tight with a long slit up one leg. She looked like a Bond girl who later turned out to be the villain.

She insisted on doing my make-up too – she had always been a fan of makeovers, she explained – and I let her, seeing as she was way better at make-up than me. She blended golds and browns on my eyes, chose a muted pink lipstick, filled my eyebrows with a tiny brush, and drew neater winged eyeliner than I had ever been able to achieve alone.

'There,' she said, after what felt like hours but was probably more like twenty minutes. 'All done.'

I checked myself out in Rooney's pedestal mirror. I actually looked excellent. 'Wow. That's – wow.'

'Go look in the big mirror! You need to see the full effect with your dress. You look like a princess.'

I did as she said. The dress was straight out of a fairy tale – floor-length, rose-coloured chiffon with a sequinned bodice. It wasn't super comfortable – I was wearing a *lot* of tit tape – but with my wavy hair and shimmery make-up, I did look and feel like a princess.

Maybe I could even enjoy tonight. Wilder things had happened.

Rooney stood next to me in the mirror. 'Hm. We kind of clash, though. Red and pink.'

'I think it's a good clash. I look like an angel and you look like a devil.'

'Yes. I'm the anti-you.'

'Or maybe *I'm* the anti-*you*.'

'Is this a summary of our whole friendship?'

We looked at each other and laughed.

The theme of the Bailey Ball had been a huge topic of speculation at St John's College for weeks, and somehow I was one of the only people who hadn't found out what it was before the night of the ball itself. This was probably because the only friend I had in college was Rooney, and she'd refused to tell me when I asked, and I wasn't bothered enough to force it out of her.

Apparently, there'd already been a 'Circus' year, 'Alice in Wonderland', 'Fairy tale', 'Roaring '20s', 'Hollywood', 'Vegas', 'Masquerade', and 'Under the Stars'. I did wonder whether they were starting to run out of ideas.

It wasn't immediately clear what the theme was when we walked through the college corridors and out towards reception. The foyer had been adorned with flowers and the stairway had been turned into what looked like a castle wall, complete with turrets and balcony. Inside the dining hall, circular tables featured centrepieces of more flowers, but also crafted bottles of poison and wooden knives.

I only got it when I heard 'I'm Kissing You' by Des'ree playing overhead – a song I knew featured prominently in a certain 1996 Baz Luhrmann movie.

The theme was *Romeo and Juliet*.

We met Pip and Jason outside the doors to St John's. Jason gave me an awkward nod, but otherwise said nothing to me.

They both looked incredible. Jason was wearing a classic tuxedo, and it hugged his broad shoulders so perfectly that it was like it'd been custom-tailored. Pip had styled her hair extra curly and was wearing black cigarette trousers, but with a velvet tuxedo jacket in a forest green colour. She'd paired that with a pair of chunky faux-snakeskin Chelsea boots, which somehow exactly matched the colour of her tortoiseshell glasses.

Rooney's eyes flickered up and down Pip's body.

'You look nice,' she said.

Pip struggled not to do the same to Rooney in her Bond girl dress, instead keeping her eyes firmly up at Rooney's face. 'So do you.'

Dinner felt like it went on for a year, even though it was only the beginning of what was to be the longest night of my whole life.

Rooney, Jason, Pip and I had to share a table with four other people, but thankfully they were all Rooney's friends and acquaintances. While everyone else all got to know each other, I did what I always did and stayed silent but attentive, smiling and nodding when people spoke but not really knowing how to get involved in any of the conversations.

I felt lower than I had ever felt.

I wanted to snap out of it, but I couldn't.

I didn't want to be at a party where Jason hated me and Rooney and Pip were living what I would never have.

Sunil, dressed in a baby-blue tux, and Jess, who was wearing a dress covered in mint-green sequins, stopped by to say hello to us, though they mainly spoke to Rooney because she was three glasses of wine down and very talkative. When they went to leave, Sunil winked at me, which made me feel better for about two minutes, but then the brain goblins returned.

This was who I was. I was never going to experience romantic love, all because of my sexuality – a fundamental part of my being that I couldn't change.

I drank wine. A *lot* of wine. It was free.

'Only *eight hours to go!*' Pip cried as we filed out of the dining hall after dessert. I was absolutely stuffed with food and, to be honest, drunk already.

I shook my head. 'I'm not gonna make it till six a.m.'

'Oh, you *will*. You will. I'm going to make sure you will.'

'That sounds incredibly menacing.'

'I'll be here to flick you on the forehead if you start falling asleep.'

'Please don't flick me on the forehead.'

'I can and I will.'

She attempted to demonstrate, but I ducked out of the way, laughing. Pip always knew how to cheer me up, even if she didn't know I was feeling down in the first place.

The Bailey Ball wasn't confined to one hall – it spread throughout the ground floor of the main college building and into a marquee on the green outside. The dining hall was quickly transformed into the main dance hall, of course, with a live band and a bar area. There were several themed rooms serving food and drink, from toasties to ice cream to tea and coffee, and a cinema room that was playing all the different movie adaptations of *Romeo and Juliet* in chronological order. The corridors that we hadn't seen yet were decorated so intensively that you couldn't see the walls any more – they were covered in flowers, ivy, fabrics, fairy lights, and giant crests for 'Capulet' and 'Montague'. For one night only, we were in another world, outside the rules of space and time.

'Where shall we go first?' said Pip. 'Cinema room? Marquee?' She turned round, then frowned, confused. 'Rooney?'

I turned too and found Rooney a few paces away from us, leaning against the wall. She was drunk for sure, but she was also looking at Pip almost like she was *scared*, or at the very least nervous. Then she covered it with a wide grin.

'I'm gonna go and see my other friends for a bit!' she shouted over the crowd and the music.

And then she was gone.

'Other friends?' said Jason, confused.

'She knows everyone,' I said, but I wasn't sure how true that rang any more. She knew a lot of other people, but I was starting to realise that we were her only real *friends*.

'Well, she can fuck off, then, if she's gonna be like that,' said Pip, but her heart wasn't in it.

Jason rolled his eyes at her. 'Pip.'

'What?'

'Just . . . you don't have to keep doing that. We both know you like her.'

'What?' Pip's head snapped up. 'What – *no*, no I don't, like – I mean *yes* I like her as a *person* – I mean, I admire her as a *director* and a creative person but her personality is *very* intense so I wouldn't say I *liked* her, I just *appreciate* who she is and what she *does* . . .'

'But you fancy her,' I stated. 'It's not a crime.'

'*No.*' Pip folded her arms over her jacket. '*No*, absolutely not, Georgia, she's – she's objectively *extremely* hot and *yes* in any ordinary situation she would be exactly my type and I *know* you know that but – I mean, she's *straight* and she literally *hates* me, so even if I did, what would be the point –'

'Pip!' I said, exasperated.

She shut her mouth. She knew there was nothing she could say to hide it any more.

'I think I should go find her,' I continued.

'Why?'

'Just to check she's OK.'

Pip and Jason didn't protest, so I left to go and find Rooney.

I had a feeling that, if she continued to get even drunker, she was going to do something she regretted.

CAPULET VS MONTAGUE

Rooney was nowhere to be found. There were hundreds of students swarming the college, and it was difficult to even get through the corridors, let alone spot anyone in the crowds standing around chatting, laughing, singing, dancing. She was in there somewhere, no doubt. Rooney seemed to operate like she was a video-game protagonist in a world of non-player characters.

I hung around the marquee for a while, hoping she might show up, but even if she was here, I probably wouldn't have found her. It was packed because this was where all the fun activities were – a photo booth, popcorn and candyfloss stalls, a rodeo bull, and the main attraction: 'Capulet vs Montague', which looked like a bouncy castle with two raised platforms inside, upon which two students would battle it out with inflatable swords until one person fell down. I watched a few people play, and I really did want to have a go, but I didn't know where Rooney was and I'd have felt kind of embarrassed to ask her. I guess I had this feeling that she'd just say no.

I got another drink from the bar, which I didn't need because

I was already drunk, and stumbled aimlessly around the ball and all its various rooms. The more I drank, the more I could space out and not care about being alone, in every sense of the word.

It was hard to forget, though, when every single song that was playing overhead was about romantic love. Obviously this was deliberate – the theme was *Romeo and Juliet*, for God's sake – but it still pissed me off.

Everything started to remind me of the prom afterparty. The flashing lights on the dance floor, the love songs, the laughter, the suits and dresses.

When I had been at that party, I had felt that this was my world, and one day, I would be one of these people.

I didn't feel like that any more.

I would never be one of these people. Flirting. Falling in love. Happily ever after.

I went to curl up in the tea room, only to find myself stuck opposite a couple who were making out in the corner. I hated them. I tried to ignore them and drank my wine while scrolling through Instagram.

'*Georgia.*'

An incredibly loud voice shattered the relaxing atmosphere of the room, startling everyone in the room. I turned towards the door and found Pip there in her green jacket, one hand on her hip and a plastic cup undoubtedly full of alcohol in the other.

She grinned sheepishly at the sudden attention. 'Er, sorry. Didn't know this was the quiet room.'

She tiptoed over and crouched down next to me, spilling a drop of her drink on the floor.

'Where's Rooney?' she asked.

I just shrugged.

'Oh. Well, I have come to challenge you to a Capulet vs Montague duel.'

'The bouncy castle thing?'

'This is so much more than a bouncy castle, my dude. This is an ultimate test of endurance, agility and mental fortitude.'

'It looks exactly like a bouncy castle to me.'

She grabbed my wrist and hoisted me up. 'Just come and try it! Jason said he needed a nap already so he's gone back to Castle.'

'Wait . . . He's gone?'

'Yeah. He'll be fine, you know he's terrible at staying up late.'

I immediately felt guilty – it was my fault Jason was in a mood – and I clambered to my feet, only for the world to move around me, nearly sending me crashing back down.

Pip frowned. 'Jesus. How much have you drunk?'

'Oh,' said Pip as we entered the marquee.

At first, I assumed she was referring to the state of the marquee. When I had come in here at the start of the night, it had been shiny and exciting, colourful and new. Now it looked like a run-down fairground. The floor was sticky and scattered with trampled popcorn. The stalls were less busy and the staff operating them looked tired.

But Pip wasn't referring to any of that, which I realised when we were approached by Rooney in her Bond villain dress.

She was still, impossibly, wearing her heels, and she must have just touched up her make-up, because she looked radiant. Highlighter shimmering, contour as sharp as a knife, she smiled down at Pip with wide, dark eyes.

She was also obviously quite drunk.

'Excuse me,' she said, smirking. 'Who invited you? You're not a John's student.'

Pip smirked right back, immediately going along with the joke. 'I snuck in. I'm a master of stealth.'

'Where did you go?' I asked Rooney.

'Oh, you know,' she said. She put on a voice that made her sound like a rich heiress. 'I've just been *around,* darling.'

'We were just about to have a bouncy castle battle,' said Pip. 'You can join us. Someone's about to get absolutely wrecked.'

Rooney smiled at her with a hint of menace. 'Well, I do love wrecking people.'

'*OK,*' I found myself saying. If I had been sober, I probably would have just let this play out, but I was drunk and tired and fed up with both of them, and every time they gazed at each other with that fiery passion that bordered love and irritation, I wanted to die because that would never happen to me. I looked at Pip, whose bow tie was askew and her glasses too far down her nose, and at Rooney, whose foundation was not hiding the flustered blush on her skin.

And then I looked between them at the 'Capulet vs Montague' challenge.

'I think you two should go first,' I said, pointing at it. 'Against each other. Just to get it out of your system. Please.'

'I'm in,' said Rooney, meeting Pip's glare with knife eyes.

'I . . . OK,' Pip spluttered. 'Fine. But I'm not gonna go easy on you.'

'Do I look like the sort of person who likes it when people *go easy* on me?'

Pip's eyes drifted down Rooney's dress, then quickly back up. 'No.'

'Well then.'

This was becoming absolutely unbearable, so I walked up to the guy operating the contraption and said, 'These two want a go.'

He nodded wearily, then gestured at the two raised platforms. 'Climb on.'

The two girls didn't speak as they clambered on to the bouncy castle, Rooney kicking her heels off as she went, and then on to the two raised platforms. This was clearly more difficult than either of them had anticipated – Pip's skinny trousers were only slightly more practical than Rooney's tight dress – but they made it, and the guy handed them each what looked like a swimming pool noodle.

'You have three minutes,' he droned, gesturing to the countdown timer on display at the back of the bouncy castle. 'The aim is to knock the other person off their platform before the time runs out. Are you ready?'

Rooney nodded with the intense focus of a tennis player at Wimbledon.

'Fuck yeah,' said Pip, gripping her noodle.

The guy sighed. Then he pressed a button on the floor, and a beep sounded three times. A countdown.

Three. Two. One.

Start.

Rooney went straight for the jugular immediately. She swung the noodle wildly towards Pip, but Pip saw it coming and blocked it with her own noodle, though not without wobbling on her platform. The platforms were circular and could only have been half a metre in diameter. This probably wasn't going to last very long.

Pip laughed. 'Not fucking around, then?'

Rooney grinned. 'No, I'm trying to *win*.'

Pip thrust her noodle forward in an attempt to push Rooney backwards, but Rooney swerved her torso, doing an almost ninety-degree bend to one side.

'All right, *gymnast*,' said Pip.

'Dance, actually,' Rooney shot back. 'Until I was fourteen.'

She swung the noodle at Pip once again, but Pip blocked it. And the fight began.

Rooney swung this way and that, but Pip's reflexes only seemed to have been sharpened by the alcohol she'd drunk, which made no sense whatsoever. Rooney swiped left, Pip parried, Rooney swiped right, Pip dodged. Pip jabbed forward, trying to push Rooney back by the shoulder, and for a moment, I thought it was all over, but Rooney regained her balance with a sly grin, and the battle continued.

'Your concentration face is *so funny*,' said Rooney, laughing. She did an impression of Pip's scrunched-up expression.

'*Er*, not as funny as your face is gonna be when I win,' Pip shot back. But there was a hint of a smile on her face too.

There were more swings and jabs and at one point they were having a full-on lightsaber battle. Pip prodded Rooney in the side and she nearly went down, saving herself at the last second by using her noodle as a crutch, which made Pip laugh so hard she nearly fell off on her own.

That was when I realised that they were *enjoying themselves*.

That was also when all the alcohol rushed to the top of my head and I felt like I was going to fall over.

I stumbled as carefully as I could over to the side of the marquee and sat down against the fabric to watch the finale.

I couldn't help but notice that Rooney, as ruthless as she appeared from her wild, large swings, was strategically avoiding Pip's face so as not to hit her glasses. Pip, however, was out for blood.

'Why are you so *bendy*?' Pip cried as Rooney dodged another jab.

'Just one of my many charms!'

'*Many* charms? Plural?'

'I think you know all about them, pipsqueak.'

Pip swung her noodle at Rooney, but Rooney blocked it. 'You are a fucking *nightmare*.'

Rooney smirked back. 'I am and you *love it*.'

Pip released what could only be described as a war cry. She jabbed the noodle at Rooney, then again, and then a third time, knocking the girl back slightly each time, and on the fourth, Rooney went down, falling perfectly backwards from the podium and down on to the bouncy castle, letting out a short scream as she went.

'YES!' Pip cried, holding her noodle aloft in victory.

The guy operating the bouncy castle stopped the timer and gestured vaguely at Pip. 'Glasses wins.'

Pip leapt off the podium and started bouncing next to Rooney, making it hard for her to get up. 'Having some trouble down there, mate?'

Rooney tried to get to her feet but just ended up tumbling back down again as Pip bounced next to her. 'Oh my *God*, stop –'

'I thought you were a dancer! Where's your coordination?'

'We didn't dance on *bouncy castles*!'

Pip finally slowed down her bouncing, coming to a halt and holding out a hand to help Rooney up. Rooney looked at it, and I could see her considering, but she didn't take it, instead standing up on her own.

'Good game,' she said, one eyebrow raised. Then she walked away – or, rather, clambered away across the bouncy castle and rolled over the edge on to solid ground.

'You're not gonna be a sore loser, are you?' Pip called after her, also dropping down and rolling off the contraption.

Rooney tutted so loud even I heard her from across the marquee.

'Oh.' Pip grinned. 'You are. I should have guessed.'

Rooney started cramming her feet back into her heels. She probably wanted to regain her significant height advantage against Pip.

'Hey!' Pip raised her voice, calling after her. 'Why d'you hate me so much?'

Rooney stopped.

'Yeah, that's right!' Pip continued, raising her arms. 'I said it! Why d'you hate me? We're both drunk so we might as well just get it out there! Is it because I was Georgia's best friend first so I'm in the way?'

Rooney said nothing, but she finished putting on her heels and stood up to her full height.

'Or do you just hate who I am as a person?'

Rooney swung round and said, 'You are very stupid. And you should have let me win.'

There was a pause.

'Sometimes I get to have what *I* want,' said Pip with unnerving calmness. 'Sometimes, I get to be the person who wins.'

I barely had time to think about the statement, because Rooney was about to erupt. She scrunched her hands into fists, and I could sense a real argument was coming, drink-fuelled and embarrassing to look back on. I needed to stop it. I needed to end this before it got any worse. These were the only two friends I had left.

So I hauled myself to my feet, which was a task in my dress.

I opened my mouth to speak. To try and bring this to a halt. Maybe even to try and help.

But what actually happened was all the blood rushed to my head. Stars tingled at the corner of my vision and my hearing went fuzzy.

And then I passed out.

DEFEATED

I regained consciousness to find Pip patting my face slightly too hard.

'Oh my God oh my God oh my God,' she was stammering.

'Please stop slapping me,' I mumbled.

Rooney was there too, the annoyance completely gone from her expression and replaced by serious concern. 'Holy shit, Georgia. How much did you drink?'

'I . . . fourteen.'

'Fourteen what?'

'Fourteen drinks.'

'No, you *didn't*.'

'OK, I can't remember how much I drank.'

'So why did you say fourteen?'

'Sounded like a good number.'

We were interrupted by a few other students peering over Pip and Rooney's shoulders, asking politely if I was OK. I realised I was still lying on the floor, which was awkward, so I sat up and reassured everyone that I was fine and had just had a bit too much to drink, which they chuckled at and went on with their evening. If I hadn't been absolutely pissed out of my head, I would have been deeply embarrassed, but thankfully I was, and the only thing going through my mind was how much I wanted to throw up.

Rooney pulled me to my feet, one arm round my waist, which seemed to annoy Pip for some reason.

'We should go chill in the cinema room for a bit,' said Rooney. 'We've still got six hours to kill. We can get you sobered up.'

Six hours? Sober was the last thing I wanted to be right now.

'*Noooo*,' I mumbled, but Rooney either ignored me or didn't hear me. 'Let me go. I'm fine.'

'Clearly you are not, and we're going to sit on a beanbag with some water for the next half an hour whether you like it or not.'

'You're not my mum.'

'Well, your real mum would thank me.'

Rooney supported most of my weight as we walked through the floral, twinkling corridors of college, Pip trailing behind us. Nobody spoke until we reached the door of the cinema room and a loud voice behind us cried, '*PIP!* Oh my God, hi!'

In my hazy state I peered behind me at the voice. It belonged to a guy leading a large group of people who I didn't recognise, most likely because they were from Pip's college.

'Come hang with us,' the guy continued. 'We're all going to dance for a bit.'

Pip shuffled awkwardly. 'Oh – er . . .' She turned back to look at me.

I didn't really know what to say, but thankfully Rooney spoke for me. 'Just go. She'll be fine with me.'

I nodded in agreement, giving her a wobbly thumbs-up.

'OK, well . . . erm . . . I'll meet you back here in, like, an hour?' said Pip.

'Yeah,' said Rooney, and then we turned away, and Pip was gone.

'Here,' said Rooney, handing me a large glass of water and a toastie in a folded-up napkin as she slumped down next to me on a beanbag.

I took them obediently.

'What's in this?' I said, waving the toastie.

'Cheese and Marmite.'

'Risky choice,' I said, biting down into it. 'What if I hated Marmite?'

'It was the only filling they had left so you're gonna eat it and make do.'

Thankfully, I love Marmite, and even if I didn't, I probably would have eaten it anyway because I was suddenly *ravenous*. The nausea had passed, and my stomach felt painfully empty, so I munched on the toastie while we watched the movie that was currently playing on the screen.

We were the only people in the room. Distantly we could hear the thumping of the DJ's music in the dance hall, which was no doubt where most people were. There was also some chattering coming from the room opposite, which was serving free tea and toasties, and occasionally loud laughter and voices would drift past the door as students went about their night together, doing whatever to pass the time until the end of the ball at dawn. It didn't feel like a ball any more – it felt like a giant sleepover where nobody wanted to be the first to go to sleep.

The movie was the best adaptation of *Romeo and Juliet* – Baz Luhrmann's nineties one with Leonardo DiCaprio. We hadn't missed much – Romeo was walking moodily along the beach – so we settled down into the beanbag to watch, not speaking.

We stayed that way, engrossed, for the next forty-five minutes.

That was roughly how long it took me to sober up a little and for my brain to start working again.

'Where'd you go?' was the first thing I said.

Rooney didn't look away from the screen. 'I'm right here?'

'No . . . earlier. You left and then you were gone.'

There was a pause.

'Just hanging out with some people. Sorry. I . . . yeah. Sorry about that.' She glanced at me. 'You were OK, though, right?'

I could barely remember how I'd spent the time between dinner and the bouncy castle battle. Wandering through the dance hall, sitting in the tea room, exploring the marquee but not having a go on any of the stalls.

'Yeah, I was fine,' I said.

'Good. Did you dance with Jason?'

Oh. And there was that.

'Nope,' I said.

'Oh. How come?'

I wanted to tell her everything.

I was going to tell her everything.

Was it the alcohol? The buzz of the ball? The fact that Rooney was starting to know me better than anyone, all because she slept two metres from me every night?

'Me and Jason isn't going to happen,' I said.

She nodded. 'Yeah, I . . . I guess I got that impression, but . . . I just assumed you were still dating.'

'No. I ended it.'

'Why?'

'Because . . .'

The words were on the tip of my tongue. *Because I am aromantic and asexual.* But it sounded clunky. They still felt like fake words in my brain, secret words, whispered words that didn't belong in the real world.

It wasn't that I thought Rooney would react badly – she wouldn't react with disgust or anger. She wasn't like that.

But I thought she would react with awkwardness. With confusion. An *er, OK, what the fuck is that?* She would nod politely once I explained it, but in her head she would be thinking *Oh my God, Georgia's really weird.*

Somehow, that felt almost as bad.

'Because I don't like guys,' I said.

As soon as I said it, I realised my mistake.

'*Oh,*' said Rooney. 'Oh my God.' She sat up, nodding, taking this information in. 'That's OK. Fuck. I mean, I'm glad you *realised.* Congrats, I guess?' She laughed. 'It seems *way* better to not be attracted to guys. Girls are much nicer all round.' Then she made a pained expression. 'Oh my *God.* I spent *so much time and energy* trying to set you up with Jason. Why didn't you *say* anything?'

Before I had time to respond, she interrupted herself.

'No, sorry, that's an idiotic thing to say. Obviously you were working shit out. That's fine. I mean, that's what university is *for,* isn't it? Experimenting and figuring out who you actually like.' She patted me firmly on the leg. 'And you know what this means? Now we can focus on finding you a nice *girl* to date! Oh my *God.* I know so many cute girls who would like you. You *have* to come with me on a night out next week. I can introduce you to *so* many girls.'

All the time she was monologuing, I felt myself getting hotter and hotter. If I didn't speak up, I was going to lose my nerve and start going along with this new lie and then I'd have to go through the whole trying-to-date thing again.

'I don't really want to do that,' I said, fiddling with the now-empty toastie napkin.

'Oh. OK, yeah. Sure. That's fine.'

Rooney sipped on her own glass of water and spent a few moments watching the screen.

Then she continued. 'You don't have to get into dating right now. You've got *so* much time.'

So much time. I wanted to laugh.

'I don't think I will,' I said.

'Will what?'

'Date. Ever. I don't like girls either. I don't like anyone.'

The words echoed around the room. There was a long pause. And then Rooney laughed.

'You are *drunk*,' she said.

I was, a little, but that wasn't the point.

And she'd laughed. That annoyed me.

That was how I'd expected her to react. That was how I expected everyone to react.

Pitying, awkward laughter.

'I don't like guys,' I said. 'And I don't like girls. I don't like anyone. So I'm never going to date anyone.'

Rooney said nothing for a few moments.

And then she said, 'Listen, Georgia. You might feel that way right now, but . . . don't give up *hope*. Maybe you're going through a rough patch at the moment, like, I don't know, the stress of starting uni or whatever, but . . . you *will* meet someone you like one day. Everyone does.'

No, they don't, was what I wanted to say.

Not everyone.

Not me.

'It's a real thing,' I said. 'It's a . . . it's a real sexuality. When you don't like anyone.'

I couldn't say the actual words, though.

It probably wouldn't have helped if I had.

'OK,' said Rooney. 'Well, how do you *know* that you are . . . that? How do you know that you won't meet someone one day who you really like?'

I stared at her.

Of *course* she didn't understand.

Rooney wasn't the romance expert I'd thought she was. I was pretty sure I knew more than her at this point.

'I've never had a crush on anyone in my life,' I said, but my voice was quiet and I didn't even *sound* confident, let alone feel confident about who I was. 'I . . . I like the idea of it, but . . . the reality . . .' I trailed off, feeling a lump in my throat. If I tried to explain it, I knew I would just start crying. It was still so new. I'd never tried to explain it to anyone before.

'Have you kissed a girl, then?'

I looked at her. She was looking at me level-headedly. Almost like a *challenge*.

'No,' I said.

'So how do you know you don't like that?'

Deep down, I knew this was an unfair question. You didn't *have* to try something to know for sure you don't like it. I knew I didn't like skydiving. I definitely didn't need to try that out to prove it.

But I was drunk. And so was she.

'I dunno,' I said.

'Maybe you should give it a go before you . . . you know. Completely reject the idea that you could possibly find someone.'

Rooney laughed again. She wasn't *trying* to do it in a mean way. But that was how it felt.

I knew she just wanted to help.

And that sort of made it worse.

She was trying to be a good friend, but she was saying all the wrong things because she didn't have the faintest idea what it was like to be me.

'Maybe,' I mumbled, leaning back into the beanbag.

'Why don't you try with me?'

Wait.

What?

'What?' I said, turning my head to face her.

She rolled to one side so her whole body was facing mine, then held up both hands in a gesture of surrender. 'I literally just want to help. I absolutely don't like you that way – *no offence* – but you might be able to get a sense of whether it's something you might like. I want to help.'

'But . . . I don't like you like that,' I said. 'Even if I *was* gay, I wouldn't necessarily feel something just because you're a girl.'

'OK, maybe not,' she said with a sigh. 'I just don't want to see you give up without *trying*.'

She was annoying me, and I realised that it was because what I was doing wasn't 'giving up'.

It was acceptance.

And maybe, just maybe, that could be a good thing.

'I don't want you to feel like you're going to be sad and lonely forever!' she said, and that was the moment I broke a little.

Was that all I would be? Sad and lonely? Forever?

Had I doomed myself by daring to think about this part of me?

Was I just accepting a life of solitude?

As soon as those questions hit me, they opened the floodgate to all the doubts I thought I'd been fighting off.

Maybe it was all just a phase.

Maybe this was giving up.

Maybe I should keep trying.

Maybe, maybe, maybe.

'Fine, then,' I said.

'You wanna try?'

I sighed, defeated, *tired*. I was so tired of all this. 'Yeah. Go on, then.'

It couldn't really be any worse than the one with Jason, could it?

And so she leant in.

It was different. Rooney was used to deeper, longer kisses of an entirely different type.

She led. I tried to imitate her.

I hated it.

I hated it just as I had hated the kiss with Jason. I hated how close her face was to me. I hated the feeling of her lips moving around against mine. I hated her breath on my skin. My eyes kept flickering open, trying to get a sense of when this was going to be over, while she put her hand on the back of my head, pulling me closer to her.

I tried to imagine doing this with a person I liked, but it was a mirage. The harder I tried to think about that scenario, the quicker it disintegrated.

I was never, ever going to enjoy this. With anybody.

It wasn't just a dislike of kissing. It wasn't a fear or nervousness or 'not meeting the right person yet'. This was a part of me. I did not feel the feelings of attraction, of romance, of desire, that other people felt.

And I wasn't ever going to.

I really hadn't needed to kiss anyone to work that out.

Rooney, on the other hand, was going for it, which I assumed was what she did with everybody. The way she kissed made it feel like she really did like me, but I realised suddenly that I knew her better than that. It was never about the other person. She was using this to make her feel good about herself.

I didn't have the energy to start to understand what that meant.

'Oh,' said a voice from behind us.

Rooney moved away from me instantly, and I, hazy and a little weirded out by this whole situation, turned to see who it was.

I should have guessed, really.

Because the universe seemed to have it in for me already.

Pip had her jacket folded over one arm and a toastie in her other hand.

'I . . .' she said, then trailed off. She was looking at me, eyes wide, then at Rooney, then back at me again. 'I brought you a toastie, but . . .' She looked at the toastie. 'It – er, fucking hell.' She looked back at both of us. 'Wow. Fuck you both.'

PAPER FLOWERS

Rooney leapt to her feet. '*Hang on*, you literally don't understand what was just happening.'

Pip's stare hardened.

'I think it's pretty plainly obvious what was just happening,' she said. 'So don't try and insult me by lying about it.'

'I'm not, but —'

'If this was a thing, you could have at least told me about it.' She turned her stare to me, her face scarily blank of emotion. 'You could have at least told me about it.'

And then she walked out of the room.

Rooney wasted no time in running after her, and I quickly followed. I needed to explain. Rooney needed to explain.

Everyone just needed to stop lying and acting and pretending all the time.

Rooney grabbed Pip's shoulders just as she got to the end of the corridor and pulled her round to face her.

'Pip, just *listen* —'

'To WHAT?' Pip shouted, then lowered her voice as a few passing students turned round curiously. 'If you're seeing each other fine, just go and fuck each other and enjoy yourselves, but you could have at least done me the courtesy of informing me so I could try and put a stop to *my* feelings and not be absolutely fucking *crushed* right now –' Her voice broke and there were tears in her eyes.

I wanted to explain, but I couldn't speak.

I had ruined my friendship with Jason and now I was destroying my friendship with Pip too.

'I don't – we don't – we're not together!' Rooney gestured to me wildly. 'I swear! It was my fucking idea because I'm an idiot! Georgia's just been figuring shit out and I've just been making stuff worse, making her date Jason as an experiment when she never really wanted to do that, and now this –'

It felt like the walls shattered around us. Pip clenched her fists. 'Wait . . .' She turned to me. 'You – Jason was just an *experiment?*'

'I . . .' I wanted to say no, he wasn't, I thought I liked him, I genuinely *wanted* to fall for him, but . . . was that a lie?

Pip's face crumpled. She took a step towards me, and now she was *shouting.* 'How could you *do that? How could you do that to him?'*

I stepped back, feeling tears forming. Don't cry. Do not cry.

'Stop blaming her!' Rooney shouted back. 'She was figuring out her sexuality!'

'Well, she shouldn't have done that with our best friend who'd only just got out of a relationship that made him feel like an actual piece of SHIT!'

She was right. I'd fucked up. I'd fucked up so bad.

Rooney physically put an arm in between me and Pip. 'Stop trying to make this about something else when we know what this is about!'

'Oh yeah?' Pip's voice lowered. There were tear stains down her cheeks. 'What's this about, then?'

'About the fact that *you hate me*. You think I'm taking Georgia away from you and because she's one of your only *two friends*, you *despise me* because you think I'm replacing you in her life.'

There was a silence. Pip's eyes widened.

'You don't know anything,' she said hoarsely, and turned round. 'I'm leaving.'

'Wait!' I said. The first fucking thing I'd said.

Pip turned back, struggling to say anything through her tears. 'What? Got anything to say?'

I didn't. I couldn't form the words.

'That's what I thought,' she said. 'You never have anything to say.'

And then she was gone.

Rooney went right after her, but I stayed where I was in the corridor. The walls around me were made of paper flowers. Above me were twinkling fairy lights. Students passed, laughing, holding hands, wearing stylish suits and sparkly dresses. The song playing overhead was 'Young Hearts Run Free' by Candi Staton.

I hated all of it.

SURVIVOR

I wandered through dimly lit corridors and raucous crowds. I stood at the edge of the dance hall as the band were finishing their set, playing a slow song so all the couples could hold each other and sway. It made me feel sick.

Rooney and Pip were nowhere, so I went back to my room. It was the only thing I could think to do. I looked at myself in the mirror for a long time, wondering if this was the moment when I would just collapse, I could just let it out and start sobbing because I had fucked it all up. I had fucked *everything* up in my quest to understand who I was. Despite the fact that Pip and Jason had so much to deal with on their own, I had only truly been thinking about myself.

But I didn't cry. I was silent. I didn't want to be awake any more.

I went to sleep for a few hours, and when I woke up I could hear the thumping of people having sex in the room above me.

This was, perhaps, the final straw.

Was everyone just having sex and falling in love all the time? Why? How was it fair that everyone got to feel that except me?

I wished everyone would stop. I wished sex and love didn't exist.

I stormed out of the room, not even taking my phone with me, ran up the stairs to the corridor above two at a time, not quite knowing what I was going to do when I got there, but I could at least see whose room it was and maybe at a later date I could track them down and tell them to stop being so loud . . .

When I reached the point in the corridor that was above my room, I stopped, and stood very still.

It was a utility room. Inside: six washing machines and six dryers.

One of the washing machines was on. It was making a rhythmic thumping sound against the wall.

Back in my room, I realised that it was only ten minutes until 6 a.m. – the time of the fabled 'Survivors Photo'.

I'd just go and have a look. See how many people had made it.

The answer was not very many. Of the hundreds of students that had been bustling around college earlier, there could only have been about eighty left, and they'd all congregated in the dance hall. A tired-looking photographer was waiting for the drunk, sleep-deprived students to organise themselves into rows. I didn't know whether to join them or not. I felt like a bit of a fraud, since I'd basically napped through the last five hours.

'Georgia!'

I turned, scared that I'd face Jason or Rooney or Pip, but it was none of them.

Sunil approached me from the dance hall's doorway. His tie was undone, his baby blue jacket was slung over one arm, and he looked unnaturally awake for 6 a.m.

He clapped his hands on to my upper arms and shook me a little. 'You *made it*! You made it to six a.m.! I'm very impressed. I gave up at midnight when I was a fresher.'

'I . . . had a nap,' I said.

Sunil grinned. 'Good shout. Got to be strategic about these things. Jess went for a nap a couple of hours ago but hasn't resurfaced, so I think she's failed again this year.'

I blinked. I didn't know what to say to him.

'So, no one else make it? Rooney? Pip? Jason?'

'Uh . . .' I looked around. Neither Rooney, Pip nor Jason were anywhere to be seen. I had no idea where anyone was. 'No. Just me.'

Sunil nodded. 'Ah, well. You'll get to brag tomorrow.' He wrapped an arm round my shoulder and started walking us towards the throng of students. 'You're a *survivor*!'

I tried to smile, but it just turned into a lip wobble. Sunil didn't see, too busy leading us onward.

I blinked again.

And then I said it.

'I think I might be . . . asexual. And also aromantic. Both of them.'

Sunil stopped walking.

'Yeah?' he said.

'Uh . . . yeah,' I said, looking at the floor. 'Um. Don't really know what to do about that.'

Sunil stayed very still for a moment. Then he moved, his arm dropping away from me and turned so that he was standing directly in front of me. He put his hands on my shoulders and bent a little so that our faces were level.

'There's nothing to *do*, Georgia,' he said softly. 'There's nothing to do at all.'

And then the photographer started getting impatient and shouted at everyone to get organised, so Sunil marched us over to the scrum and we squeezed into the third row next to a couple of his friends, and as he turned away to chat to them, only then did I realise that what I'd said was undeniably true. I knew that now.

Sunil turned back, squeezed my shoulder and said, 'You're gonna be OK. There's nothing you have to do except *be*.'

'But . . . what if what I *am* is just . . . nothing?' I breathed out and blinked as the photographer took the first shot. 'What if I'm nothing?'

'You're not nothing,' Sunil said. 'You have to believe that.'

Maybe I could do that.

Maybe I could believe.

PART FOUR

VERY OPPOSITE PEOPLE

The morning after the Bailey Ball, Rooney came back to our room at nearly midday. I'd still been asleep, but she kicked the door open so hard that it slammed against the wall, then said something about having slept at some guy's place, before kicking off her shoes, pulling her dress over her head, and standing in the centre of the room, staring at Roderick the house plant, who was basically close to death. And then she got into bed.

She didn't say anything about what had happened with me or with Pip.

I didn't want to talk to her either, so as soon as I was up and dressed, I went to the library. I walked right up to the top floor where there were tables tucked behind long cases of books on finance and business. I stayed there until dinnertime, finishing one of this term's assignments, not thinking about anything that had happened. I was definitely not thinking about anything that had happened.

When I got back, Rooney awoke, just in time for dinner in the college cafeteria.

We walked down there together, saying nothing, and we ate

together sitting next to a group of students I recognised as Rooney's acquaintances, but she still said nothing.

When we got back to our room, she changed into her pyjamas, got right back into bed, and fell asleep again. I stayed awake, staring at Pip's jacket in the corner of the room – the one she'd left here in Freshers' Week. The one I'd kept forgetting to give back to her.

When I woke up in our room on Sunday, I felt disgusting, realising I hadn't showered since before the Bailey Ball.

So I showered. I got dressed in a fresh T-shirt and a warm cardigan, and I exited the room, leaving Rooney alone in bed, only her ponytail poking out of the top of her duvet.

I went to the library again with the intention of getting another essay done. My first assignments of my university life were all due next week before the winter holidays, and I still had a lot to do. But once I'd swiped into the library with my campus card and found a vacant table, I just sat there with my laptop, staring at my old message threads with Pip and Jason.

I drafted a separate message to each of them. It took two hours. To Jason, I sent:

Georgia Warr

I'm so, so sorry for everything. I didn't properly think about how this would affect you – I was only thinking about myself. You are one of the most important people in my life and I took advantage of that without thinking. You deserve someone who worships you. I honestly wish that I did feel that way but I can't – I literally am not attracted to anyone, no matter their gender. I've tried really hard to be, but I'm just not. I'm so sorry for everything.

To Pip, I sent:

Georgia Warr
Hey, I know you're not talking to me, and I understand why, but I just want you to know the facts: Rooney kissed me because I've been very confused about my sexuality and she wanted to help me see if I liked girls. This was a very dumb thing for both of us to do – it didn't help me in any way whatsoever, wasn't really what I wanted to do at all, and we were both drunk. We're really not into each other and both seriously regret it. So I'm really really sorry.

Both of them read the messages within the hour. Neither of them responded.

Despite us living literally in the same bedroom, the first proper conversation I had with Rooney after the events of the Bailey Ball came on the Monday before the end of term in an introduction to drama lecture. I was sitting alone near the back, which was my usual spot, when she appeared in my peripheral vision and sat down next to me.

She was in her day look – leggings, a St John's polo shirt, hair in a ponytail – but her eyes were wild as she stared at me and waited for me to say something.

I didn't want to talk to her. I was annoyed at her. I knew that what had happened was my fault as well as hers, but I was angry at how she'd reacted when I'd tried to explain my feelings.

She hadn't even tried to understand.

'Hello,' I said flatly.

'Hi,' she said back. 'I need to talk to you.'

'I . . . don't really want to talk to you,' I said.

'I know. You don't have to say anything if you don't want to.'

But then neither of us could, because we were both interrupted by the professor starting her lecture on Pinter's *The Birthday Party*.

Instead of leaving the issue, Rooney withdrew her iPad from her bag, opened up a notes app, and laid it on the table in front of us, close enough to me so that I could see the screen. She started tapping, and I assumed she was just taking notes on the lecture, but then she stopped and pushed the screen towards me.

I'm so, so sorry about what happened at the bailey ball. It was entirely my fault and I was a fucking dick to you when you were trying to tell me something important.

Oh. OK.

That was unexpected.

I looked at Rooney. She raised her eyebrows and nodded at the iPad, gesturing for me to respond.

What was I supposed to say?

I cautiously raised my hands and began to type.

okay

Rooney paused, then tapped furiously at the keyboard.

I know we were drunk but that's literally not an excuse for the way I acted. You know when straight guys find out that a girl is gay and they're all like 'haha but you haven't kissed me so how do you know you're gay'. That is basically what I did to you!!!

This whole time I've been pestering you about finding a relationship and kissing people and getting out there . . . I kept telling you to try with Jason and when you tried to tell me you didn't actually want any of that, I didn't even listen. And then I thought kissing would be a good idea because I always think kissing just solves everything!!!!

You've been figuring out your sexuality for months and I did everything wrong. EVERYTHING.

I had so many ideas about how people should feel about romance and sex and all that, but . . . it's all just bullshit and I'm so sorry

I'm literally so dumb and I'm an asshole

I WANT YOU TO TELL ME I'M AN ASSHOLE

I raised an eyebrow and then typed,

okay you're an asshole

Rooney actually grinned at this.

R – Thank you

G – no problem

I hadn't even expected her to apologise, let alone understand why what she'd done had been bad.

But she had.

I decided to be bold and type out:

so as it turns out, I am aromantic asexual

Rooney gave me a look.

It wasn't the 'what the fuck is that?' look that I expected.

It was a curious look. Curious. A little concerned, maybe, but not in a bad way.

Just honestly wanting to know what's going on with me.

yeah I was confused about it too haha
    it means i'm not attracted to anyone romantically or sexually
    no matter their gender
    sorta been figuring that out lately

Rooney watched me type. Then she took a moment to think before she responded.

R – Wow . . . I didn't even know that was a thing!!! I always assumed it was like . . . you like guys or girls or some sort of combo

G – haha yeah same
    hence all the confusion

R – It sounds really difficult to figure out . . . I'm proud of you!!!!!!

It was far from a perfect response to someone coming out. But it was so distinctly Rooney that it brought a smile to my face.

R – Are you feeling okay about it?

G – to be honest not really.
    but
    i think i will be
    in time?
    like . . . realising and accepting that this is who i am is the
first couple of steps and i have done that now i guess??

Before typing a response back, Rooney simply put her head on my shoulder and rested it there for a few seconds, in lieu of a real hug, which would have been a bit difficult in the middle of a lecture.

R – I guess I can't really relate but I'm here for you. Like, if you ever wanna rant about it or just talk things through!!

G – really??

R – Georgia. We are friends.

G – oh

R – I mean, we have KISSED. Sort of. Platonically made out.

G – i'm aware

R – Sorry about that. Again. Was it really horrible for you????

G – i mean. it did feel a little bit disgusting yes

R – Oh!!

G – no offence

R – No I like it. you're definitely the anti-me

G – we are very opposite people, yes

R – Very refreshing

G – love that for us

R – Tasty

G – delicious content

R – 10/10

We both started giggling, and then we couldn't stop, until the professor shushed us and we looked at each other, grinning. Everything might have been shit still, I'd hurt my two best friends and I knew I had so far to go before I could even begin to like who I was, but at least I had Rooney sitting next to me, laughing instead of crying.

AROMANTIC ASEXUAL

The internet is a blessing and a curse. Googling 'aromantic asexual' unleashed a quantity of information I was not mentally or emotionally prepared for. The first time I searched it, I quickly exited the window and didn't search again for a whole day.

My animalistic instinct was *this is stupid.*

This is fake.

This is a made-up internet thing that is stupid and fake and absolutely not me.

And yet, it was me. Sunil and Jess were not the only ones. There were thousands of people on the internet who identified this way and were very happy to do so. In fact, people had been using the word 'asexual' as a sexual identity since as far back as 1907. So it wasn't even an 'internet thing' at all.

Sunil had explained it pretty concisely, to be fair. The internet informed me that asexual simply meant little-to-no *sexual* attraction, and aromantic meant little-to-no *romantic* attraction. On a more intense internet dive, I discovered there was actually a lot of debate over these definitions because people's experiences and feelings could be so vastly different, but at that point, I decided to log the hell off again.

It was too much. Too confusing. Too new.

I wondered whether Sunil had ever felt like this about his own asexuality, and after I scrolled down his Instagram for a while, I found he had a blog. It was called 'Diary of a Cellist at Durham', and it had posts about all sorts of things – studying music, Durham activities, his daily routine, his role in Pride Soc and in the student orchestra. He'd also posted a few times about asexuality. One post stuck out to me, where he'd written about how he'd initially found it difficult to accept his asexuality. Sexuality in general was very taboo in Indian culture, he'd explained, and when he'd looked for support, he'd found that the asexual community – even online – was incredibly white. But after finding a group of Indian asexuals online, he'd started to feel proud of his identity.

Sunil had no doubt been on a very different journey to me, and a lot of things that he'd dealt with, I would be shielded from due to being white and cis. But it was reassuring to know that he too had felt some anxiety about being asexual. People didn't always love who they were right away.

I soon found the courage to continue googling.

It turned out that lots of asexual people still wanted to have sex for all sorts of different reasons, but some felt totally neutral about it, and others – what I'd originally thought – literally despised it. Some asexual people still masturbated; others didn't have libidos at all.

It also turned out that lots of aromantic people still wanted to be in romantic relationships, despite not feeling those feels. Others didn't ever want a romantic partner.

And people identified as all sorts of combinations of romantic and sexual – there were gay asexuals, like Sunil, or bisexual aromantics, like Jess, or straight asexuals, pansexual aromantics, and loads more. Some asexual and aromantic people didn't even like splitting up their attraction into two labels, and some just used the word 'queer' to summarise everything. There were words I had to google like 'demisexual' and 'greyromantic', but even after googling I wasn't sure exactly what they meant.

The aromantic and asexual spectrums weren't just straight lines. They were radar charts with at least a dozen different axes.

It was a lot.

Like *a lot* a lot.

The crux of it all was that I did not feel sexual or romantic feelings for anyone. Not a single goddamn person I had ever met or would ever meet.

So that really was me.

Aromantic.

Asexual.

I came back to the words until they felt real in my mind, at least. Maybe they wouldn't be real in most people's minds. But I could make them real in mine. I could do whatever the fuck I wanted.

I whispered them sometimes under my breath, until they felt like a magic spell. Pictured them as I fell asleep.

I'm not sure when I realised that I was no longer feeling melancholic distress about my sexuality. The *woe is me, I am loveless* mood had just gone.

It was anger, now.

I was so angry.

At *everything*.

I was angry at fate for dealing me these cards. Even though I knew there was nothing wrong with me – lots of people were like this, I wasn't alone, love yourself, whatever – I didn't know how to get to the point where this would stop feeling like a burden and instead feel like something *good*, something I could *celebrate*, something I could *share with the world*.

I was angry at every single couple I passed in the street. Every single pair I saw holding hands, every single time I saw that couple down the corridor flirting in the kitchen. Every time I saw two people cosying up in the library or in the cafeteria. Every time one of the authors I'd liked posted a new fanfiction.

I was angry at the world for making me hate who I was. I was angry at myself for letting these feelings ruin my friendships with the best people in the world. I was angry at every single romance movie, every single fanfic, every single stupid OTP that had made me crave finding the perfect romance. It was because of all of that, no doubt, that this new identity felt like a loss, when in reality, it should have been a beautiful discovery.

Ultimately, the fact that I was angry about all of that just made me angrier because I knew I *shouldn't* feel angry about any of these things. But I did, and I'm trying to be honest about it, OK? OK.

TRUE LOVE

The reality of the situation with Pip and Jason only sank in when they both dropped out of the Shakespeare Society on the same day. The last day of term.

They didn't even do it in person.

I didn't have high hopes that they would attend our rehearsal on that Friday before Christmas, but Rooney and I went along anyway, unlocked the room, switched on the electric heater, and moved the tables to one side. Sunil turned up none the wiser, wearing a coat that was basically a blanket and a smile on his face. We didn't know what to tell him.

Ten minutes after they should have arrived, Pip messaged the group chat.

Felipa Quintana
Hey so me and Jason have decided we're not gonna be in the play any more, too much other work and stuff. Find some other people to replace us.

Sorry

I saw it first, then passed my phone to Rooney.

She read it. I watched as she bit down on the insides of her cheeks. For a moment, she looked furious. Then she passed my phone back to me and turned round so neither me nor Sunil could see how upset she was.

Sunil saw the message last. He looked up at us with a confused expression and asked, 'What – what happened?'

'We . . . we all had an argument,' I said, because I didn't know how to explain what an actual clusterfuck this small group of people had become while Sunil was an innocent bystander just wanting to take part in a fun theatre society.

And it was all because of me.

I have always felt lonely, I think.

I think a lot of people feel lonely. Rooney. Pip. Maybe even Jason, though he hasn't said so.

I'd spent my teenage life feeling lonely every time I saw a couple at a party, or two people kissing outside the school gate. I'd felt lonely every time I read some cute proposal story on Twitter, or saw someone's five-year-anniversary Facebook post, or even just saw someone hanging out with their partner in their Instagram story, sitting with them on a sofa with their dog, watching TV. I felt lonely first because I hadn't experienced that. And I felt even lonelier when I started to believe I never would.

This loneliness – being without Jason and Pip – was worse.

Friends are automatically classed as 'less important' than romantic partners. I'd never questioned that. It was just the way the world was. I guess I'd always felt that friendship just couldn't compete with what a partner offered, and that I'd never really experience *real love* until I found romance.

But if that had been true, I probably wouldn't have felt like this.

I loved Jason and Pip. I loved them because I didn't have to think around them. I loved that we could sit in silence together. I loved that they knew all my favourite foods and they could instantly tell when I was in a bad mood. I loved Pip's stupid sense of humour and how she immediately made every room she entered a happier place. I loved how Jason knew exactly what to say when you were upset and could always calm you down.

I loved Jason and Pip. And now they were gone.

I had been so desperate for my idea of true love that I couldn't even see it when it was right in front of my face.

HOME

I pressed a cold hand against my car, which was as far up the drive of our house as it could get. I'd missed my car.

There were three other cars on our driveway and four more parked on the pavement outside, which told me one thing: all of the Warr family had congregated at our house. This was not an unusual occurrence around Christmas at the Warrs', but a family party on December twenty-first was a little premature, and it was not exactly the environment I wanted to return to after my university term from hell.

'Georgia? What are you doing?'

Dad was holding open the front door for me. He'd picked me up from the station.

'Nothing,' I said, dropping my hand from my car.

There was a sort of cheer from the twenty-or-so members of my family socialising in the living room as I entered. I guess that was nice. I'd forgotten what it was like to be around that many people who knew who I was.

Mum gave me a big hug. My older brother, Jonathan, and his

wife, Rachel, came over for a hug too. Then Mum wasted no time in making me take everyone's tea and coffee orders and informing me of the hour-by-hour schedule for the next week, including the fact that my aunt, uncle and cousin Ellis would be staying here until Boxing Day. Like a big family sleepover.

'You don't mind Ellis sharing your room, do you?' Mum asked.

I wasn't thrilled by this turn of events, but I liked Ellis, so it wouldn't be too bad.

My bedroom was exactly the same as I'd left it – books, TV, stripy bedsheets – apart from the addition of a blow-up mattress for Ellis. I flopped straight on to my bed. It smelt right.

Even by the end of term, university hadn't felt like home.

'Come on, then!' Gran squawked at me as I squeezed on to the sofa next to her. 'Tell us everything!'

By 'everything' she definitely didn't mean how I'd utterly destroyed the very small number of friendships I'd had, begrudgingly realised that I wasn't straight and was in fact a sexuality that very few people in real life have heard of, and realised that the world was so obsessed with romantic love that I couldn't go an hour without hating myself because I didn't feel it.

So instead I told her, and the other twelve family members listening in, about my lectures ('interesting'), my room in college ('spacious'), and my roommate ('very nice').

Unfortunately, Gran liked to pry. 'And what about friends? Have you made any nice friends?' She leant towards me, patting me slyly on the leg. 'Or met any nice young *men*? I bet there are lots of lovely boys in Durham.'

I didn't hate Gran for being like this. It wasn't her fault. She had been raised to believe that it was a girl's primary aim in life to get married and have a family. She had done just that when she was my age, and I think she felt very fulfilled because of it. Fair enough. You do you.

But that didn't stop me from being deeply, deeply annoyed.

'Actually,' I said, trying as hard as I could to keep the irritation out of my voice, 'I'm not really interested in getting a boyfriend.'

'Oh, well,' she said, patting my leg again, 'plenty of time, my love. Plenty of time.'

But my time is now, I wanted to scream. My life is happening right now.

My family then launched into a conversation about how easy it was to get into a relationship at uni. In the corner, I spotted my cousin Ellis, sitting quietly with a glass of wine and one leg crossed over the other. She caught my stare, smiled a small smile, and rolled her eyes at the group around us. I smiled back. Maybe, at least, I would have an ally.

Ellis was thirty-four and used to be a model. A legit *fashion* model who did runway shows and magazine adverts. She gave that up in her mid-twenties and used the money she'd saved to spend a couple of years painting, which, as it turned out, she was very good at. She's been a professional artist ever since.

I only saw her a couple of times a year, but she always caught up with me when we did see each other, asking me how school was, how my friends were, if there'd been any recent developments in my life. I'd always liked her.

I don't know when I started to notice how Ellis was sort of the butt of the joke in our family. Every time she and Gran were in the same room, Gran would manage to drag the conversation back to the fact that she wasn't married yet and hadn't provided the family with any cute babies for them to coo over. Mum always spoke about her like she had some sort of tragic life, just because she lived by herself and had never had a long-term relationship.

I'd thought she had a super-cool life. But I guess I had always wondered whether she was happy. Or whether she was sad and alone, desperately wishing for romance, just like I had been.

'No boyfriend, then?' Ellis asked me as I slumped down next to her in the conservatory that evening.

'Tragically, no,' I said.

'Sounding a little sarcastic there.'

'Maybe so.'

Ellis smiled and shook her head. 'Don't worry about Gran. She's been saying the same things to me for the past fifteen years. She's just scared she's going to die without a great-grandchild.'

I chuckled, even though this was something I thought about and felt a little bad about. I didn't want Gran to die unhappy.

'So . . .' Ellis continued. 'There haven't been any . . . girlfriends? Instead?'

It took a moment for me to realise that she didn't mean 'girlfriend' in the platonic sense of the word. She was asking me if I was gay.

Which, you know, massive props to Ellis. If I had been gay, this would have been a bloody amazing moment for me.

'Um, no,' I said. 'Not really interested in girlfriends either.'

Ellis nodded. For a moment she looked like she was going to ask something else, but then she just said, 'Fancy a bit of *Cuphead*?' So we turned on the Xbox and played *Cuphead* until everyone went home or went to bed.

ELLIS

The Warrs are one of those terrible families where Christmas Day present-opening is banned until the late afternoon, but that year I didn't mind too much, having other things on my mind. I hadn't asked for anything in particular, so ended up with a big stack of books, an assortment of bath products I'd probably never use, and a sweatshirt from Mum featuring the phrase 'Fries before guys'. The family had a good laugh about that one.

After presents, the grandparents all fell asleep in the conservatory, Mum got into an intense chess match against Jonathan while Dad and Rachel prepared the tea. Ellis and I played a bit of *Mario Kart* before I snuck off to my bedroom to chill out and check my phone.

I opened my Facebook message chat with Pip.

Georgia Warr
merry christmas!! i love you, hope you had a good day yesterday
xxxxx

It was still unread. I'd been drunk when I sent it midway through Christmas dinner. Maybe she just hadn't seen it yet.

I checked her Instagram. Pip's family celebrated Christmas primarily on Christmas Eve, and she'd been posting a lot of Instagram stories. She'd posted a photo in the early hours of the morning – her family walking along the street on their way back from Midnight Mass.

i fell asleep in church lol

And she'd posted another photo half an hour ago of her in her family kitchen, putting a doughball into her mouth.

leftover buñuelos get the FUCK inside my belly

I thought about responding but couldn't think of a funny thing to say.

Since she posted that half an hour ago, she had probably seen my message on her phone. She was just ignoring me.

She still hated me, then.

I was tucked up in bed by 10 p.m. Overall, not a bad Christmas Day, despite having lost my best friends and the way my singleness was becoming an ongoing family joke.

One day I would probably have to just tell them.

I don't like guys. Oh, so you like girls? *No, I don't like girls either.* What? That doesn't make any sense. *Yes, it does. It's a real thing.* You just haven't met the right person yet. It'll happen with time. *No, it won't. This is who I am.* Are you feeling OK? Maybe we should get you an appointment with the GP. *It's called being 'aromantic asexual'.* Well, that sounds fake, doesn't it? Did you hear about that on the internet?

Ugh. OK. Didn't really want to venture into that conversation any time soon.

I was heading downstairs to get some water when I heard the raised voices. At first, I thought it might just be Mum and Dad bickering at each other, but then I realised the voices were, in fact, Auntie Sal and Uncle Gavin. Ellis's parents. I hung back on the stairs, not wanting to interrupt.

'Look at Jonathan,' Auntie Sal was saying. 'He's got it *sussed*. Married, his own house, his own business. He's set for life.'

'And he's a decade younger than you!' Uncle Gavin added.

Oh. Ellis was there too.

I wasn't super close to Auntie Sal and Uncle Gavin. Same as Ellis, really – they didn't live close by, so we only saw them a few times a year at family gatherings.

But they always seemed a little more uptight than my parents. A little more traditional.

'I'm aware,' said Ellis. Her voice took me by surprise. She sounded so tired.

'Doesn't that bother you at *all*?' asked Auntie Sal.

'What is there to bother me?'

'That Jonathan is growing up, starting a family, making plans while you're still . . .'

'Still what?' snapped Ellis. 'What am I doing that's so bad?'

'There's no need to shout,' said Uncle Gavin.

'I'm not shouting.'

'You're getting *older*,' continued Auntie Sal. 'You're in your mid-thirties. You're passing your dating prime. Soon it's going to get harder and harder for you to have children.'

'I don't want to date, and I don't want children,' said Ellis.

'Oh, come on, now. Not this again.'

'You are our *only* child,' said Uncle Gavin. 'Do you know what that's like for us? You are the *sole* carrier of my surname.'

'It's not my fault you didn't have any more children,' said Ellis.

'And what, that's it for us? No more children in the family? We don't get to be grandparents? That's the thanks we get for raising you?'

Ellis sighed loudly.

'We're not trying to *criticise* your . . . life choices,' said Auntie Sal. 'We know it's not about us, but . . . we just want you to be *happy*. I know you think you're happy now, but what about ten years from now? Twenty? Forty? What will your life be like when you're Gran's age, without a partner, without children? Who is going to be there to support you? You'll have *no one*.'

'Maybe I would be happy,' Ellis shot back, 'if you hadn't spent my entire life brainwashing me into thinking that finding a husband and having babies is the only way for me to feel my life is worth anything. Maybe then I would be happy.'

Auntie Sal went to interrupt, but Ellis cut her off.

'It's not as if I'm actively rejecting people, OK?' Ellis sounded on the verge of tears now. 'I don't like anyone like that. I never do. This is just who I am and one way or another, we're all going to have to put up with it. I can still do amazing things with my life. I have friends. And I'll make new friends. I was a successful model. Now I'm an artist and my paintings are selling really well. I'm thinking about going to uni to study art, since I never got to go the first time. I have a really nice house, if you could ever be bothered to visit. If you tried, and I mean really *tried*, you could actually be proud of all the things I've done in my life and all the things I'm going to do.'

There was a long, horrible silence.

'What would you say,' said Auntie Sal, speaking slowly as if choosing her words, 'to thinking about trying therapy again? I'm still not sure we found the right therapist last time. If we kept looking, we could find someone who could really help.'

Silence.

And then Ellis said, 'I don't need fixing. You don't get to do that to me again.'

There was the sound of chairs scraping the floor as someone stood up.

'Ell, don't do this,' said Uncle Gavin. 'Don't have a strop like last time.'

'I am an adult,' said Ellis. There was a contained fury in her voice that reinforced the statement. 'And if you're not going to respect me, then I am not going to be around you.'

I watched, hidden in the darkness at the top of the stairs, as Ellis sat down on the bottom step to put her shoes on. Then she pulled on her coat, calmly opened our front door, and stepped outside.

Before I could think twice, I raced to my room, grabbed my dressing gown and slippers, and ran after her.

I found her sitting in her car, vape pen hanging from her mouth but with seemingly no intention of smoking anything.

I knocked on the window, which made her jump so hard that the vape pen flew out of her mouth.

'Holy fucking *shit*,' she said after turning on the ignition and rolling down the window. 'You scared the absolute poo out of me.'

'Sorry.'

'What are you doing out here?'

'I . . .' Maybe this was a bit awkward. 'I heard your parents being shitty to you.'

Ellis just looked at me.

'I thought you could use some company,' I said. 'I dunno. I can go back inside, if you want.'

Ellis shook her head. 'Nah. Get in here.'

I opened the door and hopped inside. She actually had a really nice car. Modern. Way more expensive than my elderly Fiat Punto.

There was a silence as I waited for her to say something. She located her vape pen, slotted it neatly into the compartment in front of the gear lever, and then said, 'I'm in the mood for a McDonald's.'

'On Christmas Day?'

'Yeah. I just really want a McFlurry right now.'

Thinking about it, I was actually really up for some chips. I guess it *was* a 'fries before guys' day.

I also wanted to talk to Ellis about everything I'd just heard. Especially about 'not liking anyone'.

'We could go to McDonald's,' I said.

'Yeah?'

'Yeah.'

So Ellis started the car, and off we went.

PLATONIC MAGIC

'Oh my God, *yes*,' said Ellis, dunking the plastic spoon into her McFlurry. 'This is what Christmas Day has always been missing.'

'Agreed,' I said, already halfway through my chips.

'McDonald's. She never lets me down.'

'I'm not sure that's the slogan.'

'It should be.'

We were parked in the restaurant's car park, which was almost entirely empty apart from us. I'd messaged Mum and Dad about where I was, and Dad sent back a thumbs-up emoji, so they probably weren't bothered. Being in the car in my pyjamas and dressing gown did feel a bit wrong, though.

Ellis had chatted to me the whole way there about the most mundane topics. It was only a fifteen-minute drive, but for that whole fifteen minutes I hadn't been able to get in much more than a 'yeah' or an 'mmhm' of agreement. I hadn't been able to ask anything I really wanted to ask.

Are you like me? Are we the same?

'So,' I was finally able to say while she was mid-spoonful of ice cream, 'your parents.'

She made a grunting noise. 'Oh, yeah. Jesus, sorry you had to hear *any* of that. It's very embarrassing that they still treat me like I'm fifteen. No offence to all the fifteen-year-olds out there. Even fifteen-year-olds don't deserve to be spoken to like that.'

'They sounded . . .' I searched for the word. '. . . unreasonable.'

Ellis laughed. 'Yeah. Yes, they did.'

'Do they get at you about that stuff a lot?'

'Whenever I see them, yeah,' said Ellis. 'Which is less and less these days, to be honest.'

I couldn't imagine seeing Mum and Dad less and less. But maybe that's what would happen to me, if I never got married or had children. I would just be phased out of my family. A ghost. Only popping up at occasional family gatherings.

If I came out to them, would they make me get therapy, like Ellis's parents had?

'Do you ever believe them?' I asked.

Ellis was clearly not expecting this question. She took a long breath in, staring at her ice cream.

'You mean, do I ever feel like my life is worthless because I won't ever have a partner or children?' she asked.

It sounded worse when she put it like that. But I wanted to know.

I needed to know whether I would always feel uncomfortable with this part of myself.

'Yeah,' I said.

'Well, firstly, I can have children whenever I want. Adoption exists.'

'But what about having a partner?'

She paused.

And then she said, 'Yes, I do feel like that occasionally.'

Oh.

So maybe I was always going to feel like this.

Maybe I would never feel comfortable with this.

Maybe –

'But that's just a feeling,' she continued. 'And I *know* it's untrue.'

I blinked up at her.

'Having a partner is what some people want. For others, it's not. It took me a long, long time to figure out that that's not what I want. In fact . . .' She hesitated. But only for a moment. 'It took me a long time to realise that it's not even something I *can* want. It's not a choice for me. It's a part of me that I can't change.'

I was holding my breath.

'How did you realise?' I asked eventually, my heart in my mouth.

She laughed. 'It's . . . well, are you in the mood for me to condense my entire life into one conversation over a Christmas Day McDonald's?'

'. . . Yes.'

'Ha. OK.' She took a spoonful of ice cream. 'So . . . I never had any crushes when I was a child. Not any real ones, anyway. Sometimes I confused friendship for them, or just thinking a guy was really cool. But I never really fancied anyone. Even celebrities or musicians or whatever.'

She raised her eyebrows and huffed out a sigh as if this was all a minor inconvenience.

'But the thing *was*,' she said, 'everybody else I knew got crushes. They dated. All my friends talked about hot boys. They all got boyfriends. Our family has always been big and loving – you know, your parents and my parents and our grandparents and everyone else – so that was always what I saw as the *norm*. That was all I knew. In my eyes, dating and relationships were just . . . what people did. It was human. So that's what I tried to do too.'

Tried.

She had tried too.

'And this continued into my late teens, and then into my twenties. Especially when I got into modelling, because *everyone* was getting with each other in modelling. So I would force myself to do it too, just to be involved and not be left out.' She blinked. 'But . . . I hated it. I hated every fucking second of it.'

There was a pause. I didn't know what to say.

'I don't know when I started to realise that I hated it. For a long time, I was just dating and having sex because *that's what people did*. And I *wanted* to feel like those people. I wanted the fun, exciting beauty of romance and sex. But there was always this underlying feeling of *wrongness*. Almost *disgust*. It just felt wrong on a fundamental level.'

I felt a wave of relief that I had never let myself go that far.

Maybe I was a little stronger than I thought.

'And yet, I kept trying to like it. I kept thinking, *maybe I'm just picky. Maybe I haven't met the right guy. Maybe I like girls instead. Maybe, maybe, maybe.*' She shook her head. 'Maybe never came. It never got here.'

She leant back into the driver's seat, staring ahead at the soft glow of McDonald's.

'There was the fear too. I didn't know how I was going to function in this world alone. Not just alone now, but *endlessly* alone. Partnerless until I die. You know why people pair up into couples? Because being a human is fucking terrifying. But it's a hell of a lot easier if you're not doing it by yourself.'

I guessed that was the crux of it.

I could, on a base level, accept that I was like this. But I didn't know how I was going to deal with that for the rest of my life. Twenty years from now. Forty. Sixty.

Then Ellis said, 'But I'm older now. I've learnt some things.'

'Like what?' I asked.

'Like the way friendship can be just as intense, beautiful and endless as romance. Like the way there's love everywhere around me — there's love for my friends, there's love in my paintings, there's love for myself. There's even love for my parents in there somewhere. Deep down.' She laughed, and I couldn't help but smile. 'I have a lot more love than some people in the world. Even if I'll never have a wedding.' She took a big spoonful of ice cream. 'There's definitely love for ice cream, let me tell you *that*.'

I laughed and she grinned at me.

'I was hopeless about being like this for a long time,' she said, and then shook her head. 'But I'm not any more. Finally. *Finally* I'm not hopeless any more.'

'I wish I could be like that,' I said, the words tumbling out of my mouth before I could stop them.

Ellis raised a curious eyebrow at me. 'Yeah?'

I took a breath. OK. Now or never.

'I think I'm . . . like you,' I said. 'I don't like anyone either. Romance-wise, I mean. Dating and stuff. It's . . . I just can't feel any of it. I used to want it — I mean, I still think I do want it sometimes. But I can never *really* want it, because I don't feel that way for anyone. If that makes sense.'

I could feel myself going redder and redder the more I spoke.

Ellis said nothing for a moment. Then she ate another spoonful of ice cream.

'That's why you got in the car, isn't it?' she said.

I nodded.

'Well,' she said. She seemed to realise the magnitude of what I'd admitted. 'Well.'

'It's a real sexuality,' I said. I didn't even know if Ellis knew it *was* a sexuality. 'Just like being gay or straight or bi.'

Ellis chuckled. 'The *nothing* sexuality.'

'It's not nothing. It's . . . well it's two different things. Aromantic is when you don't feel romantic attraction and asexual is when you don't feel sexual attraction. Some people are just one or the other, but I'm both, so I'm . . . aromantic asexual.'

That wasn't the first time I'd said those words. But every time I said them, they felt a little more at home in the air around me.

Ellis considered this. 'Two things. Hm. Two in one. Buy one get one free. Love that.'

I snorted, which made her genuinely laugh, and all the nerves that had been constricting my chest eased.

'Who told you about those, then?' she asked.

'Someone at uni,' I said. But Sunil wasn't just someone, was he? 'One of my friends.'

'Are they also . . .?'

'They're asexual too.'

'Wow.' Ellis grinned. 'Well, that makes three of us.'

'There are more,' I said. 'A lot more. Out there. In the world.'

'Really?'

'Yeah.'

Ellis stared out of the window, smiling. 'That would be nice. If there were lots out there.'

We sat in silence for a moment. I finished eating my chips.

There *were* more of us out there.

Neither of us were alone in this.

'You're . . . very lucky to know all of this,' said Ellis suddenly. 'I'm . . .' She shook her head. 'Ha. I guess I'm a bit jealous.'

'Why?' I asked, confused.

She looked at me. 'I just wasted a lot of time. That's all.'

She chucked her empty McFlurry pot into the back seat and turned on the ignition.

'I don't feel lucky,' I said.

'What do you feel?'

'I don't know. Lost.' I thought of Sunil. 'My friend said I don't have to do anything. He said all I need to do is *be*.'

'Your friend sounds like a wise old sage.'

'That just about sums him up.'

Ellis started driving us out of the car park.

'I don't like doing nothing,' she said. 'It's boring.'

'So what do *you* think I should do?'

She gave this some thought for a moment.

Then she said. 'Give your friendships the magic you would give a romance. Because they're just as important. Actually, for us, they're *way* more important.' She glanced to one side at me. 'There. Was that sage-like enough for you?'

I grinned. 'Very sage-like.'

'I can be profound. I *am* an artist.'

'You should put this in a painting.'

'You know what? Maybe I will.' She raised a hand and twinkled her fingers. 'I'll call it *Platonic Magic*. And no one who isn't like us – wait, what was it? Aro . . .?'

'Aromantic asexual?'

'Yes. No one who isn't aromantic asexual will understand it.'

'Can I have it?'

'Do you have two thousand pounds?'

'Your paintings are selling for *two thousand pounds*?'

'They sure are. I'm pretty good at my job.'

'Can I get student discount?'

'Maybe. Just because you're my cousin. Student cousin discount.'

And then we were laughing as we reached the motorway and I thought about the magic that I could find, maybe, if I looked a little harder.

MEMORIES

Magic was not what I found when I returned to my college room on the afternoon of January eleventh. What I found instead was most of Rooney's possessions scattered around the floor, her wardrobe wide open, her bedsheets several metres away from her bed, Roderick a worrying shade of brown, and the aqua rug inexplicably crammed into the sink.

I had just unzipped my suitcase when Rooney entered wearing pyjamas, looked at me, looked at the rug in the sink, and said, 'I spilled tea on it.'

She sat on her bed while I tidied her possessions, squeezed the water out of the rug, and even snipped most of the dead bits off Roderick. The photo of Mermaid-hair Beth had fallen on the floor again, so I just stuck it back on the wall, without saying anything about it, while Rooney watched, expressionless.

I asked about her Christmas, but the only thing she said was that she hated spending time in her home town.

Then she went to bed at seven o'clock.

So, yeah. Rooney was clearly not in a great place.

To be fair, I understood why. The play wasn't going to happen.

Her unspoken thing with Pip was not going to happen. The only thing she really had was — well, me, I guess.

Not a great consolation prize, in my opinion.

'We should go out,' I said to her at the end of our first week back at uni.

It was the early evening. She glanced at me over the top of her laptop screen, then continued what she was doing — watching YouTube videos. 'Why?'

I was seated at my desk. 'Because you like going out.'

'I'm not in the mood.'

Rooney had made it to two of our six lectures that week. And when she *had* come, she had simply stared ahead, not even bothering to get her iPad out of her bag to take notes.

It was like she just didn't care about anything any more.

'We could . . . we could just go to a pub, or something?' I suggested, sounding a little desperate. 'Just for one drink. We could get cocktails. Or *chips*. We could get chips.'

This prompted an eyebrow raise. 'Chips?'

'Chips.'

'I . . . would like some chips.'

'Exactly. We could go to the pub, get some chips, get some fresh air, then come back.'

She looked at me for a long moment.

And then she said, 'OK.'

The nearest pub was packed, obviously, because it was a Friday night in a university town. Thankfully we found a tiny beer-stained table in a back room and I left Rooney to guard it while I procured us a bowl of chips to share and a jug of strawberry daquiri with two paper straws.

We sat and ate our chips in silence. I actually felt very calm, considering the fact that I was technically on a 'night out'. All around us were students dressed up for the evening, ready to spend a couple of hours in a bar before heading out to clubs later. Rooney was wearing leggings and a hoodie, while I was wearing joggers and a woolly jumper. We probably stuck out quite a lot, but compared to the hell of Freshers' Week, I was extremely relaxed.

'So,' I said, after we'd sat in silence for over ten minutes. 'I've been sensing that you are not having a great time right now.'

Rooney stared at me blankly. 'I enjoyed the chips.'

'I meant generally.'

She took a long sip from the jug.

'No,' she said. 'Everything's shit.'

I waited for her to open up about it, but she didn't, and I realised I was going to have to pry.

'The play?' I said.

'Not just that.' Rooney groaned and leant over the table on one hand. 'Christmas was *hell*. I . . . I spent most of it meeting up with my school friends and, like . . . *he* was always there.'

It took me a moment to realise who she meant by 'he'.

'Your ex-boyfriend,' I said.

'He ruined so many things for me.' Rooney started stabbing the fruit in our cocktail jug with her straw. 'Every time I see his face I want to scream. And he doesn't even think he did anything *wrong*. Because of him, I – God. I could have been a much better person if I'd never met him. He's the reason I'm like this.'

I didn't know what to say to that. I wanted to ask her what happened, what he did, but I didn't want to force her to revisit bad stuff if she didn't want to.

There was a long silence after she spoke. By the time she spoke again, she had successfully skewered all of the fruit in the jug.

'I really like Pip,' she said in a very quiet voice.

I nodded slowly.

'You knew?' she asked.

I nodded again.

Rooney chuckled. She took another sip.

'How come you know me better than anyone?' she asked.

'We live together?' I said.

She just smiled. We both knew it was more than that.

'So . . . what are you gonna do?'

'Uh, nothing?' Rooney scoffed. 'She hates me.'

'I mean . . . yes, but she misinterpreted the situation.'

'We made out. There's not much to misinterpret.'

'She thinks that we're a thing. That's the reason she's angry.'

Rooney nodded. 'Because she thinks I'm taking you away from her.'

I almost groaned at the stupidity. 'No, because she likes you back.'

The look on her face was like I'd taken a glass and smashed it over her head.

'That's – that's just – you're just wrong about that,' she stammered, going a little red in the face.

'I'm just saying what I see.'

'I don't want to talk about Pip any more.'

We fell into silence again for a few moments. I knew Rooney was smart about this sort of thing – I'd watched her effortlessly navigate relationships of all kinds since the first day I met her. But, when it came to Pip, she had the emotional intelligence of a single grape.

'So you like girls?' I asked.

The scowl on her face dropped. 'Yeah. Probably. I dunno.'

'Three wildly different answers to that question.'

'I dunno, then. I guess . . . I mean, I questioned whether I liked girls a bit when I was younger. When I was thirteen, I had a crush on one of my friends. A girl. But like –' she made a shrugging gesture '– all girls do that, right? Like, that's common, having little crushes on your female friends.'

'No,' I said, trying not to laugh. 'Nope. Not all girls do that. Example A.' I gestured to myself.

'Well. OK, then.' She looked to one side. 'I guess I like girls, then.'

She said it with such nonchalance, it was as if she'd realised her sexuality and come out in the space of about ten seconds. But I knew her better than that. She'd probably been figuring it out for a while. Just like I had.

'Does that make me bi?' she asked. 'Or . . . pan? Or what?'

'Whatever you want. You can think about it.'

'Yeah. I guess I will.' She was staring at the table. 'You know, when we kissed . . . I think I did that because there's always been this part of me who's wanted to . . . um, you know. Be with girls. And you were just a safe option to try it out because I knew you wouldn't hate me forever. Which was a really *shit* thing to do, obviously. God, I'm so sorry.'

'It was a shit thing to do,' I agreed. 'But I can relate about accidentally using people because you're confused about your sexuality.'

We'd both fucked up in a lot of ways. And while our sexuality confusion wasn't an excuse, it was good that we both realised our mistakes.

Maybe that meant we'd make less of them going forward.

'I never had any gay or bi friends at school,' Rooney said. 'I didn't really know anyone openly gay, actually. Maybe I would have figured it out sooner if I had.'

'My best friend has been out since she was fifteen, and it still took me years to figure myself out,' I said.

'True. Wow. Shit's tricky.'

'Yup.'

She snorted. 'I'm at uni for three months and suddenly I'm not straight any more.'

'Mood,' I said.

'Love that for us, I guess?' she asked.

'Love that for us,' I agreed.

I got us a second cocktail jug – cosmopolitan – and nachos.

We were halfway through the jug when I told Rooney my plan.

'I'm going to get Jason and Pip to come back to the Shakespeare Soc,' I said.

Rooney crushed a particularly cheesy nacho into her mouth. 'Good luck with that.'

'You're welcome to help me.'

'What's your plan?'

'I mean . . . I haven't got quite that far yet. There will probably be a lot of apologising involved.'

'Terrible plan,' said Rooney, chomping down on another nacho.

'It's all I have.'

'And if it doesn't work?'

If it didn't work?

I didn't know what would happen then.

Maybe that would be it for me, Jason and Pip. Forever.

We finished the nachos – it didn't take long – and the cocktail jug, before heading towards the pub door, both of us feeling a little bit fuzzy. I was ready to sleep, honestly, but Rooney had fallen into a chatty mood. I was glad. Alcohol and chips definitely weren't the healthiest solution to her problems, but she seemed a little happier, at least. Job done.

That mood lasted the thirty seconds it took us to get to the door, and then it was gone. Because standing just outside, surrounded by friends, was Pip Quintana herself.

For a brief moment, she didn't see us. She'd had a hair trim, her curly fringe just meeting her eyebrows, and she was dressed up for a night out – stripy shirt, tight jeans, and a brown aviator jacket that made her look like one of the guys from *Top Gun*. With the bottle of cider in one hand, it was a look.

I could practically feel the wave of horror spill from Rooney as Pip turned round and saw us.

'Oh,' said Pip.

'Hi,' I said, having no idea what else to say.

Pip stared at me. Then her eyes flitted to Rooney – from her messy ponytail down to her mismatched bed socks.

'What, on a date, or something?' said Pip.

This immediately annoyed me. 'Clearly we're not on a date,' I snapped. 'I'm wearing joggers.'

'Whatever. I don't want to talk to you.'

She started to turn back round but froze as Rooney spoke.

'You can be mad at me, but don't be mad at Georgia. She's done nothing wrong.'

This was absolutely untrue – Pip had heavily implied that she liked Rooney, and then I'd kissed Rooney anyway. Not to mention everything I'd done to Jason. But I appreciated the support.

'Oh, *fuck off* with that taking-the-blame shit,' Pip spat. 'Since when are you suddenly trying to be a *good person*?' She swung round so she could speak right to Rooney's face. 'You're selfish, you're nasty, and you don't give a shit about other people's feelings. So don't come up to me and try to pretend to be a good person.'

Pip's friends had all started murmuring, wondering what was going on. Rooney stepped forward, teeth gritted and nostrils flaring like she was about to start shouting, but she didn't.

She just turned round and walked away down the street.

I stayed still, wondering whether Pip was going to say anything to me. She looked at me for a long moment, and I felt like my brain rushed through the entirety of our past seven years of friendship, every single time we'd sat next to each other in lessons, every sleepover and PE lesson and cinema trip, every time she'd cracked a joke or sent me a stupid meme, every single time I'd almost cried in front of her – didn't, *couldn't*, but *almost*.

'I just can't believe,' she said, through an exhale. 'I thought – I thought you cared about my feelings.'

Then she turned away too, rejoining a conversation with her new friends, and all of those memories smashed around me into tiny pieces.

LOVE RUINS EVERYTHING

Rooney spent the whole walk back to college tapping away on her phone. I didn't know who she was messaging, but when we got to our room, she quickly changed into a nicer outfit and I knew she was going out.

'Don't,' I said, just as she reached the door, and she stopped, and turned round to face me.

'You know what I've learnt?' she said. 'Love ruins everything.'

I didn't agree, but I didn't know how to argue with a statement like that. So she left and I just said nothing. And when I walked towards my bed, I found the photo of Mermaid-hair Beth on the floor again, partially crumpled like Rooney had ripped it off the wall.

YOU DESERVE JOY

I went to Pride Soc's January social at the Student Union alone. It was our third week of term, and I tried to lure Rooney into coming with me, but she'd been spending most nights out in town clubbing, returning around 3 a.m. with dirty shoes and messed-up hair. It was up to me to find Pip and there was a chance she'd be at a Pride Soc event.

If I could just *talk to her*, I figured, she would understand. If I could just get her to listen to me for long enough to explain, then everything would be OK again.

The instant regret I felt upon showing up to the social was almost enough to send me running right back to college. We were in the biggest room in the Student Union. At the head of the room was a projector screen displaying all of Pride Soc's upcoming events for the term. Music was playing, people were dressed casually, gathered in circles or sitting at tables to chat and catch up over some snacks.

It was a social. In which the point was to *socialise*. I was at a gathering with the specific purpose of socialising. On my own.

Why the absolute Jesus had I done this?

No. OK. I was brave. And there were cupcakes.

I went to get a cupcake. For emotional support.

Sunil, Jess and hopefully Pip were there, so there *were* people I knew. I searched around and quickly found Sunil and Jess in the centre of a group of people having a loud conversation, but didn't want to disturb them when they probably had lots of things to do and lots of people to talk to, so left them to it and continued on my search for Pip.

I walked around the room three whole times before concluding that she was not there.

Great.

I got my phone out and checked her Instagram, only to discover that she was posting in her story about a movie night with her friends at Castle. She wasn't even planning to attend this event.

Great.

'Georgia!'

A voice made me jump — Sunil's voice. I turned to find him striding towards me, wearing loose culottes made out of a jersey material that looked simultaneously very cool and very comfy.

'Sorry, did I make you jump?'

'N–no, no!' I stammered. 'It's fine!'

'I just wanted to see whether anything had happened with the Shakespeare Soc?' he asked, with an expression so hopeful that it actually hurt my heart. 'I know you lot had an argument, but . . . well, I was just hoping that, maybe . . . you'd sorted it out, or something.' He smiled meekly. 'I know it was just a bit of fun, but . . . I was really enjoying it.'

The look on my face was probably answer enough, but I told him anyway.

'No,' I said. 'It's . . . it's still all . . .' I made a gesture with my hands. 'It's not happening.'

'Oh.' Sunil nodded as if he'd expected it, but his obvious disappointment made me want to cry a bit. 'That's really sad.'

'I'm trying to make things right,' I said instantly. 'I'm actually here because I wanted to find Pip and see if she'd reconsider.'

Sunil glanced around the room. 'I don't think I've seen her.'

'No, I don't think she's here.'

There was a pause. I didn't know what to tell him. I didn't know how to make any of this better.

'Well . . . if there's anything *I* can do,' said Sunil, 'I'd – I'd like to help. It really was nice to just have something *fun* to do that wasn't stressful. Everything's a bit stressful for me at the moment, what with third year and Pride Soc and Lloyd is determined to be a perpetual annoyance in my life.' He glanced quickly towards where the ex-president, Lloyd, was sitting at a table with a group of people.

'What's he been doing?'

'He's just been trying to weasel himself back on to the society exec.' Sunil rolled his eyes. 'He thinks his opinions are *vital* to the society because my perspective is *too inclusive*. Can you believe that? *Too inclusive?* This is a society for queer and questioning students, for God's sake. You don't have to take a test to get in.'

'He's a dickhead,' I said.

'He is. Very much so.'

'Is there anything I can do to help?'

Sunil laughed. 'Oh, I don't know. Spill a drink on him? No, I'm joking. You're sweet, though.' He shook his head. 'Anyway – Shakespeare Soc. Is there any way I can help resolve the situation?' He looked almost desperate. 'I . . . It really was the most fun I've had in quite a while.'

'Well . . . unless there's a way you can get Jason and Pip to talk to me and Rooney again, I don't think there's really any way it's happening.'

'I could talk to Jason,' he said instantly. 'We chat on Whatsapp occasionally. I could get him to come to a rehearsal.'

I felt my heart race with hope. 'Really? Are you sure?'

'I really don't want this play to fall apart.' Sunil shook his head. 'I really didn't have any *fun* hobbies before. Orchestra is stressful and Pride Soc doesn't count as a hobby, and they're fun, but they're *work*. This play . . . it was just *joy*, you know?' He smiled, gazing down. 'When we started rehearsing, I . . . honestly, I was a little concerned it was a waste of time. Time I should be using studying and doing things for my other societies. But making friends with you all, acting out fun scenes, having pizza nights and everyone's silly messages in the group chat – it was just joy. Pure joy. And it took me so long to feel like I deserved that. But I do! And this is it!' He let out a bright, carefree laugh. 'And now I'm oversharing!'

I wondered whether he was a little tipsy, before remembering that Sunil didn't drink alcohol. He was just being earnest.

It made me want to be earnest too.

'You do deserve that,' I said. 'You . . . you helped me so much. I don't know where I would be or how I would feel if I hadn't met you. And . . . I feel like you've done that for a lot of people. And it's been hard sometimes. And people haven't always checked up on *you*.' I felt embarrassed by what I was saying, but I wanted him to know. 'And even if you'd done none of that . . . you're my friend. And you're one of the best people I know. So you do deserve that. You deserve joy.' I couldn't stop myself from smiling. 'And I like it when you overshare!'

He laughed again. 'Why are we being all emotional?'

'I don't know. You started it.'

We were interrupted by Jess and another of Sunil's vice-presidents, who had come to summon him to the front of the room. Sunil had to make a speech.

'I'll message him,' he said, as he walked away.

That was when I knew that I could not rest until I got the Shakespeare Soc back together. Not just because I wanted Pip and Jason to be my friends again – but for Sunil too. Because, despite his hectic life and all the important things he had going on, he'd found joy in our stupid little play. And months ago, at that Autumn Pride Soc formal, Sunil had been there for me in a moment of crisis, even while he was stressed out and dealing with assholes. Now it was my turn to be there for him.

I hung around for Sunil's speech. On the sidelines, with a cupcake and a full glass of wine.

Sunil got up on stage, tapped the microphone, and that was enough for the attendees to start applauding and whooping. He introduced himself, thanked everyone for coming, and then spent a few minutes going through all the upcoming events for the term. The film night this month would be *Moonlight*, the Pride Club Nights would be on Jan 27, Feb 16 and March 7, the Trans Book Club would take place at the Bill Bryson Library on Jan 19, the Big Queer Dungeons and Dragons group was looking for new members, and it was someone named Mickey's turn to host the Queer, Trans and Intersex People of Colour Society dinner on Feb 20 at their flat in Gilesgate.

And there were lots more. Hearing about all these things, and seeing all the people getting excited about them, made *me* feel excited in a weird way. Even though I wouldn't go to most of them. I almost felt like I belonged to something just by being here.

'I think that's covered all of this term's events,' Sunil concluded, 'so, just before I let you carry on eating and chatting, I just wanted to thank you all for what a great few months we had last term.'

There was another round of applause and cheers. Sunil grinned and clapped too.

'I'm glad you enjoyed it too! I was pretty nervous about being your president. I know I implemented some big changes, like turning the bar crawls into formals and introducing more daytime activities for the society, so I'm really thankful for your support.'

He gazed out into the distance suddenly, like he was thinking about something. 'When I was a fresher, I didn't feel like I belonged at Durham. I'd arrived hoping to finally meet some people like me, but instead I found myself still surrounded by a lot of cis, straight white people. I'd spent a lot of my teenage life very alone. And by that point, I'd got *used* to it. I spent a long time thinking this was the way things had to be – I had to survive on my own, I had to do everything on my own, because nobody would ever help me. I spent much of that first year in a really dark place . . . until I met my best friend, Jess.' Sunil pointed towards Jess, who quickly put a hand in front of her face in a half-hearted attempt to hide. There were a few more cheers.

'Jess won me over instantly with her numerous items of clothing that have dogs on them.' The crowd chuckled, and Jess shook her head, her smile just peeking out from behind her hand. 'She was the funniest and bubbliest person I'd ever met. She encouraged me to join Pride Soc. She brought me to one of the original QTIPOC dinners. And we had so many discussions about how the society could be better. And then she encouraged me to try for president, with her at my side.' He grinned. 'I thought *she* should be president, but she's told me a billion times how much she hates public speaking.'

Sunil smiled down at Jess, and Jess smiled back at him, and there was such genuine love in that gaze.

I felt dazzled by it.

'Pride Soc isn't just about doing queer stuff,' Sunil continued, and that got him some laughs. 'It's not even about finding potential hook-ups.' Someone in the crowd shouted their friend's name, which earned more laughs. Sunil laughed with them.

'No. It's about the relationships we form here. Friendship, love and support while we're all trying to survive and thrive in a world that often doesn't feel like it was made for us. Whether you're gay, lesbian, bi, pan, trans, intersex, non-binary, asexual, aromantic, queer, or however you identify – most of us here felt a sense of unbelonging while we were growing up.' Sunil looked one more time at Jess, then back out at the crowd. 'But we're all here for each other. And it's those relationships that make Pride Soc so important and so special. It's those relationships that, despite all of the hardships in our lives, will continue to bring us joy every single day.' He raised his glass. 'And we all deserve joy.'

It was kind of cheesy, maybe. But it was also one of the loveliest speeches I'd heard in my whole life.

Everyone raised their drinks then cheered for Sunil as he stepped down and Jess buried him in a hug.

That was it. That was what everything was about.

The love in that hug. The knowing look between them.

They had their own love story.

That was what I wanted. That was what I'd *had*, once, maybe.

I used to dream of a spellbinding, endless, forever romance. A beautiful story of meeting a person who could change your whole world.

But now, I realised, friendship could be that too.

On my way out of the room, I found myself nearing Lloyd's table. He was sitting with a couple of other guys, drinking their way through a bottle of wine with sour expressions on their faces.

'It's so pathetic the way he feels like he needs to bring up asexuality literally every time he does one of these,' Lloyd was saying. 'Next thing you know, we'll be getting any old cis-hets joining who think they're mildly oppressed.'

The way he said it sent a shot of cold hatred into the pit of my stomach.

But I was feeling brave, I guess.

As I walked past, I let my now half-full cup of wine gracefully tip in my hand and over the back of Lloyd's neck.

'WH–what the FUCK!?'

By the time he'd swung himself round to see who had just poured wine over him, I was already halfway to the door with a massive smile on my face.

JASON

Sunil Jha
JASON IS IN.

Georgia Warr
SERIOUSLY

Sunil Jha
YEP. He agreed to come along as a personal favour to me.
But he said he's still not sure about rejoining ☹

Georgia Warr
okay
so
i have an idea about how to win him back

'No,' said Rooney, once I explained my idea to her. She was
on her bed. I was watering Roderick, who was not half as
voluminous as he once had been due to the dead bits I'd chopped,
but wasn't *quite* dead, as I'd previously thought.

'It'll *work*.'

'It's stupid.'

'It's not. He has a good sense of humour.'

Rooney was sprawled in her going-out clothes eating breadsticks straight from the packet, something that had recently become her pre-night-out routine.

'The Shakespeare Soc is finished,' she said, and I knew she believed it. She wouldn't be going out all the time if she hadn't given up on it completely.

'Just trust me. I can win him back.'

Rooney gave me a long look. She crunched a breadstick loudly.

'OK,' she said. 'But I get to be Daphne.'

I skipped my lectures the next day to go on a costume hunt. It took most of the morning and a solid chunk of the afternoon. Durham had one costume shop down a tiny alleyway, and they didn't have exactly what I was looking for, so I ended up trawling the clothes and charity shops for whatever I could find to create makeshift costumes. Rooney even joined me after lunch, sunglasses on to hide the bags under her eyes. She'd been sleeping in till midday most days lately.

I sacrificed a lot of my allowance for this month to get everything, meaning I'd have to live off cafeteria food for the next couple of weeks, but it was a worthy sacrifice, because once Rooney and I arrived early at our rehearsal room and changed into our costumes, I knew that this was the best idea I had ever had in my life.

'Oh, this is the cosplay of my *dreams*,' said Sunil as I handed him a bright orange jumper, a red skirt and some orange socks.

We finished changing, and then we waited.

And I started to think this may have been a terrible idea.

Maybe he wouldn't find it funny. Maybe he'd take one look at me and then leave.

There was only one way to find out.

'What is going on?' Jason asked, stepping into the room and frowning at our odd get-ups. I'd missed him. *God,* I'd missed him and his fluffy jacket and soft smile. 'Why are you – what are you do –'

His eyes widened suddenly. He clocked Sunil's skirt. My oversized green T-shirt and brown trousers. Rooney's little green scarf and purple tights.

'Oh my God,' he said.

He dropped his bag on the floor.

'Oh. My. *God,*' he said.

'Surprise!' I cried, holding out my hands and the dog plushie I'd found at one of the high street charity shops. Rooney flipped her hair back and posed as Daphne, while Sunil shouted 'JINKIES!' and pushed up his Velma glasses.

Jason put his hand on his heart. For a second, I was terrified that he was annoyed or upset. But then he smiled. A big, toothy smile. 'Why the actual HELL – literally what the FUCK. WHY THE FUCK ARE YOU DRESSED AS THE SCOOBY GANG?'

'There's a fancy-dress club night tonight,' I said, grinning. 'I . . . I thought this would be fun.'

Jason approached us. And then he just started laughing. Slowly, at first, but then louder. He took the dog plushie from my hand and looked at it, and then it was almost hysterics.

'Scooby's –' he gasped through his laughs – 'Scooby's supposed – to be – a Great Dane – and this – is a pug!'

I started laughing with him. 'It was the best I could do! Don't laugh!'

'You've cast Scooby –' he literally started wheezing – 'you've cast Scooby as a *pug* – what is this – absolute defamation?'

He doubled over, and then we were just cry-laughing while he was holding the tiny pug plushie.

It took a few minutes for us to calm down, Jason wiping the tears from his face. In that time, Rooney had taken the final items of clothing we'd bought today out of the carrier bag and held them up to Jason – a white jumper, orange scarf and blonde wig.

He looked at them.

'My time,' he said, 'has come.'

'So you really like Scooby-Doo?' Sunil asked Jason later that night, once we'd made it to the club. It was packed full of students dressed as everything from superheroes to giant whisks.

'More than most things in this world,' said Jason.

We danced. We danced *a lot*. And for the first time since getting to this university, I actually enjoyed it. *All* of it. The loud music, the sticky floor, the drinks served in tiny plastic cups. The old classics this club was playing, the drunk girls we befriended in the bathroom because of the pug plushie I'd been carrying around, Rooney slinging her arm over my shoulder, tipsy, swaying along to 'Happy Together' by The Turtles and 'Walking on Sunshine' by Katrina and the Waves, Sunil grabbing Jason by the hands and forcing him to do the macarena even though he thought it was cringey.

Everything was better because of my friends. If they hadn't been there, I would have hated it. I would have wanted to go home.

I kept an eye on Rooney. There was one point in the night where she started drunkenly chatting and laughing with another group of people, students I'd never even seen before, and I wondered whether she was going to do her thing and abandon us.

But when I grabbed her hand, she turned away from them and looked at me, her face flashing different colours under the lights, and she seemed to remember why she was here. She remembered that she had us.

And I pulled her back to where Jason and Sunil were jumping up and down to 'Jump Around' by House of Pain, and we started jumping, and she smiled right in my face.

I knew she was still hurting. I was too. But for a moment she seemed happy. So, so happy.

All in all, I had one of the best nights of my university life.

'I'm screaming,' said Rooney, with a mouthful of pizza as we walked through Durham back to our colleges. 'This is the best thing I have ever had in my mouth.'

'That's what she said,' said Jason, which set Rooney off on a laughing fit that quickly turned into a coughing fit.

I bit into my own pizza slice, agreeing with Rooney. Something about a hot takeaway pizza in the middle of the night in the freezing northern winter was, to be frank, heavenly.

Jason and I walked side by side, Rooney and Sunil walking a little way ahead, engaged in discussion about the best pizza place in Durham.

I hadn't yet had a chance to talk to Jason one-on-one. Until now. I didn't really know how to start. How to apologise for everything. How to ask if there was a chance we could be friends again.

Fortunately, he spoke first.

'I wish Pip was here,' he said. 'She would have loved tonight.'

It wasn't what I expected him to say, but as soon as he did, I realised how right he was.

Jason snorted. 'I have such a clear vision of her dressed up as Scooby-Doo, doing the Scooby-Doo voice.'

'Oh my God. Yes.'

'I can literally *hear it*. And it's terrible.'

'She would be terrible.'

We both laughed. Like everything was back to normal.

But it wasn't.

Not until we talked about it.

'I'm . . .' I started to say, but stopped myself, because it didn't feel like enough. Nothing I could say felt like enough.

Jason turned to face me. We'd just reached one of the many bridges that stretched over the River Wear.

'Are you cold?' he asked. 'You can borrow my jacket.'

He started to take it off. God. I didn't deserve him.

'No, no. I was gonna say . . . I was gonna say I'm sorry,' I said.

Jason pulled his jacket back on. 'Oh.'

'I'm so sorry for . . . everything. I'm just so sorry for everything.' I stopped walking because I could feel myself welling up and I didn't want to cry in front of him. I really, really didn't want to cry. 'I love you so much and . . . trying to date you was the worst thing I've ever done.'

Jason stopped walking.

'It was pretty bad, wasn't it?' he said, after a pause. 'We were very shit at it.'

This made me laugh, despite everything.

'You didn't deserve to be treated like that,' I continued, trying to get it all out now while I had the chance.

Jason nodded. 'That is true.'

'And I need you to know that it was nothing to do with you – you're – you're perfect.'

Jason smiled, and attempted to flip the hair of his wig. 'Also true.'

'I'm just – I'm just different. I just can't feel that stuff.'

'Yeah.' Jason nodded again. 'You're . . . asexual? Or aromantic?'

I froze. 'What – wait, you know what those are?'

'Well . . . I'd heard of them. And when you messaged me I made the connection and then I went and looked them up and, yeah. That sounded like what you were describing.' He looked alarmed suddenly. 'Am I wrong? I'm so sorry if I got it wrong . . .'

'No, no – you're right.' I let out a breath. 'I-I am. Uh, both of them. Aro-ace.'

'Aro-ace,' Jason repeated. 'Well.'

'Yeah.'

He slotted his hand into mine and we resumed walking.

'You didn't reply to my message, though,' I pointed out.

'Well . . . I was really upset.' He stared at the ground. 'And . . . I couldn't really talk to you while I was . . . still in love with you.'

There was a long pause. I had no idea what to say to that.

Eventually, he said, 'D'you know when I first realised I liked you?'

I looked up at him, not sure where this was going. 'When?'

'When you clapped back at Mr Cole that time during *Les Mis* rehearsals.'

Clapped back? I couldn't remember a time when I'd *clapped back* at a teacher, let alone Mr Cole, the authoritarian director of our school plays in the sixth form.

'I don't remember that,' I said.

'Really?' Jason chuckled. 'He was shouting at me because I'd told him I had to miss a rehearsal that afternoon to go to a dentist appointment. And you were there, and he turned to you and said, *Georgia, you agree with me, right? Jason is Javert, he's a key role and he should have organised his appointment for another time.* And you know what Mr Cole was like – anyone who disagreed with him was officially his enemy. But you just looked him in the eyes and were like, *Well, it's too late to change it now, so there's no point shouting at Jason about it.* And that just shut him right up and he stormed away to his office.'

I *did* remember this incident. But I didn't think I'd been particularly forceful or bold. I'd just tried to stand up for my best friend who was clearly in the right.

'It just made me think . . . Georgia might be kind of quiet and shy, but she'd stand up to a scary teacher if one of her friends was being shouted at. *That's* the sort of person you are. It made me feel certain that you truly cared about me. And I guess that's when I started . . . you know, falling for you.'

'I still care about you that much,' I said immediately, even though I didn't think what I'd said to Mr Cole was particularly special or brave. I still wanted Jason to know that I cared about him exactly as much as he'd thought in that moment.

'I know,' he said with a smile. 'That's partly why I needed some space away from you. To get over you.'

'Did you get over me?'

'I . . . I'm trying. It's going to take time. But I'm trying.'

I subconsciously withdrew my hand from his. Was I making this worse for him just by being around him?

He noticed this happen and there was a pause before he spoke again.

'When you told me why you dated me, I . . . I mean, obviously I was crushed,' he continued. 'I felt like . . . you just didn't care about me at all. But after I got your message, I think I started to realise that you've just . . . you've been so confused about stuff. You really thought we could be together, because you *do* love me. Not in a romantic way, but just as strongly. You're still that person who stuck up for me to Mr Cole. You're still my best friend.' He glanced at me. 'You and me not being a couple doesn't change that at all. I haven't lost anything, just because we're not dating.'

I listened, stumped, taking a moment to figure out what he meant.

'You're OK with – with just being friends?' I asked.

He smiled and took my hand again. '"Just friends" makes it sound like being friends is worse. I think this is better, personally, considering how terrible that kiss was.'

I squeezed his hand. 'I agree.'

We reached the end of the bridge, crossing back into a cobbled alleyway. Jason's face ducked in and out of darkness as we passed the streetlamps. When his face came into the light again, he was smiling, and I thought, possibly, I was forgiven.

SORRY

Sunil peered at Jason's framed photo of Sarah Michelle Gellar and Freddie Prinze Jr for a solid few seconds before tapping it and asking, 'Would somebody like to explain this, please?'

'It's a really long story,' said Jason, who was sitting on his bed.

'It's a good story, though,' I added. Me and Rooney were on the floor with Jason's pillows as back rests, though Rooney was having a small power nap.

'Well, now I'm even more intrigued.'

Jason sighed. 'How about I explain once we've actually decided what we're doing about Pip?'

It was a week after our Scooby-Doo outing. With Jason back in the Shakespeare Soc, things were looking up, and we'd actually been able to have a proper rehearsal.

But we couldn't do the show without Pip.

And it wasn't just about that, anyway. The society was important to all of us, but our friendship with Pip was more important. *That* was what needed saving.

I just didn't know exactly how I was going to do that.

'We're talking about Pip?' said Rooney, who had apparently just woken up.

Rooney was still going out most nights and returning in the early hours. I didn't know whether I *could* stop her, or if I even *should*. She wasn't doing anything wrong, technically.

I just got the sense that she only did it to numb everything else.

'I thought we were rehearsing,' I said.

'There's no point carrying on with rehearsals if Pip isn't coming back,' Jason stated, and there was silence as we all realised that he was right.

Sunil perched on Jason's desk and folded his arms. 'So . . . do you have any suggestions?'

'Well, I've been talking to her, and –'

'Wait, you've been *talking to her*?' Rooney said, sitting upright.

'It's not *me* she has a feud with. We're still friends. We're at the same college.'

'You can get her to come back, then. She'll listen to you.'

'I've tried.' Jason shook his head. 'She is *angry*. And Pip doesn't forgive easily.' He looked at me and Rooney. 'I mean . . . I sort of understand why. What you both did was incredibly idiotic.'

Jason *knew about the kiss*. Of course he did – Pip probably told him everything. I felt myself go red out of sheer embarrassment.

'What did you do?' Sunil asked curiously.

'They kissed and Pip saw,' said Jason.

'*Oh.*'

'Um . . . can we explain our side of the story about that?' Rooney asked.

'I mean my guess is that you were drunk and it was Rooney's idea,' said Jason. 'And you both instantly regretted it.'

'OK, that's . . . that's fairly accurate.'

'So what should we do?' asked Sunil.

'I think Georgia and Rooney are just going to have to keep trying to talk to her until she's willing to listen. Maybe one at a time, so she doesn't feel like you're ganging up on her.'

'When?' I said. 'How?'

'Now,' said Jason. 'I think one of you should go to her room and just apologise to her face. You haven't actually tried apologising in person yet, have you?'

Neither Rooney nor I said anything.

'That's what I thought.'

An idea flashed into my mind. 'Pip's jacket. One of us should go and give her back her jacket.'

Rooney snapped her head round to me. 'Yes. That's been in our room for, like, *months.*'

'Want me to run back and get it?'

But Rooney was already getting to her feet.

Once she returned from St John's with Pip's denim jacket in hand, Rooney demanded that she be the one to go to talk to Pip. She didn't even let me argue with her – she just swung the door open, stepped outside, and said, 'Which way is her room?'

Rooney still blamed herself for the whole thing, it seemed. Even though Pip had many more reasons to be angry with me.

I went with her part of the way, but stopped round a corner a few metres away so I could listen to the conversation. It was evening, and dinner had finished, so hopefully Pip would be there.

Rooney knocked on Pip's door. I wondered what she was going to say.

Was this a terrible idea?

Too late.

The door opened.

'Hi,' said Rooney. And then there was a noticeable silence.

'What are you doing here?' asked Pip. Her voice was low. It was strange hearing Pip so genuinely sad. I hadn't heard her like that very much before . . . all of this.

'I . . .'

I expected Rooney to launch into a big speech of some sort. To deliver a heartfelt and forceful apology.

Instead, she said, 'Um – your . . . jacket.'

There was another silence.

'OK,' said Pip. 'Thanks.'

The door creaked, and I peeked round the corner just as Rooney swung out her arm to keep the door open.

'Wait!' she cried.

'What? What do you want?' I couldn't see Pip – she was too far inside her room – but I could tell she was getting annoyed.

Rooney was panicking. 'I . . . Why is your room so messy?'

This was definitely the wrong thing to say.

'You literally cannot stop yourself from making snidey comments about me, can you?' Pip snapped.

'Wait, sorry, that's not what I –'

'Can't you just leave me alone? I feel like you're haunting me, or something.'

Rooney swallowed. 'I just wanted to say sorry. Like . . . properly. To your face.'

'Oh.'

'Georgia's here too.'

I felt my stomach drop as Rooney pointed towards where I was hiding round the corner. This hadn't been the plan.

For someone who supposedly knew a lot about romance, Rooney sure as hell didn't know how to pull off a grand gesture

Pip stepped a little way out of her room to look, her expression dark.

'I don't want to talk to either of you,' she said, her voice cracking, and she turned to go back inside.

'Hang on!' I was surprised by my own voice leaving my mouth, and by the way I scrambled towards Pip's room.

And there she was. Her hair was fluffy and unstyled, and she was wearing a hoodie and jersey shorts. Her bedroom was extremely messy, even for her. She was clearly upset.

But she wasn't as angry as the other week outside the pub.

Was that progress?

'We thought it might be better if just one of us spoke to you,' I blurted. 'But – um, yeah. We're both here. And we're both really sorry for . . . you know. Everything that happened.'

Pip said nothing. She waited for us to continue, but I didn't know what else to say.

'That's it, then?' she said, eventually. 'I'm supposed to just . . . forgive you?'

'We just want you to come back to the Shakespeare Soc,' said Rooney, but this was, again, *definitely* the wrong thing to say.

Pip laughed. 'Oh my God! I should have guessed. This isn't even about me – you just need your fifth member for the fucking *Shakespeare Society*. Oh my *God.*'

'No, that's not what –'

'I have no idea why you care so much about your stupid play but why the *fuck* would I put myself through that with someone who made me think there was the *tiniest* chance she liked me back, and then decided to get off with my best friend?' Pip shook her head. 'I was right all along. You just hate me.'

I waited for Rooney's inevitable comeback, but it didn't arrive.

She blinked several times. I turned to look at her properly, and realised she was about to cry.

'I *did* like –' she began to say, but stopped, and her face just *crumpled.* Tears started falling from her eyes, and before she could say anything else, she turned abruptly and walked away.

Pip and I watched her disappear round the corner.

'Shit, I . . . I didn't mean to make her cry,' Pip mumbled.

I had no idea what to say now. I almost felt like crying too.

'We really are sorry,' I said. 'We − *I'm* sorry. I meant everything I said in my message. It was just a weird, drunk mistake. Neither of us like each other like that. And I've apologised to Jason too.'

'You talked to Jason?'

'Yeah, we . . . we talked about everything. I think we're OK now.'

Pip said nothing to that. She just looked down at the floor.

'I really don't care if you don't want to come back to the Shakespeare Soc,' I said. 'I just . . . I just want us to be friends again.'

'I need some time to think.' Pip went to shut the door, but before she did, she said, 'Thanks for bringing my jacket back.'

BETH

Rooney had stopped crying by the time I returned to our room.

Instead, she was changing into going-out clothes.

'You're going out?' I asked, shutting the door behind me and flicking the light switch. She hadn't even bothered to turn the light on.

'Yeah,' she said, pulling a bardot top over her head.

'Why?'

'Because if I stay here,' she snapped, 'then I'll have to sit and think about everything all night, and I can't do that. I can't just sit and be with my thoughts.'

'Who do you even go out with?'

'Just people in college. I have *other friends*.'

Friends who don't ever stop by for tea, or come over for movie nights and pizza, or check in with you when you're feeling rough?

That's what I wanted to say.

'OK,' I said.

★

Her normal bullshit, was what I'd been telling myself. That was how I justified it all, really. The skipped lectures. The sleeping in until the afternoon. The clubbing every night.

I didn't take any of it seriously, *really* seriously, until that night, when I woke up at 5 a.m. to a message reading:

Rooney Bach
can your let me in im outside coellge
Forgotmy key

It had been sent at 3.24 a.m. The college doors were locked between 2 a.m. and 6 a.m. – you needed your key to get back into the main building.

I often woke up in the early hours and checked my phone, before very quickly going back to sleep. But this panicked me so much that I leapt out of bed and immediately called Rooney.

She didn't pick up.

I put on my glasses, dressing gown and slippers, grabbed my keys, and ran out of the door, my mind suddenly filled with visions of her dead in a ditch, choked on her own vomit, or drowned in the river. She had to be fine. She did stupid stuff all the time, but she was *always* fine.

The main reception hall was dark and empty as I thundered through it, unlocked the door, and ran out into the dark.

The street was empty, apart from a figure sitting on a low brick wall a little way ahead, huddled into herself.

Rooney.

Alive. Thank God. Thank *God*.

I ran up to her. She was just wearing the bardot top and a skirt, despite the fact that it had to be like five degrees outside.

'What – what are you *doing*?' I said, feeling inexplicably angry at her.

She looked up at me. 'Oh. Good. Finally.'

'You . . . Have you just been *sitting here* all night?'

She stood up, attempting to be nonchalant, but I could see the way she was clutching her arms, trying to control her violent shivering. 'Only a couple of hours.'

I wrenched off my dressing gown and gave it to her. She wrapped it round herself without question.

'Couldn't you have called someone else – one of your other friends?' I asked. 'Surely *someone* was awake.'

She shook her head. 'No one was awake. Well, a couple of people read my messages, but . . . they must have ignored them. And then my phone died.'

I was so alarmed by this that I couldn't even think of anything else to say. I just let us back into college and we walked to our room in silence.

'You can't just . . . You need to be more careful,' I said as we entered the room. 'It's not safe to be out there on your own at that time.'

She started changing into her pyjamas. She looked exhausted.

'Why do you care?' she whispered. Not in a mean way. A genuine question. Like she honestly couldn't fathom what the answer was. 'Why do you care about me?'

'You're my friend,' I said, standing by the door.

She didn't say anything else. She just got into bed and closed her eyes.

I picked up her discarded clothes from the floor and put them in her wash basket, but then realised her phone was in her skirt pocket, so I fished it out and put it on charge for her. I even poured a little bit of water into Roderick's planter. He really was looking a little perkier.

And then I got into bed and wondered why I cared about Rooney Bach, queen of self-sabotage, the love expert who wasn't. Because I did. I really, really did care about her, despite how different we were and how we probably wouldn't have ever spoken if we hadn't been roomed together and all the times she'd said the wrong thing or made a mess of a situation.

I cared about her because I liked her. I liked her passion for the Shakespeare Society. I liked the way she'd get excited about things that didn't matter very much, like rugs or plays or college marriage. I liked the way she'd always genuinely wanted to help me, even though she'd never actually known the right thing to say or do and had given much worse advice than I'd initially realised.

I thought that she was a good person, and I liked having her in my life.

And I was starting to realise that it was unfathomable to Rooney that someone could feel that way about her.

I was woken up again two hours later by the sound of Rooney's phone ringing.

We both ignored it.

When it rang the second time, I sat up and put my glasses on.

'Your phone's ringing,' I said, my voice croaky from sleep.

Rooney had not moved. She just made a grunting noise.

I rolled out of bed and stumbled over to where Rooney's phone was on charge on her bedside table, and looked at the caller ID.

It read: *Beth*

I stared at it. I felt like I should know who this was, somehow, like I'd seen the name before somewhere.

And then I realised that it was the name of a person half a metre in front of me, in the only photo Rooney had put up on the wall next to her bed. A photo that was a little crumpled from all the times it had fallen off the wall and been trodden on.

The photo of thirteen-year-old Rooney and her best friend from school. Mermaid-hair Beth.

I swiped to answer the call.

'Hello?'

'*Hi?*' said the voice. Beth. Was this Beth? The girl in the photo with dyed red hair and freckles?

Did she and Rooney still talk to each other? Maybe Rooney *did* have other friends who checked in with her, I just didn't know about them.

And then Beth said, '*I got some missed calls from this number last night and I just wanted to check who this was, in case it's an emergency or something.*'

I felt my mouth drop open.

She didn't even have Rooney's number saved.

'Um –' I found myself talking. 'Sorry – this actually isn't my phone. This is Rooney Bach's phone.'

There was a pause.

'*Rooney Bach?*'

'Uh, yeah. I'm her uni roommate. She . . . she was pretty drunk last night, so . . . maybe she drunk-called you?'

'*Yeah, I guess . . . sorry, this is really weird. I haven't seen her for . . . God, it must be like five years. I don't know why she even still has my number saved.*'

I stared at the photo on the wall.

'You don't still talk to her?' I asked.

'*Uh, no. She moved schools when we were in Year Nine and we didn't really keep in contact after that.*'

Rooney had lied. Or . . . had she? She'd told me Beth was her friend. Maybe that had been true when she was younger. But it wasn't now.

Why did Rooney have a photo of a friend she hadn't spoken to for five years on her wall?

'*How is she?*' asked Beth.

'She's . . .' I blinked. 'She's OK. She's good.'

'*That's good. Is she still into theatre?*'

I didn't know why, but I felt like I was going to cry.

'Yeah,' I said. 'Yeah, she is. She loves theatre.'

'*Aw. That's nice. She always said she wanted to be a director, or something.*'

'You should – you should message her sometime,' I said, trying to swallow the lump in my throat. 'I think she'd like a catch-up.'

'*Yeah,*' said Beth. '*Yeah, maybe I will. That'd be nice.*'

I hoped she would. I desperately hoped she would.

'*Well . . . I'll hang up then, as this isn't an emergency or anything. I'm glad Rooney's doing well.*'

'OK,' I said, and Beth ended the call.

I put down Rooney's phone. Rooney herself hadn't moved. All I could see of her was the back of her head, her ponytail falling out, and the rest of her covered up by her floral duvet.

EMERGENCY MEETING

What I'd thought was a mask was actually a wall. Rooney had a solid brick wall round some part of her that nobody was allowed to know.

She'd spent the year knocking my own wall into pieces. I deserved a chance at doing the same to her.

So I called an emergency meeting of the Shakespeare Society.

We were going to get Pip back. And Rooney was going to help, whether she liked it or not.

It was a Saturday, and we agreed to go out for mid-morning coffee. Jason had an early rowing practice, Sunil had an orchestra rehearsal, and Rooney would not get out of bed until I slapped her on the back of the head with her aqua rug, but somehow we all made it to Vennels Café by eleven o'clock. I finally knew what Vennels was.

'That . . . is a *lot*,' said Sunil, once I explained my plan. 'I could get Jess involved. She plays the viola.'

'And I'll ask my rowing captain if we can borrow some stuff,' said Jason, tapping his fingers over his mouth. 'I'm sure he'd say yes.'

'I . . . I don't want to bother anyone,' I said. The thought of other people having to help felt kind of embarrassing.

'No, Jess will actually be *upset* if I don't ask her to take part,' said Sunil. 'She's obsessed with stuff like this.'

'What about Rooney?' said Jason to Rooney. 'What do you think?'

Rooney was slumped back in her chair and clearly did not want to be awake.

'It's good,' she said, trying to sound enthusiastic but failing dismally.

Once Jason and Sunil headed off to their own things – Jason had a study group and Sunil was meeting some friends for lunch – Rooney and I were left alone. I thought we might as well stay here and have some food, since she hadn't had any breakfast and we didn't have anything else to do.

We ordered pancakes – I went for savoury; she went for sweet – and chatted for a while about mundane topics like our coursework and the upcoming reading week.

Eventually, though, she cut to the chase.

'I know why you're doing this,' she said, her gaze level with mine.

'Doing what?'

'Making me go out for breakfast and help you with the Pip thing.'

'Why's that, then?'

'You feel sorry for me.'

I put my knife and fork neatly on to my empty plate. 'No, actually. Wrong. Utterly wrong.'

I could tell she didn't believe me.

And then she said, 'You spoke to Beth on the phone.'

I froze. 'You were awake?'

'Why'd you answer the phone?'

Why had I answered the phone? I knew most people would have just let it go to voicemail.

'I guess . . . I hoped she was calling to check up on you,' I said, and I didn't know how much sense that made.

I had just wanted Rooney to know that someone had called. That someone cared. But Beth wasn't that person. She didn't care any more.

'Was she?' asked Rooney in a small voice. 'Calling to check up on me?'

I could have lied.

But I didn't lie to Rooney.

'No,' I said. 'She didn't have your number saved.'

Rooney's face dropped. She looked down, to one side. She took a long gulp of apple juice.

'Who is she?' I asked.

'Why do you have to do that?' Rooney leant on to one hand, covering her eyes. 'I don't want to talk about it.'

'That's fine. I just want you to know that you can.'

I ordered another drink. She sat in silence with her arms folded, seemingly trying to cram herself further into the corner of the room.

It took two weeks of intense planning.

In the first week, we coordinated the time and place, and Jason went on a mission to sweet-talk the captain of his rowing team into letting us use what we needed. After we sent him to barter with a four-pack of beers, he returned with a smile on his face and a spare key to the boathouse, and we celebrated with pizza in Jason's bedroom.

In the second week, Sunil brought Jess along to a rehearsal. Although I didn't feel I knew her very well, having only spoken to her a couple of times, she immediately demanded to know where I'd got my jumper – it was beige with multicoloured Fair Isle patterns – and we proceeded to bond at length over our shared love for patterned woolly jumpers.

Jess was completely in favour of taking part in our scheme, despite the number of times I told her it was OK if she was too busy. And when she took out her viola and Sunil took out his cello, I realised why she was so keen – they clearly *loved* playing music together. They started running through the piece, chatting about it as they reached difficult parts and making little notes on the sheet music.

Both of them seemed different here, as opposed to at Pride Soc, where they were constantly running around, organising everything, being *the president* and *the vice-president*. Here, they could just be Sunil and Jess, two best friends who liked making music.

'Don't worry, we'll get it perfect before Sunday,' Sunil promised, with a big smile on his face.

'Thank you,' I said, but it really didn't feel like enough thanks for what they were doing.

Rooney begrudgingly agreed to take control of a tambourine. The first couple of times we ran through it together, she just stood there, tapping it against her hand, looking down at the ground.

But as we got closer to Sunday, she started to get a little more into it. She began bobbing on the spot as we ran through the piece. Sometimes she even sang along, just a little bit, like she was sure nobody could hear her.

By the end, I almost thought she was having fun.

We all were, really.

We were all having so much fun.

And *this was going to work.*

THE NIGHT BEFORE

The night before that Sunday, Rooney did not go out.

I wasn't sure why. Maybe she just didn't feel like it. But for whatever reason, she looked up from her laptop screen as I returned from the shower and asked, 'Wanna watch YouTube videos and eat biscuits?'

I squeezed into her bed, which was, like last time, pretty uncomfortable, so I said without thinking, 'What if we moved our beds together?' and Rooney said, 'Why not?' So, we did. We both pulled our beds into the centre of the room, squishing them together to make one giant double bed, and started watching TikTok compilations while making our way through my packet of chocolate digestives.

'I'm really nervous about tomorrow,' I confessed halfway through the third video.

'Same,' said Rooney, crunching a biscuit in her mouth.

'Do you think she'll like it?'

'I honestly have no idea.'

We didn't say anything else for a little while, and we soon finished the biscuits too. When the fourth video ended, Rooney didn't go to find a new one, so we just lay there silently in the light of the screen.

After some time – maybe a few minutes, maybe longer – she asked, 'D'you think it's weird I've still got that picture of Beth?'

I rolled my head to face her.

'No,' I said. That was the truth.

'I do,' she said. She sounded so tired.

'If she couldn't be bothered to keep in contact when you moved schools then she doesn't deserve you,' I said. I was angry at Beth, honestly. I was angry at her for making Rooney care so much about someone who didn't care about her.

Rooney huffed a tiny laugh into her pillow. 'It wasn't her. It was me.'

'What d'you mean?'

'When I was in Year Nine . . . that's when I met my ex-boyfriend.'

'The . . . horrible one?'

'Ha, yeah. There was only one boyfriend. And he was horrible. Not that I realised that at the time.'

I didn't say anything. I waited and let her tell the story.

'He went to a different school. We would text each other all day every day. I was instantly obsessed with him. And I . . . I soon decided that the best thing would be for me to move to his school.' She snorted. 'I just screamed at my parents until they let me move schools. I made up lies that I was being bullied, that I had no friends. As you can imagine, I was the actual worst child alive.'

'And Beth was from your old school?'

There was a pause, before Rooney said, 'Beth was the only real friend I ever had.'

'But . . . you stopped speaking to her . . .'

'I know,' said Rooney, rubbing one eye with her fist. 'I just . . .

I thought having a boyfriend was the *best thing ever*. I thought I was in love. So I immediately gave everything up. Beth. Everyone else I knew at school. My whole life was at that school. I had . . . hobbies. Me and Beth did all the school shows. I went to the drama club. I'd always pester the head of drama to let us do a Shakespeare and she'd always give in. I was . . . happy. I was actually happy.' Her voice quietened. 'And I gave all of it up to be with my boyfriend.'

And Beth had forgotten her. Rooney had remembered, Rooney had never stopped thinking about what her life would have been like if she hadn't chosen 'love' over everything else. She'd never stopped imagining what it would have been like to grow up with someone who really, genuinely cared about her.

'My life was just horrible throughout the three years we dated. Well, I say *dated*, if you're not counting the ten billion times he broke up with me, then decided we should get back together. And all the times he cheated on me.' Rooney's eyes were damp. 'He decided everything. He decided when we would go to parties. He decided we should start drinking and smoking and going to clubs using fake IDs. He decided when we would have sex. And I just kept thinking . . . as long as he was happy, then I must be living my dream. This was *love*. He was my *soulmate*. This was what everyone wanted.'

And this had gone on for *three years*?

'It took *everything* for me to break up with him.' A single tear rolled down her cheek and on to the pillow. 'Because . . . breaking up with him meant accepting that I'd made a really, really bad mistake. It meant accepting that this was completely my fault and I'd . . . I'd fucked up my own life. I'd lost my best friend for nothing. And I could have been so happy, but love ruined me.'

She broke down. She just started crying and she couldn't stop, so I held her. I wrapped my arms round her and I held her tight and wanted to kill the guy who had done this to her, who was probably out there living his life and not giving a single fucking thought to any of this. I wanted to rewind time and give her the life she deserved because I loved her, and she was a good person. I knew she was a good person.

'It's not your fault,' I whispered. 'You have to believe that.'

She wiped frantically at her eyes, which didn't help much.

'Sorry,' she said hoarsely. 'This always happens when I talk about . . . stuff.'

'I don't mind you crying,' I said.

'I just . . . I hate the idea of people knowing me because . . . surely then they'll hate me the same way I hate myself.'

'But I don't,' I said. 'I don't hate you.'

She didn't reply. She kept her eyes closed. And I don't know when we both fell asleep but we did, tangled up like that in our makeshift double bed, and I knew there was no easy way to fix this, but I hoped she felt safe, at least. Maybe I would never be able to replace Beth, and maybe Rooney would take a long time to dig her way out of these feelings, and maybe there was nothing I could do to help at all. But I hoped she felt safe with me.

YOUR SONG

Sunday arrived, and I was wearing a full suit and tie – borrowed from one of Sunil and Jess's friends, as I didn't own anything nearly this cool myself – staring down at a rowing boat.

It wasn't one of the racing boats – it was wider, made for casual trips down the river, so we'd all actually fit in with the instruments and it'd be unlikely that anyone would fall out. But I was still starting to feel like this was a terrible idea.

'This was a terrible idea,' I said to Jason, who was standing next to me at the riverbank wearing a large, bright-yellow life jacket over his own suit and tie. It was a look.

'It's not a terrible idea,' he said. 'It's a very good idea.'

'I've changed my mind. I want to die.'

'Is it the boat you're afraid of or what happens after we all get in the boat?'

'All of the above. I regret that a boat was ever involved.'

Jason swung an arm round me and gave me a squeeze. I rested my head against him.

'You can do this, OK? I mean, you're absolutely fucking insane for doing this, but this is literally going to go down in history. Honestly, I wouldn't be surprised if it went viral.'

I shot him a panicked look. 'I do *not* want this to go viral. I want to do this and then never think about it again. No one is allowed to post this on YouTube.'

'OK. It won't go viral. We can forget this day ever happened.'

'Thank you.'

'Life jacket?'

'Yes, please.'

He helped me into a life jacket. Bright purple.

Rooney approached us, also in a suit, with a navy life jacket on, holding her tambourine.

'You ready?' she asked.

'No,' I said.

Sunil and Jess were behind us, instruments in hands. Sunil shot me a strong thumbs up.

'Everything will be fine,' said Sunil.

'And if it's not,' said Jess, 'at least we'll have had fun!'

'Now get in the fucking boat,' said Jason.

I sighed and got in the fucking boat.

We had spoken to one of the few people I knew was friends with Pip. Or, rather, Jason had. Jason was friends with him on Facebook and had messaged him asking if he could get Pip to arrive at Elvet Bridge at five o'clock exactly – roughly the time the sun would start to set. The guy agreed.

I'd done seven school shows and four youth theatre productions. I'd gone to university three hundred miles away from home, I'd agreed to share a room with a stranger, I'd gone clubbing for the first time despite knowing I'd hate it, and I'd come out to four whole people.

Somehow, none of that was as scary as this.

But I was going to do this. For Pip.

To show her that I loved her.

Jason – who I realised suddenly had built up a lot of muscle strength since joining the rowing club – rowed the five of us down the river. It wasn't far from John's to Elvet Bridge, but we started to draw a lot of attention as we approached the town centre, rowing along in our suits and ties with musical instruments stored cautiously at our feet.

There was absolutely no need to do this from a boat other than for dramatic effect. And I was regretting it a little. But, overall, I knew that Pip would love this. Pip loved anything that was a little ridiculous and theatrical.

The others were all laughing and gabbling excitedly, which I was glad for, because I was so nervous I couldn't even talk. It was freezing too, but at least the adrenaline was keeping me warm.

The bridge slowly approached from the distance. Sunil kept checking his watch to make sure we were on time.

'Nearly there,' Jason murmured from behind me.

I turned to him, feeling comforted by his presence.

'It's gonna be amazing,' he said.

'Yeah?'

'Yeah.'

I tried out a little smile. 'Thanks for helping.'

Jason shrugged. 'We're friends.'

I grinned. 'Let me know if you need any help with any elaborate platonic gestures of your own.'

'I will.'

And when I turned back and looked up at the bridge, Pip was there.

Her eyes were wide behind her glasses. The winter wind was whipping her hair into a mess of dark curls. She was bundled in a thick Puffa jacket, standing next to her friend who, thankfully, had brought her here on time.

She was looking down at me, mouth open, absolutely baffled.

I just grinned. I couldn't help it.

'Hi!' I called up to her.

And then she grinned back and shouted, 'What the fuck?'

I turned to everyone on the boat. Sunil, Jess and Rooney had picked up their instruments, ready to begin. They were waiting for me.

'Ready?' I said.

They nodded. I counted them in.

And then, with three accompanists, I stood on a boat on the River Wear and sang 'Your Song' – the version specifically from *Moulin Rouge* – to Pip Quintana, who didn't yet know me as well as I wished she did, but despite that, was one of my favourite people I had ever met.

THE OPPOSITE OF CURIOUS

We didn't actually perform the full three minutes thirty-nine seconds of 'Your Song', instead keeping it to a safe ninety seconds so the whole thing didn't become *too* embarrassing and awkward for anyone involved. But I was probably still going to look back on this and cringe for the rest of my life.

When the song ended, we'd drawn quite a large crowd of onlookers from Durham's town centre, and Pip's smile was so wide and bright that all I could think about was that she looked like the sun. Our performance had done its job.

Jason nudged me in the side.

I looked at him, feeling how much my face was burning. 'What?'

'You need to ask the question.'

Oh yeah.

I grabbed the megaphone we'd brought with us from the bottom of the rowing boat – carefully, so I didn't just fall into the water, which was becoming an ever-increasing danger by this point – and held it up.

'*Pip Quintana*,' I said, and it came out so loud through the megaphone that I made myself jump.

Pip looked incredibly flustered and still did not seem to know what was going on. 'Yes?'

'*Will you be my college wife?*'

The look on her face told me that she was not expecting that question.

Then she smacked her palm on to her forehead. She *realised*.

'YES!' she shrieked at me. 'AND I HATE YOU!'

And then people just started applauding. All the random people who'd paused on the bridge and by the river to watch – a lot of students, but also local residents of Durham too – clapped, and a few of them cheered. It was a whole thing. Like in a movie. I prayed none of them had filmed it.

And then Pip started to cry.

'Oh fuck,' I said. 'Jason?'

'Yes?'

'She's crying.'

'Yes, she is.'

I started patting Jason on the arm. 'We need to get to shore.' Jason grabbed the oars. 'On it.'

When we got to shore, Pip had already run down the steps from the bridge, made her way down the path and on to the grassy riverbank, and when I got out of the boat, she ran into me and hugged me so aggressively that I stumbled backwards, fell, and suddenly both of us were sitting waist-deep in the River Wear.

Somehow, it didn't seem to matter at all.

'Why are you *like this*?' was the first thing Pip said to me, furiously rubbing tears from her eyes, new ones replacing them just as fast.

'Like . . . what?' I asked, genuinely confused.

Pip shook her head, sitting back from me a little. '*This.*' She laughed. 'I never would have done something like this. I'm too much of a dumbass.'

'You're not a dumbass.'

'Oh, I am. Big, big dumbass.'

'You're talking to someone who is waist-deep in a river in February right now.'

She grinned. 'Shall we continue this conversation elsewhere?'

'That would be nice.'

We ended up getting back into the boat – with Pip, this time – and rowing all the way back to St John's. Pip was so excited by this that she nearly capsized the boat and it took Jason and me quite a lot of effort to convince her to sit down and stay still, but we made it to college without any accidents.

Rooney sat right at the back, trying not to look at Pip. I noticed Pip glancing back a few times, almost like she might say something to her, but she didn't.

Before we all disbanded on the college green, I thanked everyone for helping me.

'All in the spirit of love,' replied Sunil, slinging an arm round Jess.

He was right, I supposed.

All of this was for love, in one way or another.

Pip and Rooney finally acknowledged each other's existence when Pip said, 'You were good . . . on the tambourine.'

She'd meant it as a genuine compliment, but somehow it sounded like an insult. Rooney just said, 'Thank you,' and then mumbled something about having someone to meet in town, tore off her lifejacket, and left before Pip could say anything else.

The last person to say goodbye was Jason. He gave me a tight hug, then walked away, the bottom of his trousers damp and water droplets on his sleeves.

And then it was just Pip and me.

It didn't even need to be said that Pip would stay and talk with me that afternoon. She just did.

It reminded me of the way we were the first year we met. Age eleven. That was the year we went everywhere with each other, trying to figure out if there was anyone else we could invite into our inner circle, and eventually realising that, for now, it was just us.

I took her up to my bedroom. Rooney wasn't there – she really had gone into town, and I had a feeling she wouldn't be back for a while – but our beds were still pushed together, the sheets unmade, and everything from last night came back in a sudden rush. Rooney's confession. The tears.

I realised suddenly that this was probably not the best impression to give Pip, who had been angry at me and Rooney because she thought we were an item.

'Um,' I said. 'This is not – we weren't –'

'I know,' said Pip. She smiled at me, and I knew then that she believed me. 'Hey, has Roderick shrunk?'

She walked over to Roderick and crouched down. Despite the amount of leaves I'd had to cut off, he actually seemed to have grown since I last watered him. Maybe he wasn't totally dead after all.

Pip shivered suddenly, which was when I remembered that both she and I were pretty much drenched from the waist down.

I dug out a pair of joggers for her and some pyjamas for me, and when I turned round, Pip was practically ripping her jeans from her legs in her haste to get out of them.

My joggers were comically long on Pip, but she rolled them up and soon we were huddled on the carpet, our backs against the side of the bed, with mugs of hot chocolate and a blanket over our legs.

I knew I needed to be the first to say something about everything that had happened, but I was still so bad at having deep conversations or talking about my emotions in any way that it took a few minutes of Pip chatting aimlessly about her course and her nights out with friends before I said what I really wanted to say.

Which was, 'I'm sorry. I know I've already said that, but, yeah. I really am.'

Pip looked at me.

'Oh,' she said. 'Yeah.'

'I completely understand you not talking to me after the whole thing at the Bailey Ball,' I continued, not quite able to look her in the eye. 'I'm sorry for . . . you know, what happened. It was a shitty thing to do. For . . . several reasons.'

Pip said nothing for a moment. Then she turned away and nodded.

'Thanks for saying that,' she said, awkwardly flattening her curls. 'I . . . I think I knew right away that it was a mistake for both of you, but . . . yeah. It still hurt.'

'Yeah.'

'I just . . .' She looked up at me, right in the eyes. 'OK. We're being honest, right?'

'Yeah. Of course.'

'Well . . . I did like Rooney. I really did.' She tilted her head back. 'I know I never outright said it, but . . . I didn't want to admit it to myself. But you knew, right? I mean, you said you knew.'

I had known. That's what made this situation so awful.

'Yeah,' I said.

'I . . . I didn't want to admit it, because, like . . .' She laughed. 'I am so fucking *done* with liking straight girls. Literally my *whole* teenage life I spend pining after straight girls, maybe getting like one kiss from a slightly curious girl who immediately goes back to her boyfriend, and then I come to uni hoping to finally meet a solid range of other queer girls . . . and I just immediately fall for a straight girl again.' She smacked her forehead with one hand. 'Why am I the actual *dumbest gay alive?*'

I grinned. I couldn't help it.

'Shut up,' said Pip, also grinning. 'I know. I *know*. I was doing *so well*. I joined Pride Soc and LatAm Soc and I even went to a couple of those stupid Ultimate Frisbee games, but like . . . I was *still* making the same mistakes. Then when you and her kissed, I just – it just felt like the biggest betrayal from both of you.'

I hugged her. Tight. 'I'm sorry. I'm so sorry.'

She hugged me back. 'I know.'

We stayed like that for a long time.

Then she said, 'I just don't understand *why* the kiss happened. Like . . . I don't think I've ever been so genuinely shocked by anything in my life.'

I felt myself go a bit red. 'Didn't Rooney explain?'

'To be honest, I was so pissed off that I barely listened to what she was saying.' She huffed out a laugh. 'And by the time I calmed down, it was kind of too late.'

'Oh.'

Pip looked at me. 'Georgia . . . I don't want to . . . *force* you to talk about anything that you don't want to talk about. Like, that's not what people should do to anyone, especially their friends, and especially about things like . . . like sexuality.' Her voice grew softer. 'But . . . I at least want you to know that you *can* talk to me about it, if you *want* to, and I promise I would understand.'

I felt frozen.

She knew something was up.

She'd known for ages, probably.

'I don't know whether you'd understand,' I said in a very small voice.

Pip paused, then let out a short, exasperated chuckle. 'I'm not sure if you're aware of this fact, Georgia Warr, but I am an exceptionally humungous lesbian with a lifetime of experience in gay thoughts.'

I laughed. 'I know. I was there all through your Keira Knightley phase.'

'Erm, my Keira Knightley phase is still ongoing, thank you very much. I've still got that poster in my room at home.'

'*Still?*'

'I can't throw it away. It represents my gay awakening.'

'You can't throw it away because she's hot, you mean.'

'Maybe so.'

We both grinned, but I didn't know where to go from there. Should I just say it? Should I find an article for her to read? Should I just drop this whole topic because she'd never understand?

'So,' said Pip, twisting her body round so she was facing me. 'Keira Knightley. Thoughts?'

I snorted. 'Are you asking me whether *I* fancy Keira Knightley?'

'Yup.'

'Oh.' So this was how we were doing it. 'Well, um, no.'

'What about . . . girls in general?'

Pip held her mug in front of her mouth, staring at me with quiet cautiousness.

'No,' I murmured.

I guess I was sure about that now. But it still felt almost impossible to admit. For Pip, at least, it probably would have been easier to understand if I *did* like girls.

'So . . . the thing with Rooney . . .' Pip looked down. 'Was it . . . were you just curious, or . . .?'

Curious. I wanted to laugh. I was, and always had been, the opposite of curious.

'*Desperate* is the word I would use,' I said before I could stop myself.

Pip frowned, confused. 'Desperate for what?'

'Desperate to like someone.' I looked at Pip. 'Anyone.'

'Why?' she whispered.

'Because . . . I don't. I can't. I can't like anyone. Not boys, not girls, not anyone.' I ran a hand over my hair. 'I just . . . can't. I never will.'

I waited for the words that would inevitably follow. *You don't know that. You'll meet someone one day. You just haven't met the right person.*

But all she said was, 'Oh.'

She nodded slowly in that way she did when she was thinking hard about something.

I was just going to have to say the words.

'It's called aromantic asexual,' I said on an exhale.

'Oh,' she said again.

I waited for her to say something more, but she didn't. She just sat there, thinking really hard.

'Thoughts?' I said, letting out a small, nervous laugh. 'Do I need to look it up on Wikipedia for you?'

Pip snapped out of her little thought bubble and looked at me. 'No. No Wikipedia needed.'

'I get that it sounds weird.' I could feel myself going red. Would I ever stop feeling embarrassed about explaining this to people?

'It's not weird.'

'It sounds weird, though.'

'No, it doesn't.'

'It does.'

'*Georgia.*' Pip smiled, a little exasperated. 'You're not weird.'

She was the first person who'd said that to me.

I hated that I still felt, sometimes, underneath it all, that I wasn't normal.

But maybe getting over that would take time.

Maybe, little by little, I could start to believe that I was OK.

'A bit wordy, though, isn't it?' Pip continued, leaning back on to the side of the bed. 'Eight whole syllables. Bit of a mouthful.'

'Some people call it aro-ace for short.'

'Oh, that's *way* better. That sounds like a character from *Star Wars.*' She made a dramatic gesture with one hand. '*Aro Ace.* Defender of the universe.'

'OK, I hate that.'

'Come on. You like space.'

'No.'

We were just joking, but I sort of wanted to scream. *Take me seriously.*

She could tell.

'Sorry,' she said. 'I don't know how to talk about serious things without making it into a joke.'

I nodded. 'Yeah. It's fine.'

'Did you . . . feel like that all through school?'

'Yeah. I wasn't really aware of it, though.' I shrugged. 'Just thought I was super picky. And my fake feelings for Tommy were a bit of a red herring.'

Pip rested her head against my sheets, waiting to hear more.

'I guess . . . I always felt, like . . . uncomfortable when I tried to have feelings for anyone. Like, it just felt wrong and awkward. Like what happened with Jason. I knew I didn't like him like that because when we tried to do anything romantic, it just felt . . . *wrong*. But I guess I thought that everyone felt like that and I just needed to keep trying.'

'Can I ask a dumb question?' Pip interrupted.

'Er, yeah?'

'This is going to sound bad, but, like, how do you know you won't find someone one day?'

This was the question that had been plaguing me for months. But when Pip asked me it then, I realised I knew the answer. Finally.

'Because I know myself. I know what I feel and . . . what I have the capability to feel, I think.' I smiled weakly at her. 'I mean, how do you know you won't fall for a guy one day?'

Pip made a face.

I laughed. 'Yeah, exactly. You just *know* that about yourself. And now I know too.'

There was a pause and I could hear my own heart thumping in my chest. God, I couldn't wait until talking about this didn't give me high adrenaline and nervous sweats.

Suddenly, Pip slammed her empty mug down on the carpet and cried, 'I can't believe neither of us realised this earlier! For fuck's sake! Why the fuck are we like this!'

I picked up her mug, slightly alarmed, and put it safely out of the way on my bedside table. 'What d'you mean?'

She shook her head. 'We were literally going through the same thing at the same time, and *neither of us realised*.'

'Were we?'

'Well, I mean, with some minor details changed.'

'Like the fact that you like girls?'

'Yes, like that. But *apart from that*, we were both trying to force ourselves to like guys, we were both struggling with the fact that we didn't have crushes on the people we were supposed to, we were both feeling . . . I dunno . . . *weird and different*! And *neither of us liked guys*! And — oh my *God*, I was the one coming to you like, *oh no, sad, I think I'm gay and I don't know what to do* all the while you were in such an intense state of repression that you literally thought you were straight despite the fact that doing anything with guys made you want to *vom*.'

'Oh,' I said. 'Yeah.'

'Yeah!'

'Are we both dumbasses?'

'I think we are, Georgia.'

'Oh no.'

'Yes. That's the takeaway from this conversation.'

'Great.'

And then Pip started to laugh. And that made me laugh too. And then we were laughing hysterically, the sound echoing around the room, and I couldn't remember the last time Pip and I had laughed together like this.

We'd missed dinner, so we decided to have a little picnic with all the snacks I kept in my room — of which there were plenty. We sat on the floor and ate supermarket-brand cookies, a half-empty family-size packet of caramelised onion crisps, and bagels that were definitely almost stale, while watching *Moulin Rouge*, of course.

It was similar to last night, watching YouTube videos with Rooney. If I could spend every night of my life eating snacks and watching something silly in a giant bed with one of my best friends, I'd be happy.

My future still terrified me. But everything seemed a little brighter when my best friends were around.

We didn't talk any more about identities and romance and feelings until the film had nearly finished, when we'd moved on to the bed and had been curled up in my bedsheets in silence for the better part of an hour. I was dangerously close to falling asleep.

But then Pip spoke – her voice soft and quiet in the low light of the room.

'Why did you college propose to me?' Pip asked.

There'd been a lot of reasons. I'd wanted to make a big gesture, I'd wanted to cheer her up, I'd wanted her to be my friend again, I'd wanted to make things right. I was sure Pip knew all those things too.

But maybe she needed to hear it out loud.

'Because I love you,' I said, 'and you deserve magical moments like that.'

Pip stared at me.

Then her eyes filled with tears.

She leant on to one hand, covering her eyes. 'You fucking dick. I'm not drunk enough to cry while having emotional conversations with friends.'

'I'm not sorry.'

'You should be! Where the fuck are *your* tears!'

'I don't cry in front of anyone, my dude. You know this.'

'I'm making it my new mission in life to make you cry with emotion.'

'Good luck with that.'
'It's going to happen.'
'Sure.'
'I hate you.'
I grinned at her. 'I hate you too.'

MESS

I woke up groggily the next morning to the sound of the bedroom door opening, and when I raised my head, I was unsurprised to find Rooney creeping in wearing last night's clothes – the full suit she'd worn as part of the proposal.

This was a relatively normal occurrence by this point, but what was *not* normal was the way Rooney froze in the middle of her aqua rug and stared at the space next to me on the double bed – Rooney's side – which was occupied by Pip Quintana.

Pip and I had been chatting so much last night that by the time Pip realised she should probably go back to her own college, it was bordering on midnight, so I'd lent her some pyjamas and she'd stayed over. Both of us had utterly forgotten about the fact that things could be quite awkward between Pip and Rooney if they were in the same room.

There were a very obvious few seconds of silence.

And then I said, 'Morning.'

Rooney said nothing for a moment, and then started very slowly taking off her shoes and said, 'Morning.'

I felt movement next to me and turned to look, grabbing my glasses from my bedside table. Pip was awake, her own glasses already on.

'Oh,' she said, and I could see the colour filling her cheeks. 'Um, sorry, I – we probably should have asked you if –'

'It's fine!' Rooney squawked, turning away from us and rummaging frantically in her toiletries bag for a packet of make-up wipes. 'You can stay over if you want!'

'Yeah, but – this is your room too –'

'I don't really care!'

Pip sat up. 'O-OK.' She started clambering out of the bed. 'Um, I should probably go anyway, I've got a lecture this morning.'

I frowned. 'Hang on, it's like seven a.m.'

'Yeah, well, I-I need to wash my hair and stuff, so –'

'You don't have to leave because of me!' said Rooney from the other side of the room. She was facing away from us, scrubbing her face with a make-up wipe.

'It's not because of you!' said Pip much too quickly.

Both of them were panicking. Rooney started changing into her pyjamas just to give herself something to do. Pip began to gather up her own clothes from yesterday while determinedly keeping her eyes averted from Rooney, who was now just wearing pyjamas shorts.

I really, really wanted to laugh, but for both their sakes, kept my mouth shut.

Pip spent much longer than she needed to gathering her belongings and, thankfully, by the time she dared to turn round, Rooney had a pyjama top on and was sitting at her desk, attempting to look casual by scrolling through her phone.

'Well . . .' Pip looked at me, almost disoriented. 'I'll . . . see you later?'

'Yeah,' I said. I clenched my lips together so that I didn't laugh.

Pip went to leave the room, but suddenly looked down at the pile of clothes she had in her hands and said, 'Oh, shit, erm, I think – these aren't mine?' She pulled out a pair of leggings with the words 'St John's College' on them. Rooney's.

Rooney glanced over, feigning nonchalance. 'Oh, yeah, those are mine.' She held out a hand.

Pip had no choice but to approach Rooney and hand them over.

Rooney's eyes stayed focused on Pip's as she slowly approached. Pip held out the leggings and dropped them into Rooney's open hand from a height that suggested she was nervous to put her hand anywhere near Rooney's skin.

'Thanks,' said Rooney.

An awkward smile. 'No problem.' Pip hovered next to Rooney's desk. 'So . . . were you out last night, or . . .?'

Clearly Rooney was not expecting this. She clenched the leggings in her hand and said, 'Oh, yeah! Yeah, I was just . . . me and some friends went out to Wiff Waff and then stayed in their room.' Rooney pointed out of the window. 'In a different building. I couldn't be assed to walk back here.'

Pip nodded. 'Cool. Wiff Waff . . . that's the table-tennis bar, right?'

'Yeah.'

'That sounds fun.'

'Yeah, it was good. I get so competitive, though.'

Pip smiled. 'Yeah, I know.'

From the look on her face, this statement seemed to shake Rooney to her core.

'Yes,' said Rooney, strained, after a long pause. 'So . . . you and Georgia had a sleepover?'

'Oh, yeah, erm –' Pip suddenly blanched. 'I mean – just a platonic sleepover. Obviously. We didn't – Georgia's not –'

'I know,' said Rooney quickly. 'Georgia's not into sex.'

Pip's mouth twitched. Rooney using the word 'sex' seemed to have sent Pip on to another level of panic.

'Georgia's right here,' I said, literally unable to keep the giant smile off my face by this point.

Pip stepped back, her cheeks tinged red. 'Um . . . anyway, yeah, I'd better go.'

Rooney looked dazed. 'OK.'

'I . . . well, it was nice to . . . um . . . yeah.'

'Yeah.'

Pip opened her mouth to say something more, then shot a panicked glance towards me, and then she was out of the room without another word.

We waited a few seconds until we heard the door at the end of the corridor shut.

And then Rooney exploded.

'Are you FUCKING JOKING ME, GEORGIA? Could you not have done me the tiniest courtesy of WARNING ME that the girl I like was going to BE HERE when I got back?' She started pacing back and forth. 'Do you think I would have waltzed in here wearing fucking LAST NIGHT'S CLOTHES with last night's make-up smeared all over my FUCKING face had I known that Pip Quintana was going to be here with the most FUCKING adorable bedhead I have ever seen in my FUCKING life?'

'You're going to wake up the whole corridor,' I said, but she didn't even seem to hear me.

Rooney collapsed on to her side of the bed face first. 'What sort of impression am I supposed to make wandering back into my own college room at seven a.m. like I've just been out fucking some person I never want to speak to again?'

'Were you?' I asked.

She lifted her head and gave me a sharp look. 'NO! For fuck's sake! I haven't done that since before the Bailey Ball.'

I shrugged. 'Thought I'd check.'

She rolled on to her back, spreading out her limbs as if willing herself to melt into the sheets. 'I'm a mess.'

'So's Pip,' I said. 'You're kind of made for each other.'

Rooney made a low grunting sound. 'Don't give me false hope. She's never going to like me after what I did.'

'Do you want my opinion?'

'No.'

'OK.'

'Wait, yes. Yes I do.'

'Pip likes you back and I think you should actually try talking to her normally again.'

She rolled on to her front. 'Absolutely impossible. If you're going to offer ideas, please offer realistic ones.'

'Why is that impossible?'

'Because I'm shit and she deserves better. I can't fall in love, anyway. I'll get over this. Pip should be with a *nice* person.'

The way she said it – light and casual – I could have easily mistaken it for a joke. But because I understood Rooney on a slightly deeper level by this point, I knew she wasn't joking at all.

'Dude,' I said. 'I'm the one who *can't* fall in love. I think you just don't want to.'

She made a 'harrumph' noise.

'Well?' I asked. 'Are you aromantic?'

'No,' she grumbled.

'There. So stop erasing my identity and tell Pip you like her.'

'Don't use your identity to make me admit my feelings.'

'I can and I will.'

'Did you see her bedhead?' Rooney mumbled into her pillow.

'Er, yes?'

'She looked so fluffy.'

'She'd probably murder you if you called her fluffy.'

'I bet she smells really nice.'

'She does.'

'Fuck you.'

We were interrupted by notification sounds from both of our phones.

A message in our Shakespeare Soc group chat. The one that hadn't been used since before the new year – 'A Midsummer Night's Dab'.

Felipa Quintana
Forgot to say-
I would like to rejoin the Shakespeare Soc
If you'll have me
I can learn my lines in two weeks!!!

We lay there on the bed, reading the messages at the same time.

'We're doing the play,' said Rooney breathlessly.

I didn't know whether she was thrilled or terrified.

'Are you OK with that?' I asked. I thought this was what she'd wanted. She'd been devastated when Pip and Jason had left and the society crumbled. It had sent her spiralling for *weeks*.

Rooney was so good at pretending she was fine. Even now I sometimes failed to spot when she was spiralling. And after her breakdown the other night, and the situation with Pip, and all of the feelings I knew she was fighting, and the ones I was still dealing with too . . .

Were we going to be OK?

'I don't know,' she said. 'I don't know.'

WE KEPT THE BEDS TOGETHER

'*Against my will*,' Pip said, rolling her eyes while leaning against a pillar that I had spent a whole morning crafting out of cardboard and papier mâché, '*I am sent to bid you come in to dinner.*'

Rooney was lounging on a chair, centre-stage. '*Fair Beatrice,*' she said, standing up with a flirty expression. '*I thank you for your pains.*'

We had ten days until the play.

This was definitely not enough time to finish staging all of the scenes, learn all of our lines, and prepare costumes and set. But we were trying anyway.

Pip's expression remained unbothered. '*I took no more pains for those thanks than you take pains to thank me: if it had been painful, I would not have come.*'

Rooney stepped closer, slotting her hands into her pockets and smirking down at Pip. '*You take* pleasure *then in the message?*'

Before today's rehearsal, Rooney had spent a solid twenty minutes changing outfits and doing her hair before I straight-up asked, 'Is this about Pip?'

She denied it loudly and at length, before saying, 'Yes. Fine. What do I do?'

It had taken me a moment to realise that she was asking for my help. With romance.

Just as I had done all those months ago in Freshers' Week.

'*Yea, just so much as you may take upon a knife's point and choke a daw withal,*' Pip scoffed back, folding her arms. '*You have no stomach, signor: fare you well.*' And then she turned and whisked off stage.

Me, Jason and Sunil clapped.

'That was good!' Pip said, a smile on her face. 'That was good, right? And I didn't forget the *choke a daw* bit.'

'You were *OK*,' said Rooney, eyebrows raised.

I had given Rooney all the advice I could think to give. *Be yourself. Talk to her. Maybe try saying nice things sometimes.*

Well, she was trying, at least.

'That means a lot coming from you,' said Pip, and Rooney turned away so we couldn't see her expression.

Five days before the play, we ran through the entire thing. We messed up several cues, Jason smacked his head on the top of the paper-mâché pillar, and I completely blanked my final speech from *A Midsummer Night's Dream*, but eventually we made it to the end, and it wasn't a complete disaster.

'We actually did it,' said Pip, her eyes wide as we all finished clapping each other. 'Like, we might possibly pull this off.'

'Don't sound so surprised,' Rooney scoffed. 'I am actually a good director.'

'Excuse me, we are *co*-directors. I get some of the credit.'

'No. Incorrect. I removed your directorship when you decided to abandon us for two months.'

Pip's mouth dropped open, and she whipped her head round to me to see my reaction. 'Is she allowed to joke about that yet? Surely we're not at the point where we can joke about our feud yet.'

'I can joke about what I want,' said Rooney.

I was busy stacking chairs. 'I'm not getting involved,' I said.

'No,' said Pip, turning back to Rooney. 'I refute this. I want my co-directorship back.'

'You're not having it!' said Rooney, who had started pushing the pillar to one side of the room.

Pip walked right up to Rooney and poked her on the arm. 'Too bad! I'm taking it back!'

She went to poke her again, but Rooney ducked round the pillar and said, 'You'll have to fight for it, then!'

Pip followed her, increasing the speed of her pokes so that she was basically tickling Rooney. 'Maybe I will!'

Rooney tried to bat her away, but Pip was too fast, and soon Pip was basically chasing her around the room, both of them shrieking and swatting at each other.

They were smiling and laughing so much that it made *me* smile.

Even though I still wasn't sure whether Rooney was really OK.

We hadn't spoken again about what she'd told me that night we moved the beds. About Beth and her ex-boyfriend and her teenage life.

But we kept the beds together.

We rehearsed our play and we ate in the cafeteria, and Rooney stopped going out at night. We sat together in lectures and walked to and from the library in the cold and we watched *Brooklyn Nine-Nine* one Saturday morning until noon, buried in the covers. I waited for her to break again. For her to run away from me.

But she didn't, and, still, we kept the beds together.

She took down the photo of Beth. She didn't throw it away — she just put it inside one of her notebooks where it could stay safe. *We should take more photos,* I thought. *Then she'd have something else to stick on the wall.*

I felt that there was something we weren't saying. Something we hadn't addressed. I had figured out who I was, and she had told me who she'd been, but I could feel that there was something more, and I didn't know whether it was her keeping things inside or whether it was me. Perhaps both. I didn't even know whether it was something we needed to talk about.

Sometimes I woke up in the night and couldn't go back to sleep because I started thinking about the future, terrified, having no idea what it would look like for me now. Sometimes Rooney would wake up too, but she wouldn't say anything. She would just lie there, shuffling a little under the duvet.

It was comforting when she did wake up, though. When she was just there, awake with me.

It all came to a head the night before the play.

Me, Pip and Rooney gathered together for one final rehearsal in Pip's bedroom. Sunil, who was an expert at speeches, had memorised everything weeks ago, and Jason had always been quick to learn his lines, but the three of us felt like we wanted one last chance to go through everything.

Pip's bedroom was not any tidier than the last time I'd been here. In fact, it was actually a lot worse. But she *had* managed to clear a small patch of carpet for her and Rooney to act in and had created a comfy area on the floor near her bed, piled with cushions and snacks for us to chill out on. I sprawled on the cushions while they went over their scenes.

'You're saying that line wrong,' said Rooney to Pip, and it was like we were back in the first week we all met. 'I say *do you not love me* and you say *why, no, no more than reason*, like – like you're trying to conceal your feelings.'

Pip raised an eyebrow. 'That's exactly how I'm saying it.'

'No, you're being like '*no more than reason?*' like it's a question.'

'I'm definitely not.'

Rooney gestured at her with her copy of *Much Ado About Nothing*. 'You are. Look, just trust me, I know this play –'

'Excuse me, I also know this play and I'm allowed my own interpretation –'

'I know, and that's fine, but like –'

Pip raised her eyebrows. 'I think you're just scared of me outshining you on stage.'

There was a pause while Rooney realised that Pip was joking.

'*Why* would I be scared of that when I'm *clearly* the superior actor?' Rooney shot back, snapping the book shut.

'Wow. Presumptuous, much.'

'Just stating the facts, pipsqueak.'

'Roo,' said Pip, 'come on. You *know* I'm a better actor.'

Rooney opened her mouth to shoot back a retort, but the sudden use of a nickname seemed to take her so off-guard that she couldn't even think of a comeback. I don't think I'd ever seen her so genuinely flustered until that moment.

'How about we take a break?' I said. 'We could watch a movie.'

'Um, yeah,' said Rooney, not looking at Pip as she joined me on the stack of cushions. 'OK.'

We put on *Easy A* because Rooney had never seen it, and – though not quite up there with *Moulin Rouge* – it was one of my and Pip's favourite sleepover movies.

I hadn't seen it for a while. Not since before coming to Durham.

'I'd forgotten this movie is about a girl who lies about not being a virgin for social clout,' I said, once we were about half an hour in. I was sitting between Pip and Rooney.

'AKA, the plot of at least eighty per cent of teen movies,' said Rooney. 'So unrealistic.'

Pip snorted. 'You mean you *didn't* lie about sleeping with a guy and then walk around with the letter A embroidered on your corset when you were seventeen?'

'Didn't have to lie,' said Rooney, 'and I can't sew.'

'I don't get why so many teen movies are about teenagers who are obsessed with losing their virginity,' I said. 'Like . . . who actually cares?'

Pip and Rooney said nothing for a moment.

'Well, I think quite a lot of teenagers do care about it,' said Rooney. 'Take Pip, for example.'

'Excuse me!' Pip exclaimed. 'I don't – I'm not obsessed with losing my virginity!'

'*Sure* you're not.'

'I just think having sex would be *fun*, that's all.' Pip faced the screen again, going a little red. 'I don't care about *being a virgin*, I just – sex seems fun, so I'd like to start having it sooner rather than later.'

Rooney looked over at her. 'I mean, I was joking, but that's good to know too.'

Pip went even redder and stammered, 'Shut up.'

'But why are, like, most teen movies focused around the fact that teenagers feel like they're going to die if they don't lose their virginity?' I asked, then almost immediately figured out what the answer was. 'Oh. This is an asexual thing.' I laughed at myself. 'I forgot other people are obsessed with having sex. Wow. That's really funny.'

I suddenly realised both Rooney and Pip were gazing at me

with small smiles on their faces. Not pitying or patronising. Just kind of like they were happy for me.

I guess it *was* a development that I could laugh about my sexuality. That had to be progress, right?

'It's a good movie, but I think it'd be better if the main romance was gay,' said Pip.

'Agreed,' said Rooney, and we looked at her.

'I thought you'd be into this sort of adorable post-John-Hughes hetero romance,' said Pip. 'The straights eat this shit up.'

'They do,' Rooney agreed, 'but fortunately I'm not straight, so, yeah.'

There was a long, long silence.

'O-oh,' Pip choked. 'Well – well, that's good then.'

'Yeah.'

'Yeah.'

We finished the rest of the movie in extremely awkward silence. And when it was done, I knew it was time for me to go. To step away and let this happen.

They tried to get me to stay, but I insisted. I needed to sleep, I told them. They could go through their last scene on their own.

I guess I felt a little lonely as I walked out of Castle. I walked down the corridors, out of Pip's block, across the green and back towards St John's. It was dark and cold at nearly 1 a.m. I was alone.

I was alone now.

When I got back to my room, I put Universe City on YouTube while I changed into my PJs, took my contacts out, brushed my teeth, and checked on Roderick, who really did seem to be doing better these days. And then I snuggled into my half of the bed, wrapping the covers round me.

I fell asleep for half an hour but woke up in a sweat, my mind filled with flashes of nightmares about apocalyptic futures and all my friends dying, and rolled my head automatically to check for Rooney, but she wasn't there.

It was harder to fall back to sleep when she wasn't there.

I woke up with my head feeling like TV static and a stomach full of bees, which was a given for show day. But none of that compared to the feeling of dread that washed over me as I checked my phone to find I had a huge stream of messages from Pip.

The first ones read:

Felipa Quintana
GEORGIA
EMERGENCY
I'VE FUCKED UP
ROONEY HAS GONE

HORNY AND CONFUSED

Felipa Quintana
Okay I know it's 7am and you're definitely asleep but oh my god you are going to murder me when I explain what just happened

Oh my GOD sflkgjsdfhlgkj okay

WOW

Sorry I literally cannot process

Okay. right. so

Everything was fine last night, like, once you left we just went through our last scene.

(I mean fine by our standards, like obviously talking to her is just full of tension every time)

But by the time we finished it was suuuper late, it was like 3am so I offered to let her sleep in my room – as in, in my bed with me – and she said YES

This was definitely not a good idea because I did not sleep for one SINGLE minute my dude

She woke up again at like 5am and went to get some water, and when she got back I knew she could tell I was awake so we just started talking while lying in bed

And idk if it was because we were just tired or what but like . . . it was different, we weren't bantering, we were just talking about stuff. Like first about the play and then about our lives at school and all sorts of deep shit. She told me . . . man we talked about a lot of really personal stuff for like . . . at least an hour, maybe more

She told me she thinks she's pansexual!!!!! She said she just doesn't think she really has a gender preference and that felt like the right word for her!!!! She said you already kinda knew about it

We'd been talking for ages and then we were just quiet for a while and then she was like – and I QUOTE – she literally said 'I know it seems like I hate you but it's actually the opposite'

Georgia, I died

I was like 'yeah . . . . me too' while trying not to actually scream

And then she just leaned in and KISSED ME

ADKLGJSHDFKLGJSLDFGSLFJGSLDF

She immediately moved away with this expression like she was scared she'd made a mistake

But obviously she had NOT made a mistake and she could see it on my fucking face

And then she leaned in again and we literally started MAKING OUT

Like I'm talking proper making out

So I'm just like holy fuck how is this happening, I'm literally deceased, and we just make out in my bed for like twenty minutes

UM this story gets a bit nsfw from here on I am very sorry about this but if I don't tell someone what happened then I will die

So after a while she kneels up and just like . . . takes her t-shirt off. And I'm like. Oh my god

And then I'm thinking OKAY she wants to go further than just making out??

And I'd be okay with that??? I also want to do that?????

She like . . . lies back down and is like 'is this okay?' and I'm like hell yeah please proceed

(I didn't actually use the phrase 'please proceed' during my first sexual encounter. I think I just nodded very enthusiastically.)

So obviously I've never done anything sexual with anyone and she's like . . . just about to put her hand in my pyjama shorts and I'm nervous as hell but extremely up for it lol

But then she pulls back and she's like 'oh my god' and she jumps off me and just starts freaking out, like, pulling her clothes on and packing up all her stuff and being like 'I'm so sorry I'm so sorry' and I'm just lying there horny and confused like 'um'

And then she's like 'shit, I mess everything up' and then she just like RUNS out of my room

SHE IS GONE

I've called her and messaged her but I have no idea where she is, is she back at yours???

I'm so worried and confused and the play's today and I'm just freaking out a little bit, I think I might have upset her and ruined everything

But also I think I need to get a couple of hours of sleep now because otherwise I may pass out on stage this afternoon

So um

Yeah

Message me when you wake up

Georgia Warr
i'm awake
oh my god

I WILL FIND HER

Georgia Warr
she's not here
don't panic
i will find her

I called her first and sat there in our bed, listening to the phone ringing, waiting.

It went through to voicemail.

'Where are you?' I said instantly, but didn't know what else to say, so I just hung up, hurled myself out of bed, put on the nearest clothes I could grab, and ran.

This could not be happening.

She was not abandoning us on the day of the show.

She was not abandoning me.

I ran all the way to the bottom of the stairway before realising that I had literally no idea where to look. She could be *anywhere*. A library. A café. Somewhere in college. Someone's flat. Durham is small, but it wasn't possible to search a whole city in one day.

But I had to try.

I ran all the way to the theatre first. She'd probably just decided to meet us there, maybe gone to get a Starbucks first. We'd all agreed to meet there at 10 a.m. – our performance was at 2 p.m. – and it was 9.30 now, so she was probably just a bit early.

I crashed into the door in my attempt to open it. It was locked.

That was when I started to get scared.

She'd left Pip in the middle of the night. Where had she gone after that? I would have woken up if she'd come back to our room. Had she gone to see one of her many friends who didn't seem to care about her? Had she gone to a club? The clubs didn't stay open that late, did they?

I crouched down on the pavement, trying to breathe. Shit. What if something bad had happened? What if some man had pulled up in a car and grabbed her? What if she'd been walking along the bridge and fallen in?

I pulled my phone out of my pocket and called Rooney again.

She didn't pick up. Maybe she didn't even have her phone with her.

I called Pip instead.

'Did you find her?' was the first thing she said when she picked up.

'No. She's . . .' I didn't even know what to tell her. 'She's . . . gone.'

'Gone? What – what do you mean *gone*?'

I stood up, looking around as if I might suddenly see her up the street, running towards me in her sports leggings, her ponytail flying behind her. But I didn't. Of course I didn't.

My voice broke. 'She's just gone.'

'This is my fault,' said Pip instantly, and I could hear how devastated she was, and how much she truly believed what she was saying. 'This is – I shouldn't have – she probably didn't even – it was way too soon for us to even –'

'No, it's my fault,' I said. I should have been looking out for her. I should have seen this coming.

I knew her better than anyone.

Anyone in her whole life.

'I'll find her,' I said. 'I promise I'll find her.'

I owed her that.

I ran to the club that we went to in Freshers' Week, when she'd told me to search for someone I fancied while she went off to get with a guy. Years ago, that felt like.

It was closed. Of course it was; it was a Saturday morning.

I went to Tesco, like I might just see her browsing cereal options, and I walked around the square like she might just be sitting on a stone bench, scrolling on her phone. I crossed Elvet Bridge and stormed into the Elvet Riverside lecture hall building, not even sure if they opened it at the weekend but not caring, having no idea why she would be here on a Saturday morning but hoping, hoping. *Praying*. I went up to the Student Union to find it locked, and then I couldn't run any more because my chest hurt, so I walked to the Bill Bryson Library, went inside, stood on the stairs and just shouted 'ROONEY!' once. Everybody turned round to look at me, but I didn't care.

Rooney wasn't there. She wasn't anywhere.

Were we not enough for her in the end?

Was I not enough?

Or had we just got through to her, only for something terrible to happen to her?

I called her again. And it went to voicemail.

'Did something happen?' I asked.

I hung up again. I had no idea what else to say.

Back outside the library, my phone started to ring, but it was only Jason.

'What's going on?' he asked. 'I'm at the theatre and no one else is here except Sunil.'

'Rooney's gone.'

'What do you mean gone?'

'Don't worry, I'll find her.'

'Georgia —'

I hung up and tried Rooney a third time.

'Maybe the you from Freshers' Week would have left us. But not now. Not after everything.' I felt a tightness in my throat. 'You wouldn't have left me.'

When I hung up that time, I realised my phone only had five per cent battery left, because I'd failed to put it on charge last night.

The wind whipped around me on the street.

Should I call the police?

I started walking back towards the town centre, all the 'what if's circling around my head. What if she'd gone home? What if she'd fallen in the river and died?

I stopped in the middle of the pavement, a memory suddenly flashing in my mind so hard I felt like I got whiplash.

On that first night out in town, Rooney had put herself on Find My Friends on my phone. I hadn't used it at all in the end, but . . . would it work now?

I nearly dropped my phone in my haste to get it out and check, and sure enough, there on the map was a little circle with Rooney's face in it.

She was, apparently, in a field, by the river, maybe a kilometre away in the countryside.

I didn't even let myself think why. I just started running again.

I hadn't thought about what Durham might be like outside the city centre. All I'd known for the past six months was university buildings, cobbled streets and tiny cafés.

But it only took ten minutes for me to find myself in big, endless greenery. Long fields stretched out ahead as I followed the small, worn footpaths and tracked the little Rooney dot on my phone, until my phone screen went black and I couldn't any more.

By that point, I didn't need it. The dot had been by the river, next to a bridge. I just needed to get to the bridge.

It took another fifteen minutes. At one point I was scared I was truly lost, with no Google Maps to help me, but I just kept going, following the river, until I saw it. The bridge.

The bridge was empty.

The surrounding footpaths and fields were too.

I just stood there and looked for a moment. Then I walked across the bridge and back, like Rooney might be sleeping down on the riverbank or I might see the back of her head bobbing in the water, but I didn't.

Instead, when I reached the footpath again, I saw light glint off something on the grass.

It was Rooney's phone.

I picked it up and turned the screen on. All of my missed calls were on there. Lots from Pip too, and even a couple from Jason.

I sat down on the grass.

And I just cried. From exhaustion, from confusion, from fear. I just sat in a field with Rooney's phone and cried.

Even after everything, I couldn't help her.

I couldn't be a good friend to her.

I couldn't make her feel like she mattered in my life.

'GEORGIA.'

A voice. I looked up.

For a moment I thought I might be dreaming. Whether she was a projection from my mind of what I wished was happening right now.

But she was real.

Rooney was running across the bridge to me, a Starbucks in one hand and a bunch of flowers in the other.

GRAND GESTURE

'Oh my *God*, Georgia, why are you — what's wrong?'

Rooney collapsed on to her knees in front of me and stared at the tears flowing out of my eyes.

Pip had cried in front of me dozens of times. It didn't take much to set her off. Often it had been warranted, but sometimes she cried just because she was tired. Or that one time she cried because she made a lasagne and then dropped it on the floor.

Jason had cried in front of me a few times. Only when really bad things happened, like when he realised how horrible Aimee was to him, or we watched really sad movies about old people, like *The Notebook* and Pixar's *Up*.

Rooney had cried in front of me a few times too. When she first told me about her ex. Outside Pip's door. And when we moved the beds together.

I'd never cried in front of her.

I'd never cried in front of anyone.

'Why . . . are you . . . here . . .?' I managed to stammer out in between heaving breaths. I didn't want her to see me like this. God, I didn't want anyone to see me.

'I could ask you the same thing!' She dropped the flowers on the ground and placed her Starbucks cup carefully on the footpath, then sat down next to me on the grass. I realised she was wearing different clothes from last night – she was now in different leggings and a sweatshirt. When had she gone back to our room to change? *Had* I slept through her coming back?

She wrapped an arm round me.

'I thought . . . you were . . . in the river,' I said.

'You thought I'd fallen in the river and *died*?'

'I d-don't know . . . I was scared . . .'

'I'm not *dumb*, I don't just go around jumping in rivers.'

I looked at her. 'You frequently stay at strangers' houses.'

Rooney pursed her lips. 'OK.'

'You *locked yourself out of college at five a.m.*'

'*OK*. Maybe I'm a bit dumb.'

I wiped my face, feeling a little calmer. 'Why was your phone here?'

She paused. 'I . . . walk out here sometimes. After nights out. Well . . . usually the mornings after. I just like coming out here and . . . feeling like everything's calm.'

'You never told me.'

She shrugged. 'I didn't think anyone would really care about it. It was just my thing that I did to clear my head. So I came out here this morning and at some point I dropped my phone, and I didn't realise until I was all the way back at college – you must have already left by that point – so I just got changed and ran back here and . . . now we're both here.'

She still had her arm round me. We stared out at the river.

'Did Pip tell you what happened?' she asked.

'Yeah.' I tapped my foot against hers. 'Why'd you run?'

She let out a deep breath. 'I'm . . . very scared of . . . getting close to people. And . . . last night, with Pip, I . . .what we *did* – well, what we were about to do, I-I just started to think that I was doing what I normally did. Having sex to just . . . detach myself from feeling anything real.' She shook her head. 'But I wasn't. I realised almost as soon as I left. I realised I . . . it would have been the first time with someone I actually . . . cared about. With someone who cared about me too.'

'She's really worried about you,' I said. 'Maybe we should get back.'

Rooney turned to me.

'*You* were really worried about me too, weren't you?' she said. 'I've never seen you cry before.'

I clenched my teeth, feeling the tears welling up again. *This* was why I didn't cry in front of people – when I started, it took me ages to stop.

'What's going on?' she said. 'Talk to me.'

'I . . .' I looked down. *I didn't want her to see me.* But Rooney was looking at me, eyebrows furrowed, so many thoughts churning behind her eyes, and it was that look that made me start spilling everything out. 'I just care about you so much . . . but I've always got this fear that . . . one day you'll leave. Or Pip and Jason will leave, or . . . I don't know.' Fresh tears fell from my cheeks. 'I'm never going to fall in love, so . . . my friendships are all I have, so . . . I just . . . can't bear the idea of losing any of my friends. Because I'm never going to have that one special person.'

'Can you let me be that person?' Rooney said quietly.

I sniffed loudly. 'What d'you mean?'

'I mean I want to be your special person.'

'B-but . . . that's not how the world works, people always put romance over friendships –'

'Says who?' Rooney spluttered, smacking her hand on the

ground in front of us. 'The heteronormative rulebook? *Fuck* that, Georgia. Fuck that.'

She stood up, flailing her arms and pacing as she spoke.

'I know you've been trying to help me with Pip,' she began, 'and I appreciate that, Georgia, I really do. I *like her* and I think she likes me and we like being around each other and, yep, I'm just gonna say it – I think we really, really want to have sex with each other.'

I just stared at her, my cheeks tear-stained, having no idea where this was going.

'But you know what I realised on my walk?' she said. 'I realise that I *love you*, Georgia.'

My mouth dropped open.

'Obviously I'm not romantically in love with you. But I realised that whatever these feelings are for you, I . . .' She grinned wildly. 'I feel like I *am* in love. Me and you – *this* is a fucking love story! I feel like I've found something most people just don't get. I feel at home around you in a way I have never felt in my *fucking life*. And maybe most people would look at us and think that we're *just friends*, or whatever, but I know that it's just . . . so much MORE than that.' She gestured dramatically at me with both hands. 'You *changed me*. You . . . you fucking saved me, I swear to God. I know I still do a lot of dumb stuff and I say the wrong things and I still have days where I just feel like *shit* but . . . I've felt happier over the past few weeks than I have in *years*.'

I couldn't speak. I was frozen.

Rooney dropped to her knees. 'Georgia, I am never going to stop being your friend. And I *don't* mean that in the boring average meaning of 'friend' where we stop talking regularly when we're twenty-five because we've both met *nice young men* and gone off to have babies, and only get to meet up twice a year. I mean I'm going to pester you to buy a house next door to me when we're forty-five and have finally saved up enough for our deposits. I mean I'm going to be crashing round yours every night for dinner because you *know* I can't fucking cook to save my life, and if I've got kids and a spouse, they'll probably come round with me, because otherwise they'll be living on chicken nuggets and chips. I mean I'm going to be the one bringing you soup when you text me that you're sick and can't get out of bed and ferrying you to the doctor's even when you don't want to go because you feel guilty about using the NHS when you just have a stomach bug. I mean we're gonna knock down the fence between our gardens so we have one big garden, and we can both get a dog and take turns looking after it. I mean I'm going to be here, annoying you, until we're old ladies, sitting in the same care home, talking about putting on a Shakespeare because we're all old and bored as shit.'

She grabbed the bunch of flowers and practically threw them at me.

'And I bought these for you because I honestly didn't know how else to express any of that to you.'

I was crying. I just started crying again.

Rooney wiped the tears off my cheeks. 'What? Don't you believe me? Because I'm not fucking joking. Don't sit there and tell me I'm lying because I'm not lying. Did any of that make sense?' She grinned. 'I am *extremely* sleep-deprived right now.'

I couldn't speak. I was a mess.

She gestured at the bunch of flowers, which had pretty much exploded in my lap. 'I really wanted to do some grand gesture like you did for Pip and Jason but I couldn't think of anything because you're the brains in this friendship.'

That made me laugh. She wrapped her arms round me, and

then I was just half laughing, half crying, happy and sad at the same time.

'Don't you believe me?' she asked again, holding me tight.

'I believe you,' I said, my nose all bunged up and my voice croaky. 'I promise.'

PART FIVE

IT'S BEEN FUN

Neither of us were at the level of fitness where running all the way back to the city centre was a good idea, but that's what we did anyway. Our play was due to start in under two hours. We didn't have a choice.

We ran all the way along the river, me with the flowers in my hands and stopping to pick them up every time I dropped one, and her with nothing but a phone, a Starbucks cup, and a grin on her face. We had to stop and sit down several times to catch our breath, and by the time we got to the town square, I truly thought my chest was going to implode. But we had to run. For the play.

For our friends.

When we got to the theatre, we were both soaked in sweat, and we burst in through the doors to find Pip sitting at a table in the foyer, her head in her hands.

She looked up at us as I literally fell on to the ground, sounding like an astronaut running out of air, while Rooney did her best to adjust the mess that was her ponytail.

'Where,' said Pip, very calmly. 'The fuck. Have you been?'

'We . . .' I started to say, but then I just let out a wheeze.

So Rooney spoke for us.

'I panicked after last night and Georgia tracked my phone but I'd lost my phone in a field and she ran all the way there and then I went back there because I knew I'd dropped it somewhere near the field and then I ran into her and I had these flowers because I wanted to tell her how much I appreciated her and everything she's done for me this year and then we talked about everything and I told her how important she is to me and also —' Rooney stepped forward towards Pip, who was staring, wide-eyed — 'I also realised that I really, truly like you and I haven't felt like that for anyone in a long time and it really scared me and that's why I ran away.'

'Um . . . O-OK,' Pip stammered.

Rooney took another step forward and put one hand on the table in front of Pip.

'How do you feel about me?' she asked, completely straight-faced.

'Um . . . I . . .' Pip's cheeks went red. 'I . . . I also . . . really like you . . .'

Rooney nodded vigorously, but I could tell she was getting a bit flustered. 'Good. Just thought we should be clear about it.'

Pip stood up, her eyes never leaving Rooney. 'Right. Um. Yeah. Good.'

I had, by this point, managed to get to my feet, and my lungs no longer felt like they were about to explode. 'We should go and find Jason and Sunil.'

'Yes,' said Rooney and Pip simultaneously, and the three of us started walking into the backstage area of the theatre, Rooney and Pip just slightly behind me.

As I turned a corner, I said, 'Are they in a dressing room, or . . .?' and when I got no answer, I glanced back, only to find

Rooney and Pip vigorously making out, Rooney having pushed Pip up against a dressing-room door, both of them seemingly unbothered that I was literally *right there*.

'Hey,' I said, but they either didn't hear me or chose to ignore me.

I coughed loudly.

'HEY,' I repeated, louder this time, and they reluctantly broke apart, Rooney looking a little irritated and Pip adjusting her glasses, looking like she'd just been punched. 'We have a play to perform?'

Jason and Sunil were sitting on the edge of the stage, sharing a packet of salted popcorn. As soon as they saw us enter, Jason raised both his arms in triumph, while Sunil said, '*Thank God.*' Jason then ran over, picked me up, and carried me all the way on to the stage while I laughed hysterically and tried to escape.

'We're doing it!' he said, spinning us around. 'We're doing the play!'

'I feel like I'm going to cry,' Sunil said, and then stuffed three more pieces of popcorn into his mouth.

Rooney clapped her hands loudly. 'No more time for being happy! We need to get changed before people start arriving!'

And so we did. Jason and Sunil had already arranged all our costumes, props and set backstage, so we all got changed into our first set of costumes, then spent ten minutes arranging the set we'd managed to craft with our limited resources – my papier-mâché pillar, which we placed on the centre-left, and a garland covered in stars that we somehow, after much deliberation between Jason and Rooney, managed to attach to one of the backdrop rails. When we hoisted it up, it looked like little stars were raining down from the ceiling.

We also had a chair in many of our scenes, but the best thing we could find was a red plastic thing in the wings. 'I have an idea,' said Rooney, and she leapt off the front of the stage to grab the flowers that I'd left on a front-row seat. She brought them up on to the stage and started sellotaping flowers to the chair.

By the time she'd finished, the chair had been transformed into a throne of flowers.

It was ten minutes until our performance when I started to wonder who was actually going to attend this show.

Obviously Sadie had been invited, since she was judging it. And I could guess that Sunil would have invited Jess. But would that be it? Two audience members?

I peeked out from behind the curtains and waited, and soon I was proven very, very wrong.

First, a few people I recognised from Pride Soc showed up. Sunil immediately went out to greet them, and eventually gestured for the rest of us to come say hi. Moments later, another small group of people arrived, and Sunil introduced them as his friends from his orchestra. They all started rambling about how much they'd been looking forward to this.

I didn't know whether that scared me or excited me.

Next, Sadie arrived with a couple of friends. She came to say a quick hello before sitting down in the front row, the most intimidating choice of seat possible.

Soon after, Jess arrived, and after saying hi to the Pride Soc gang, went to see Sadie. They hugged and sat down together, seeming to be good friends. University was a small world.

A gaggle of large boys showed up and I had no idea who they were until Jason went over to greet them – they were a few of his rowing teammates. And then two other people showed up, again complete strangers to me, but Pip ran over to them, hugged them and then introduced them as Lizzie and Leo, two friends she'd made at LatAm Soc.

I didn't have anyone who came along specifically to see me. Neither did Rooney.

I didn't mind, though. Who I had here – these four people – was enough.

And despite my lack of contribution, we had an audience. Enough to fill up three whole rows of seats.

Maybe that wasn't a lot. But it felt like a lot to me. It felt like what we were doing *mattered*.

At three minutes to two, the five of us gathered in the right wing and huddled up.

'Does anyone else feel like they need to shit?' asked Pip.

'Yes,' said Rooney immediately, while Sunil said, 'Well, I wouldn't exactly put it like that.'

'We're going to be *fine*,' said Jason. 'Everyone relax.'

'You telling me to relax makes me even less relaxed,' said Pip.

'Whatever happens,' I said, 'it's been fun, right? It's all been fun.'

Everyone nodded. We all knew it had.

Whatever happened with the play, with the society, with our strange little friendship group . . .

It had all been so much fun.

'Let's do this,' said Jason, and we all put our hands in.

GOOD NIGHT

Jason was on stage first. With a microphone and dressed as Romeo – in brightly coloured contrasting prints.

'This is just a little pre-show announcement,' he said. 'Firstly – thank you everyone for coming. Very nice to see such a large and impressive turnout, no doubt thanks to our incredibly extensive publicity campaign.'

There were some chortles in the audience.

'Secondly, I just wanted to inform you that we've had some . . . mild issues, trying to prepare this play. We had some . . . cast disputes. And we've had to rush through some of the final scenes. Everything is fine now, we hope, but . . . it's been quite the journey getting here. There've been a lot of tears and heated WhatsApp messages.'

There were more chuckles in the crowd.

'For those of you who don't know,' Jason continued, 'we at the Shakespeare Society decided that for our first ever show, we would perform a selection of scenes rather than just one play. All of these scenes are, in one way or another, about love – but we leave it up to you to interpret what sort of love these scenes are depicting.

Pure, toxic, romantic, platonic – we wanted to explore all sorts. In any case, it's going to be quite a bit shorter than a regular play, so we'll all get out in time for a late pub lunch.'

Some whoops from the crowd.

'Lastly,' said Jason, 'four of us wanted to say that we're dedicating this performance to the person who managed to bring us all together after everything sort of fell apart.'

He turned and looked at me in the wings, his eyes finding mine.

'Georgia Warr is the reason this play is even happening,' he said. 'And it might just be a small play, but it matters to all of us. Quite a lot. And Georgia deserves to have something made just for her. So, this one's for you, Georgia. This is a play about love.'

It was a bit of a mess, but it was wonderful. We started with a comedy, Rooney and Pip going on as Benedick and Beatrice, and soon the audience were in stitches. I somehow found myself hearing the story of *Much Ado About Nothing* as if I had never heard it before. It was alive in front of me. It was beautiful.

Twelfth Night was up next. Which meant it was nearly time for me to go on.

And that's when I realised I was fine.

No nausea. No running to the bathroom like *Romeo and Juliet* in Year 13.

I was nervous, sure. But a normal level of nervous, mixed with excitement to perform, to *act*, to do the thing I really, really enjoyed.

And when I went on and did my 'Come away, death' speech, I really did have fun. Jason and Sunil went on after me as Orsino and Viola, and I watched from one side, smiling, relieved, *happy*. I'd done it. *We'd* done it.

Jason and Rooney did some *Romeo and Juliet*, making it look as passionate as if they really were dating. Then all of us did some *King Lear*, where Lear tries to figure out which of his daughters loves him the most. And then I was Prospero with Sunil as Ariel from *The Tempest*, both of us needing the other but wanting to be free from our magical bond.

Rooney and Pip came back and did more *Much Ado*, where Benedick and Beatrice finally admit they love each other, and when they kissed, the audience roared with applause.

And finally, we ended with *A Midsummer Night's Dream*. Or, rather, I did.

I sat in the throne of flowers and read the final lines to conclude the play.

'*So, good night unto you all.*' I smiled gently at the faces of the audience, hoping, praying this had all been enough. That this wouldn't be the last time I performed with my best friends. '*Give me your hands if we be friends, and Robin shall restore amends.*'

Sunil dimmed the stage lights, and then the audience were on their feet.

We took our bows as the audience cheered. This wouldn't go down in university history. This wouldn't be anything special to anyone else. People would forget about this, or just remember it as that kind of weird but interesting student play they saw one time.

Nobody else in the universe would see this play.

But I guess that made it ours.

'It was a *mess*,' said Sadie, eyebrows raised, and arms folded. 'Your scene transitions were questionable at best, and your staging was . . . very unusual.'

The five of us, who were sitting in a row on the edge of the stage, collectively drooped.

'*But* −' she continued, holding up a finger − 'I did not dislike it. In fact, I thought it was very creative, and definitely more interesting than if you'd come on and done a very average, abridged version of *Romeo and Juliet*.'

'So . . .' Rooney spoke up. 'Was it . . . are we . . .'

'Yes,' said Sadie, 'you can keep your Shakespeare Society.'

Pip and Rooney started screaming and hugging each other. Sunil put a hand to his chest and whispered, '*Thank God*,' while Jason swung his arm round me and grinned, and I realised that I was grinning too. I was happy. I was so, so happy.

After Sadie left, Rooney was the first to hug me. She clambered over the others and just fell on top of me, pushing me down on to the stage and wrapping her arms round me, and I laughed, and she laughed, and we were both just laughing and laughing. Pip joined us next, shouting, 'I want to be included,' and leaping on top of us. Sunil rested his head on Rooney's back, and then Jason wrapped his body round the four of us, and we all just stayed like that for a moment, laughing and babbling and holding each other. At the bottom of the scrum, I was basically being crushed, but it was comforting, in a weird way. The weight of all of them on top of me. Around me. With me.

We didn't have to say it, but we all knew. We all knew what we'd found here. Or, I did, at least. I knew. I'd found it.

And this time there was no big declaration. No grand gesture. It was just us, holding each other.

THE HOUSE

The house was on a street corner. A Victorian terraced building, but not an aesthetically pleasing one, and it had worryingly small windows. The five of us stood outside, staring up at it, nobody speaking. No one wanted to say what we were all thinking: it looked kind of shit.

A month after our play performance, me, Rooney, Pip and Jason realised that we did not have anywhere to live next year. Durham University's college accommodation was primarily for first-year students and a few third- and fourth-year students – second-years were generally expected to find their own place to live. So most freshers had formed little groups around December and January, gone house hunting, and signed rental agreements.

Due to the drama of this year, we had totally missed the memo. And by the end of April, most of the university-arranged rental accommodation in Durham was already completely taken for the next academic year, which left us having to trawl through dodgy adverts on private landlord websites.

'I'm sure it's nicer on the inside,' said Rooney, stepping forward and knocking on the door.

'You said that about the last three,' said Pip, arms folded.

'And I'll be right, eventually.'

'Just to say,' said Sunil, 'maybe we should reconsider how bothered we are about having a living room.'

Although Sunil was in his third year, he'd decided at the last minute to return next year to do a master's degree in music. He still had no idea what he wanted to do with his life, which I thought was very relatable and understandable, and he said he loved being at Durham and wanted to stay for a little while longer.

But Jess was leaving at the end of the year. In fact, most of Sunil's third-year friends were. As soon as we discovered this, we asked him to live with us, and he said yes.

The door opened and a tired student let us in, explaining that everyone was out at lectures except her so we could walk around and look in any of the rooms we wanted. We all headed into the kitchen first, which doubled up as the living room with a sofa on one side and the kitchen counters on the other. It was all very old and well used, but seemed functional and clean, which was all we needed. We were students. We couldn't be picky.

'It's actually not bad,' said Sunil.

'See?' said Rooney, gesturing around. 'I told you this would be the one.'

Jason folded his arms. 'It's quite . . . small.' The top of his head was very close to the ceiling.

'But no black mould,' Pip pointed out.

'And there's enough room to have everyone here,' I said. By 'everyone', I meant the five of us, plus the others who'd been coming along to our rehearsals – well, they weren't really rehearsals any more. It wasn't like we had another play to prepare for this year, and we were all getting busy with exams and coursework, so we usually just met up to chat, watch movies, and get takeaway food. Every Friday night in my and Rooney's room.

Sometimes Sunil would bring Jess along, or Pip would bring her friends Lizzie and Leo. Sometimes half the Castle men's rowing team showed up – loud boys who scared me at first, but were actually quite nice when you got to know them. Sometimes it'd just be the original five, or fewer if we were busy.

It had become a ritual. My favourite university ritual.

'And this is the *perfect* place for Roderick!' said Rooney brightly, pointing at an empty corner next to the sofa arm.

We headed towards the two downstairs bedrooms, which were both pretty ordinary. Jason and I peered into the second one. It was almost as messy as Pip's current bedroom.

'I always wanted a downstairs bedroom,' said Jason. 'I don't know why. It just seemed cool.'

'You'd be right next to the road.'

'I think I'd like it. Ambient noise. And look!' He pointed at a patch of empty wall above the bed – enough room for a framed photograph. 'The perfect place for *Mystery Inc.*'

It'd been Jason's birthday the week before. One of his presents from me: a framed photograph of the whole Scooby-Doo gang. All five of them.

'I'd like a downstairs room,' said Sunil, who'd appeared behind us. 'I like being close to the kitchen. Easy snack access.'

Jason glanced at him warily. 'As long as you're not practising cello late at night.'

'You mean you *don't* want to listen to my beautiful music in the early hours of the morning?'

Jason laughed and headed upstairs, leaving Sunil and me to wander into the first bedroom, careful not to touch any of the current occupant's stuff.

And then Sunil said, 'I wanted to run an idea by you, Georgia.'

'Yeah?'

'Well, I'm only going to be Pride Soc president for a couple more months, and before I have to step down . . . I wanted to set up a new group within Pride Soc. A society for aromantic and asexual students. And I suppose I wondered . . . whether you'd want to be involved. Not necessarily as president of it, but . . . well, I don't know. I just wanted to ask. No pressure, though.'

'Oh. Um . . .' I immediately felt nervous about the idea. I still had days where I wasn't brimming with confidence about my sexuality, despite all the days where I felt proud and grateful that I knew who I was and what I wanted. Maybe the bad days would become less and less common, but . . . I didn't know. I *couldn't* know.

Maybe a lot of people felt like that about their identity. Maybe it would just take time.

'I don't know,' I said. 'I'm not even out to my parents.'

Sunil nodded understandingly. 'That's OK. Just let me know after you've thought about it.'

I nodded back. 'I will.'

He gazed into the bedroom at the way the evening light was hitting the floor. 'It's been a good year, but I'm looking forward to stepping down. I think I deserve a more restful year, next year.' He smiled to himself. 'It'd be nice. To have a rest.'

There were three more bedrooms upstairs, and Pip and Rooney immediately beelined for the most obviously large one.

'I'm having this one,' said Pip and Rooney simultaneously, then glared at each other.

'I need more room,' said Rooney. 'I'm like a whole foot taller than you.'

'Um, firstly, that's a lie, you are only a few inches taller –'

'At least six inches.'

'And secondly, I need more room because I have way more clothes than you.'

'You're both going to be sleeping in the same room loads anyway,' Jason muttered, rolling his eyes, and Pip shot him a look that mixed embarrassment with alarm while Rooney immediately went bright red, opened her mouth, and began to protest.

Rooney had still been spending nights out of our room. The first time it happened after the play, I was scared that she'd gone back to heavy drinking and clubbing with strangers, but when I eventually confronted her about it, she timidly revealed that she was spending all of those nights in Pip's room. And the clothes she kept leaving there were a bit of a giveaway.

She'd spend nights in our room too, though. Lots of nights. It wasn't like she'd replaced me, or I was less important.

She was one of my best friends. I was one of hers. And we both understood what that meant now.

Once Rooney had finished berating Jason for bringing up her sex life and Jason had tactically retreated towards the bathroom, I watched as Rooney and Pip stood together in the doorway. Rooney gently touched Pip's hand with hers, and Rooney leant towards her and whispered something I couldn't hear that made Pip grin wide.

I stepped away to peer inside another of the bedrooms. This one had a big sash window, a sink in the corner, and whoever lived here had stuck polaroid photos all over one of the walls. The carpet was kind of odd – it had a bold red pattern that reminded me of Gran's curtains – but I didn't dislike it. I didn't dislike any of it.

It wasn't fancy, or anything. But I could really imagine myself living here. I could imagine all of us here, starting a new academic year, coming home and slumping on the sofa next to each other, chatting in the kitchen in the mornings over bowls of cereal, crowding into the biggest bedroom for movie nights, falling asleep in each other's beds when we were too tired to move.

I could imagine all of it. A future. A small future, and not a forever future, but a future, nonetheless.

'What d'you think?' asked Rooney, who'd come to stand next to me in the doorway.

'It's . . . OK,' I said. 'It's not perfect.'

'But?'

I smiled. 'But I think we could have fun here.'

She smiled back. 'I agree.'

Rooney returned to continue arguing with Pip over the largest bedroom, but I just stayed there for a moment, looking at what might be my future living space. After months of sleeping next to one of my best friends, I was a little nervous about going back to a solo bedroom. Sleeping in a silent room with just my thoughts.

I had time to get used to the idea, though.

Until then, we would keep the beds together.

ACKNOWLEDGEMENTS

This book was the most difficult, frustrating, terrifying and liberating thing I've ever made. So many wonderful people helped me through this journey:

Claire Wilson, my incredible agent, who has received more than her fair share of emotional emails. My editor, Harriet Wilson; my books' designer, Ryan Hammond; and everyone else at HarperCollins who has worked on this book – thank you for your tireless efforts and support for my stories, despite me needing to extend almost every single deadline I was given. Emily Sharratt, Sam Stewart, Ant Belle and Keziah Reina for their editing, insight, and beta-reading, often under very speedy time constraints. My writer soulmate, Lauren James, who has put up with the brunt of my woes regarding this book and helped me so much with structure and pacing. My friends and family, in real life and online. And my readers who have cheered me along. Thank you so, so much, everyone.

And thank you to all who have picked up this book. I really hope you've enjoyed this story.

FURTHER RESOURCES ON ASEXUALITY AND AROMANTICISM

AVEN (The Asexuality Visibility and Education Network): https://www.asexuality.org/

What Is Asexuality?: http://www.whatisasexuality.com/

Aces & Aros: https://acesandaros.org/

AZE, a journal publishing asexual, aromantic, and agender writers and artists: https://azejournal.com/

AUREA (Aromantic-spectrum Union for Recognition, Education, and Advocacy): https://www.aromanticism.org/

Indian Aces: https://www.facebook.com/IndianAces

Asexual resources at the Trevor Project: https://www.thetrevor project.org/trvr_support_center/asexual/ .

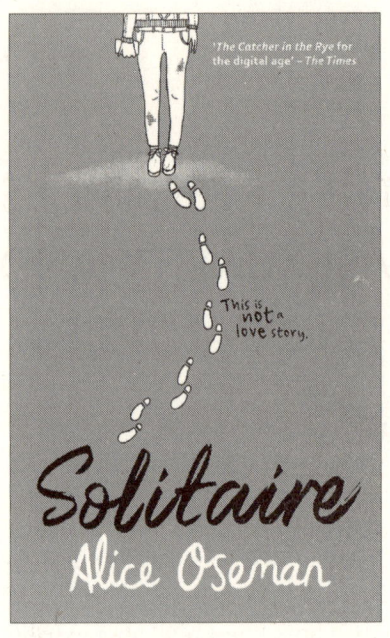

'The Catcher in the Rye for the digital age' – The Times

This is not a love story.

Solitaire

Alice Oseman

My name is Tori Spring. I like to sleep and I like to blog. Last year I had friends. Things were very different, I guess, but that's all over now.

Now there's Solitaire. And Michael Holden.

I don't know what Solitaire are trying to do. And I don't care about Michael Holden. I really don't.

"*The Catcher in the Rye* for the digital age" – *The Times*

Frances is a study machine with one goal. Then she meets Aled, and for the first time she's unafraid to be herself. So when the fragile trust between them is broken Frances is caught between who she was and who she longs to be.

Frances is going to need every bit of courage she has.

For Angel, life is about one thing: The Ark – a pop-rock trio of teenage boys taking the world by storm. Being part of The Ark's fandom has given her everything she loves – her friend Juliet, her dreams, her place in the world.

Jimmy owes everything to The Ark. He's their frontman – and playing in a band with his mates is all he ever dreamed of doing.

But dreams don't always turn out the way you think and when Jimmy and Angel are unexpectedly thrust together they find out how strange and surprising facing up to reality can be.

Read the Heartstopper novellas...

Read Alice's graphic novel series...